TO THE MANOR BORN

MATTHEW SPEISER

Black Rose Writing | Texas

ISBN: 978-1-68513-273-6
PUBLISHED BY BLACK ROSE WRITING
www.blackrosewriting.com

Printed in the United States of America
Suggested Retail Price (SRP) $22.95

To the Manor Born is printed in Book Antiqua

*As a planet-friendly publisher, Black Rose Writing does its best to eliminate unnecessary waste to reduce paper usage and energy costs, while never compromising the reading experience. As a result, the final word count vs. page count may not meet common expectations.

PRAISE FOR
TO THE MANOR BORN

"Speiser's command of historical events frames this compelling story of antagonistic societies shaped by the absence of United States victory in the Civil War. A turbulent and engrossing world."
–Gary W. Gallagher, author of *Causes Won, Lost, and Forgotten*

"Speiser's deep knowledge of the Civil War era shines through in this captivating tale."
–Dr. Melissa Blair, History Department Chair, Associate Professor of History, Auburn University

"A riveting journey through an unthinkable turn in American history. *To the Manor Born* is bold, it's honest, and you can't put it down."
–Dr. Mario Dell'Olio, author of *Letters from Italy*

*To my mom and dad, who taught me to study the past
and who assured me it was once as uncertain as the future.*

TO THE MANOR BORN

CHAPTER 1

July in Virginia.

The Planters were the ones in charge, but the sun bore down like a god. It turned the air into soup, dew from below, humidity from above, and Atticus Brooke shut his eyes and saw red spots dancing in his vision. The sweat pooled at the nape of his neck; stale salt coated his lips. He crouched amid the cotton stems and wiped his chin.

He'd been patrolling the furrows since dawn, scraping the soil for scraps, grabbing whatever wisps the modules had missed. After all, such was the nation's latest mantra: faster, faster, always faster – leaf-drop, re-growth, double harvest – the same at every plantation across the commonwealth, and this, the largest one of all. Richmond's propagandists had honed their message, and the technicians had finally caught up: nitrogen levels cut in half; new desiccants patented; herbicides replaced with hormonals. The soil was vanquished at last. The twenty-first century had made the fields its own.

He squinted from the sting in his eyes, and longed for sleep. Stupidly, he'd stayed in quarters past the morning alarm, and it'd cost him a whole week's lunches. He was lucky it hadn't brought on a beating. Over by the veranda, the overseers were still watching him, mouths stiff, boots to their knees, sharp eyes glinting. On either side, his fellow indents were in every direction, hunched by the thousands, nestled amid the muted green and snow-white trenches closer in.

But why look? Rosewood Manor was in his blood, stenciled there from birth, carved out by every century that had come before. He knew every inch: the sweeping porticoes up behind him, cooled by the geothermal pipelines he'd helped install; pastures drenched in honeysuckle and ringed with lilies; down below, the indentures' quarters, sinking in the mud like a slum; all of it bathed now in summer gold. The field borders were marked by an ancient stone wall on one end, clumps of primrose on the other, the soft scent of fresh-cut grass to boot. The finches' songs floated past, and fine elms blocked a rolling horizon. Apple blossoms crowded the front pastures. Overhead, the pillowy clouds turned pink, and the horseflies grew noisy.

There'd been no screams today, not yet at least, no whippings curdling the air. But he listened carefully to make sure – hearing nothing but the roar of the nearest module, trolling Field 19 now, shaking the earth with its drums, cables screeching. Folks said there were better machines in the North, and maybe so. But that wasn't the point. It never had been.

He glanced left.

There she was, just a few yards off, half-hidden by a line of stems that had escaped the mechanical reaper. Her fingertips were bleeding, sliced by the bolls' edges; the wool-cord basket hitched to her belt was banging against her thighs. Her brown eyes were flecked green in the sun, and she'd tied back her thick hair with a soiled white ribbon.

Clara Brooke.

Like all indents born on the property, she shared the Planter's surname. Atticus took note of her thin lips pursed in concentration, a study in how to cloak a well of thoughts always simmering underneath.

"What?" she suddenly whispered, glancing over, squinting back.

He grinned. It was that whisper which gave him reason enough to live.

"What do you want, you crazy fool!"

And now he had to stifle a laugh, hiding his face in the crook of his elbow, winking as she angled back to work. The nearest overseer was approaching – pudgy-faced, with nothing but a scrim of yellow hair on his pate, and a paunch hanging over his belt – and as he got close, Atticus could smell him, soaked in sweat. "No foolin' around," the fellow grumbled, and he placed a hand on his holster.

Atticus tightened, set to do something, though he didn't know what. But Clara simply shifted right, finishing the patch and moving to the next – until the overseer, relaxing his grip, exhaled, shuffled back to the row's edge, and settled down with his canteen.

• • •

It was later, well after sunset, when the signal had been given and the indents were back in their quarters for supper, that Atticus heard thunder in the western hills. But rain held off, and the air stayed thick.

At least food was waiting. It would be served in the long hall at the ridge's base, flanked by the fields on one side and dilapidated sheds on the other, all rotting walls and sagging stoops, dating back to the days when they'd still been called slaves. No food was permitted in the cabins themselves – mice scurried over their feet each night anyway – so the indents ate in the so-called banquet hall, underneath a pockmarked tin roof. The space could hold a thousand at a time, and the lines formed as soon as the whistle sounded, always crowding at the front, while the cooks ladled corn meal and lard over rice.

In the hall's corners, flickering ghost-like beneath the fluorescent light, the overseers still glared. Unblinking, unbending, the same as always: they had all the cash and all the tech, all the weapons on their side. Yet still they watched. From the line, Atticus ignored them, scanning the room for Clara instead.

There'd be no one else to eat with, he knew: his pals from boyhood had all been stationed in other residential sectors – the Planter kept young men apart – and his cabinmates were rotated constantly, always over seventy years old. Until eventually, he spotted her, close to the door.

Only it was then there was a loud pop – a fist striking flesh – and a shout, and Atticus tilted his head to see, knowing at once that one of the overseers must've snapped: sipping whiskey all day, unwilling to let a clean target go to waste. Everyone else was nudging forward now too, squeezing in, looking for a view – shoved in turn by the overseers behind them, smelling blood, no doubt seeking someone else to take down. Here was one of them now, eyes smarting, cheeks flushed. George Something-or-other, Atticus recalled: a father killed in the latest skirmishes up north. He had a red face, and a scar down his cheek that he swore had come from a Union admiral. "You wanna get your hands dirty?" the fellow shouted over in staccato. Though before he could swing, the crowd pressed him aside, and Atticus found his reprieve.

Reinforcements were arriving through the door, fifty now, maybe more, swarming in beneath the old timber frame. In an instant, the room was pulsing, and knowing what was coming, Atticus shoved through. At last, he reached Clara, pushing closer like a fish against the current.

"Why're you still here?" she shouted impatiently. "You'll get blamed, Atti!"

He gave a shrug, but knew she was right. The young men were always used to make an example. From behind, an awful electric buzz had begun.

It was the tasers.

"Run," Clara urged. "Go."

He nodded. The shouts were growing, the white men choosing their next marks. "Uprisers!" one of them was bellowing. "Uprisers!"

It was enough to set the others off, and Atti took an elbow to the side. "All right," he grunted, grimacing, breaking Clara's gaze. "All right," he said again. And sliding past the buffet, grabbing a slice of stale bread, he shoved it in his mouth and sprinted out.

• • •

Turning from the banquet hall, wary of guard dogs and motion detectors, Atticus stayed low as he looped back toward the cabins. Up ahead, in a grassy patch beyond the next ridge, he spotted a stray overseer – renegade or runt it didn't matter – scrolling on his phone.

Atti spun away. He scanned the clouds, checking for surveillance drones, darting down the next dip in the grass, nearer the cotton quadrants, no longer quite sure where he should head. He breathed deep, glad simply to be free from the scrum and out of trouble, listening to the clomp of his boots, keeping in rhythm with the treefrogs nearby.

In the moonlight now, the main house loomed before the horizon, nursing the same manic longing as the nation at large. Its double doors had been widened, part of some latest renovation; curb lights transformed its front drive into all but a runway; in the garden, contorted sculptures had been sheared out of the hedges, twisting like mangled ghosts.

Suddenly, Atti heard a shout, and spinning back, he saw the same figure he'd spotted before, now standing just a dozen feet off. "Why're you out, boy?!" the overseer yelled over. He must've been more alert than he'd let on, using his phone for infrared spotting, not just checking the latest scores.

"Just getting some air."

"You want me to call General Brooke?"

That sounded like a bluff. Still, why test it? "Figured I'd better get free of the banquet hall crowd, that's all. I got lost in the night."

The overseer didn't budge. "Ain't you lived here long enough to know your way 'round?"

"Just got too far out, sir. I told you."

Now the overseer cocked his head.

Atti could see him thinking, and he was certain the man's bitterness was at work. It wouldn't be long before this was marked up in an incident report. And sure enough, only a second later, the fellow's phone was back out. Atti exhaled. There'd be an adjudication hearing, he was certain – followed by lavatory duty, loss of canteen, maybe even solitary – and he cursed silently at his luck, as the rain arrived at last. The moon slipped behind its cover, the fields glistened, the first drops landed loudly, and the overseer let loose a sigh, as if it were Atti's fault for getting him wet.

CHAPTER 2

General Franklin Brooke was watching television in Rosewood Hall's main parlor. Past the room's entrance, the vestibule gleamed beside a double stairwell; nearer in, the shelves bowed under the weight of unread volumes. Opal-shaded sconces crowded the restored molding. Up above, things were even grander: a grooved ceiling, plasterwork flowers, pillared balconies that ran laps around the atrium. Chandeliers glittered over the corridors; gilt-framed portraits boasted ancestors who'd defended the nation's cause: bearded, long-haired souls, delighting in their pride.

Franklin's thoughts were elsewhere. Outside, came a clatter of thunder; in here, the lamps rattled. But he took no note. He was still on edge after hearing about the indents' food riot the night before, and the news on the television screen wasn't helping. Despite the best efforts of the censors, the anchors were betraying their nerves, reporting on the skirmishes at the border, sharing rumors of Resistance meetings in the capital.

He needn't truly worry, of course. Border tension was constant. Skirmishes were bound to flare up. What's more, the stubborn stories of Resistance were tiresome, limited to a fringe of rabble-rousers who always ended up captured. But it was never good when the television took note. It only unleashed discomfort – encouraging those who wanted to shut down a free press entirely.

Franklin leaned back on a maroon velvet cushion, glad when he heard Cathryn returning from the hall. She'd left to check on the indents in the kitchen – really, she'd needed an escape from the news – and he smiled as she glided in. She was as sure-footed as ever, no matter the world stirring madly around her, blue silk with a violet waistband, aster blossoms tucked in her graying hair. Her posture never sank; her green eyes never wavered.

•   •   •

As she took his hand now, Cathryn gazed down on the powerful face before her, far more lined than when Franklin had first done his wooing. His beaten-up boots were set firmly on the floor, broad shoulders perched tight. Even under the strain, he remained elegant, silver hair a bit too long, uniform as finely fitted as ever. He'd agreed to keep it on for the night, and she was pleased: four gold stars on his collar, tidy gray buttons lining his front. She watched as he drummed his fingers against the armrest, waiting.

"I'm sorry, darling," he finally said, gesturing toward the television. His dark eyes, ever-vigilant, weren't without care. "It's these reports."

"You think there's any truth to them?"

"No more than usual. It's the same war as ever." He left it there.

Cathryn nodded. Her husband didn't share details, but she knew enough to register that border-skirmishes didn't amount to real news. They went back to the Confederacy's earliest days; she'd learned of them even as a girl, back in the North, before any of this – before Franklin. The border would never calm down. Not so long as the two Americas refused to let it.

Still, it was clear Franklin was distracted. He hadn't been sleeping; he'd skipped his dawn walks, taking morning calls in his office instead. His official trips to the front had grown more frequent, with private flights and staffers galore, and various corporate entities in tow, usually on their way to visiting their offices along the coast, down in the Gulf, in the islands – always leaving the problems to him: calming CEOs' nerves, he told her, even as they seemed to be riling his in turn.

She stroked his hair. There was nothing that could be fixed tonight anyway; and there was certainly no benefit in staring at the talking heads. She found the remote.

"Leave it on."

"Come now, dear. You know everything already from your own men."

Franklin opened his mouth once more, but said nothing. Instead, he leaned his head against her hand, and took a breath. "Still glad you said yes, my darling?"

"Always."

Though before he could respond in kind, they both turned. Rapid footsteps had emerged from the front hall.

Not a second later, their daughter Liza came swinging into the room. She'd let her dark curls fall loose on her shoulders. She was wearing a yellow hoop dress. Her alert, fine eyes were as wide as ever, the same brown as her hair. And both her parents smiled. Her chin was broad, cheeks soft and cheerful, so that her expression was open, without undoing the sharpness of her gaze.

"Oh father," she proclaimed upon entering. "You needn't wear your uniform just for Kevin!"

Franklin shrugged. "I voted for undershirt and pajamas, before I was vetoed." It was charming, if not entirely true. For there was no denying he still cared what others thought. He'd shaped his life around service to the Cause, yes. Yet he'd never quite denied the accoutrements that came with it.

"Let's go down," Liza answered, moving past the Stars-and-Bars on his lapel, the way they matched the shine in his hair. "He's nearly here."

Cathryn stepped forward first. "We'll form a greeting line."

"For God's sake, must we?"

"Until he proposes, dear, it's the only way."

"Stop it, mother. We're friends. As you know."

"You're perfect for each other."

Liza bristled. The fact was, she wondered sometimes if Kevin wasn't more perfect for them. He was her oldest, dearest friend, it was true. He was thoughtful and kind, and she could talk to him all day and night. But couldn't he also be just as enraging as they were? It wasn't that he didn't wonder about the world. After all, it was he who pored through treatises on every subject, ordering books from overseas gray markets whenever they were blocked online, paying whatever price was demanded. He'd discuss them the instant he had a chance, inviting Liza to join in, to forgo acting like a proper belle and ponder the mysteries of life. And yet – whenever she pushed him toward precision, he'd turn quiet instead, raise an eyebrow, swallow a thought. It was right there in his gaze: the constant hint of restraint. Always and forever, she knew he was holding back. Like her parents indeed, when it counted anyway, never quite pursuing what mattered.

Perhaps that shouldn't have been surprising. Kevin Donleau was a gentleman, and the world expected a certain protocol from him. If he offered an untoward joke, he'd immediately proffer an apology. When he got animated, he'd clear his throat. He was unfailingly, unimpeachably polite.

If only he weren't quite so wealthy, Liza thought, if he weren't so trapped into being a perfect noble, he might instead register some of those ideas swirling in his head, not just the ones about history or art, but about the rest of it too, about the rules and rites and rituals and routines, the ideas she was certain were there, burning alongside the comments he'd let slip – about everything from traffic patterns to rural design, anything but the real meat underneath.

Not that she'd dare mention any of that now, of course. Her mother couldn't possibly understand – she was far too busy auditioning as the truest Confederate in the land. And father? Beneath all his trappings of power, he was more like Kevin than even he knew: afraid to truly talk, for fear he might stumble upon his own thoughts. Besides, why start an argument? It would just end with her hurrying out, flushed and irritated, as though she were the only person who ever wondered what the indents were thinking, or questioned the concept of aristocracy, or simply found her sundresses stifling.

Her mother followed a step behind, leading Franklin by the hand, and they entered the main hall. It was cavernous and impressive and unabashed, and it always made Liza think of the house's history, stretching back to the Confederate Revolution. The front door was wide with iron trim, and the windows at its sides were high, like those in a church. Now, as she reached the foot of the marble stairwell, the door chimes rang out, and one of the indents, an old man with narrow shoulders, sprung out from the kitchen while she and her parents waited.

The door squeaked open, and there was Kevin, standing on the portico, wearing coattails but no hat, smiling eagerly. He was tall and thin, handsome despite his lankiness, with sandy brown hair that swung over his forehead and fine blue eyes that focused hard on whomever he was addressing. He was only a year older than Liza, but somehow it'd always seemed like more.

He bowed now, and extended his arm. "General Brooke." He shifted toward Cathryn. "And ma'am, it's wonderful to see you, as ever."

"Why thank you Kevin. And you as well, I'm sure."

But Liza was already easing to his side.

"Shouldn't we stay for tea?" he asked.

"Absolutely not!" She winked farewell to her parents as she said it – so that they couldn't help but accept – and guided them across the porch instead, out to the front lawn. "Let's just go eat at your place."

"That suits me fine," he replied with a grin, and as he waved goodbye over his shoulder in turn, Liza finally relaxed.

•   •   •

The Donleau Plantation was only a half-mile from the Brookes' driveway, and Liza would've simply walked there herself, if custom allowed. It was the main seat in the hamlet of Crotelle, and had been for ages. Kevin had grown up there; later, after he'd completed his years in the service and his parents had moved to North Carolina – retreating from the unrest of Virginia and its borders – he'd stayed on, and they'd granted the plantation title to him in full. Ever since, he'd embraced the place's peace, reading and thinking and taking long walks, barely keeping up any real crop management, living instead off his trust funds and investments. Rather than relying upon the indents – they'd all moved south with his parents – Kevin paid a few scattered yeomen to run the place.

Liza was more than aware of the contrast to her own family. Her father had long acted as though he possessed infinite funds when he didn't, spending his life focused on government work, without tending to the business side of Rosewood Manor. If not for subsidies, her family would've reached serious financial waters years before. Not that they were alone; it was Kevin's family that was the exception, not hers, one of the few with enough inherited wealth to turn public funds away. The subsidies were widespread among the Planters, a never-ending spigot thanks to all the taxes on yeomen. To Liza, it had long been clear this not only sustained the nation's celebrated agrarian splendor, but also blocked its profit and progress. That didn't mean she'd trade it in for the polluted skies that were said to dominate the U.S. But she did wonder about a system that put perennial pride over policy.

They were walking through the white gate at the Donleau Plantation's edge, when Kevin turned. "What're you thinking?"

"Oh just about how much money you have…"

He laughed. His fine eyes twinkled.

"Don't you believe me?"

"I do believe you're one of a kind. The only Confederate who actually speaks her mind."

Liza wasn't sure she did anything of the sort, but she didn't say so. Instead, bathing in the still summertime air, she clasped Kevin's arm as they strolled toward the main house, steady and serene atop a hilltop all its own. It was a place Liza had always adored, ever since she'd been a little girl.

If folks didn't know better – and most didn't – they'd assume Kevin's family had far less money than hers, not more. Unlike her own parents, renovating constantly, the Donleaus had let their house age gracefully, a testament to its storied history. The cypress-shingled roof was nearly black, darkened by years of rain and sun; the thin blue shutters were warped at the corners. A slanted porch circled the house, and in the rear a winding lake held off the surrounding fields, rows of lazy red maples dotting their edges. At this hour, with evening approaching, the more distant pastures had already grown hidden under the shadow of the sky. But Liza was comforted just to know they were there.

She realized Kevin was holding her hand.

For a moment, it made her nervous. It wasn't that they'd never walked like this before – they had, millions of times as children, a million times more ever since – but now, in the warmth of dusk, it seemed different.

He paused. "Is something wrong?"

"Nothing. I'm just distracted."

"I hear the border skirmishes are getting bad."

"My father says they're not much worse than usual."

"That's what he always says."

"Why?" Liza asked. "Do you disagree?"

Kevin thought for a moment. "It's true the news reports are picking up. And I've seen more Confederate Guard in town, monitoring the indentures. But who knows?"

"What do you mean?"

"Only that it's worth noticing when the Guard's on alert. Spooked by the rumors of unrest, I suppose. Same as everyone else." He'd paused in the high grass. "I don't think it's just the indents that concern them. It's the Resistance too. People say it actually exists."

Liza nodded. "My father says there's no reason to worry. But he worries himself. Last week, I asked if it was true the Guard was asking after the Underground Railroad, only he wouldn't even admit it exists." She angled back. The house's lanterns flickered. Nearer in, summer blossoms reached out unrestrained, all variety of pink and purple, these manor grounds like sheets of watercolor. She exhaled. It helped her forget the nation's troubles. "We used to do this walk as kids," she mused. "Holding hands like this, just the same." She shifted back. "Except then it was normal. Now – doesn't it feel somehow unlikely?"

"Unlikely good?"

To her surprise, Liza didn't have to think. She felt at home with him. It was as simple as that. She always had. "Unlikely good."

A moment passed. Kevin waited. "Might I?" he asked, in a voice just as quiet as hers.

"Might you what?" But slowly, she nodded.

Gently, he leaned forward, and ran his hand through her dark hair. Then, clasping her chin softly, he brought his lips very near. "Yes?"

"Yes," she answered. "Yes," she said again.

It was then that he kissed her. It was a soft, lovely kiss, and Liza closed her eyes, realizing she didn't want it to end. The fact was, they'd never actually done this before. She knew her mother wouldn't believe that – she hardly believed it herself – and it felt so natural now, it was hard to imagine it was even true.

When they pulled apart, Kevin was smiling.

Liza breathed in the Virginia grass and nectar, and felt her home all around her – its solidity – its certainty of place.

"Come," he said. "Let's go in. After we eat, I'll walk you back before they get worried."

It was enough that Liza smiled too. She was glad to see his eyes so filled with pleasure, and knew hers must be too. Supper would be perfect. No silly grand restaurant. Just sandwiches on the wooden table in his kitchen. And for once, she questioned nothing at all, joining him for the stroll inside, holding his hand once more.

CHAPTER 3

Two days passed before Atticus had a chance to tell Clara about getting caught running from the banquet hall. They'd missed each other at mealtimes, and they'd been assigned to separate fields for labor. But on the third evening, he spotted her waiting for dismissal from supper, and he hurried over.

"Hey you."

"Atti! Where've you been?"

"I know – I'm sorry. Let's manage a walk."

She didn't hesitate. Leaving him in place, she sprang up and strode toward a group of overseers against the nearest wall. One of them glanced over: a bear of a man, his face smeared with sweat, a wink that flashed like a dart.

"What is it?" he said, breath thick with tobacco.

"Bathroom?"

"Sure," he muttered, and Clara exited through the hall's main door.

Atti watched, impatient, and forced himself to return to his table and count to a thousand in his head. When he could wait no longer, he hurried to the room's other side, finding another overseer – this one middle-aged and bored, with patchy hair the color of manure. He was whittling a twig into a point.

"Sir? Toilet break?"

"Don't be long."

Relieved, he ducked out before they could recognize him as the indent who'd been spotted sprinting in the fields. He knew where to go. A manmade lake sat a hundred yards from the banquet hall. During the Revolution, there'd been Confederate soldiers encamped at Rosewood, and they'd dug it out as a swimming hole. Now it just lay awkwardly, cutting into the fields and requiring pumps for filling. It was beyond the indent cabins, forbidden except on Christmas – though of course by then it was too cold – tucked away by a ridge and rarely looked after. Atti and Clara had stolen many a moment there, ever since they'd been small.

He found her at the north end, among the reeds, and she smiled. Together now, they walked along the water's edge, knowing it took only five minutes for a lap. There was still a hint of light in the air. The breeze was alive with the sound of crickets.

"I got nabbed the other night, you know. Running from that brawl."

"I heard," Clara answered. "Where?"

"Field 5. Persuaded the overseer I'd gotten lost."

"He bought that?"

"Seemed to. No sentence yet."

"No news is good news."

"Hope so."

She stopped walking. "I was proud of you, though." Her voice had turned serious. "I was glad you didn't fight."

Atti hesitated. "So what's wrong then?"

"Nothing." But she'd stepped closer, and he felt himself tighten.

He'd dreamt of her stepping to him like this, pictured it a thousand times, wished for her to look at him with earnest, intent eyes just the way she was doing now.

"I've been meaning to ask you something, is all," Clara said next, and Atti was suddenly certain she was even more beautiful in the night than the day, the nape of her neck, that grace in her stride, how she couldn't hide her perfect shape beneath the cotton of her dress. "Do you want to kiss me, Atti?"

He gulped outright at that, aware his mouth felt dry. "Well sure," he replied, determined to hold onto her question. "I always want to kiss you, Clara."

"You do?" She'd placed his hands in hers, he realized. "You want to kiss me now?"

This time, Atti didn't say anything at all. He just took her in his arms as he'd always imagined doing, and pressed his lips to hers.

She moved up against him, and he kissed her again, with everything he'd always felt – love even enough for marrying, he suddenly thought – love enough for crowding out obstacles and good sense and a nation that had them in its grips. Gone now was the banquet hall, the grumbles from the overseers, the slander of the world. Gone was everything but this. Lifting his hand to her hair, he was conscious only of her.

Until all at once, the world came rushing back.

•   •   •

They sprinted over, listening as the shouts turned to screams. When they got close, they saw a small boy, an indenture, on the ground outside the main door. He was weeping at the feet of an overseer, who was clenching a fist. The kid wore a torn long-buttoned shirt; his round cheeks were soaked with tears. The guard was strapping but soft – red hair sheared too close, freckles dotting his brow. No one was else was near, and the banquet hall doors had been locked to prevent anyone from interfering. The boy was bleeding from his shoulder; his sobs were becoming whimpers.

Atti shouted without thinking. "What could he possibly have done?!"

The overseer looked up, surprised. He was taller than most, with an undone strap on his denim overalls, temples sweating like streams, cheeks billowing; it was as if he needed to prove his strength, and had picked a child for doing so. "You shouldn't be out of the hall."

Meeting his eye – seeing the broken expression on the man's face – Atti felt his heart jabbing against his ribs, a hammer swinging straight to his throat. He knew he should be silent. "We were on bathroom break."

"You oughtta get inside with everyone else."

But Atti stepped forward. "Why?" Something within him had been stretched, nearer to snapping than ever before. "So you can get on with kickin' a kid?"

Clara pulled him back.

The overseer spat. "This child was stealing bread." But at that, instead of another kick, he turned to the hall, and tapped in a code by the door. "Get out of my sight," was all he snarled now. And thank God, he was gone.

Clara knelt by the boy's side. "Where's your ma, son?" Her breaths were shallow, her voice tight in a way Atti had never heard before. She checked the lad's joints, and helped him stand.

The boy couldn't have been more than seven or eight, and he looked up, wiping his face with his wrist. "Back at the youth hall," he managed, lips shaking as he pointed toward a smaller shed fifty yards south.

Clara nodded, and Atti stood behind her, knowing he'd made a mistake, that he'd been showing off, that it'd be hard to avoid the shackles for challenging a white man. Together, they helped the boy straighten up, confirming no bones seemed broken, and ordered him to go find his mother at supper.

There was no point asking if it was true he'd stolen bread. Of course he had. Who hadn't? Worse, he'd no doubt known he'd be beaten for it – probably had been before, and would be again. And as they watched the boy limp down the hill, both Clara and

Atti remembered their own childhoods, full of encounters just the same, days defined by helplessness, lessons from elders that they'd better take care: the beginnings of a rage that such ruin could ever seem normal.

Now, they turned toward the hall, avoiding eye contact with the overseers as they were let back in. Inside, some of the indents had started to sing. The tune was an old favorite, something they called the "Republic Hymn," though no one knew if that was quite right. It was said the lyrics had come from the U.S, traveling down from the distant past. All anyone really knew was that it was illegal, and that whites never sang it.

Still, the overseers usually let the indents bellow the words as loudly as they wanted, figuring that singing – even singing like this – was better than riots. And standing at the edge of the room, Atti and Clara joined in:

While God is marching on.
Glory, glory, hallelujah!
As He died to make men holy,
Let us die to make men free.

Chapter 4

That night, well after moonrise but well before dawn, Atti snuck over to Clara's cabin. The overseers had long since finished taking roll and drifted off to sleep, leaning their backs against the outer cabin walls, using their ammunition pouches as pillows.

He'd been lying awake in bed for hours, until it had become clear: he couldn't wait another moment. Not after that kiss at lake's edge. For wasn't it Clara who made him matter? Wasn't it she who gave him any bit of breath amid all the awful wrong of it all – who lent him any patience, any hope that he'd ever be able to negotiate through this place – so long as she was with him? Thinking again of how her lips had felt, the soft whisper that had come from the back of her throat, he knew he had to get back to her.

Questioning his own recklessness even as he rolled from his cot, Atti slid silently to the floor and placed his feet on the rough planks below. He tiptoed past the overseers and walked, quickly, steadily, toward the ramshackle cabin that awaited in the next quadrant over. To him, it was the palace of a princess, and moving past another clump of overseers, holding his breath when one of them stirred, Atti slowed his pace, peering at the worn-out buildings beneath the moonlit sky. As he approached, he caught a sliver of movement past the next corner, and ducked behind the nearest outhouse.

It smelled of rot – enough that his eyes watered, and he wiped them with his sleeve. Loose cinderblocks were scattered below, damp with the juices of old sewage. He peeked back up. The shift in the shadows had just been a rat, he realized: crouched beyond the path, belly low to the ground. But as it scurried away, Atti stayed put, zeroing in once more on the cabin he needed – its small stoop in front, warped walls above – and staying silent, he monitored the horizon for a sign that sun-up might be nearer than he wished. Another minute passed, then another. The nearest overseers were snoring loudly, and heart pounding, Atti finally stepped forward once more, keeping his eyes locked on Clara's cabin, checking for extra surveillance, needing to be certain. At long last, he moved towards its door.

Exhaling silently, he stepped inside. There were only three beds, and hers was in the middle. He could make out the rise-and-fall of two older women sleeping by the wall, and he ducked further in – only to see that Clara was awake, watching him in the dark. "Atti," she whispered.

"Did I startle you?"

"I knew you'd come."

"You did?"

"Only you can't stay." Clara paused, then sat up and pulled him close.

Her tongue brushed his lips, then found its way in; his thoughts evaporated. Trying to remain quiet, he climbed into the bed alongside her, kissing not just her lips now, but her neck and shoulders and back. "Why not?"

"The others will be up soon." But she'd gripped him still tighter.

Carefully, he undid the ties that kept her nightdress held up, warm cotton against his palms, as she took in his silhouette in turn, kissing his forehead and chest, and soon every other place too.

"I'm sorry about all my scars."

"I'm sorry about mine."

He kissed her again. "Don't be," he said into her ear. "I love you, Clara."

"I love you back," came the reply, and for just a moment, he pulled away to look, taking in her face glistening against the shadows, before they kissed again, holding each other with burning quiet, as the moon started to lower in the sky.

. . .

Afterwards, as they lay atop the cheap fiberfill mattress, stroking each other's arms, Clara turned from Atti's shoulder. "You have to go."

"Already?"

"The other women and I have been meeting over morning porridge." She hesitated. "To divvy up labor for the elders."

She felt guilty over lying, especially now, especially after this, but Clara knew the truth wouldn't do either. Not yet. Not before discussing it with the others at least. Besides, she already guessed what they'd say: that it was best for Atti not to know, that his impulsiveness could lead to something rash.

"That's kind of you," he murmured, closing his eyes. His fine lips let loose that familiar smile; his breaths were calm and cool.

She kissed him softly, then placed her hand on his brow. "Don't drift," she said. "I'll see you later today. Give it five minutes - then slip out yourself." With that, she stood and stepped off, confident the overseers were still asleep outside.

The truth was, Clara was already thinking of the meeting to come. The previous winter, she'd been voted Keeper of the Council, and the agenda was hers. There was lots to cover: the weapons shipments had been arriving in heaps from the North, and she'd need to confirm they were being properly hidden in the fields. Nor had she yet assigned leaders for gathering guns on the day of the uprising, let alone for assembly and distribution. What's more, there was the never-ending dispute over making contact at nearby plantations – the others thought it premature, but she aimed to prepare links anyway: to be used after the fact, if not before.

After all, the rebellion would spread. She had to believe it. No one had ever attempted an uprising on the Brooke plantation in all its years, and the Planter wouldn't be ready. As long as they moved quickly, finishing their work before any Confederate Guard got involved, they could take over the property. Once they had control, the plantation's other indents would join in. They had numbers on their side.

Clara took in a breath. No matter what, her life was about to change. She wouldn't be staying in this cabin much longer, and glancing once more toward Atti, she felt a twinge.

Only if not her, then who?

It'd been this way since she'd been a little girl. Learning her letters from a white-haired preacher – leading nightly lessons in secret, the next cabin over – she'd put them to use: writing up requests and placing them on the overseers' doors, seeking shorter hours for those who were sick, larger shares of apples for those who were hungry. Her mother had told her to stop, to sit back and avoid the gamble, to wait and pray like the others. For a time, she'd even listened. But then her mother had been sold away. And the need to speak up had become a compulsion.

Lacing her boots, Clara worked to bottle her impatience. It was too much to keep in. Yet she trusted her own judgment, and took solace in the knowledge that when the day did arrive, and the secret was out at last, all the others would be right there with her, and Atti first among them.

CHAPTER 5

The following Sunday, Rosewood Manor's weekly brunch finished in the dining room just as the midday sun crested. At the room's center, opposite an enormous bay window, Franklin and Cathryn Brooke sat at one end of an oval table, basking in the air-conditioned chill and waiting while the indents cleared dishes. White-gloved and swift, the staff paraded past, carrying piles of porcelain scraped clean. Outside, a leisure garden beckoned; beyond that, the views of cotton-dappled fields rolled on forever.

When the indents finished, Cathryn spoke first. "I just don't understand." Her voice was quiet.

"I've told you, my dear. The subsidies have simply decreased. It's difficult these days for Richmond. It's asking too much to support all our commonwealth's Planters." Franklin paused. "The border trouble's real. We'll be needing more men at the front."

"And soldiers' wages to be taken off our backs?"

"Of course not." It wasn't so as bad as she feared. He could always apply for funds as a member of high command. In the meantime, better to avoid the optics, and take the pinch with along everyone else – only a few thousand dollars a month. "We'll be more than alright. We can trim back the tree line, expand the crop margins; we'll have the indents sell some of their trinkets, if need be. Worse comes to worse, we'll rent out the lower pasture to yeomen. They can host a concert, stage a wedding."

"Don't be gauche."

"I only mean we'll do what we must."

"You don't know what it is to be tight on money, Franklin."

"No. Nor shall I now."

She gave a snort. "Everyone fighting for every last scrap. That was Yankeedom. Pinching, saving. Never an inkling of community. No thought for order or civility. It's no good, Franklin. It's not something to be offhand about."

"So you've told me."

"It's the abolitionists," she pressed. "I *know* northerners. I know what they're made of. It's their propaganda that fuels all the trouble. They feed off the conflict. They stir it up."

"That doesn't mean we can ignore it." He poured another glass. "For it's precisely that venom we must fight. It snakes in easier than ever – their viruses pierce our firewalls; their satellites override our censors. Misinformation, false flag operations, corrupted newsfeeds. It all comes streaming through. And it means billions from Treasury – that's atop funding for the Guard."

"So they punish us in the meanwhile?"

"Who's they, darling? Richmond?" He tried a grin. "I am them, and they are me."

"Don't condescend."

He sighed, and took a sip of his punch.

"I mean it. I know what people whisper."

"Not anymore."

"Please."

"Not for years."

But she was shaking her head. "'*Once a Yank, always a Yank. Rotted from birth. Cold as New England ice.*'" She lifted a glass of her own. "I don't need protection, Franklin. I never did."

"Enough now." He reached out his hand. "You're more than the rest of us put together. More than any sad sack inheriting his acres, certainly. Anyone who knows you knows your spine, Cathryn – what you chose. What you renounced." He took her in: that fine gray hair tied tight behind her neck, green eyes darkened by the room's shadow.

It'd been twenty years, and still she didn't like talking about all she'd left behind. He wondered sometimes what her old life had become – no doubt she wondered too, though she never let on. Word had come last Christmas that her mother had passed, and her father moved to a home. Yet when Franklin had offered to find her a pass – for crossing the border, for visiting the cemetery at least – she'd refused. *What's gone is gone,* she'd insisted. *Love conquers all.* Clichés upon clichés, too much pain for actual grappling.

"Come now, Franklin." She was fighting off the concern in his gaze – the pity even. "Don't you worry – " she placed her hand upon his, and eventually offered a wink. "Look at you, my darling. It was never about that uniform, you know. No matter how handsome."

"What then?"

"Everything you are, naturally. Loyalty. Good sense."

"Charm beyond measure?" He was glad when a smile emerged.

"I mean what I say, though." She shifted in her chair. "Remember. All this – " she gestured toward the property outside – "it comes from what you do, not simply how you were born."

He chuckled.

"I speak because I must."

"I'm glad you speak." He leaned close, and winked back. "It's the Yank in you, after all."

This time, however, no smile came. "Think on it, Franklin. When Unionists marched on our squares, when indents were running their own papers out west for God's sake – when New York threatened our dollar! – who has it always been to save us?"

He shushed her. "Take care now. The indents will hear you, darling."

"Oh, Franklin. Missing Liza's recitals so you could give your speeches, galvanize our forces, round up intel? Remind the politicians of all you've done – make them listen – use your sway! They owe you. Always the gentleman, Franklin. Yet don't neglect your mettle beneath."

"My wallet, you mean."

"Well so be it. This plantation needs its cash."

"So does the Cause."

She rolled her eyes. "You believe the saints of yore ever had to choose? Between cash and country? Lee – Jackson?" But now she stopped, seeing him wince as she took their names in vain. "Fine then. Have another drink with me."

"Maybe something lighter."

She nodded, and moved toward the antique sideboard, fetching some lemon-water to wash away the liquor. "I only mean the plantations are everything."

"Of course."

"They're the soul of the nation."

"Yes, my love." He sighed. "But remember why else you left your country."

"As I say. I left for you."

"But also because you couldn't stay. Because respect for wisdom and history had been forgotten. Because their schooling is a free-for-all, and their society is founded upon nothing but rage. You're the one who made sure I understood that." His voice had gained an edge. "Because the masses must be checked, or else we face chaos. Because aristocracy has proven the better theory, and our government holds it together."

"Please do not lecture me on my own choices, Franklin."

He bit his lip. When he stumbled, he knew better than to plant his flag. Still, every word he said was true. As a boy, he'd read every book he could find. And Cathryn had only confirmed what he'd learned. The fact was, the U.S. had always been a land of greed and sin, blitzing its own citizens in the name of profit, living the lie that gold could make men free, that cities brought clarity, that utopian ideas were the same as good sense.

It was why the original Union had lasted but three generations, crumbling under the weight of its own lies. The Confederate Revolutionaries had tried to save it, reaching back for its original vision: liberty rooted in order, making good at last upon the promise of a City on a Hill, understanding, as Athens itself had once understood, that for free life to function, man must not overestimate his own capacity for self-government. Thank God then southerners had grasped equity was the enemy of freedom, discipline the antidote to fear.

Refusing surrender, they'd finally managed it, stabilizing the border after a decade of struggle. The new Confederate nation had grown quickly after that, blossoming right into the next century, when a rising generation of leaders had codified what until then had been bound up only in southern hearts, re-writing the Constitution, recognizing that the rights of citizenship worked best on a graduated scale, that only those properly prepared warranted the reins of power.

Unhindered by wild notions of populism, the nobles had borne their God-given responsibility, ushering the C.S.A. into its golden age. Voting had ceased for yeomen, office-holding too. Plantations had been expanded. Slavery preserved. The Confederate Guard had been founded for enforcing it all.

At long last, military victories had emerged in Missouri and Kentucky, extending the South's borders westward. From there, Confederates had marched further, drawing the old Mason-Dixon Line straight through the Mississippi, across the Plains and the Rockies, all the way to California, where citizens had picked their sides.

Only then had the armistice been reached. Battlefields were ceded to guerrillas, the Yanks grown exhausted. The war hadn't really ended, it was true, but the guns had been put away. All-out fighting settled into a steady simmer. A modicum of quiet had arrived, which people could call peace.

Both countries had turned inward to lick their wounds; the Yanks to their factories, the Rebs to their farms. The dueling American nations had signed their agreement respecting the border. By the time of the Second World War, while the U.S. razed its land and brutalized its people, all for the sake of steampipes and gas lines, the Confederacy cemented its status as the planet's largest exporter of foodstuffs, grain, and cotton.

Moreover, neutrality in that new, latest conflict had revealed the South's real might, as both sides across the ocean had begged – then bribed – Richmond's leaders for allegiance. The ultimate decision to stand against the world's tyrants had been not only virtuous but shrewd, infuriating northern abolitionists, undercutting their years of invective aimed at linking Confederate aristocracy with global totalitarianism – forcing them, briefly, to stand as allies.

Victory, then, had exceeded expectations. The young nation's cotton blockade had proven its economic weight, bolstered by the West's pledge to abandon India's suppliers after the war. What's more, the brief alliance with the U.S. had diminished the American continent's conflict in the eyes of Europe, putting the two countries on equal footing at last, defining the Confederacy as a proper superpower, no longer just a younger brother gone astray. Moral clout had been granted.

In the years since, northern climate-denial had only helped, as the Confederacy had led the way in solar and wind innovation, gearing up to make trillions, all while pointing a righteous finger at Yankee worship of banks over biosphere.

Foreign affairs had given a boost in the meantime. South Africa's apartheid had provided a new waystation for virtue-signaling. Palestine too.

Still, Franklin knew glory and strength could be fleeting. History taught that also. The era of Confederate confidence was the one into which he'd been born. There was no assurance it would be the one to see him off. It was up to his generation to maintain the project. Wearing the uniforms of their ancestors, they had their own leg of the race to run: silencing the nuclear threats from D.C. and San Francisco, muffling those on their own side who'd rather throw those same threats back in return; avoiding the riots and congressional shouting matches of the U.S.; sustaining instead a land of loyal yeomen and happy indents, faced with none of the challenges that came when man tried to alter God's intentions.

So Franklin had been taught. And so he continued to believe.

For who was he to deny the rock-solid results of stability? After all, hadn't Confederate custom and dignity been borne out? The laborers remained in fields and on factory floors, singing their songs of rebellion without seeing out their own lyrics' call; yeoman race-loyalty had been made clear; no-divorce laws were validated in poll after poll, proving Confederates the happiest population on earth.

Not that there hadn't been changes. But to Franklin's mind, these had served as release-valves, keeping pressure in check, allowing the foundation to hold. They'd emerged upon his entrance into the armed forces, following his stint at university. After vanquishing dictators across the globe, rebeldom's postwar heroes had ushered in the new sharecropping system, transforming the slaves into something closer to citizens. The new so-called indentures would never be paid, certainly, but nor would they be fully owned anymore. Legally, their bodies were henceforth to be their own. It was their *labor* that shifted into statutory possession of the white Planters.

It'd been a concession made under international lobbying. The old guard had been enraged, of course, but the new leaders had claimed flexibility on behalf of tradition. The hope in elite circles had been that this would be enough.

And boy had it. In the decades since, the rest of the world had watched with impatience but not interference, as it'd grown clear that no indenture would ever successfully pay off his debt. For how could they? The cabins they used, the food they ate, the plots where they raised their children – none of it belonged to them. Side-wages were illegal. Personal bank accounts forbidden. Savings of more than a hundred dollars confiscated. Each day they devoted to the Planters was another upon which they borrowed. As it stood now, they remained in bondage and always would. Order was maintained. The hard-liners were placated.

Alas, the end of slavery somehow hadn't ended U.S. abolitionism, let alone U.S. aggression. It hadn't even undone the Underground Railroad – that network of homes and businesses taking in runaway indentures, still managing to duck the Confederate Guard, seduced by propaganda-infused nonsense about freedom to the north. The internet had resurrected the damned thing from the history books, providing communication, carving out an illegal path straight to Maryland, then from there to the true-blue Union states of the coast.

More worrying yet, the vaunted Confederate military had begun to show cracks. Franklin could never acknowledge as much publicly, but it was increasingly hard to deny. There were even reports of U.S. victories in the border skirmishes nearby – those that would never make the nightly news. To the west, U.S. secret forces had repeatedly raided the Confederacy, stealing indentures, even kidnapping officials for interrogation. The biggest fear was that the U.S. would recognize such successes for what they were: evidence of the Confederacy's weakened defense apparatus, strained by the nation's small population and growing lack of funds. For had it not become clear that the treasured Confederate agriculture couldn't sustain itself forever? The Planter-subsidies had exploded in size; the taxes on yeomen had grown in turn.

Franklin shuddered to think of the U.S. military mobilizing and unleashing another full-scale war. Wiping the silver hair from his forehead, he exhaled, noticing the glass of lemon-water that Cathryn had placed in front of him.

"Dear?"

"Hm?"

"Didn't you hear me?"

He glanced up.

"I asked if you'll end up selling an indenture."

He rubbed his eyes, snapping his thoughts back to the here-and-now. "Why would I do that, darling?"

"To draw extra revenue, of course. To pay the overseers."

.   .   .

Neither of them had noticed Liza standing in the doorway, arms folded, looking suspicious. It was only when she spoke that they spun their heads. "What is it you're on about?" she wanted to know.

"Oh don't eavesdrop, Liza." Cathryn's northern way with words clipped her vowels; the consonants seemed to take over entirely. "We were just discussing the plantation's finances. And whether to sell a slave."

"They're not slaves, mother."

"You know what I mean. Their labor is ours to do with as we please."

From his seat, Franklin looked at his daughter. Her brown eyes were fixed, her shoulders steady. He understood her reluctance, for he too hated the idea of transporting these people against their will. But then, she didn't have to worry about financial realities. "It's true," he explained – a weariness in his voice that betrayed his age. "There's no reason to over-dramatize it. It'd be a business transaction. The corporations down south are always interested. I'll give one of them a call."

"You can't, father."

"Excuse me?"

"People say they're horrid. They don't act with near the same care as we do."

"Don't generalize, Liza darling."

But her voice was rising. "Couldn't you just sell something else – one of the cars? A section of land?"

"Don't be silly." Franklin frowned. He hadn't even committed to the idea, yet here he was defending it. "Your mother's right. Proceeds from a single indent would get us what we need."

"At the least, we should limit our luxuries first." Liza had stepped closer. "I don't need so many dresses for the season's balls. I can repeat a gown. Not to mention your anniversary party. Why don't I downsize it? No one would notice."

At that, however, Cathryn cleared her throat. "Young lady. You've grown up in the luxury of this place, without ever experiencing its alternative."

Liza paused. "So it's the party? That's what's forcing you to sell an indent? You need a cash injection?" When no reply came, she turned back to her father instead. "You can't just invite fewer guests? You'd rather sell a whole person away?"

• • •

She wanted to believe he'd speak up – that his heart would rise to the fore. But gazing upon him now, Liza could tell this battle was already lost. It was true he was a man who cared about others. But there was also the fact of how he'd built his life – embracing the ease of Rosewood, the parties and balls providing a welcome balance against his trips to the capital and meetings with other captains of the nation.

She braced herself.

He seemed to have lost an inch in the past year, and Liza frowned to look upon him, having observed the passage of time in his gout as well, in how he squinted when he read, in his stride slowed to a shuffle. Now, seeing him stoop, she could suddenly imagine a much older man indeed.

Franklin met her eye. "I'm sorry Liza," he said calmly. "But this is for the best. And it works out besides. I've been informed there's an indenture who's liable to be trouble."

She swallowed back her disappointment.

"Please don't worry darling. From what the overseers tell me, a change could serve this fellow well. He was caught running about the other night, spewing some tale about getting lost. This same fellow all but picked a fight with a white man for punishing a young indent over thieving. Then came reports he'd been spotted among the ladies' cabins." He shook his head. "We can't have it, Liza. Discipline will help the poor soul. Given our situation, I've half a mind to say the whole thing is God's will."

Liza looked toward the old wooden floor. "What's this 'poor soul's' name then?" she asked softly. Somehow she felt saying it aloud might at least lend the man his own humanity.

Her father shrugged. "He's called 'Atti,'" he answered. "And I'm sorry darling, but I'm gonna sell him."

CHAPTER 6

Ever since 1900, when it had moved from Washington D.C. – far too close to the border, officials had finally concluded – the U.S. capital had resided in New York City. There, amid the glinting steel and miles of crisscrossing pavement, in the heart of the city's energy and grit on Sixth Avenue, the world's tallest buildings housed the federal government. The structures varied in age – some had been converted, others were newly constructed – but all were enormous, home to thousands of staffers, darting between their offices and the sidewalks, grabbing coffees and overpriced sandwiches, answering texts on tiny screens, running the bureaucracy on everything from taxation to war.

Because this new capital city hadn't been born as such, it still retained its old points of pride, preserving them around its newly purposed heart. Despite the noisy motorcades snarling traffic, regular life endured. Downtown, the crowded, self-important bars still partied through the night. East and West, hospitals and public housing grids ran up against the gorgeous, polluted rivers. Up north, beyond the oasis of Central Park, tenements bordered the grand old houses of luxury.

The Government District began at 44th Street, with a sparkling new skyscraper that served as headquarters for the Primary Intelligence Office. Its analysts tended to the nation's foreign policy as a whole, but its largest division, filling the top thirty floors, focused on the Confederacy. There, thousands of young workers monitored reports from border cameras and field commanders, filed data on the Underground Railroad, and stayed alert for information from interrogated Confederates.

Ted Mercer and Raj Hayworth were but two among them.

All summer, they'd been sifting through the border updates for anything that seemed unusual. It was tedious work, examining bullet-points about the latest skirmishing, tallying numbers of prisoners, mapping possible soft spots in the face of incursions, writing up bid-solicitations for the latest sections of the newly proposed border wall. But at least the growing tension meant something might change.

That was enough to drive Ted onward as he sat at his computer and scanned PDFs: the latest recruiting numbers, cell phone shots of U.R. hiding spots, weekly casualty counts at the front. Regarding this last item: until recently, the numbers had been categorized by month instead, but with the violence getting worse – more escaped runaways making dashes near the trenches, Confederate forces ever jumpier, U.S. intelligence raids more common – the government had adapted.

Ted managed to find it interesting. He'd long dreamed of working for the feds, and after college, had applied for whatever positions were posted. With the help of his father, Manhattan's most sought-after contracts lawyer – not to mention his activist-donor mother who'd raised him on stories of their vaunted Union heritage – he'd fast-tracked right here: one ancestor allegedly felled at Bull Run, another serving as military governor in Delaware, and now him, typing and scrolling for his country.

His desk-mate and oldest school chum, Raj, was sitting just a few feet off. It happened to be 1pm on a Wednesday, which meant a new weekend was finally closer than the last one, and Raj had taken note. "You know," he murmured now, rubbing his black beard, aware it might eventually need a trim. "You could mark down half of those reports as mine – just say I went through them...."

Ted cracked a smile but kept at it. "C'mon, buddy. It wouldn't help the cause."

"I forgot. With privilege, cometh principle." They both snorted. For Raj, a job was a job. His family had never had time for American creed; they'd been too busy ducking American hypocrisy. His mother had come from Mumbai, meeting his New Jersey-born father at Princeton, obtaining a green card through marriage. When Ted had gotten him this gig, he'd taken it. Now, he spent most of their days poking fun at the piety of Northern whiteness. It wasn't that he sympathized with the Confederacy, of course. But he didn't dwell on it either.

Ted glanced back up, his prep school looks still fully intact: hair cast blonde by the sun, sea-blue eyes amused, the same shade as the polo shirt buttoned to his collar. "You just gonna watch me all day?"

"Four more hours."

"Three. It's last Wednesday of the month: senior staff meetings at day's end. We get to leave early."

Raj exhaled. Finally, he returned to the reports, beginning with an account from the night before of Union special forces taking thirty Confederate Guard agents prisoner. They'd require funding for transport. "The fighting's picking up," he mused.

"Sure is."

"You think it'll ever turn into anything more?"

"I think it might." Ted paused. "I hope it does."

"What does that mean?"

"Why not properly fight those bastards down there? Remind them what we think of them."

Raj just shook his head. Still, their friendship endured. Ted was a loyal soul. It wasn't just his country he stuck by – he was good to anyone who was important to him. And together, they stayed tethered to their screens.

Chapter 7

Liza Brooke had never ventured far from Rosewood Manor. Her life at home was easy enough, her days in central Virginia routine, her citizenship rights as a woman so limited that inertia kept her immobile.

Over time, though, she'd grown restless. And recently, it'd gotten worse. With her parents' worries over money, the very notion of expensive parties seemed more ridiculous than ever, and all the harder to enjoy. Yet what else to do? She'd long ago made it through all the interesting books in her father's library – antebellum novels, military histories, the occasional government study on climate – and the digital world was so heavily censored, there was nothing left worth finding on her computer either.

School, meanwhile, had ended before university, as it did for all young women. Friends were hard to come by; those she retained from the primary grades and debutante balls were largely to be seen only at the galas now, with chaperones and custom guarding them at all times. Only the Donleau mansion sat within walking distance. More and more, then, she thought about taking a trip, curious to see something more of her country, to venture beyond the walls of her family's circumstance.

After all, stories from her father about distant government meetings seemed no more accessible than the fairy tales he'd once told at her bedside; news about the border had become so airbrushed as to grow dull. Conversations with the indents were forbidden. Civilian air travel wasn't allowed for women on their own. Sometimes it felt like government ads assailing the U.S. - its class warfare, the warped notions of its wild masses - were all she actually knew of the outside world beyond Crotelle.

The fact was, she wouldn't need to go a great distance. A trip to Richmond would suffice. Just driving through the yeomen counties on the way would bring plenty of new sights. Then there'd be the city itself. It was so infamous for urban bustle that some worried it echoed too much of the U.S.

So it was, lying in bed one Thursday night, Liza found herself again pondering a getaway. Borrowing one of her father's cars wouldn't be too difficult - he barely touched them, always getting chauffeured by government drivers instead - and while nobles were discouraged from leaving their neighborhoods, always amid concerns about provoking class strife, a stray weekend away was now-and-again permissible.

She leaned against her headboard. Her mind throbbed, and she listened to herself breathe. She looked down, and studied her feet, poking up from the lambswool throw below.

In fact, part of her disquiet was because of Kevin. They'd kissed several more times, and she suspected they'd do so again soon. He still made her feel safe, and warm, and happy too. But that wasn't all. He also still made her think. For all his stoicism, Kevin still enjoyed questions. The other week, over lunch, he'd contemplated what a yeoman might make of the inside of a noble's mansion. A few days later, he'd gone so far as to wonder aloud whether the Confederate Guard knew how much people made fun of them.

If she invited him along, she'd get to see those brilliant blue eyes study the world in real-time. After all, Kevin was always reading antique books about foreign lands and long-ago moments. To him, learning itself was the adventure; he could become energized just staring up at the sky. She'd love to be with him as he experienced something more.

Already, Liza knew he'd seen places she never had. He'd gone to university a full hour away in Charlottesville. More exotically, he'd lived his year of military service at a base in West Texas. He'd spent his time there studying cartography, stuffed full with too many orders for sightseeing, he'd said, but Liza could tell from the way he still marveled over its dry heat and flat terrain that he'd been dazzled simply by being somewhere far away.

And so, after she'd eventually dozed off and morning had arrived, she knew what to do. She showered swiftly, then put on her most comfortable dress, regretful as ever that women weren't allowed to wear shorts in summer, before passing through the kitchen without even grabbing toast. Walking briskly, she shot straight from the house's main hall, ignoring the indents offering her a ride, and down to the road to tell Kevin of her grand plan.

She found him at a picnic table on the front pasture, under a maple tree, reading a yellowed newspaper he'd probably located in his family's archives, studying forgotten morsels. It was typical of him, she thought, getting absorbed in what was most distant; it was why she'd come. Even in the morning shade, the temperature was creeping toward 90 degrees, but Kevin always preferred natural breeze to manmade air-conditioning. He had to be one of the few nobles who spent his summer days outside like an indent – albeit in the shade, finding a spot simply to sit – and Liza smiled at his stubbornness. Perhaps he wasn't just an armchair-philosopher after all, she thought. For here he was, adhering to his principles.

He looked up, and put the newspaper down with a smile right back.

. . .

Kevin had always adored Liza of course. Growing up, they'd been best of friends. But ever since he'd returned from service, it'd been even more. He'd looked forward to every last instant with her. They had anything and everything to talk about: gossiping about their parents, even confiding in each other their guilt over their easy upbringings, pondering the heat and the climate change that government spokesmen were always going on about.

Now he stood, admiring her as she got close. Her dark hair gleamed in the morning sun; her eyes were as sparkling as the day. She had on a fine opal necklace and a soft dress covered in pink flowers, and he couldn't help but think that somehow the nation's troubles couldn't touch her. It was as if there were at least some things on earth that could be relied upon – and Liza was one of them.

He was falling in love, he was sure. Kissing those lips was a wonder each time – like a dream. Her gaze was buoyant, her smile beyond imagining. He only wished he could explain how much it meant to him. Yet for all his ability to pontificate about an author's latest screed or a newsman's deficiencies on camera, he found that he hemmed and hawed whenever it came time to express his feelings to Liza. It was as though the stakes were too high, and he just couldn't match them with his words.

Instead, he simply waved. "Should we go in?"

She replied with a laugh. "What about your love of summer heat?"

"You'd stay out here with me?"

"How could I say no to bees and sweat?" And she let him kiss her indeed, before taking his hand as they started a stroll around the grounds, green fields beckoning them forward.

"So I've had an idea," Liza announced as they walked. "I want to go on a trip – and I want you to come with me."

He raised his eyebrows.

"I've never seen my own country, you know. I've never even seen half my own commonwealth! Why not drive around, the two of us? We could take it in for real. Not from government textbooks, or the news, but with our own eyes. I know you've gone farther than I have, Kevin. But going together would be divine. I know it would."

His grin hadn't faded.

"What?" she asked.

"Gimme a moment. I'm just admiring the way you talk." Her noblewoman's accent came out most when she was happy – lilting and melodious and elegant.

"You talk just the same!"

"It doesn't sound as good coming from me."

"Well won't you come?"

"Tell me more. What is it you want to see?"

"Our capital, for one. The center of the nation. I want to find out what it is that gets those Yanks so mad."

"It's pretty straightforward, I'd say. Every society has its problems – wealth and poverty, discord and cover-ups, oppression even. I suppose that's the enemy's job: focus on the problems and leave out the rest."

"Oh stop. I still want to see it myself, decipher it on my own, don't you?"

He hesitated. "I'm sorry. You're right, Liza. I'm lucky I've gotten to." It wasn't fair that women didn't get to travel for university or service, he knew; he oughtn't be offhand about it. But change wasn't such a lighthearted matter either. "It's just not that easy to get across Virginia. Not without a pass."

"If I get stopped, I'll say I forgot it."

"The Confederate Guard's stringent these days, even with nobles. They'll send you right back."

She rolled her eyes.

"Don't be mad."

"I'm not mad. But all this logic – all these words. How can someone so curious be so afraid?"

He flushed. "We're the same, really. We wouldn't know how to talk to anyone if we went, that's all. Or be with them, or behave in their yeoman shops. I've never wandered like that. Neither have you."

"Oh for heaven's sake. I just want to go on an afternoon drive!"

"You don't, though. You don't just want an afternoon drive, Liza." He took in a heavier breath. "You said so yourself. You want to see what it is about this country that makes other people so mad."

"Fine. But it's not treason either."

"Don't be silly."

"Well don't be so sincere."

But they both went silent for a while after that, looking across the sweep of gentle pastures to their right. At the edge, another line of red maples sat languidly. They were in perfect antique formation, half-a-dozen of them, trunks near as wide as cars, leaves as dark as emeralds; like a lonesome team of sentinels – sanguine, sorrowful at once – charged with guarding against time itself. "You know," she finally went on. "If you didn't want to come, you could have just said you had family obligations or something."

"Give me more credit than that."

"I'm serious."

He retrieved his smile. "You really are amazing."

"Apparently not enough to get you to Richmond."

"What if your father finds out?"

"He won't be near as worked up as you." But this time, she paused, leaning up on her toes, and she kissed him on the cheek.

"You won't stay for lunch?"

She shook her head. "Let's do it another day, and I'll tell you all about my trip."

"You don't mean you'll go alone?"

But she was already walking off.

At once, Kevin wished he had given in. But wasn't it an uneasy time to be curious about the world? What with everyone getting so tense over the border and the rumors of resistance in the cities? Watching her amble back down the driveway, already impatient to see her again, he imagined himself catching up and following along. But that wouldn't help either, unless he was going to change his mind, and so slowly he headed back toward the picnic table and newspaper, letting her disappear.

CHAPTER 8

That night at home in the Brooke study, Liza scanned websites.
The blue glow from the screen was the only light source in the
room, and its gleam cast a modern pall upon the cracked
portraits of Confederate ancestors on the walls.

She'd worked hard to ignore Kevin's protests, sorry he was
so wracked by his own thoughts, but also annoyed. To put him
from her mind, she'd taken to searching the internet for a map
of Virginia. Normally that would be no easy task, with databases
blocked by the government and travel surveilled. But Liza had
logged on using her father's name and password, scrawled out
on a notepad by the keyboard. His clearance meant she had the
widest berth: she still couldn't access certain sites – non-
Confederate media remained off-limits – but maps weren't a
problem. Eagerly, she jotted down directions.

As she was finishing up, a small alert appeared in the upper
corner of the screen. She glanced at the flashing banner. *Reports
from Richmond*, its rigid black font proclaimed. *Resistance
Meetings. Insurrectionist activity*. That was it.

The words were intended for her father, and Liza knew she
ought to look away. Still, she lingered an extra moment. He
never shared about his job, speaking only vaguely about
summonses to Richmond – for dull-sounding strategy sessions
on blocking Union raids, or endless discussions about yeomen

taxes. Yet the little bits he offered were also how Liza knew anything at all. It was how she'd learned that Congress was worried about a rise in runaways, and how she'd gleaned that the president had been increasing Guard recruitment, amid concerns over criminality in the capital.

She read the alert once more, wondering what "Resistance" could actually mean. All her life people had talked only of loyalty and heritage. Teachers back in school had treated government decrees like sacred texts. Her parents toasted the founding generation all but every night. Parties were always leashed to historical holidays – Secession Day, Memorial Day, the Song of the South Festivals. If there were any doubts about the nation at all, they'd been kept private.

So what was this?

What would it be like to come upon a city where such a thing was real, where there were enough people curious about the way things were that the government actually sent out a notice?

It certainly wasn't that Liza wished ill upon her own country. She'd been brought up the same as everyone else, to admire the Confederate heroes of the past, to know that those who ran things were continuing their legacy. Only – wasn't this evidence that there wasn't a monopoly on how to think?

She shut the computer and stuffed the handwritten directions in her pocket.

·   ·   ·

The next morning, she drove out, leaving her sleeping parents at daybreak.

Peering out from her father's car, a Carolina-constructed BMW 7-series, she marveled at mist-strewn views ahead. Following her coordinates, gripped by the rush that came with discovery, she soon passed farther from the estate than she'd ever been, leaving the Piedmont's gated manors behind and coming upon two-room huts in their place, wrapped in unglazed windows and half-collapsed porches. Here now were yeomen children, in wheat sacks for clothing, rolling hoops along spotted hay; grown folk too, tending vegetable-gardens and laundry lines, fetching firewood from large stacks, eyeing her sedan with suspicion.

She slowed to avoid the little ones, and as she did, one of the men wandered over, hauling a bundle of celery root, squinting up past sallow brown cheeks, not a tooth left in his grimace. His shoulders looked to have once been sturdy. His neck matched the crinkled linens behind him.

"Can't help you," Liza murmured, wishing now she hadn't cracked the windows, making sure she didn't steer into the gullies.

"You a Planter gal then?" He had a gravelly voice, like simmered milk.

"Just a passer-through."

"What about a Christian?" someone else called, and Liza glanced toward the porches at the roadside and the emaciated visages staring back.

"Just can't help," she repeated. For if she did – what then? She'd be alone among them, wholly dependent on their grace. Some piece of her wished to pull the car over anyway, to learn more, but even then, what could she ever really know of their lives? And what could she possibly offer? She had no cash, only credit cards and digital payment apps on her phone. What would father say if he saw a sum wired to a family in the valley?

It just wouldn't do.

Pressing the accelerator, marking proud green hills in the distance, Liza shook off the moment, passing privies and rotting compost piles as she held her breath, no longer listening to their pleas. In time, the dusty road eased wider, and the homes receded from the curbs, tin roofs and forgotten faces – children who seemed as withered and weathered as their parents – giving way to paved-over boulevards and cream-colored sidewalks. Poverty wasn't what she'd come to see, after all, and she could always ask her father to invite some yeomen to the house if she really wanted information. In the meantime, the city awaited. Adventure still beckoned.

The car clattered onward, and eventually she was entering the capital region. Now there were different sorts of houses – aluminum canopies and white grated doors, gray stoops, wide driveways – and the crowds were growing as well: boys playing ball on the corners, women walking small dogs. Until there it was – the capital itself – lording over the horizon, and Liza leaned forward on the wheel, gazing upwards at what was coming, alive and electric and immense.

She blinked as she got close, ogling the lines of cars vying for position against crunched vistas of apartments and office complexes. Craning her neck, she marveled at the slim tops of buildings farther off, all while pushing onward toward the coast, through a growing rush of concrete, hustle, and horns.

In time, the streets grew even more clogged, with more traffic than she'd ever seen. Liza kept the car close to the curb, nervous and excited at once by the thrill of competing for space with so many others. Richmond City, the stuff of magazines and film, and here she was smack in the middle of it. She'd seen photos of the place, sure, but to be confronted by it in real time, in real space, was something else entirely.

She wished Kevin were there to see it too, but already she was eager to share it with him when she got back. She could picture his gaze as he peppered her for details, and she smiled to think of his earnest nods as he listened to her descriptions. Gradually, she was letting go her grudge.

Closer to the city center then, and the roads began to slow. She sought signs for parking, and soon spotted an underground garage. It seemed to spiral downward forever, as if to the center of the earth, and Liza almost grew dizzy angling through its maze. But at last, she found a spot.

Taking a breath, she stepped from the car. The low ceilings and shimmering florescent light made it feel like some massive cement cave. But it was also a springboard to all that beckoned, and trekking back up the garage ramp by foot, she strode into the sun. The air was a swirl of noise and exhaust. A six-lane boulevard extended before her. The walls ahead were cluttered with windows. The cars were small, with non-existent trunks and tiny windshields. There were steel bridges and roaring buses, and the murmur of hurried voices. Her own world was far slower than this one, she thought, and she found herself clenching her fists by her sides.

Every inch of this city occupied every history book she'd ever opened. Once upon a time, its citizens had defied hunger and sieges during the Revolution, then had rebuilt and regrown the whole place over the ensuing decades. But as Liza stepped forward, she wasn't focused on the shadows of past greatness, but rather a propulsion here to the future. On block after block, there was more life than she thought possible. Cafés, bus depots, apartment high-rises.

To be sure, in between, monuments abounded, saluting the eras that had come before. Here were sculpted heroes like Wilson and Lee, founding fathers like Davis, modern stars too – presidents and Planters – including, she realized with a flush, her own father, cast in bronze. He was right there on the next corner. The sculptor had gotten the dignified profile just right – though he'd missed the warmth of the gaze, replacing it with a generic humility that didn't remind Liza of anyone at all.

More striking than the monuments, though, more even than her own family's place among them, were the *people*. Expertly dodging cars and trams, they somehow didn't look like the locals Liza normally saw. Half of them were faced down, stuck to their gadgets, tiny phones they were gripping like comfort blankets. Yet in the same instant they all seemed so *sure* – every step the thrust of a dagger, every swivel a pirouette.

Certainly, there were men here her father's age, wearing full Confederate regalia – no doubt he knew half of them – walking with purpose, as if these pulsing streets were nothing more than an inconvenience to be dealt with between tasks. And she saw a few noblewomen like herself, some in semi-formal wear, displaying the hoop skirts that were the staple of official Confederate fashion, others simply donning sundresses. But most of all, there were Confederate Guard agents everywhere, young and certain and in command.

Their powder blue uniforms, lined with silver buttons and complemented by wool-lined kepi hats, made them instantly recognizable. Liza still feared the Guard as much as anyone did, no matter how many harmless old grammar school classmates she knew who had enlisted; their power was too real, the stories too haunting. And as she watched these men now, chattering in their Chesapeake cadences and Tidewater drawls, marching swiftly in their high black boots – strapping and wet from the heat, smirks and sneers buried beneath their caps – Liza couldn't help but confirm there was a menace to their clout, an excess strength infusing their struts. No matter their youth, they had a puffed-out swagger in all they declared to the world.

In technical terms, the Confederate Guard was the nation's security force. Liza's own father insisted that was the extent of it. But everyone knew the agents did far more than protect the influential. They were the ones in charge of both foreign and domestic intelligence, always on the lookout for whispers of dissent. Only nobles were permitted to enlist – not merely outranking local yeomen police, but granted extralegal rights – questioning, ID'ing, and imprisoning dissidents, using any means they chose. Liza had even heard stories of Planters themselves being snatched from their homes, without warning and at strange hours, facing interrogation about everything under the sun, from Underground Railroad stations to issues seemingly minor – the discovery in a nearby town dumpster of a U.S. pamphlet, or a shopping order placed to an international store.

In every town in Confederate America, people worked hard to avoid these agents. There were tales of torture, disappeared citizens, inmates returned unable to speak – or spending the rest of their lives sharing nothing but murmured platitudes about the majesty of the South. But avoidance would certainly be impossible here. Back home, there'd be one or two uniformed corporals on a corner. Here, on one half-block, she could count fifteen. People in all directions were quietly glancing over their shoulders as they passed, the way they might toward a threatening dog – only to encounter a new batch on the very next curb.

It wasn't just the agents pouring out from every crevice, however. It was the yeomen too. These were far from the first Liza had ever seen, of course. Her family's milkman delivered bottles every other day, and low-level staffers visited her father weekly. Not to mention the overseers who patrolled every square of Rosewood's acreage. Yet never had she felt so obviously outnumbered. Not like this.

Here, hundreds were strolling, chatting, resting, smoking – twisting about among their superiors. A few were yelling, some laughing, all of them loud. Their words were rough and thick; she could hear it in the hard "b's" and "t's," the casual vowels, and easy intonation. Some of the men wore regular army uniforms; others merely sauntered past in jeans and sneakers, with ragged shirts and missing buttons. But Liza's jaw dropped most of all at the yeomen ladyfolk. There were no hoop dresses. No sundresses either. Their skirts were form-fitting, shockingly so, their tops low-cut. She didn't know whether to laugh or scold, and instead she just gawked.

Everywhere too, she saw indentures. There were as many in her view now as in a whole quadrant back at Rosewood. Some seemed to be on errands for their owners. But others were in groups of eight or ten, bound together by shackles and tracked by GPS tablets sewn to their belts or latched to pendants strapped tightly around their necks. At first, she wondered at such large groups. She knew of course that the Confederacy had millions of indents; her family's plantation alone had more than a thousand. Once, when she'd been a girl, father had let slip that the nation might even be home to more black Confederates than white – though the census wouldn't ever officially confirm it, and no one really wanted to know.

But this was enough to make such talk seem real.

One indent woman began pointing, saying something frantic about a journey, though as soon as Liza stepped forward to hear, the woman was hustled off with the rest. There were no children in these groups, no elders either, just the young and the strong – were they runaways? Recently caught? And then one of the men in the nearest gaggle – only a few feet distant – looked directly Liza's way. The creases by his eyes deepened; he lifted a gnarled finger, crooked in all the wrong places – like a paper clip half-straightened, hinting at some terrible past abuse that made her wince. "Tears of pity don't do us any good," he suddenly said, and she was sure she heard some of the men snicker by his side.

As they went, Liza stayed stuck. She couldn't imagine an indent talking that way back home, voicing any opinion at all, let alone an opinion about her – directly to her, no less! – and she shook her head, stunned by this city, its clatter and din, its sense of pandemonium brimming just offstage, as if roaring barely out of earshot. Her thoughts returned to Kevin, to his reluctance and his doubts – probably sipping a tall glass of lemonade under the shade of his trees at this very moment – and again she wanted to get back and tell him of all that she'd seen.

Instead, across the street, she saw a small corner pub that looked popular – men and women crowding the door, a mixture of nobles and yeomen – with a brightly painted sign out front. "Village Field Tavern," it declared, and needing a moment to pause, she set forth.

．　　．　　．

Instantly, she appreciated the place's relative peace after the commotion of the streets. The pub had high wooden ceilings and heavy, smoke-filled air, and there was a water cooler in the corner where she was able to fill a cup. Smoothing back her hair, Liza took a sip.

An ornate bar was in the corner, antique no doubt, mostly blocked by revelers at its counter. A menu on a chalkboard listed all manner of traditional Confederate fare, chops, beefsteaks, clams, boiled eggs. But before she could even think about ordering, a tall man was suddenly standing right in front of her.

He had a dark beard and dancing even darker eyes. His shoulders were broad, pushing against a brown woolen jacket, his chestnut hair gone shaggy, with a hint of red when it caught the light. He stepped smoothly forward, and bowed – handsome in a way he clearly understood: lips on the brink of a smile, gaze glinting – looks, Liza was already certain, that made every day far too easy for him.

"How do ya' do, darlin'," he began, and the pure fun with which he said it, poking away at the mannerisms of nobles everywhere, made her smirk despite her uncertainty. "You look like you need a laugh," the man went on, and with a wide grin, he stuck out his hand. "I'm Dale Birch."

Liza shook cautiously. She'd met plenty of confident Confederates in her time, but usually they oozed insensitivity. Not this one. His smile was broad and earnest, his voice self-assured but kind.

"I'm Liza," she said. "Liza Brooke. Pleased to meet you."

"Just water today?"

"Isn't it a bit early for anything else?"

"That's your excuse?"

"I'm also driving – back to Crotelle." She paused. There was a directness to his questions that had her sharing more than she intended.

"Your hometown?"

"More or less. I'm from Rosewood Manor."

"You don't say." Dale took her in. "I've been out there a few times – gorgeous country."

"It is."

For just a moment, he was quiet. Then his smile returned. "I sound like a bourgeois ass."

This time, Liza laughed loudly. "You're very honest."

Dale shook his head. "Dunno about that."

There was certainly something about him, she thought. His words came out easy, quicker than those of most Virginia gentlemen – a nonchalance and poise somehow mixed together – the timbre of his voice rich but not loud, the kind that forces you to listen.

Now he was leaning closer again, his jaw grown tighter, though still his dark eyes danced. "Would you mind if I did something stupid?"

"Well I don't know," Liza replied, feeling her heart pick up its pace, flummoxed that a stranger should have such an effect. "It would depend."

It was his turn to laugh. "You thought I was gonna kiss you!"

She gasped. Was everyone so forward in this city? The indents, the nobles, everybody in between?

"Truth is, Ms. Brooke, I had in mind something even more reckless." He squinted towards her. "I was fixing to ask you downstairs."

She found herself nodding, and she placed her glass on a table.

He shook his head with another smile. "My friends would kill me if they'd any idea how long we'd known each other."

But with that, Dale reached out his hand. He led Liza to the rear of the room, where light bulbs swayed from strings, and clouds rose from rolled cigarettes, guiding them towards a crooked stairwell in the corner and a narrow door at its base.

Kevin Donleau never once entered her mind.

CHAPTER 9

Beyond the staircase door, they stepped into a tight hallway. The floorboards were narrow-cut, the walls empty except for a stained mirror; another door stood closed on the far end, with voices coming from behind. Dale pushed this one open too.

The sounds grew louder.

"*Another!*" someone was shouting. "*It's early yet!*" There was an out-of-tune piano playing loudly.

The barkeep was busy, in a white apron and black tie, hair greased so tight it looked frozen in place. The customers were swinging to the syncopation – the bass line caressing the melody, the men doing the same to the gals. This wasn't the Confederacy Liza knew. "They're wild," she declared.

"They're the future," Dale responded from her side.

But the bartender was shouting their way. "Nice garb, stranger!" and he laughed as he took in Liza's sundress. "You here to make trouble?"

She stepped forward. "No trouble at all." She hesitated. "Mint julep?"

"Yes, ma'am," and he started mixing, then slid over two tin cups.

"We'll start a tab," Dale announced, and the bartender marked down their order.

Next, Dale led them over to a table by the wall: two women, a blonde and a brunette, stood nearby; opposite them sat a fellow with thin cheeks, and a rounder, quieter type, who looked drunker than he intended, sliding down in his chair. Liza frowned. She was being too easily led about, acting as if she had no power to stop it. Yet on she walked. It was as though the world she'd accessed all her life was becoming undone in an instant, and she couldn't help but gape.

"This here is Liza," Dale was shouting to the others. "Be polite."

"Great dress," the heavy one slurred. "I'm Raymond."

"I'm Walter," added the other. "Guard-rank Captain, at your service" – they all cackled, as though such a joke were nothing at all – "and this is Dorothy" – the blonde woman winked – "and that's Louise."

Louise was staring at Liza's sundress. "Aren't you a hoot!"

"Excuse me?"

"You sound just like my grammy!" the young woman howled back – and Liza stared in turn. "Oh no, dear – I mean no harm by it: it's just so charmingly bygone! You're new to Richmond then?"

But Liza only took a gulp from her drink, the noise rising, the faces melding into a raucous tableau. She noted Dale was grinning widely as ever, as he took her hand back in his, and they lowered into the stools that awaited. She was self-conscious at how close they were, balancing her glass on the table's edge, fidgeting with the sprig of mint in her cocktail.

"Thanks for inviting me," she managed.

He tilted his head a millimeter closer and lifted his cup. "To shared destiny," he murmured. "And the path from there."

Liza drank in turn. The room had become a cresting, colorful wave, as if all around them were eager souls, defying the staidness of their own lives, thinking only of the next round, the next yarn, the next burst of jokes and joy. Leaning forward on the table, Liza took them all in. Their city accents were harried and clipped, but their ease was contagious; they were swapping stories, sharing in simple fun. Somewhere along the line, someone passed a platter of salted ham and pretzels. The crowds grew thicker. The piano crescendoed.

She felt herself tapping her thumbs to its rhythm. Dale bent in nearer than ever. "Would you like to dance?"

She tilted away.

"C'mon, Ms. Brooke – what's the downside?" And before she knew it, she was standing along with him. He put his hand around her waist. "What do you think?"

"I think I'd never get away with this back home," but her lips parted into a smile, and she turned her face to his as she placed a hand on his shoulder.

They shifted forward in the bar's uneven light. "You have to know, Ms. Brooke, I'd never ask a gal to dance the very first day I met her." His voice went hushed. "You're just the most riveting one I ever encountered."

"That's the juleps talking."

"I swear it's not."

For a long second then, it was as if the piano had gone quiet, and the dance floor belonged only to them.

"I've an idea," Louise suddenly announced from their side.

"Impossible!" Charlie yelled, and the others cackled.

"I do!" she protested. "Listen here!" She slammed her glass on the table. "We each write a poem. Then we read them aloud!"

Liza waited for the table to erupt once more. But the others were actually nodding, pulling out pencils for scribbling on napkins.

"Any spares?" she asked, pushing away from Dale, glad suddenly for the distraction. And as someone passed one over, they both sat back down. Still, the warmth of the moment lingered, and for now at least, she avoided his gaze. She grinned at the others, and started scribbling.

Charlie faced her a moment later, his small eyes aglimmer. "Guests first."

"It's pretty short," she said. Her confidence surprised her, but she cleared her throat and began: "*A Night, or A Year,*" she recited. "*Or Four. Or Forever.*" She looked up.

"I like it," Walter abruptly declared, and the others laughed.

Dale was nodding. "Me too," he said, his voice rumbling through the crowd, though he'd glanced away. Near the back wall, several young men were playing billiards, and now, as Liza watched, Dale gave them a longer look. One bent toward an electrical outlet, lifted it from the wall's base, and pressed a small button. To her surprise then, yet another narrow door, a hidden one, was sliding from the corner, opening along grooves she'd thought were seams in the woodwork.

Dale faced back. "You liked our dance, yeah?"

"What if I did?"

"Well this is even better," and with a wink, he led her onward.

Waving a hasty farewell to the others, they stepped ahead – until, to her surprise, as soon as they'd reached the next room, the door shut behind them with a click, notched back into the wall once more. The air in here was even heavier, a fog; the crowd was denser, more muted; wooden crates had been stacked by the corner. In the middle, another bar awaited, quieter and less fully stocked than the one they'd just left. A young woman glanced up from behind it, a cotton wrap upon her shoulders, long strands of pearls around her neck. "Ah," she proclaimed. "My friends – let's welcome Dale Birch. Give him a hand!"

In an instant, it seemed like the whole room was applauding.

Liza stared, heart clanging against her ribs. All at once, she recalled the alert on her father's computer. The warning about "*Resistance.*"

For what else could this be? A secret room beyond a basement speakeasy beneath a Richmond pub?

She froze. She didn't belong here. It was dangerous and ridiculous to stay, and she knew she should turn, head outside, never look back. If she was smart, she'd never even *think* back. This Dale Birch was a stranger, after all – he'd lied, brought her in here on false pretenses.

Yet why wasn't she leaving? Could it really be just the booze? – or the sheer excitement of being somewhere impossible?

After all, wasn't that why she'd come to this city at all?

Then – Dale climbed atop the bar.

"Folks," he began, straightening himself out, standing tall. "I know why you're here."

The room grew quiet – Liza most of all.

"I love the Confederacy," he continued. "And so do you. But we love it because it's the land of our fathers and grandfathers, not because we're told to love it – not because of the government's fearmongering about northern chaos being the alternative. We love it because it's our home. We love it because of its good food, and good drink…"

There was warm, widespread laughter.

"We love it because of what it's supposed to be. A place where people go about their lives, enjoy their families, don't ever bother over what the authorities think they oughtta be doin'. That's what this country was designed for, that's what it claims to stand for. Federalism – localism! Not top-down hypocrisy."

Liza realized she was holding her breath.

"Unfortunately for us, that ain't what it's become," Dale said next. "Hell, nobles see the truth just as much as anyone else. Aristocracy ain't freedom for everybody – it's freedom for a few. *That's* what needs changing. This country can still restore rights to its people, not just Planters. We can still be a southern republic!"

The crowd erupted into its loudest applause yet, and Liza felt as if she was going to faint. Certainly, she'd questioned the Confederacy before, pressing her father about indents' hours, about censorship on the news. But this was different. To put it all so pointedly, so publicly...

It was insane.

Dale had finished. He was jumping down from the bar, allowing another young man to take his place. Stepping toward Liza, accepting slaps-on-the-back and handshakes along the way, he grinned. "Well, Ms. Brooke? How'd I do?"

She tried to find her voice.

"You alright?"

She cleared her throat. "You said a hell of a lot."

"Why thank you."

"But no mention of indents?"

"Ah – you were paying attention! Too much at once, and you'll lose 'em, you see."

"Nothing about women either."

This time, he guffawed – a big laugh that Liza was already getting used to. "So you'd advise more audacity next time?"

"No, no, please – "

"It's alright, Ms. Brooke."

Her thoughts were tumbled. She flushed. "What about all those Guard outside?"

"It's a risk," he shrugged. "But worth taking, no? "

"You only just met me, Mr. Birch."

"Am I wrong?" His voice steadied. "I like you, Liza. That much I knew straight away."

"That's enough?"

"I felt you could see this and keep it to yourself. You saying I have bad instincts?"

"You act like any of this is normal."

"It could yet be." His grin stayed in place. "Come back and see, whenever you like. Look me up. I'm usually at this bar. Or when I'm not, they've got my number." He didn't ask for hers in turn – then again, no noble ever would. It seemed some Confederate niceties were respected even here. "C'mon," Dale said then. "I'll show you out."

She nodded, quiet now, turning again toward the door. Somehow, being here with him, sparked by all his confidence and dash, she felt herself waver. Here was someone magnetic and glib, so unlike Kevin and her parents, she finally concluded, and she felt electrified by him, not knowing what he would say next, or what he was thinking, or why.

Stop it, she ordered herself.

It was a relief when they reached the wall.

Dale knocked once, then waited. A separate knock came from the room outside; then the door slid open as before, and he turned to Liza. "I'm gonna stay on for a bit."

She stuck out a hand. But he didn't take it. Instead, he offered a hug, as though he'd known her for ages. Shocked, she gingerly hugged him back.

"See you 'round," he said, spinning away with another wink.

Liza spun too, back through the bar they'd danced in, back up the stairs, and into the city outside. Somehow, she felt lighter and burdened at the same time.

She'd witnessed treason. Real treason – not just silent doubts in one's own mind. Enough to scare anybody.

But also: what a thing! To know the world was as complex as it seemed. To know that so many others were filled with questions too.

The sun struck her face. The streets were jammed even more than before, flanked by fine columns and older brick façades. The walk to the car was short, along fine blocks, with silver birches hanging over their sidewalks. But as she kept her gaze fixed ahead, it was as if the earth itself seemed to wobble now – from the alcohol, sure, but not just that. It was the very same city she'd seen that morning, yet in the meanwhile, her entire life had just turned upside down.

She wanted to race back down and see Dale again, to affirm he was real. That she had met a man who spoke in public using words people weren't even allowed to whisper in private. But then, her parents would worry – how they would shudder if they knew where she'd been! – and she knew in turn she'd better make it home before dark, when the roads would become harder to drive, and her father would start to fret she was truly missing.

CHAPTER 10

Nighttime had arrived by the time General Franklin Brooke met with the indent.

He'd finished supper with his wife and daughter – Liza had spent the day on a ridiculous, unsanctioned visit to Richmond, driving all the way there and back just to see the place – and now he was in his office, on the mansion's second floor. He sat behind an oversized oak desk, silver laptop at its edge, a yellow porcelain lamp in the corner, brass fixtures overhead. It wasn't a large room, with bookshelves full of military histories along three of the walls, and a fine square-paned window spanning most of the fourth.

The fellow in question was supposed to be escorted up at seven o'clock sharp, and Franklin had summoned him on the theory that even an indent had a right to learn his own fate directly. It was a rare thing for a Planter to engage in conversation with an indenture, but in this case, it also seemed the right thing to do. The indents were Confederates in their own way, after all, with a place in the hierarchy as sacred as his own. They'd been there from the start, a cornerstone of the infant country's strength. Their station supported all the others, and for that, they deserved a certain justice. He would explain his decision as best he could, avoid overwhelming the poor fellow with too much financial detail, and that would be that.

Of course, there were those who'd be horrified by how he was conducting himself. The fire-eaters in Congress screamed constantly about the dangers of giving the indents anything – even a Sabbath, for fear they'd somehow swipe a whole slew of benefits to follow – about the northern mistake of ignoring the need for order. Franklin saw the point. After all, U.S. miscalculation on the matter had grown obvious in its dysfunction as a nation – the boiling chasms between parties, classes, cities versus farms, its rampant prisons – everything the Confederacy had worked to avoid.

All the same, Franklin couldn't deny what he'd witnessed in his own indents at Rosewood Manor – in their songs at dusk, their children bounding about during breaks, women whispering soft blessings, men toiling with pride. Unlike most generals in the army, or ministers in government, he was at his plantation often enough to see the truth for himself: that the indents were far more than the docile shadows depicted in books, nothing like the untamed menaces of which propagandists warned. Sometimes, when he wandered his fields, and witnessed black women from nine to ninety carrying crops, his mind traipsed even further, daring him to think of his own Cathryn and Liza. It was a sacrilegious comparison of course. One he could never admit. But one he couldn't deny.

For he was certain he'd even seen something like fully enriched souls.

As ever, he tried to shake off such thoughts, reminding himself of his earliest lessons from school, that the indents were to be saved from themselves – and from the deprivation of the U.S. – by Confederate grace and good sense. He worked to recall that when he saw them heaving for breath, it was said they were showing no more than satisfaction from a hard days' work; that when he saw their smiles, it was not that they were joking at his expense, but that they were content.

The buzzer on the desk rattled. "Let him in!" he called. The door handle turned.

And there he was: wearing gray cotton pants and a sweatshirt, ankles braced together by iron, dark eyes anxious. He was breathing deep; his Adam's apple was pressed past his shirt collar; his lean face was strained. Placing his hands before him, the indent bowed his head.

A lifetime of training ensured that Franklin would never stand in greeting. Instead, he leaned back. "Atti," he said. "That's your name, isn't it boy?"

The indent nodded.

"Why do they call you that?"

"Just suppose that's what I get called, sir. Never really thought to think about it. Been called that all my life."

"I suppose it's a silly question. No doubt your momma named you. I wouldn't know how to explain my own name either."

"Yes sir." The indent hesitated. "But my full name's Atticus, sir."

Franklin nodded, peering back. "Well." He gathered himself. The full name had given him pause. It seemed to harken back to a more sophisticated age, as if indents could ever really know of such things. "I'm the one summoned you in here, and I won't keep you in suspense as to why. You've heard about our country's border troubles?" – there was no response – "how they're causing strain?" Franklin cleared his throat. "We're all a bit strapped these days, is the point. Have to take some measures."

"Measures how, sir?"

"Well, Atti, you'll have to be going." Best to put it plainly, he thought. "Off to another plantation, I mean." The words lingered. A breeze picked up outside. "One with more resources than we've got here at Rosewood. It's why I've decided to sell your labor, Atti: not only to support our own efforts, but to contribute to production farther south. I've heard some wonderful things about the plantations down that way: they're mighty large, with plenty of work to go round. It seems to me that they're the future. So that's where you're headed. I'll make sure you have time for farewells, a few days anyhow, before the papers clear and the lawyers run their eyes through everything. I'm sure the change will suit you. It's lovely country."

Finally, the Planter stopped talking.

• • •

Atticus could barely move. He felt the blood rushing from his face, and the world growing lopsided. His teeth clenched without his say-so, and his throat went dry. He stiffened his neck, trying not to crumble or burst entirely, and somehow, the first thought that occurred to him was that the Planter had never once aimed an ounce of attention his way, not until now.

He'd heard before about the Deep South, about mysterious places like Mississippi. Word had always been that things there were somehow even worse, if such a thing were possible, not better: that the Confederate Guard was more common, the Planters issuing regular beatings just to ensure order, that indents weren't even allowed to get married.

Such tidbits lingered in tales told after supper, in accounts shared in whispers. Everyone knew that getting sent down there was always a path that lurked, though no one wanted to dwell on it. Ever since the Labor Laws of the 1960s, indent-sales had been illegal. But that didn't have any real meaning: the Planters could still auction off an indent's labor.

Atti blinked. A dizziness was taking over. But he didn't look away.

He'd heard the buyers were hardly ever individual patrons. They were massive corporations, conglomerates that owned plantations near the Gulf, where few Planters still operated on their own, as at Rosewood. Family wealth had thinned out in the Confederate basin, and nobles there hadn't been able to sustain their lifestyles or their landholdings – even with the government subsidies. Too much single-crop dependency, it was said, prone to bad harvests and rising hurricanes. Thus the massive corporate buy-ups in recent decades.

He knew as much because the whites complained about it. They made a big fuss, often within earshot, about how the conglomerates went against the true spirit of the Confederacy, undercutting proper power, mistreating overseers to boot.

He realized the Planter was looking to the door. It was a done deal, then, as quick as it was cruel. Atticus would lose the only home he'd ever known. He'd arrive in the Deep Confederacy and get to test the rumors for himself, about outlawed group suppers, old whipping posts still active, indent families torn apart.

His throat caught.

He pictured Clara. He pictured her as if she were standing right there with him, until his breath thinned. He had tears now, running down his face in quiet, but in his mind's eye still he could see her sharp grin, her solid stance amid the cotton rows, how she laughed over suppers, and kissed him with such gentle force.

For he knew the truth. All the dreams in the world, all the ideas he'd ever had about building some make-believe life far away from this – none of it meant anything without Clara.

Taking a small step forward, inhibited as much by custom as by the shackles at his feet, Atti resolved to change the Planter's mind. He had to try.

"Please sir," he said quietly, respectfully as could be. "Please – have I done something to deserve this?"

The Planter straightened in surprise, pupils darting back-and-forth like a current. "Don't you worry, boy." It was as if he refused to use a name – epithets only, forever. "It's plain. We need revenue. Money still matters, no matter how much we Confederates try and deny it. We all work for our country's prosperity, and that starts with doing one's part. You included."

Atticus glared back, a crush suddenly upon his chest. For God's sake, the man sounded as if he thought he were being kind. "Sir, I just need to say – " Atti's jaw tightened. "It feels more than a bit like punishment."

But at that, he'd gone too far. The Planter stood. "You forget yourself." He cleared his throat roundly. "You're a decent slave, a hard worker, but I'm told you've been known to overstep, and here you are proving it. I can't take back the sale. It's done. I thank you for your service – I wish you the best." The Planter nodded curtly, and clicked his heels. Then, short as that, he marched from the room, walking along the wall to ensure as much space between them as possible, leaving Atti alone.

Outside, a sudden downpour had started, hammering the window panes across the way, sending wind blasting through their cracks. The light bulbs flickered.

But Atti scarcely noticed. He hadn't even heard the Planter's last few words, or the formalities at the close. He'd been stuck instead on one word alone: it had slipped out. Right there, like a bullet.

So it wasn't just the indents who used it, he thought. Planters did too.

Slave.

There it had sat, in all its crisp, awful honesty. Forsaking every ounce of progress the so-called New Confederates claimed. Right off the Planter's lips – even a man like General Brooke, young enough he didn't remember life before the reforms.

Atti stared at the empty desk the General had left behind, its antique wood, the scuffed floor below. These too were pieces of property. Same as him. Parts of a house he'd served all his life, but hadn't ever been allowed to call home.

In a few weeks, he'd never see any of it again.

He heard the overseer's approach from the hall, and squeezed away the tears that seemed a betrayal. Sorrow would give too much credit to this world. He'd rather feel rage.

He couldn't dare mourn the loss of this prison.

He didn't want to admit his old life might yet be better than where he was going.

He refused to accept the injustice of owing his captor for bringing Clara into his existence in the first place.

Taking a slow, wobbly breath, Atti turned. Already, something in his soul told him he couldn't take this. He had to prevent it – for himself, and for her. And just as sure, he suspected what he had to do, even if he didn't yet know how.

• • •

General Brooke walked down the hall toward bed. Angry with himself for feeling guilty, annoyed at the indent for acting so impetuous, he tried to feel right about his decision. After all, everyone had an allotment in life. That much was clear. It was how things had always been. It was the way of the Confederacy.

He sighed, knowing he should sleep. Hundreds of emails would be awaiting him the next day. More troops were to be deployed at the borders, and he'd have to decide on numbers. Confederate Guard training was to be expanded, and he was the one to approve it. Endless discussions would resume about revamped yeomen taxation and covering the debt. In the meantime, a troublesome sold-off indent was simply not worth his time.

He saw his daughter coming up the carpeted stairwell. "You're headed to bed then?" he asked with affection.

"Yes father," came the reply. She was keeping her voice flat, as though aping his calm. But her pupils burned. "Did you just sell that indent?"

Franklin shifted his balance. He was unsure what to say. "You shouldn't ask about such affairs, Liza. It's not proper."

She stepped forward and joined him in the hall. Warm light seeped from the cut-glass lamps at their side. "Virginia's hills are as much home to him as they are to us."

"Nonsense."

"You won't admit it?"

"Don't make it bigger than it is, Liza. I know your generation likes to talk, but that doesn't do us much use."

She nodded slowly then, but didn't push. Instead, after a moment, she stepped closer and surprised him by opening her arms.

Grateful for a daughter's love, he hugged her good night.

"Sleep well, father." And letting go, she shuffled off, making her way to her room.

CHAPTER 11

Atti had made his decision before he'd even left the Planter's study.

He was going to escape. He couldn't stay at the plantation – it was as simple as that – for if he did, he'd be shipped south and would never see Clara again. The United States wasn't so far off just yet. There was still a way out.

He'd heard life up there really was possible. Word was even a black man could be paid for work. With money then, he might find a way to buy Clara's freedom; he could even disguise his identity and buy her directly. These were just ideas, he knew. But they were better than being sold. At least they'd give him a chance.

As soon as he arrived at his cabin, he began planning in earnest. He'd already seen that there weren't near as many drones as folks believed, that come nightfall the overseers were on alert, but also that darkness could be an ally. He reminded himself he knew this place. He knew every hedge, every turn of the fields.

Sitting on the edge of his cot, he looked toward the floor. In the moonlight, he could just make out his threadbare shoes against the century-old planks. He listened as the bats squeaked on the eaves outside, and to the other men, already snoring. He even said a prayer of thanks to the Lord. After all, on most plantations, it would be impossible to run. Many indents had surveillance chips surgically implanted in their ankles. Not here. Some said it was because General Brooke actually believed his indents were happy. Others maintained he was too busy with government work to bother with it. There was even a theory he disliked ideas that evoked anything the least bit modern.

Whatever the case, it was a blessing. The idea of running had always been as distant as the stars. Now at last, Atti properly envisioned it. His sale had given him conviction.

He heard a brush of dirt from outside, and recognized the sound immediately. He looked up.

"Hi there," Clara whispered as she peeked her head through the door. Her thick hair hung to her shoulders, and she had on the same loose cotton shirt as always; her eyes were puffy, her smile broad.

Atti stiffened. He'd assumed it would be tomorrow before he would have to tell her all that had occurred – the cruelty crashing down upon him, his crazy plan in response.

"I came by earlier," she said next. "You were missing."

He opened his mouth to explain, but no words came. It wasn't that he was afraid to tell her. He just wasn't sure how to start.

She walked to the cot and sat down beside him, staying hushed, so as not to wake the old men, or disturb the overseers past the wall. "What's wrong?"

There was nothing to do but answer. "I'm being sold."

Now, she didn't respond. She just sat still, for such a long time that Atti wasn't even sure she'd heard him. He turned to repeat it – then saw a swirl of tears darkening her pupils. Moving nearer, he remained quiet instead, and bent to kiss her cheeks dry. A lump rose in his throat, and he bit his lip, forcing control. He placed his hand on hers. "I'm sorry to spring it on you. I just found out myself."

She nodded. "What will you do?"

"I'm going to run." His words sliced the air. Hearing them aloud made the idea even more real.

"Run away?"

"I have to."

Somehow, Atticus could tell she wasn't surprised. "Yes. It's the only thing," she answered now. She was pulling something from her trouser pocket – a paper of some kind, which she tried to keep from crinkling. "It's a map of Virginia." She was looking down upon it, her words unspooling more quickly now. "I don't know how old, but I'm told it's still accurate. It stops at the northern border, but that'll be more than fine: that's Maryland. Contested territory. There'll be Yanks there, maybe even stops on the Underground Railroad to direct you – they're supposed to be marked with the blue shingle, but who knows? – once you've gotten that far, you're safe. The darker areas mark forest. Always stick to those. There's Guard everywhere, naturally, but they're mostly in the towns and fields, same as here. In the forest, you can hide. The agents get lazy amid the trees. They're just kids, you know – younger than us – remember that. And they won't be as desperate as you. That's an advantage, Atti. Just get north. Never stop moving north, and stick to that forest."

Atti, however, had stopped listening. He was eyeing her instead – that sharp gaze, illuminated in the moonlight.

Clara paused in turn. Her frown was sympathetic. "Don't worry, Atti. The map doesn't include any words – you won't have to read it. Just follow the shading."

He shook his head. He wasn't worried about reading – besides, she'd been teaching him well; he'd picked up enough to get by. "No," he offered now.

"What then? I thought you said you were ready."

"Only – I'm wondering why you've got a map in the first place."

She looked surprised, and started folding it back into a small square, placing it behind a tiny shelf over his cot. "Is it that odd? To have a map, I mean?"

"'Course it's odd! What if an overseer found it?"

"I always carry a map – in case of a situation like this."

Atti tilted his head. "How come you never mentioned it?"

"We were never running away!" Clara exhaled. After a moment she leaned close, so that their foreheads were touching. "It's just –" She stopped. "I just want to say…" She glanced up, meeting his eyes. Atti felt his own heart slam in turn. "You have to go, Atti. I know that. But I'm going to miss you. I'll just miss you so much." Then, before he could reply, she kissed him.

Atti wrapped his arms tightly around her. The moon had drifted behind a cloud, and in its absence, her face was slipping away. "I wish I could take you with me." His brown pupils flitted across hers. He could no longer keep his lip from quivering.

She nodded against his cheek. "I'll be with you in prayer the whole time. Don't forget."

"That's just it. You're the reason I need to go, Clara. So that I'll see you again."

"But if you can't get back to me, or if something happens – "

"It won't – "

"But if it does, Atti. If it does – know that I love you. That I'll be at your side, that I'll think of you every day and dream of you every night."

Her eyes were wetter than before, and Atti kissed her once again. The tears were warm and heavy, and he realized they were mixing with his own, as sobs threatened to creep up his throat, all while he clung to this hope, that the two of them could still make it – bottle the damage, find cover from the blast – all life's pieces and pain come to rest now on a precipice, in danger of becoming memories alone. "Clara, I'll see you again," he said, kissing her harder and longer than before, trying to remain quiet. "I know that I will."

. . .

Silently, they made love then, trying to keep the small cot from shifting against the floor. Clara pressed her body to his, so that she could feel his chest, hard and smooth, close against her own. Raising her legs, wrapping them around him, she pushed their bodies together. The nighttime breeze came through the door as they held each other, rocking back and forth, whispering again that they loved each other, that they would miss each other, that they would see each other again. And when it was over, and they both lay on the bedframe quietly, Atti caressed the hair behind her ears, and held her close, expressing what he couldn't quite manage with words. The hours passed like minutes, and he tried to resist them, until at last he was falling asleep. He'd told himself not to, knowing that as soon as he did, morning would arrive. He wanted so badly to force the night to linger on. But he allowed himself to rest, sinking into the joy of having her in his arms, the warmth of her body, the magic of the night melding with the heartache of knowing it had to end.

. . .

Clara felt Atti drift off. His breathing slowed beneath hers, and she knew she was alone.

It was then that she felt her guilt.

Usually, she kept it at bay. After all, her instincts had kept her out of trouble, and gotten her the respect of the other indents. She made quick decisions, but careful ones too. So that even recently, as the risk had grown, she'd stuck with her choices, knowing that to look back would only undermine her.

But lying there with Atti, she wasn't so sure. The others still argued he should be kept out of the plans, and Clara had still agreed. They all recognized he was sharp, creative-minded, energized – as much as any of them. Yet they also knew Atti wasn't afraid of his own emotions – that he was still too willing to feel. If anything, they worried he'd be too eager. It was that which made him popular: his sentiments were clear, be they in a smile or scowl, in how he'd light up over a story at supper, or growl at the hell that greeted them every day. But then – where was the discipline in that? How would he respond when something went wrong – when weapons didn't arrive, meetings were canceled, an overseer looked suspicious?

Turning over in bed, she watched him sleep.

She'd almost opened up to him when he'd asked about the map. He'd looked so earnest – so curious to know.

He'd deserved an answer. He was a good man with a strong heart. He managed to give the world the benefit of the doubt, even when confronted with its evil. Now he was showing his courage too, choosing to run.

Instead, she'd kissed him. She still couldn't divulge the plan without the others' approval. More than that: she didn't have the right to electrify him with more hope than he had a right to possess.

For so long, she'd kept her involvement from him, never mentioning the meetings, never sharing her knowledge of those in the North, never hinting at the coming rebellion.

Tonight, she kept it from him still.

CHAPTER 12

Walking to Rosewood Manor, Kevin Donleau was nervous. He'd thought about calling ahead, but had quickly decided it'd be better just to show up like old times. He hadn't seen Liza since she'd invited him to Richmond – all but storming off when he'd refused. Really, he felt embarrassed. She'd seen how frightened he was of his own thoughts, and then she'd gone off and shown how unafraid she was of hers.

So it was he found himself on this narrow dirt road, a week later, making his way from his house to hers. It was less humid than usual, and he paused before reaching the Brooke property, listening to the finches and admiring the light turned thin and golden. A fine blue lake sat within view; proud hills loomed in the distance – a set of soft peaks, green at their base, mist circling above.

It could have been 150 years earlier, he thought. Only the occasional murmur of a distant cotton press provided any hint that modernity had arrived, and even that blended into the breezes through the trees nearby. The road, like every other non-interstate in the Confederacy, had never been paved. It was barely wide enough for two cars. Overhead, there were no wires; they'd all been buried underground.

None of this was by accident of course. The government spent enormously to preserve the atmosphere of the Old

Confederacy. Officials focused on developing the cities without making any changes to the countryside that dominated. It was all aimed at recalling the Revolution, setting the Confederate nation apart from the world. As other countries raced against each other toward their own demolition, trampling God's pastures with iron and steel, the Confederacy held onto an older aesthetic, founded on an agrarian ideal, a self-understanding of rural paradise.

It was this mindset that had produced the anti-sprawl regulations, the prohibitions against immigration, the simmering controversy over two-child laws – this last one a clash of Confederate ideals, pitting Christian believers and race-demagogues against fetishizers of the sparsely populated past. Dizzying zoning restrictions protected antique halls. The Park Bureau mandated open spaces everywhere you looked.

Most surprising, the Old South Policy was now finding overlap with larger trends around the world. The Confederacy had long pushed for sustainable fuel, far before the United States had ever made mention of the idea. For generations, the Confederate Congress had subsidized research into solar energy and electric cars. There were those who worried labs in schools and universities would threaten the farming ethos that made the country what it was. But the consensus was that these initiatives ultimately preserved the rural environment – and brought in profit to boot. Energy helped everyone, and robust new companies even offered their products to other nations – at least those sufficiently independent-minded to do business with Confederates. Car batteries, solar panels, water disinfectors – these were just some of the celebrated exports. Yankee spluttering on the matter only made the money all the more satisfying.

It seemed obvious to Kevin that without the profits from sustainable energy, the Confederacy would already have imploded, chewed up by the dual fangs of constant taxation and sanctimonious Planter tradition. Without population-growth, not to mention cars – automobiles were rationed, with waiting lists in every district – without major train lines or skyscrapers, it would've been hard to expect growth. It was clean energy that had filled the gap. Kevin had learned in the army about towns in Louisiana and Texas cordoned off for facilities – dirt roads and endless pastures be damned – that had thrived. In a circular way, the old guard and the new were perfect allies. It was Planters' obsession with the rural past that had led to green technology in the first place.

Soaking in the Virginia quiet, he contrasted it now with the video footage he'd seen in school of hazy northern highways and metal-skinned buildings clawing at the horizon. At least his own country had avoided that. There were no U.S.-style smokestacks here, no factory fumes doing God knows what to the citizens nearby. This was what led to the glory of a Virginia night, when the only glow came from the stars; or allowed for the sheer pleasure of listening to the pitter-patter of rain on silent villages across the South; it was how sheep still grazed in the cities. It was why a walk like this one could awaken the spirit. Such was the grandeur of a country that genuinely believed itself the keeper of God's bounty.

The Confederacy was not without sin. How could it be? It was made of men. But at least, for a time, it had achieved something. It hadn't made itself beautiful, but neither had it destroyed the beauty bestowed upon it. And the peace that came with the preservation of forests gave Kevin hope. It spoke to the potential of the place, if not the reality, to the fact that there was something worth holding onto. A place so true to God's canvas could not be irredeemable.

Turning right, realizing he'd lost track of time, Kevin faced the main house at Rosewood. There it was, a quarter-mile up. Six chimneys topped the roof, erected long before central heating. The glass in the windows was so wavy, it was almost opaque.

Still, despite its three centuries, the place remained grand. Just now, it was cloaked in a lingering morning mist all its own, ringed by a new portico announcing the family's success. Magnolia trees stood out front like proud statues. In back, the cotton fields stretched to the end of the world, indents like specks in the distance.

Kevin saw Liza's mother on the porch as he approached. She wore a formal blue hoop dress and was sipping tea. "Mrs. Brooke!" he called, reaching the gate that stood in front.

Cathryn looked up and smiled. "Good morning! Where've you been hiding all week?"

He laughed. "Not hiding, Mrs. Brooke – just home reading, like always." It was largely true. He'd discovered a fine history of Imperial Rome in his library.

She stood, hands on hips, smiling wide. "Well while you're here, take some beans from the leisure-garden. I can't control them. All these years, and I'm still not ready for Virginia growing season."

Kevin smiled. Her reference to her northern background intrigued him, and he was glad for the company. Still, he glanced toward the house.

"Oh, I'm sorry, Kevin. Here I am, going on. Liza's gone to town for a dress her father ordered – there are things even the garden can't produce! You've just missed her."

"That's alright," he offered. "Might I do anything for you here?"

·   ·   ·

Cathryn curtsied, happy to accept the offer. Kevin was an unusually cerebral young man, but he was also good-natured, and he clearly cared deeply about her daughter. Then there was his family: ancestors who had served in the first government after the Revolution, and helped write the commonwealth's Constitution. Their tobacco fortune was immense, one of the oldest there was. Watching him in his coattails, Cathryn noted his aristocratic bearing came naturally. He probably wasn't even aware of his square posture, or the gentle way he enunciated his consonants. He was a noble among nobles, and it wouldn't be at all bad if Liza ended up with him.

After all, as Cathryn had come to learn, family meant everything in the Confederacy. Really, it was the only thing that had allowed her into the country to begin with. Certainly people had always liked Franklin – but not enough to warrant a northern bride. It was his heritage they liked even better. A direct line to the military gods of old.

"Thank you truly," she said to Kevin now. The midday heat would soon arrive, and the quicker she could go back to air-conditioning, the better. She gestured to the small garden at their side – neat rows of tomatoes, peppers, beans. "Anything you find that's ready – " and she led them to the brick path cutting through its center.

They got to work, kneeling down, freeing the vegetables that were starting to crowd each other, piling them in a pair of empty oak-splint baskets she'd laid out. It was soothing work, and she was glad for the company. The sun was getting higher, the breeze beginning to fade. Until eventually, Kevin paused, wiping his brow with his sleeve. He looked over, quiet, thoughtful. She glanced back.

He cleared his throat. "You said you still weren't used to the growing season here?"

Cathryn was surprised. No one ever made direct reference to her roots, but in picking up on a stray remark, Kevin had just come awfully close.

"I only mean – I was just wondering if the weather was much different in the U.S."

Well there it was, she thought. Back home, it had exclusively been "the North," everyone clinging to the ridiculous idea that what had been their country's southern half would one day return. Here, it was always and forever the "U.S."

She offered a cautious shrug. "The weather varied," she said after a moment. "Nearer the border, it wasn't so different from what you're used to. But farther up, winters were long, just the way people say. There was cold rain right into June, and fall always surprised you." She hesitated. "Nothing like down here, of course. Down here makes for better living – and better gardens too." That was more than she'd meant to utter, she realized. She turned back to the plants.

But Kevin was peering right back. "Was there really proper countryside?"

"Of course there was." Cathryn picked a short green squash. "Mind you, it's not so vast and unmarked as this. But there were plenty of spots where you could still see trees and grass. Even Yanks can't totally ruin God's plan for the world." She let slip a faint smile. "I had a friend whose family used to spend summers in Vermont – that's way up at the northern end, in New England – they had a house on a beautiful little pond. In summer, we'd swim it from end-to-end, then come inside and make stews in evening. I remember the kitchen. It had a red wooden floor, and a yellow bench by the window. There were Holland cloth shades against the screens, and on the bookshelf, a wood-case radio – always a stream of fly paper from a fixture on the ceiling. From their stoop, you could forget the chaos of everything, the hypocrisy of the country, all the cities, and just pretend. You could listen to the birds and see peace."

"Is that why you came here? For more of that?"

"No, I came because I fell in love with General Brooke." Cathryn smiled wider. "But I was delighted to discover how valued nature is, yes. Not like the North."

Kevin was nodding. "Do they really hate us then?" he asked suddenly, his blue eyes intent.

"It's been so long since I was there." She paused once more, struggling with what to say next.

"Was it that awful?"

She met his gaze. "It wasn't what you're picturing," she said quietly. "But it's true there was anger toward the Confederacy. The whole country was full of it. People could say anything they wanted, and they did. They'd get so carried away there'd be brawls in the streets, screaming on television, and it coarsened all of us. It bludgeoned us. It made us what we were. It was the kind of anger that can bubble up and explode at any point, taking the whole of society with it. Men in government were always talking about liberty, about how anyone could grow up to be anybody, but no one was happy. We were our own prisoners, Kevin, tied up by all that hate, everyone blind to what they shared, making whole battles out of whatever little slivers of difference they could find." Cathryn was talking faster now, flooded by images of what had been. "It wasn't like here, everyone occupying their God-given place. It was chaos. The yeomen were told to pursue any career at all – except they just ended up crushing each other. Black folks got told they were permitted earnings as well, but they were denied the education to get them there – the sheer hypocrisy of the place! – getting kicked aside instead. Nobles faced nothing but disrespect, no matter that they held everything together. The nation agreed on the war effort, yes, but that's all there was." She looked up, catching her breath, and smiled with forced cheer. "And here I am, all these years later, ranting like a lunatic because of it."

"Not at all."

"But I am. I am." She shook her head. "Truth be told, Kevin, there was an obsession with democracy, and it made the whole North crazy. It's why I thank God every day for Liza's father coming into my life."

.   .   .

It was indeed Liza's father who came upon both of them now.

Kevin sighed. He'd wanted more detail. All he'd ever heard out of the U.S. had come through on scrambled bits of radio, beamed in from northern satellites, and occasional slips of paper dropped by trespassing planes. Nothing ever like this, straight from someone who'd lived it. He was enthralled.

He wouldn't have a chance to question her further, though.

"What are you two on about, sweating like a couple of indents?" Franklin Brooke was laughing. He looked stout in his storm-gray frock, spatter-dashes around his ankles to keep him free from the roads' muck.

"Glad to see you, General. I hope I don't intrude."

Brooke chuckled further. "Nonsense. It's a thing I admire in you, Donleau: all the greats of history have been thinkers." He raised his eyebrows, and his silver hair shifted. "I imagine my daughter admires the same."

"You're generous to say so, sir."

"Even still, son, take care. A man can't scruple over philosophy every minute of his day. Not at the expense of making his name: running for office in his own right, offering a lady his hand. You grasp my meaning?"

"If I don't, sir, I'm sure you'll tell me again."

The general chortled once more at that – a laugh that made his chestnut eyes flicker just like his daughter's. It was sometimes easy to forget General Brooke's power, Kevin thought. He'd been Chairman of the Joint Chiefs for nearly twenty years now, far more famed than Kevin's own father – and even without a ministerial position in Congress, all those Senators, even the president, constantly sought his approval. Growing up, Kevin had grown accustomed to thinking of the General simply as Liza's dad, seeing him pad about his house in casual clothes and eat relaxed suppers with his family. "Will Liza be joining us, sir?"

Another chuckle. "Stuck in town shopping, my boy. But won't you join us on the porch without her?"

Kevin bowed in gratitude, but politely declined. He'd come back soon, he assured them. For now, his piles of books were awaiting at home, and he walked back to find them.

CHAPTER 13

Being fired had never bothered Raj Hayworth.

During college, he'd lost internships summer after summer, coming in late or leaving too early, getting high at lunch or never showing up at all, living off the generosity of friends. After graduation, the stakes had risen, but still he'd rejected the notion that anyone should care more about work than it cared about them. Even the paychecks weren't enough to convince him: after earning funds sufficient to last a month or two, he'd invariably get restless. There'd been jobs at gas stations, a bowling alley, a film editing lab at a fancy middle school. None had lasted. Eventually, thanks to his roommate Ted, he'd arrived at the latest spot, the Primary Intelligence Office.

Now that was history too.

The departure had been amicable enough. Everyone knew he'd only gotten the job because of Ted's father, and it turned out that wasn't enough to keep it. A senior analyst, well-intentioned if zealously patriotic, had called Raj into her office, told him how much everyone liked him, apologized for what was about to happen, then informed him he'd have to go. His tardiness had been increasing, and the higher-ups had noticed.

Without protest, Raj had walked right out, and into the bustle of midtown New York. Walking north, he'd dodged the weaving packs of office workers, through the shadows of skyscrapers and the garbage heaps that took over the city in summer. Cars grumbled, and barges curled in from the rivers, and he shuffled on past the gutters stained with oil, sausage vendors shouting at the corners, the traffic belching exhaust faster than the wet breeze could clean it.

There were two-ton trucks on every block, blue-clad soldiers drilling past in a hurry: everyone clattering in staccato, all sliced vowels and fast-paced localisms – *"atta boy!"* – *"gimme a break!"* – a special Big Apple language all its own. Farther up, jumbled-together apartment blocks beckoned, and more shops too: display windows with the highest fashions – old-style slouch hats, knit berets – crowds staying thick. On bulletin boards at the bus stops, there were notices of every stripe – flyers about the draft, broadsides about keeping alert for spies, postcards of the capitol buildings flapping in the city wind.

He rolled his eyes. The work hadn't been so terrible, really. He'd even begun to accept that the place actually stood for something, defending the border, battling the slavery of the South. But the day-to-day experience of watching footage from security cameras, listening to phone-taps from eighteen-year-old Confederates yapping about their farms and bigotry, had gotten old. That's when Raj had started sleeping even later than usual.

He turned off Sixth Avenue and spotted his favorite pizza joint, when he heard a set of extra-hurried footsteps approach behind him.

"Hey," Ted called out, catching up.

Raj spun back, greeting his friend with a sigh. "Hey."

"So it's true? You really got let go?"

"Sure did."

"Goddamn Raj. That was dumb."

"What are you hot about? I'll call your dad and apologize."

"That's not the point. This opens you up to the draft."

"Settle down." He didn't want to hear it. "Only if I'm unemployed eight weeks."

But Ted was now walking fully beside him. "For Christ's sake, buddy, you can't be so cavalier about this."

"You better get back – I'll see you after work."

"You really will get conscripted."

"I told you – I'll find something."

"Don't you care?"

"About what?"

"About any of it. About your job. About your country."

"Don't be an ass. I'm as much a part of this place as you are."

"That's not what I'm saying."

Raj calmed himself with a long breath. "Look, I get it."

"By all means, explain away."

"You're angry I don't get caught up in it like you. But Ted, there ain't nobody like you. Who else has got eight uncles in Congress? Who else can trace both sides back to Gettysburg? My people were fighting off the viceroys when yours were whooping Rebs. My mother barely knows who Lincoln was. I didn't grow up with this crap."

"That's fine."

"Is it?"

"I just said it was."

Raj rubbed the back of his neck. "Well good then."

"Good."

"Great."

Ted looked over. "The fighting's picking up."

"Don't worry."

"They really are shooting – and getting shot."

"I understand."

"So you said."

Raj squinted back, studying his friend in turn. "You're jealous I got fired."

"Gimme a break."

He started to smirk. "You are." The smirk was growing wider. "That's why you keep talking about me getting drafted."

"If I wanted to enlist, I would."

"Only not really. It would mean quitting your job, and pissing off your father, and screwing up your career."

Ted shook his head. "Those grunts down there have a tough job, and I'm proud to support them. But that doesn't mean I want to join them. I'm not jealous of you Raj. Just mad."

Raj gave a snort.

"Start job-hunting at least." Ted twisted back. "I'll ask around. See what's out there."

"No need." He watched then as his friend stepped off. Truth be told, he had no idea where he would find work. For now though, his stomach was still empty, and after another moment, he angled back from the chaos of cabs and crowds, deciding pizza was still the answer.

CHAPTER 14

Amid the cluster of indent cabins, it was quiet, with only the nighttime moths to distract Atti from his thoughts. Typically, even at this hour, a few whispers could be heard, perhaps the sound of quiet love-making. Tonight, it was silent.

He'd finished his packing, and was making his way through the darkness to Clara's cabin. He planned to leave for good tomorrow night, after field work, and he had to tell her so. The Planter's family was said to be planning a party, and Atti hoped it would be a distraction for the overseers. Besides, if he didn't go soon, his sale would be finalized, and there'd be no chance left at all.

Zigzagging along the narrow lanes between cabins, doubling back to avoid detection, he stayed focused. The wind was cool, steeped with the smells of fresh grass and seeds. The sky was clear, barely aglow with a quarter-moon, welcome weather for what he had planned. Hopefully it would hold.

He paused.

Hadn't he heard something? Voices from inside one of the cabins? Silently, he stepped to his side, angling for a peek past the door. There they were again – sounding urgent, rising above a whisper, swelling then falling, and Atti blinked in surprise, for it was well past curfew. A mosquito pierced the silence, circling his head, and reflexively he slapped it against his own neck.

The voices came to a stop.

For a long minute, there wasn't another sound. Then, soft footsteps emerged from the cabin's center: someone trying to be silent in turn, betrayed by loose floorboards below.

Atti bit his lip, not sure what to do.

If by some chance it was an overseer, he couldn't just stay put. That would lead to a beating; he'd be put under watch, making it impossible to get away the next evening. Worse, they'd find the packed bag beneath his bunk, with the map Clara had given him inside. There'd never been an execution on the Brooke plantation. Not in his lifetime, anyway. But that didn't mean there couldn't be a first.

Atti thought hard. He could run. But that would be noisy. He could hide, crawling around the cabin's corner. But they'd find him.

The footsteps slowed. Maybe it was just one of the old men, up to relieve himself in the night. Another second passed. A shadow appeared in the door.

Then, to his shock, Clara stepped out.

She was holding a fresh-cut switch atop her shoulder, sliced from an elm, poised as though ready to strike, and she spun her head, scanning the space before her.

"Clara!" he whispered. "What are you doing here?"

She blinked back, spotting him. "What are *you* doing here?"

"I was on my way to your cabin!"

She hesitated. "But I'm not in my cabin."

"I can see that." Atti stepped forward. He shared a grin. "Why not?"

She'd lowered the switch.

"What is it?"

Now she gestured within. "Here, come," and he nodded, stepping up.

Together, they moved inside. Squinting, he tried to see through the darkness. The cabin's regular inhabitants were elderly, awake mostly, lying in their beds or perched up against their walls – but that wasn't where his eyes were drawn. Instead, in the room's middle, he saw a group of younger indents – there had to be ten, all near his own age – gathered tightly around a pine table, jammed between a file cabinet and a broken refrigerator. His eyes began to adjust, and he could make out paper and pens, items strictly forbidden, strewn across the table's surface. The papers were full of maps, he realized, some portraying the plantation, others showing the surrounding valley. They were similar to the one Clara had given him – detailed, carefully etched, creased.

One of the young indents stood. He had a face Atti recognized from the fields, patched jeans, cheeks smooth as a boy's. But his shoulders were sturdy. Through his shirt, his chest looked chiseled from stone. "What's he doing here?" the fellow asked now. "How did he know?"

Clara answered. "He didn't. He had no idea we were here." She straightened. "Frankly, I think it's Atti owed some explanation, not us."

Atticus could see them all more clearly now, staring back. In the corner, a lad nearly seven feet tall was sitting on a splintered chair, legs splayed outward, so that he looked to be taking up half the room. Several women by his side had jaws clenched, hands clasped before them. There was a stern-faced driver whom Atti recognized from the garages – with a square head, and a thick neck – and a paler fellow too, with a finely trimmed red beard, and a gaze sharp as a schoolteacher's. Atticus turned back to Clara.

"As you know," she was saying, "Atti's not going to be here much longer. But even if things were different, it'd be time to fill him in. I'll come back shortly. Don't make decisions without me."

She angled toward the door. Still stunned, Atti followed her outside.

They strode quickly toward her cabin, keeping on the balls of their feet, listening to the snores and whirring bats, while the moon drifted behind a stray cloud. Reaching the porch, they checked their backs, then hurried in. Soon, they were sitting on her cot. Atti spoke first.

"You're planning something."

"I am," she answered. "We are."

He took a slow breath. He wasn't used to feeling speechless. "How is it possible?"

"We've been meeting a long while now – almost a year. We use the infirmary cabin because it's never guarded. The old-timers don't like the risk, but they put up with it. They don't have much time left anyway." As she spoke, he watched her closely. "It was last summer, after supper one night, when I found one of the women there, and told her I needed the place. I didn't tell her why, but once I pressed her, she went ahead and said yes. A few months later, she passed away. But the others let us continue."

He was trying to make sense of it. "A year you said?"

"Oh Atti – I wanted to tell you. You must know that. There were so many times I almost did – especially these last few weeks – "

"But you didn't – "

"It wasn't just my decision. You saw how small a group we are. When the time comes, we'll be telling everyone. We'll be needing everyone."

"Clara..."

She looked at her lap. "The thing of it is," she started. "The thing is, Atti – I *agree* with the others. You've got all that energy. And we love you for it. We do. I do." She tilted back up. "Most folks here get stunted. Beaten down and ruined. Not you. You stay in motion."

"But?"

"But that also means you rush into things." Her whisper stayed quiet. "For God's sake, you came right up to that cabin this evening, even when you heard us talking."

"You make me sound like a child!"

"No. Some folks think they know your mind, Atti, but all they really see are your feelings. If you ever got questioned, you'd fool them, I know it. I've seen you do it, telling them what they need to hear." She placed her hand on his cheek. "We owe you for who you are, Atti. I mean it. You remind us still to feel. But the fact is, it's not just us: the whites also think they can read you."

"You don't think I can handle a secret?"

"That's not what I mean." Now her voice shook. "But they search you out. They just do. Atti, I've re-thought this a thousand times, believe me. But that's how it went. I didn't want you in danger."

"What about you?" He chewed his lip.

Clara swallowed. She kept her gaze locked on his.

"C'mon," he continued. "You sure you know what you're doing?"

No answer.

"Well do you?"

"Oh Atti." Her jaw tightened. Her eyes had gone wet. "How is it can you have so much forgiveness inside?"

"That's not an answer."

She shifted closer. "Of course I'm not sure. But we're doing it anyway."

He nodded. That was how he felt about his own escape plan. "You think it can work?"

Another pause. "We're in touch with the U.S. That's where the weapons are coming from. They've been coming in for months – just a gun or two at a time, with cartridges. We've been burying them under the cabins, and they're starting to add up.

Our contact meets with us through Paul. He's the one who stood up in the cabin back there."

"Sure. I know him."

"They've told him we're not alone. That the same is happening at other plantations too, across the commonwealth. It's getting the Confederates worried. You can hear it in all their talk about border skirmishes and troops. The North's making an honest-to-goodness push."

Atticus tried to believe it. Yet wouldn't the overseers be ready for a thing like this? As soon as they got over the initial shock of armed indents, they'd rally to the cause of oppression. Not to mention Confederate Guard – they'd show no mercy. "What makes this any different, Clara? From everything that's been tried before?" After all, there'd been slave rebellions going back to the nation's earliest days – even earlier – all the way back to Nat Turner. Nothing had worked. Not really. Not the sabotage or subterfuge or strikes. Not even the outright mutiny during World War II – down in Florida, folks said, at a munitions factory – or the ghetto coup among the slaves in Georgia's Tech Valley; not the '68 Uprising after that, aided and abetted by Union spies in Richmond; certainly not the scattered field uprisings across Virginia – right into this century, if all the stories were to be believed.

Every time, they'd been crushed. Every time, the final result had been blood.

"Because we have the experience now," Clara explained. "Because we have the knowledge of our defeats. Because we know what doesn't stick – widespread movements, stabs at all-out war – and so we know what *will*. Targeted strategy. We'll occupy Rosewood, then spread outward. We turn this into the base of operations, and we do it through surprise: getting to the Planters where they are, setting up a fortress of our own – trading places and reversing the siege. We'll be taking their advantages right out from under them, don't you see? We inject them with doubt, then we exhaust them. It's their power that makes them vulnerable, Atti. They're too used to it. They won't know what to do when it's taken." She looked as though she even half-believed it.

Atticus, however, was still trying to accept that this was real – that she'd be risking her life just when he'd been planning on risking his. "How'd you get in touch with the contact?" he managed.

"That was all Paul's doing. He's always getting sent into town, fetching supplies with the overseers because they need his brawn. Four months ago, a yeoman sidled up to him while he was there – found him on the corner during the white men's break. Turned out it was a U.S. agent. They got to talking, made sure no one was watching; then the agent said plantations in the area were hatching plans for rebellions. Paul gambled and told him we'd already been doing that here, and the agent was giddy. He said that was perfect. That's when we started getting our weapons. Paul keeps meeting up with this fellow whenever he can. They hide the guns in with the regular supplies, usually grain bags, and Paul carries them back."

"You'll get yourselves killed," Atti suddenly said. The words just tumbled out.

Clara sat back. "If we don't try, Atti, nothing will change. The U.S. aid is too big to ignore: it's never happened like this, not so directly – not that I know – and if they're helping indents across the commonwealth, maybe it's across the whole country too. The weapons are real, Atti. They're weapons just like the ones the Planters have got."

"Only the Confederacy's always been here, Clara."

"Well not everyone can run off, you know. That won't work either."

He blinked. For a moment, emotion kept him from saying anything further. Instead he took her hands in his, pulling close, kissing her gently on the forehead.

"I shouldn't have said that," she said into his chest. "I love you."

He leaned his chin against her hair. "It's why I was coming over in the first place. To tell you about leaving."

She looked up. "Soon?"

"Tomorrow. Dusk."

She thought a long moment. "Good," she murmured. "That's good."

"Why? When's all this set to start?"

For a long time, she didn't move. They just stayed like that, each one leaning against the other. "I shouldn't tell you," she finally answered, and there were tears on her cheeks. "I don't want to burden you with it."

"But it's also soon?"

She took in a wobbly breath. "Please just have faith in us, Atti."

"I will." His voice wavered in turn. "I do."

Then she nodded, still facing up, her arms around him, as they kissed once more.

CHAPTER 15

In mansions across the Confederacy, parties were a staple of plantation life. Planters prided themselves on their ability to entertain with grace, glamor, and local cuisine. With a characteristic nod to tradition, women wore dazzling hoop dresses, men formal tail coats. Tables were laid with silver candelabras and multi-course feasts, and there was always time-honored line dancing after supper. The parties were as important to Planters' pride as their acreage, indent counts, even their lineage. In a life where luxury was omnipresent, where ladies were deliberately unemployed and gentlemen were occupied with acquiring titles in government and military, nobles looked to the parties for affirmation and diversion. It meant they found all sorts of reasons for hosting: birthdays, weddings, graduations, promotions. Sometimes it was simply a matter of noticing too long a gap since the last event.

Franklin and Cathryn Brooke were no exception. Their thirty-fifth wedding anniversary was the perfect occasion, set to be the largest gathering the commonwealth had seen in months. They'd set the date for the last Saturday in July, and finally, it'd arrived.

Now, after lunch, set-up was reaching a fever pitch. Specially appointed indents were preparing the tables and cooking the foods: guinea fowl, stuffed fresh peppers both hot and sweet, sausage with nutmeg and sage, venison from the woods to the west, seven varieties of cake. Franklin and Cathryn were watching over all of it, and by half-past three, they needed a break. They'd been checking the number of forks at each place setting – Cathryn didn't quite trust the indents – and now they walked hand-in-hand toward the drawing room's bay window and the red-cushioned seat at its base. Guests would be arriving at five – many wouldn't leave 'til morning – but for now, there was time for a breath.

Together, they took in the views to the south. "Here we are," Cathryn exhaled.

Franklin smiled softly. "Forever and always, my dear," and he clasped her hands. It had been four decades since they'd met – going back five years before the wedding, encountering one another in Paris. They'd both been on holiday, traveling from their respective nations, and had ended up attending the same church concert on a Saturday evening. Leaning over from the pew behind her, Franklin had asked Cathryn to supper. Seeing his Confederate uniform, she'd let him know she was visiting from Boston.

To her shock, he hadn't rescinded, and immediately she'd been intrigued: to meet an actual Confederate, and to know he wanted to meet her as well! In fact, Franklin had spent the next hour pondering whether to cancel; for sticking with it would go against every ounce of his upbringing. But the fact that she'd said yes – more than her beauty, even – had only lured him further in turn.

They'd wound their way to a set of medieval alleys and a quiet café on a jagged street of small stones, bordered on both sides by worn buildings, all slanted beams and tilting windows. The roofs had been steep and sunken, with thick wooden trim running down beige walls. Locals had wandered steadily past, chattering in rough-hewn French about the cold, hawking fabrics from narrow carts. It had all been so charming, and

Franklin and Cathryn had taken it in together beneath an awning, ordering red wine and steak. They'd ended up sitting there almost half the night.

She'd startled him at first with pointed questions about his country, eagerly sharing what she'd learned growing up – a place of tyrants and poverty, she'd told him – but somehow, he'd felt no alarm. Instead, he'd grown dazzled: by her eagerness to think aloud, her sharp conversation, her foreignness itself.

There'd been another date after that, then another one. As it turned out, they'd spent their last week in Paris all but inseparable, abandoning the friends they'd each had in tow.

The next two years had been scattered: nervous meetings in lands alien to both of them. First, a trip to Canada, then a return one to Paris, finally London – even one to Los Angeles County out in California, a territory where the formal border had all but evaporated of late, as localized war had finally fizzled out. This had led to a sort of no-man's-land on the continent's distant west coast: a welcoming, surreal escape for anonymous vacationers from both sides, where the politics from home could grow faint, at least for a moment.

It was there that Cathryn had pledged to Franklin she would move to his country, and he'd literally yelped with joy. The following month, he'd worked up the courage to tell his parents where he'd been spending his holidays. Aghast at first, then grudging, they'd eventually arranged a permanent visa for Cathryn. The engagement had come next, and though the paperwork had taken time – a visiting U.S. citizen was a rare and suspicious thing, and Franklin had not yet possessed his own sway – it had happened at last. They'd been married on a beautiful meadow, under a fine white tent, in the foothills of the Blue Ridge.

The marriage since had been a happy one. Cathryn had embraced her new life, even as Franklin had suppressed his guilt about trumping her old one. Patriotism meant everything to him: enough that no matter his disgust with the U.S., he remained in awe she'd chosen him over it.

Inheriting Rosewood Manor, they'd handled Franklin's rise with grace, staying generous to old friends, raising Liza to be both honorable and deft, all while remaining politically neutral in the government – a challenge even in a system where political parties were technically illegal. The Brookes, then, had become popular. These days, people were drawn to Franklin's status as a four-star general, but it went beyond that. His honest bearing and love of company were well-known. That in turn had helped secure his power. The Confederate Constitution's latest preamble had a number of addendums making room for informal military advisors, and there were always generals scurrying through the halls of Congress. But none had anywhere near the voice that Franklin possessed.

His talents were considerable. He displayed serenity in the face of heated debate and was a skilled organizational man as well. While commanders of earlier eras had gained their prestige on the battlefield, Franklin hadn't gotten the chance; all the immortal clashes had occurred before he was born. Nonetheless, he'd served with distinction on the border – conducting a few well-heralded raids into Maryland, blowing up cell towers, degrading fiber optic cables, generally making a nuisance – before devoting an additional six months to service in the Caribbean during the hemispheric expansion. After that, he'd streamlined military expenses, keeping up morale with his charm and chivalry, exhibiting constant diligence, filing reports, responding to consultation, knowing when to step in and side with a parliamentarian.

These days, he carried the respect of both factions in Congress. The New Confederates rightfully claimed Franklin as their own, pointing to his support for reforms regulating indent treatment and promoting energy research. But the Old Guard claimed him too. Its members were fewer in number but always louder in their constant advocacy for tradition – their devotion to agriculture and public Christianity were unfaltering – and they remained convinced that Franklin personified the best of noble heritage, whatever his views on policies.

Cathryn had long seen how people listened to him, even presidents. Every last bit of legislation required his tacit approval; tax policy went through his desk; appointments were meaningless if he hadn't signed on. That much was clear from the phone calls that came to the house – from Congress, military command, the executive offices in Richmond – all atop his trips to the capital.

Yet she also knew that Franklin didn't care nearly as much for the influence as for the human contact that came with it. Ever since they'd met, she'd admired his ability to make people feel at ease, actually listening to what they told him – no small thing for a man with power – saying yes to every supper, party, or tea. Just as people were drawn to him, so he was to them.

That morning, he'd woken with the smile of a boy at Christmas. For days, he'd been asking about guests, making reference to this or that family, chortling happily when the latest dignitary was confirmed, never taking for granted that of course everyone would attend; that this would be a crowning social event of the year; that even without genuine affection for Franklin, people would have made plans to come. To Cathryn, his humility in such matters only added to his charm. As recently as lunch, he'd glanced at the guest list and shaken his head at all the names he recognized.

That was why it was so surprising when he'd grown distracted by early afternoon. As they'd traipsed through the kitchen, then checked the tableware in the dining room, he'd turned quiet, and while Cathryn had initially kept her distance, she eventually decided to say something. For Franklin never acted this way before a party.

"What is it darling?" she finally asked, peering close.

His eyes crinkled, and he managed a smile and a frown at once. "Am I really so easy to read?"

"You certainly are."

"Well." He exhaled. "I suppose I've just been thinking on that indent."

"The one you're selling?"

"Apparently he goes by 'Atti.' This morning, I got the call from Mississippi. They've sorted out which of their plantations could use a new hand."

"That's good, no?"

"Only I'm not so certain." His voice began to trail. "What will he ever matter to them? A billion in revenue last season alone. Two million acres. Twice that much in bale-count. All thanks to the endless indents they catalogue but never know." He paused. "Do we ever consider it all?"

Now Cathryn frowned. It was a waste of a talented man's energy to worry about this kind of nonsense. "I don't suppose we should, Franklin, no. I learned that as a child. Guidance from the top is what counts. Without it, chaos and cruelty reign. Second-guessing does nothing for those poor souls."

Franklin was nodding. "We intercept a lot of U.S. propaganda through our censors in Richmond. Tales of black Americans living on their own, without us or our support. Accounts of feats in art, journalism, even business."

Cathryn raised her eyebrows.

He glanced back out the window, toward the winding stone walls near the horizon, vistas of soft green hills and mounds of uncut meadow in the distance. "A Mississippi conglomerate, of all things. With all their horrors."

"Why, we've the same up here in Virginia!"

"Not to that degree we don't." His voice was firmer. "Not on this plantation. Not here. We treat them as they ought to be treated, regardless of their capacity."

She squeezed his hand. "Enough, dear," she said. "Down there they obey the new regulations just as we do, I'm sure."

· · ·

Franklin brushed his silver hair back from his forehead. He wished what his wife was saying were true. The codes against mistreating labor were supposed to apply equally throughout the Confederacy. But she had a rosy view. She always had. She didn't see that he'd been responsible for this fellow Atti, and that now he was abandoning him. Even if the indent didn't realize the depths of the betrayal, Franklin certainly did. It indicated failure: a reneging on the implicit pledge before God to care and watch over an indent and put his labor to use for the Confederacy.

And why? It was all occurring simply because he hadn't kept his finances in order. He despised relying on the federal subsidies, but as a general, he'd never earned as much as he would have in law, let alone from graft in politics. In the meantime, he'd squandered his inherited luxury, enjoying too much the privilege of his life. The latest proof was this lavish party.

He looked once more toward his wife. He reminded himself she had good sense amid all that Yankee severity. When she said that God had given nobles the right to make decisions for a reason, surely she was right. And yet, hadn't the Good Lord also granted the capacity to doubt? "You needn't embrace so much of the Old Guard on my account, you know. Not after all this time, my love."

"What can I say, Franklin? Call it the passion of a convert."

"Only don't you ever miss it? Your old life? All you left behind?"

Cathryn winced. "You'd ask me this today? Of all days?" This time, it was her turn to look away. "When we're here to celebrate life as we chose it, Franklin? – as we built it?" Her words were swift, her voice earnest. She turned back. Her brow had creased, but her green eyes were undaunted as ever. "I love you, Franklin. I love our home. That's all there is to it."

He peered back. "And that girl in Paris who thought us all tyrants?"

"Maybe she was right," came the answer, surprising him. "But I've come to see: what land is any different?" Her gaze softened. "This one, at least, tries to make the best of it."

•   •   •

When Liza came bounding in a minute later, she curtsied.

"I just wanted to let you know I'll be taking a trip to Richmond," she informed them, as though announcing she were merely going out for a walk.

Both parents stared.

"You were only just there!" Cathryn replied.

"Well, not *just*. But yes – I've made some friends in the city, and I'd like to visit them."

"Who are they?" Franklin demanded.

"You don't know them."

"Try me. I know almost every capital family there is."

"Oh father, don't exaggerate!" Though even as she said so, Liza's heart gave a pang. The truth was, she didn't want to learn he already had an opinion of Dale Birch.

It was mother's turn again. "Regardless, dear, it's gotten too dangerous. They say the Guard's been cracking down on every corner. Nerves are frayed from the rumors of uprisings. You can't risk going and getting caught up in it."

"Oh please. We can't fall prey to tricks stirred up by U.S. intelligence."

Franklin was shaking his head. "Don't be too sure that's all it is. The border tension isn't made up. Neither are the stories of resistance in the cities. There are too many types who get encouraged every time the U.S. escalates things." He stood. "Your mother's right. Richmond is uncertain these days. The Guard grows antsy. There'll be clashes if protesters dare show their face."

"When you were my age, you were already taking trips to Europe!"

"It was a different time. The Confederacy enjoyed welcome round the world."

"That's not the point. I'm old enough to travel where I want."

"And the party?"

"I'll leave in the morning. It'll get me clear of clean-up tomorrow anyway."

In fact, Liza planned to cut out even earlier than that. It would mean driving in the dark, but it'd give her a full day once she arrived. Her parents would be so wrapped up in their guests, they'd never notice. And since no one her age was really invited, she wouldn't be missing a thing.

Her father let out one of his sighs. "At least be alert, Liza. Make sure your phone is charged." He opened his arms. "Now come here."

Liza could tell by her mother's face that she wasn't quite so ready for surrender. But surrender it was. "Thank you," she said, walking over for the embrace. "Thank you both."

CHAPTER 16

Seven hours later, the party at Rosewood Manor was fully underway, and Liza was already long gone, closing in on Richmond. She'd been right: no one had even flinched when she'd walked out. Amid cocktails and hors d'oeuvres, guests were spilling out of the mansion onto the upper-story verandas. There were pastel hoop dresses in all directions, diamond jewels, form-fitting tops that showed off the ladies' shoulders and decolletage.

A fair portion of Congress was in attendance, as were half a dozen cabinet members, a whole assortment of military officers, and – groveling as ever, always in the hope they'd prevent a shutdown of independent media altogether – the editors of the biggest Confederate periodicals, including Richmond's *Examiner*. Really, it was no surprise they'd been invited; the fact was, their voices still mattered, notwithstanding century-old legislation that'd nationalized media in order to streamline coverage. Laughter and the clatter of glasses were steady, small talk amid an endless parade of mutual compliments and empty nationalist platitudes carrying to the grounds outside, and by the time supper was completed, nobody could remember a more glamorous or better-attended occasion. Amid all the smiling faces, it was hard to detect any worry at all, to hear even a whisper of the border tensions or Resistance rumors, or remember that most of the men had spent their days in briefings about the Underground Railroad, U.S. raids, and plans for pulling back plantation subsidies.

•   •   •

Far below the buzz of conversation, Atticus Brooke was standing by a copse of junipers at pasture's edge, looking up, watching the nobles get drunk. He'd slipped from the indents' banquet hall after snagging some extra ham, now stuffed into the leather bag he'd strapped across his body. He also had a half-dozen bottles of water, a spare shirt, the map, and an extra pair of boots. He hoped it was enough. He'd be relying mostly on foraging. In the meantime, he was pleased with the party's noise, despite his revulsion at its bliss.

The daylight hours had dragged slowly by. He hadn't wanted to exert himself, going through the motions of labor, thinking constantly of Clara instead, trying not to fret over her plans, clinging to his faith as she had faith in him. A lump in his throat had lingered all afternoon.

Now, kneeling down, Atticus retreated past the patch of woods that bordered the garden terraces at the house's side, then lowered to his stomach. From there, he crawled towards the larger pastures in the rear. There wasn't yet reason to shift fully to the trees: they'd just slow him down and add to his racket.

He looked over his shoulder. In front of the mansion, a public road ran perpendicular. There were overseers manning its edge, watching as a staff of indents greeted late-arriving guests and parked their cars. Regular sentries patrolled nearby.

Atti knew he'd be reported missing by midnight at the latest, and that the Confederate Guard would be notified. But for now, he still had some time before any overseers registered he hadn't gone to bed. Most evenings, before sneaking out to Clara's, he waited for them to make their rounds. Not tonight. He'd had to move off while the party stayed loud.

He moved quickly. Finally clear of the mansion, he got on his feet but still kept close to the earth. The nobles' voices grew fainter as his feet padded the grass. Constantly, he swiveled, seeking out white men in the dark.

He prayed as he went, treading lightly to avoid tracks, aiming for the next ridge. There were tears in his eyes, he realized, as he thought once more of Clara, yet onward he pushed, knees high, heart at a roar. Sweat dripped at his temples, and the stale bread from lunch lurched in his belly.

The breeze at least was cool against his forehead, and he took it in as he passed the cotton; next came the tobacco crop, heavy aromas coating the air. Beyond that, Atti entered the quadrants set aside for food, darting through the corn stalks, then the tomato and barley. It all seemed to stretch on forever, a reminder, as if he needed it, of all he didn't own, while other men possessed the world. Still, he kept his focus, alert for trigger wires and motion-generated spotlights, ducking swiftly when he found them.

In time, the crops petered out, and Atti entered the plantation's grazing fields, employed only when cows were pastured there. The property's rear border had to be close, though he wasn't quite sure where. Whenever cattle were on hand, indents were occasionally assigned to check on them, but mostly yeomen whites were brought in for the task; the Planter didn't trust his indents with anything they weren't accustomed to.

These were also the fields, he knew, where the slave auctions had once been held. The old platforms were still intact, spaced out along the edges, and Atti skipped past them now: cement foundations, with rotting planks half-disintegrated up top. He'd heard about their use from the old-timers, though he wasn't sure if they remembered themselves or if they were simply passing along the stories, how the women would wail and the children would scream and the men would swing wildly or crumple in defeat or simply simmer in silent, impotent, infinite rage. The Brooke plantation had always been a power center, with slaves brought in from across the commonwealth, lined up right here for traders to scan.

They didn't do it that way anymore. Not since their so-called reforms. These days, instead of auction-houses, the nobles had business meetings and board tables. Instead of slave auctioneers, they had bank intermediaries. Instead of merchants taking orders, they had the conglomerates down south issuing them. And instead of yeomen with tape measures wrapped around human chattel's chests, they had spreadsheets and shorthand noting indents' ages and past transgressions.

Atti glanced across the meadow. The old auction office looked merely like a gray-shingled toolshed, which the Planter had never bothered knocking down. Folks said there'd been a lynching platform to its rear, dismantled before Atti had been born, for fear of offending modern sensibilities. But the unmarked graves below went undisturbed.

Meanwhile, the vista ahead remained empty. The party was doing its job, drawing away overseers from the plantation's border, back to the house for taking coats, or offering valet-parking for those who refused indents their keys, or providing whatever other services might garner their precious tips. Atti darted onward, as the property curved northward and the woods thickened ahead. He was sure there were surveillance cameras recording him, but hoped they wouldn't be checked for many hours at least. And he stepped onto the forest floor that awaited.

• • •

The festivities, meantime, showed no signs of ebbing. With evening turned fully into night, and dinner giving way to dessert and dancing, the guests were happily toasting each other and the Confederacy. For a moment at least, nobles could delight in their good fortune, tasting the wine shipped in from France, admiring the ancestral home, feasting on the delicacies produced by the kitchen. White-gloved indents offered champagne flutes in the foyer. Chandeliers lit the ballroom, making all the emeralds and diamonds shimmer. The symphony of banality echoed on: praise for the Guard, excitement about rearmament, appreciation for the shift in weather.

Clara Brooke, meanwhile, was delighted the whites were having such a grand time. She'd been an indent at Rosewood since birth, but only rarely had she heard parties' commotion grow so noisy. It seemed the Planter and his pals needed the release; whatever the reasons there, it was just what she'd been hoping for.

She hadn't told Atti about setting the rebellion for tonight, concerned about distracting from his own escape plans. Now, lying in her cot, she wondered how far he'd already gotten. She'd known he was leaving today, but she also knew now he hadn't been caught. Alarms would've sounded if he had. Saying a blessing for his journey, she sat up, stretched, and stepped silently from the cabin.

Everything was in order. She'd confirmed it on the way back from supper. Ten indents were stationed at their quarters' edge with AR-15s and .22 caliber cartridges, ready to charge the party at her command. Two more were already at the banquet hall, where everyone else would doubtless assemble once they heard the firing: it was where indents gathered whenever there was news of any kind – from rumors of an extended holiday, to reports of an accident in the field. Clara's hope was that tonight the overseers would head in the opposite direction, running to the mansion to see what was happening. In the meanwhile, she and the other leaders would distribute the weapons.

Over the last week, they'd collected the hundreds of guns they'd shipped in, retrieving them from their hiding spots – under floorboards, in between crop lines, at the forest perimeter – stashing them closer to quarters. In the last hour, they'd brought them to the banquet hall ridge.

It would be an enormous risk handing assault rifles to people who'd never fired them before – people who weren't expecting any bit of this. But Clara was certain the indents' conviction would keep them steady. Even if they didn't end up pulling the triggers, their appearance alone would terrify the whites.

The Planter and his guests would be drunk, distracted, even largely unarmed. With surprise on their side, the indents could swiftly swipe power. Mass-killing was not an option, no matter the temptation; it would provoke too much retaliation, Clara was sure, and provide no leverage. But holding the nobles captive could upend all society.

She told herself not to get caught up thinking about results beyond her control. The important thing was to take the plantation and disarm the overseers. Still, it was hard not to think about next steps. Clara knew indents at nearby estates had weapons too, provided by the same northern sources. They had the same numbers as well. What's more, nobles wouldn't be able to contain the news of what'd occurred, not even if contraband radios were collected and media stations censored: if nothing else, the overseers around the commonwealth would talk.

With word spreading, copycat attempts would follow. Indents on other plantations would lack surprise, it was true, but they'd have inspiration, confidence as to what was possible. And that would be surprise enough. Perhaps multiple plantations would fall. There'd be mass panic. Indents had never truly taken control of anything before.

Sneaking past a dozing guard, Clara sprinted to the infirmary cabin where she'd been holding meetings. Its old shutters clapped in the breeze. It smelled of medicine and mold, its light was uneven, evening's shadows dancing on the wood cladding. Reaching her arm beneath the stoop, she found the weapon placed there for her. She'd already received operating instructions, passed along from their northern contact, a man she'd never met but to whom she owed every shred of hope.

It was time to meet the others. They were waiting on the hill by the banquet hall, lying in the grass. Crossing the quarters, she kept her stride steady.

Paul, the strapping field-hand from Quadrant 3, was at the front. He'd become de facto second-in-command, and she was glad for it. He'd never once shown hesitation or fear in any of their meetings, and now, as she scrambled up, he gave a rapid nod. "We're all set."

"Good," she answered, crouching down next to him. "The rest of you follow."

For an instant, Clara marveled at her own power. Then she started her jog along the crest of the hill, past the hall and toward the mansion's western side. The others stood behind her, and quickly they were all running too, setting their sights on the gathering ahead, antique window panes, amber light leaking out, guests twirling to live-played rhythm and blues – thieving not only the indents' souls, Clara thought now, but their soul music too.

She lifted her gun.

No overseers had yet appeared, and she felt a burst of confidence this could actually work. The whites were close now, men and women standing tightly together on the porticos, empty glasses lining the window sills: nobles with no idea what was about to happen, no idea about the indents with guns charging at that very moment, ready to ruin their night, and hopefully their lives.

Surprising herself, Clara didn't feel afraid. She just couldn't believe how near it all finally was.

And then they'd arrived. She galloped right onto the wooden steps at the house's southeast corner, a spot she'd never been. An instant later, the enormous crack of a rifle split the night in two. She turned back, and saw Paul firing into the air.

The others joined in next, firing upwards as they ran into the house, aiming for the sky, trying to terrify the nobles before anyone could react. Everything became a rush as Clara heard shouts and bounded up the stairs onto the first-floor porch. She felt a man-made breeze for the first time in her life, drifting from ceiling fans overhead, but she scarcely registered it.

To her shock, there was no real security waiting. It turned out the overseers were back at the indent quarters, or in the main drive, or anywhere but here at the house. Clearly, it'd never occurred to the nobles that they were in any immediate danger. They were among their own, with the indents put safely to bed. Such was the world as they knew it. Uncertainty was shunted aside, frailty forgotten, all for a night of fun.

From the porch, Clara ran into the shocking chill of air conditioning, something she'd heard of but never quite believed. Its blast only added to the insanity of the moment, as the gunshots continued outside. It was then she became aware of the screaming from upstairs. Adrenalin filled her veins. The nobles knew now that their party had been shattered, that indents were arriving within.

Working to recall the floor-plans, Clara led the way toward a red-carpeted stairwell farther up. Still she hadn't fired her own gun, but she held it out in front while the others went on firing theirs, splintering walls, shredding paintings, blasting chandeliers that were now crashing down.

She spotted several indents who'd been working the party, donning tuxedos and carrying trays of glasses. They stared back, mouths agape, eyes wide. One of them, a man in his sixties at least, dropped his tray and started straight towards her, shouting over the gunfire and shouts. "Who the hell are you?!"

"Clara, Quadrant 9!"

"Well I'm Sheldon, mansion-duty, and I can't believe my eyes!"

She nodded and continued charging up the steps.

A young man in a Confederate Major's uniform – Clara could see the stripes on his arms – leapt out of the way, nearly tripping over the railing. And all at once, she knew the assault was working. His flabby face was pale and dripping with sweat, his teeth clenched, his blue eyes gripped with fear. Pointing her gun right at him, Clara felt a strength she'd never grasped in her life.

The major ducked, and she raced on by, taking three stairs at a time now, the others behind her doing the same. A moment later, they were entering the dance hall near the landing, and nobles were everywhere. Generals, captains, politicians, lawyers. Every one of them white, aristocratic, and terrified.

The band had ceased its playing. Some of the guests looked frozen in place. Others were hurrying toward the windows, seeking some escape. A few of the women were simply crumpled on the floor, whimpering. Clara snorted.

Then, making her voice heard above the noise, she issued her first order, inspired by their cowardice. "All of you! Down on the floor with the others! Do it now!" The words sounded fierce even to her, thunderous and proud and enraged, filled with the fury of generations. Their effect was immediate. The crowd slowed. More guests lowered themselves down indeed.

But at that, another voice countered her own – a familiar one from the back of the room – a white, wealthy voice. *"Young lady, what in God's name are you doing?"*

Clara spun around. It was the Planter himself. She could see him by the rear wall, arms waving beside a floor-to-ceiling window that was open to the night. His hands were outstretched, gray Confederate jacket unbuttoned, billowing white shirt untucked beneath. She could tell from his eyes that he was drunk, though he was trying hard to disguise it. His cheeks were flushed, silver hair weighed down with sweat, processing, judging. His chin was folded against his collar. He cleared his throat.

"Think about this now," he said next. "It can't end well."

Clara glared right back. She told herself she still wasn't afraid. "I swear to the heavens," she replied, her voice gone steady as stone. "I will kill you here and now if you say another word. Now lie down like everyone else."

And slowly, Franklin Brooke nodded, and Clara knew he believed her, even if she didn't believe herself. He didn't quite kneel, it was true. He just stood there, in shock or defiance or some mixture of both. But he didn't speak up again either.

Good enough, she decided.

Her eyes shifted then, scanning the room, seeing with satisfaction that every other noble was crouched to the floor just as she'd commanded – when suddenly, the scream of a siren pierced the air.

• • •

Clara flinched. The siren refused to stop, only growing louder, and she had to see what was happening. She couldn't just dart to the windows. It would be too risky to turn her back to the nobles and make herself prone. But she'd studied the mansion's layout in full, and she recalled a bedroom belonging to the Planter's daughter, just off the main hall. Shouting at the other indents to keep watch, she sprinted from the crowd at once, finding the door.

Opening it in a burst, she came upon a four-post bed, its sheets perfectly crisp and cloaked in darkness, mattress high off the ground with huge pillows and a thick blanket. She leapt right past all that, and toward a window on the far side, pediment and pilaster lining the wall beside it.

She wished she could blink away what she saw.

The entire property was encircled by vehicles. Black SUVs with the nation's banners painted on the doors. Any child would know them. Confederate Guard.

There were more coming in now too, careening in from the drive: lithium-ion-infused, cobalt-based – the 2500 HD models the Guard had made famous – a line of black electric sedans screeching in along with them, flags flapping from their hoods, at least a dozen already, speeding past the indents quarters, skidding to a halt on the front pasture. Was it possible? How could any of this have been reported so quickly? Their lights were flashing now as well, more sirens layered atop the first, a thousand different pitches and rhythms, all deafening. The whole room seemed to fill with their howl, dim shadows now overwhelmed by the red and blue from outside.

Clara spun back, away from the view. She felt her throat tighten, as her hands clenched the grip of the gun. She wasn't sure what to do.

It was a failure. That much was sure. She'd be arrested, and certainly killed.

For an instant, she wondered about killing herself instead, right then and there, saving them the trouble. She could just raise the barrel to her chin, and close her eyes. No one could stop her. It would be done.

She thought of Atti.

His grin. His handsome brown eyes, and beautiful skin.

His freedom. The hope that he could defeat this night even if she couldn't.

Paul's voice pierced the room. "They're coming, Clara," he shouted from the hall. "They're coming inside!"

She took a step forward. "There's nothing to do. They're going to win."

"We could go out firing."

"We could." She took in a breath. "But bloodshed for its own sake won't do a thing. We've made our mark."

Then, before Paul could respond, there was a crash, and she sprinted his way. He'd been tackled from behind. Confederate Guard had arrived on the landing, with others pouring in to follow. Three of them were dragging Paul across the floor, and Clara could see the rest down below, charging past the tables in lockstep, striding swiftly the way they preferred, knocking over glasses and trays, while the guests kept watch in silence.

A second later, an agent charged right at the bedroom door, pistol pointed. "Now!" he was shouting. "Drop it! You'll be shot! Drop your gun."

Clara took him in. He was barely more than a boy, rosy cheeks that probably didn't even need a shave. What kind of savagery could turn its youngest sons into executioners, while labeling her some kind of criminal? It was a miracle he hadn't already fired, she thought, and vaguely it occurred to her he must be under strict orders – that no doubt they'd need her for questioning.

"Drop it!!" he shouted again.

In a flash then, before she even could, she was surrounded by agents, and she felt herself punched on the head and ribs, as nobles jammed the hallway, gesturing, re-gaining their voices, screaming to the Guard that she was the one, she was the leader. There was a gleam of lit fury in their eyes, veins red and furious in their brows, yet still she tried to fight back, to stand and run, pulling herself loose, inching ahead – when suddenly, one of the guards held out a foot, and the whole of her body went flopping forward. It happened in an instant, but Clara could feel herself falling, a pain piercing her shoulder as she landed and cursed – then one of them had her pinned – two more snarling behind. There were orders being flung in every direction, the shadows of agents all around, dogs now as well, frantic with excitement, as one of the men stood right over her, lips curled, blue eyes eager, lifting the butt of his rifle, bringing it swiftly down square across her jaw.

It was a bitter, raging blow, as hard as anything Clara had ever encountered, yanking her neck so hard it felt as if it would fly straight from her torso. Her eyes soared upwards, and all at once, everything began to spin – the men, the dogs, the house itself. The floor wobbled, and the walls seemed to bend.

One of the agents tugged her arms behind her back, binding them together, and she realized she was being hauled across the floor, flung down the stairs, more agents twisting her legs, holding her wrists as they rushed outside.

Out of the corner of her eye, she could see them carrying other indents too, yanking them away from the shocked party guests and out onto the front lawn.

What had she done, then? What in God's name had she led them all into?

There, alongside the Guard's vehicle formation, a new line of gray vans had arrived too, their rear doors open. The agents threw Paul into one of them with a thud, the doors clanging shut behind him. Soon the very same was happening to her, the next van over. There was no point struggling, but that didn't stop her from trying.

They shoved her inside, and she hit the bed of the van with a bang, more pain crackling through her legs and up her spine.

There were no seats; the floor was hard. A wall divided the back section from the front.

Someone jerked a rough sack over her head, and she felt it tighten around her neck. Then something sharp pierced her arm, and she heard the van doors close. It felt as if someone was pinching her, deep in her flesh, deeper than seemed possible, and she yelled for it to stop. But before any sound emerged, she was instantly helpless – unable to move at all, unable even to stay awake. Her eyelids were heavy, her mind clouded.

And just as suddenly, everything went to black.

• • •

Several miles away, Atticus heard the gunfire.

Echoing off the Blue Ridge, it sounded like coal popping in a fire pit.

But that had to be it, he thought. Clara must have started the rebellion. There was no other real explanation. At once, he swerved to a stop in the woods, and listened hard. There were no more shots then, just bats fluttering, startled, through the trees above him.

Instantly, he vowed to turn back, to help in some way, even if he knew Clara wouldn't like it. But how? By the time he got there, it could be all over. For some time, he'd been scaling a hill through the forest, following ancient paths once used for logging, before the Confederacy had possessed any real roads at all.

Resuming his run, Atti aimed for the next break in the trees. When he reached the clearing's edge, he saw it was no more than a patch of overgrown grass, but at least it gave him a view, and scurrying up a slanted boulder near its center, he peered through the night. Toward the horizon, he could see flashing lights. He was certain they hadn't been there before – surely, he'd have noticed their glare against the night sky. But there was no mistaking them now: reds and blues, more each second, and he felt his heart sink deep in his chest. Someone must have alerted the Guard to the revolt, tipped them off somehow. Or maybe they'd just been nearby.

He squinted, but even with thin cloud cover, it was too dark and too distant. His heart beat faster. He prayed Clara had found a way out, that she wouldn't end up one of those arrested, and he tightened his fists in hope. Until a moment later, breathing hard, he felt vomit rising in his throat, and bending over, he let himself be sick. Heaving, panting, he shut out thoughts of what they might do to her.

Finally, when he was done, Atti gulped the nighttime air back into his lungs. He wiped his chin dry with his sleeve, and straightened back up. In the sky above, through the branches, the stars were vivid. And for a moment, he felt as though God was watching, waiting to see what he would do.

Only – it was too late to give warning about the Guard; that much was certain. They'd be starting their search for him soon as well, and he imagined what Clara would say if she found out he'd turned back, enraged at any notion of empty sacrifice – how she'd begged him to focus on going, to keep his trust in her as she demanded. And wasn't that what she'd tell him once more?

"I love you," he said softly, so quiet that his voice melted into the air around him. "Clara, I love you," he said again.

Then, angling from the clearing, Atti cut left, renewing his old pace north, pushing through tears, knowing now he had only a few hours until dawn, when he'd have to find a spot for rest. He moved on in renewed silence, under the lush trees and the dazzle of the summertime stars, pushing branches aside as he went, working hard to keep others from snapping beneath his feet.

CHAPTER 17

Byron Sampson had lived in the foothills of Virginia all his life.

His cottage was small, only two rooms plus a rickety toilet, with a leaky roof and cracked windows, peeling paint, and an interior that reeked of mildew. But to Byron, none of that mattered. The previous year, he'd finally finished paying off the bank, and now the whole thing belonged to him. No one could come in without permission. Not bankers, not neighbors, not even the Confederate Guard – assuming he didn't provoke the bastards.

Just the night before, he'd been yammering on about how proud it made him. He didn't remember much, but he remembered that. He'd been at the Crotelle Tavern with a bunch of locals he'd grown up with, and he grinned at what he could recall. At some point, he'd led a booming rendition of "Dixie Land" from atop a scuffed table, off-key and impassioned.

I wish I was in the land of cotton,
Old times there are not forgotten;
Look away! Look away! Look away! Dixie Land!!

After that, he must've gone back to the whiskey bar. He certainly didn't recall returning to the cottage – though he remembered getting sick against some crumbling wall on the way home. Probably his own chimney. Rubbing his face, he wiped away the memory and tried to wake up.

His head was pounding. He saw his boots were still on, and that he'd never pulled the sheet up over his body. The air-conditioner in the corner was creaking, its breeze coming out as lukewarm as ever. A scattered bunch of thirty-dollar bills lay on the ground. Above the door, a burned-out bulb dangled. The ceiling was black from leaks, the floor missing every other plank.

He hoped there was something left from his latest payday – a nice sum he'd made tracking down a runaway girl who'd panicked over a pregnancy. Probably by a noble, he thought, since the indents were perfectly free to get pregnant with each other. No one would run away on account of that.

He reached into his pockets and found they were empty. Damn. No doubt he'd spent a whole pile at the tavern. And stretching wide, Byron groaned as his back popped. He sat up, swallowing a wave of nausea. He stared again at his feet.

Forty-four years old, Byron couldn't remember when he'd started feeling his age. But it'd definitely happened. It wasn't just the aches in his bones, either. He could recall a time when the whole world had felt different: when being a yeoman at least meant not having to concern yourself with where things were headed. No longer. The nobles had gotten too jumpy. The TV-men spent all their time worrying about resisters and border scuffles. Even the cartoons had changed – in the old days, they'd simply poked fun at indents as simple souls who liked a good jingle; now they built them up like monsters, capable of killing an honest Confederate at any moment. It wore Byron out. The country of the Revolution was turning into a den of cowardice.

At least it was good for business. All that fear meant cash for the taking. It wasn't that nobles had begun respecting Byron's profession; the day a nobleman abandoned hypocrisy was the day he stopped being a nobleman. But at least they'd recollected they needed slave-hunters – or "Indent Monitors," anyway, as

Byron and his ilk were now officially labeled, according to the New Confederate language nobody used.

Of course, he might care more for the reforms if their facelift had provided anything besides misplaced concern for the slaves. Instead, they hadn't done a thing for yeomen: nothing for taxes, nothing concerning the draft, nothing about opening up a single new school. Just a few meaningless laws forbidding whips. And they didn't even enforce that: whippings, beatings, man-traps, bribes – so long as Byron returned the runaways half-intact, anything was acceptable. The nobles called, and he answered.

Now he reached for the painkillers on his plastic nightstand and threw back four at once. Then he shuffled to the toilet, registered it was unflushed, and relieved himself, before pivoting to the sink. It was rusty, and he'd run out of soap, but he rinsed his hands anyway. From a stained mirror on the wall, the reflection staring back was a disaster. His teeth had gone brown, and his hair, hanging nearly to his shoulders, was so greasy it looked wet. The lines on his forehead were grooves. The bags beneath his eyes looked positively alarming.

He sighed. The new job would do him good.

He'd get some fine Virginia air at least, dodge the taverns for a stretch, pad his wallet. With the house paid off, he'd used up his latest earnings too quick, passing time without purpose, waiting for someone to call. Finally, last night, someone had. It was why he'd celebrated extra hard.

Clearly, Byron's reputation had preceded him. He'd fumbled last summer, it was true – making the mistake of drinking lake water without iodine, passing out, letting slip a mother and son. He'd been tempted to track them right into Maryland, to hell with international incidents, but had ended up doing the sensible thing, retreating, apologizing, returning his funds: not out of any sense of obligation, but because it was always smart to watch after one's standing. It'd worked. The jobs had rebounded. There were still plenty of would-be runaways out there cursing his name, and plenty of Planters too – embittered he'd charged them half the cost of a slave, desperate to retain their property, but even more their impression of power.

Retreating from the mirror, he moved to the kitchen, ready for a few slabs of bacon before heading out. Breakfast would be hard to keep down, he knew. But he'd need to have his wits about him. He lit the slim stove against the chimney, grabbed a used pan from the sink, and fried the meat 'til it was crisp.

This wasn't just any Planter he was meeting, after all. It was General Franklin Brooke who'd phoned. Over from Rosewood Manor. For Christ's sake, he might be the most powerful fellow in the entire Confederacy. Damn near the richest too. The powerful ones always were.

Scarfing down the meat in three bites, sliding his chair from the table, Byron stood. He'd clean the pan later. He was supposed to get there at eleven, and the walk would be two hours. A part of him had hoped Brooke would send a car, but clearly the general hadn't considered that yeomen were forbidden vehicles of their own; on the phone, he'd simply set a time and hung up. At least it was still early. The humidity would be merciful.

Pushing open the screen door, Byron stepped into the dew-soaked grass. Past the wheelbarrows and piles of brick, straight across the un-mowed lawn, a narrow road awaited. It led to the manors, and Byron trudged over to it now.

•   •   •

Chaos had engulfed the mansion, and Franklin Brooke, who rarely became overwhelmed, was coming close. For the last hour, he'd been standing near the second-story landing, watching Guard agents still swarming about the property, collecting evidence, gathering spent cartridges in the hall, going over transcripts of interviews with the party's guests.

Even the oldest of the agents appeared to be half his age. It was obvious from their smooth, frenetic faces, no matter their sky-blue collars and efforts to speak swiftly, that they knew as little as he did about how the indents could possibly have organized an assault like this – even one that had been squashed so quickly. They were all murmuring and jotting notes on clipboards, frequently glancing his way, and Franklin suspected he was making them still more nervous.

Well, good, he thought. Let them be nervous. Whatever it took for them to do their jobs.

Eventually, he turned toward the stairs. There was only so much to be gained by glaring like this, and with a sigh, he made his way to the master bedroom. Pausing at its threshold, he eyed the rolltop desk in the corner, and the antique quartz clock on the mantle. It'd been only twelve hours since the attack, but the whole night was already impossible to comprehend, even with the broken window glass on the floor right in front of him. Gazing out the window, Franklin saw the indents back in the fields, finding renewed equilibrium in their station. To think – just a few bad seeds could spread such poison.

He wondered if it wasn't finally time to update security. He'd long maintained that doing so would betray a lack of faith, that he was too important an example for Planters everywhere. Had that always seemed naïve? Now it seemed inexcusably so. Somehow northern abolitionists had infiltrated his workers.

Cathryn remained horrified, of course, barely taking comfort that no one had been seriously hurt – something Franklin considered a miracle – going for a walk to try and find some calm. Their daughter Liza was fine, thank God. After a desperate search, she'd been located. Toll records showed she'd driven to Richmond shortly after the party's start. And while that was certainly upsetting – Cathryn was furious – what mattered was Liza was safe. They could deal with her transgression later.

Anyway, the threat had been quelled. The guests were secure; the house would be repaired. The rebellion – for that's what it had been – was over, its leaders arrested within minutes. Franklin assumed the Confederate Guard would deliver him compensation for those they'd apprehended, though he wouldn't press it.

In the meantime, the slaves were all accounted for, except one.

That lad Atticus, already pledged for sale, was gone. The scoundrel had seized the night's chaos and run off. Surveillance tape showed him slipping into the woods at the plantation's northeastern corner. Unfortunately, local Confederate Guard was now too preoccupied to be of any use. They'd issued an alert, but a solo runaway wasn't their priority.

Against his own instincts, then, Franklin had decided upon a slave-hunter.

He didn't like the idea. It'd always seemed repugnant that such a group would wait for despondent Planters to phone them up, then charge a small fortune. It was the worst of yeoman impulses, a capitalistic greed that reeked of U.S.-style thinking. Alas. He'd gotten the information for a fellow named Sampson – said to have an impressive success rate – and before bed, had made the call. He nearly hadn't dialed. But such was his duty as a Planter, Franklin knew. He couldn't just let an indent flee. It would set an intolerable precedent. The choice was really no choice at all.

•   •   •

The intercom buzzed, and Franklin told the overseer on duty to send the visitor up. Lifting his cap from the dresser, he made sure to fetch his checkbook too, finding it deep in a drawer in the sideboard. He wasn't used to needing it. On the plantation, expenses were monthly; on the road, salespeople deferred to the uniform; at work, everything was expensed. In truth, Franklin hated business dealings, or any talk of money. But then – yeomen needed payment. That didn't forgive a slave-hunter his profession, but it was worth remembering.

He waited in the hall. It would be more appropriate to meet in the study downstairs, but the Confederate Guard was still there going through records, so he stayed put, eyeing the grilles and rosettes etched into the woodwork. Until after a moment, he heard scuffling footsteps from the stairwell – and there was Byron Sampson, appearing on the landing.

Franklin studied the slave-hunter, taking in his shabby clothes and sweaty, sun-burnt face. The fellow's shirt was three sizes too big; his cheekbones jutted against his skin. His eyes were sallow and deeply set, his wispy brown hair as long as a lady's. Certainly Franklin wasn't accustomed to the sight of so much dirt on a white man, let alone the sour smell.

"Good morning, Mr. Sampson," he offered, extending his hand, his manners intact. "I'm General Brooke. Thank you for taking the meeting. Welcome to Rosewood."

•   •   •

Byron delivered his best effort at a smile and returned the handshake. The general was exactly as expected: a well-fed, well-bred son-of-a-bitch. Tucked away in his fortress, he was sporting spotless Confederate gray that matched his coiffed hair. His face was open and square-jawed – an easy mark.

Byron wondered what had occurred here. He'd spotted Confederate Guard vehicles out front, and had faced a series of insistent agents downstairs. Obviously it had to do with the vandalism – shattered windows and broken furniture by the stairwell. He bowed and tipped his cap, glad to be free of them. "It's an honor to meet you, General. Pleasure indeed."

It was time to discuss business. Franklin pulled a chair from the hall's corner and slid it over. Then he took the window seat opposite, folded his hands across his lap, crossed his ankles, and skipped the offer of a drink he would extend to a noble. "I'm new to this, and you are not," he began. "Aside from funding, what do you need?"

Byron cleared his throat. He was never sure how to query a noble. "What's the boy go by?"

"His name is Atticus. Most call him Atti. Why?"

"In case I hear word of him." Byron lowered awkwardly into the chair. He reminded himself he knew what he was doing. "Did he disable his leg device?"

General Brooke paused. "He doesn't wear one."

"Beg pardon?"

"I haven't mandated them here at Rosewood. It never occurred to me the indents would run."

"Entirely understandable, sir." Byron knew this was the right thing to say. "Most of the indents slice them right out in scenarios like this anyhow. Even when they don't, they get help from abolitionists along the way – on the U.R. The enemy's learned to muck up the signal, you see. They scramble the devices. Even the latest models."

"That so?"

"I'd complain, but it's good for business." Byron gave a wink, but the general didn't respond. "Your message said he got out yesterday evening?"

"That's right – during the incident here. You heard of it?"

"Only a touch as I arrived."

Franklin nodded. He folded his arms. "Last night, several armed indents came into the house. They were quickly apprehended of course. But you can imagine it gave my guests a terrible fright."

Byron searched for the right words. He rubbed his forehead, unable to picture it. Hell, it sounded as though the general had just admitted there'd been an uprising. "I'm sorry to hear about that sir." And he was. Nobles' showboating aside, indents were indents.

"Have we given the lad too much of a head start?"

"I can track him." Byron was glad to shift back to logistics. "He'll be slowed hunting for supplies, and he'll get disoriented. They always do. I've got more than a shot at catchin' up." He wasn't quite as confident as he appeared. The biggest challenge in Virginia remained the proximity of the U.S. border.

"Will anyone else be on the payroll?"

"No sir, I'm all on my own. Once I catch the boy, I'll stun him and bind him. Then I might hire a few locals to help load him into a rented car, but that's peanuts." Byron hesitated.

"Go on. If there's more to discuss, please say so."

He looked back. "Well, sir. I just want you to be aware, only half-refunds if I fall short.".

The General met his eyes, standing slowly. Then, taking the checkbook from his pocket, he wrote out the seventy thousand dollars they'd agreed upon, and handed it over – along with a photograph of Atticus clipped to the edge, matching the digital ones he'd already sent over.

"Appreciate that, sir. I'll be in touch."

"As will I," Franklin replied. "You can let yourself out below."

Byron turned, taking in the image resting in his palm. It showed a young black man like so many others he'd seen, with a guarded expression and eyes glinting, collar smartly snapped, cheekbones like stilts, short-cropped hair. Block letters had been stenciled across the top: *HIGH-VALUE*, they said. So this was "Atti" then.

The hunt was underway.

Chapter 18

Humidity had hit New York

Northerners liked to pretend their nation didn't suffer from stickiness and heat, but they all knew it wasn't true. For a stretch, it'd been a decent summer. But while June and July had been pleasant, August wasn't nearly so kind. Here came mosquitoes, angry crowds of tourists, and garbage at the curbs that ruined the very idea of seafood.

Rushing into the apartment on a Tuesday afternoon, Ted Mercer looked as though he'd been dunked in water. Flinging open the door, he brushed the sweat from his forehead, panting from his sprint straight from the office. The cramped common area included both kitchen and den. There were no posters hung up – a map of New York rested on the floor, betraying any good intentions behind it – and a lone lamp rested in the corner, a flimsy old thing with a cracked shade. A TV was hitched to the wall, opposite a saggy couch. On the far side were two bedrooms; to their right, a ceramic counter flanked a tiny corridor, where a two-burner stove and a half-sized refrigerator battled for space.

Raj was lying on the couch. He wore a t-shirt and soccer shorts and had positioned himself in front of the air-conditioning vents. His hair was back in a thick ponytail, beard still asking for a trim, eyes shut tight – though as Ted walked in, he allowed his hand a wave, before it flopped back to his side. A torn manila envelope sat beside him.

Ted glanced its way, then back toward his friend. "Hey."

Raj didn't open his eyes. "You were right." He arched toward the ceiling and stretched. "You were right…"

"I know."

Finally Raj squinted back. "This is terrible," he murmured. "It's terrible."

"You repeating everything today?" Ted waited for a laugh that never came. "When'd you find out?"

"An hour ago. I figured I'd check the mail before breakfast." Since losing his job, he'd developed a new morning routine: sleep in, fry some eggs, make his way to the television. Today, he'd skipped the eggs and simply ended up here.

"You didn't want to text?" Ted leaned over, unclasping his bag, and pulled out a folder of his own. He dropped it on Raj's lap.

His friend sat up. "You too?" He blinked, shimmying Ted's notice from the envelope. "I don't get it. You're not unemployed."

"That's what I said. Even the bosses were shocked. Turns out it's a massive draft day. Biggest in fifty years. It's all over the news."

"I haven't checked my phone – "

"They've already called up 150,000, and more to come. We all knew they were planning something, but no one expected this. Intel's been half cleared out – seemed like everyone under 30 got a notice – anyone with a position they think is expendable." Ted slid onto the couch too. "The higher-ups gave us the rest of the week off. Said we deserved some time before we report."

"When – Monday?"

"Yeah, you?"

"7am."

"It gives my dad a good chance. I bet he can get us stationed together. He'll talk to my uncle. The old one. He's pretty high up."

"All your uncles are high up."

"Just be happy they'll help." He'd pulled out his phone and was scrolling through the day's newsfeeds. "Both parties are on board. Lincolnians are saying it's about time. Whigs voted yes in exchange for another boost in climate spending." He rolled his eyes.

Raj turned back to the pair of envelopes. "Why today? Why all of the sudden?"

"It's been building. We've been getting reports from the Confederacy about meetings of homegrown Resisters, even reports of slaves fighting back. They're using the weapon shipments we send them. We're adding to the pressure down there."

"'We'?"

"All of us, yeah."

"You've never met a slave in your life."

"Bite me, buddy." Ted sighed. "Point is, Confederacy's got problems."

"Doesn't mean they're weak."

"The Rebs obviously disagree. They wouldn't keep sending troops themselves if they weren't worried."

"Can't be that worried. They're still God-level rich."

"BS. It's a house of cards, and they know it. All subsidies. The Planters should've diversified."

"What book told you that?"

"You saying I'm wrong?"

"Don't forget their renewables."

"Show me the profit in that."

Raj shrugged. "We're the ones spending endless money, not them – sending endless men."

"Not endless, Raj. The idea is to go in and put our foot on their throat. It's old-school. It's what we used to do all the time."

"It didn't work – that's why we stopped."

"They're weaker now."

"I don't know." He scratched the back of his head. The ponytail was half-undone. "It's the same lesson, generation after generation. We keep thinking if we nudge them just enough, they'll topple, they'll wake up and realize they're wrong and always have been."

"Every era's got to try."

"By sending citizens to get killed?"

"Don't be nasty."

"Don't be naïve. This war's going into its third century."

"Ah. There we are! Whig talking points. You steal those from Chuck Todd?"

"Don't get riled now."

"Well maybe I am. Maybe this is a hell of an opportunity."

Raj closed his eyes once more.

"Dammit Raj, gimme a break. Fighting's terrible, of course it is. But it's also coming. There's no stopping that. And I'm not gonna duck it."

Raj raised an eyebrow. "The food's gonna suck."

"The weather'll be even worse."

"It'll be like basic training all over again. With lights-out and dickhead commanders and waking up before sunrise."

Ted nodded, recalling their first stints of service. It'd only been a few years ago, but seemed longer; they'd both served their six months right out of college. Back then, there'd been only scattered border skirmishes. Half their time had been spent in West Point classrooms, studying historical feats against the Confederacy: the Rough Rider Rescue in D.C.; Baltimore's defense during the Gilded Age Siege; the race for western territory before that; the famed battles from when the war had first started. The rest of the time, they'd been drilled: marches to nowhere – across fields in West Jersey and all the way out to Ohio – regiment formation, firing guns at brightly painted targets.

Still, Raj was wrong. This time, it would be different. There'd be rules, sure – reporting to officers and remembering how to stay in position. But it wouldn't just be training. This time, they were being called up because the government actually needed them. This time, they'd see the border.

He sighed. "Alright," he offered. "We've still got a few days of freedom left. Might as well try and enjoy them."

"Any beers in the fridge?"

"I'll check."

CHAPTER 19

The ceiling in Liza Brooke's hotel room was tall, a sign of the building's age. Like so much of Richmond, it'd been built before air-conditioning, back when southerners had relied upon architecture alone to battle their summers. Standing at the mattress edge, readying for her trip home, she studied the window sills, crafted when the Confederacy had been barely more than an idea, and the elaborate wallpaper – nearly as old – with scenes of children picnicking, shepherds wandering, hounds leaping toward foxes.

It wasn't just her hotel that had survived so long, of course: the whole capital city had stood proud since the nation's founding, saved from siege thanks to the victory at Gettysburg. After that, the U.S. had abandoned its ideas of invasion, turning inward with sudden urgency, tasked instead with self-preservation. The Revolution's first phase had reached its end, and Richmond had celebrated.

Throughout the historic district, the buildings were marked with plaques. The one outside the Richmond Grand noted it had survived three fires and hosted every incoming Confederate president but Woodrow Wilson, who'd boasted his own townhouse nearby. It was the city's premier hotel, after all, lording over the main boulevard, a slender building flanked by potted plants and old horse poles, staffed by footmen in jackets welcoming the guests. Moss-dappled brick framed the hardwood doors; across the way, yellow birches lined the curb. As long as anyone remembered, it had served as the favored lodging spot for nobles, evoking the history of the nation and the grace of aristocratic power.

Yet wasn't it also stubborn? It'd remained unchanged for so many decades, Liza thought, it was almost easier to picture in black-and-white. The winding streets outside might be charming, but they were also anchors, weighing down the present with a past that would never leave. Not that such mettle came as a surprise in a country that made no room for anything new. In school rooms, periodicals, television, and speeches, in the red brick chimneys and marble statues and uniforms that never evolved, the message was always the same: the Founding Fathers' wisdom had been passed down to the nobles who now ruled in their stead.

In buildings like these, of course, people weren't supposed to wonder about such things. They weren't supposed to question claims of liberty, or consider that hoop dresses looked ridiculous instead of traditional, or acknowledge yeomen neighborhoods that'd descended into squalor and shambles.

Not when there were Confederate Guard agents on every corner.

Liza blinked. For it was here, in this aging arena at the heart of it all, that she'd at last discovered there were others who thought as she did. It was here, of all places, where she'd found Dale.

Unfortunately, it was also where she'd drawn the ire of her parents. They were beyond livid she'd traveled without telling them, skipping out on the party – missing the indents' attack in the process! – all to visit a city they'd asked her to avoid. When she'd reached her father by phone, he'd demanded she come home immediately, his voice sounding icier than she'd ever heard it. She'd pledged to drive back in time for supper.

There was a gentle knock on the door.

Liza hesitated, and looked over. But a moment later, it came again.

She swallowed, walking to the eye slot, squinting into the hall. And her heart gave a skip.

"Dale Birch!" she exclaimed at once, and she reached for the bolt.

He laughed as the door swung open. "Well, hello Miss Brooke." His dark hair was tussled from the city wind outside. "Surely you were going to tell me you were in town?"

All thought of her parents had vanished from Liza's mind. "How'd you know?"

"A friend works at the hotel – he bragged about your name on the ledger. City gossip ain't to be trifled with, you know." He grinned. "Might I come in?"

"Please!"

Dale bowed, and stepped forward. "And here you are."

But she'd stopped listening.

She was registering his clothes in full now. A fine-pressed coat of sky blue; boots to his knees; a slouch cap under his arm.

Liza heard herself gasp.

She'd been so surprised at greeting him, so distracted by that handsome beard and effortless smile, that she hadn't put it together straightaway. But suddenly there was no mistaking it.

Dale Birch was in the Confederate Guard.

He met her eye. "This?" he asked. Another laugh. "My apologies – it's just my day job. Is our reputation really so awful?"

Still, Liza was staring. It couldn't be. And yet it was. "I just didn't expect – I didn't think – " After all, she'd known plenty who'd joined the Guard, didn't she? Nobles from school days. Boys with ambition. Was it truly the case they'd all turned into monsters upon enlisting? "You just never mentioned it, Dale."

"And risk the look you're giving me now?"

She tried to restore her smile. The general rule, even for nobles, was to steer clear. The Guard wasn't known for nuance. Better to avoid them than risk being misinterpreted for cracking a joke about Congress. To think that one of them secretly spent his evenings calling for class mobility! It was incomprehensible. "What are you?" she suddenly blurted, unable to contain herself. "Some kind of double agent?

"You make it sound so grand." Again, he was chuckling. It would be irritating if it weren't so infectious. "I should have told you earlier, I know. But to be honest, I didn't figure you'd be impressed, Liza. Don't think me dishonest."

"No." She evened out her voice. "I'm just taken aback."

"I joined as a kid. Got myself stuck in it. At least for now."

It didn't make sense. Agents weren't supposed to talk this way. She shook her head. "What about your hair? Aren't you supposed to keep it short?"

"That's only for new enlistees." Dale brushed the locks from his brow, so that they settled perfectly. Then he winked.

"You're too much."

"Let me make it up to you. How 'bout a stroll? If we go now, we'll be back before the heat settles."

"My parents are expecting me."

He nodded. "I've been following the news – the whole Guard's talking about it. Half the commonwealth's been assigned to your father's plantation."

"It sounds bad."

"Sure does. Hard to believe the indents are moving faster on their discontent than the yeomen."

"I suppose that's so." She remained uneasy at Dale's openness. In the tavern, amid the electricity of free thought, it'd been thrilling. Now, alone in a hotel room, his words merely seemed blunt, careening headlong into all that was forbidden. His uniform didn't make it any easier, a steady reminder that the state was always near.

"Oh come now," he pressed. "We won't stray far – we'll have you home by dusk." He looked like a boy, eager for a gift, and she felt herself wavering. "If you let me, darlin', I'll show you the best sweet tea in town."

"Now that's unfair." She allowed the first hint of a smile.

"So you're a proper southern girl after all!"

.   .   .

The day had the air of a carnival. There were children on every block, playing leapfrog and tag, customers at market stalls haggling over peaches, soldiers drilling cheerfully in the squares. An omnibus screeched; the sun pushed aside the clouds. As they stepped from the hotel, Dale offered his arm, and Liza took it.

"I like this city," she said.

"Tell me why."

"I like its noise."

"I'll take that as encouragement."

She laughed, and hoped it covered her blush.

They turned to a quieter block, past the old sailors' pubs, and moved alongside the treasured sanctuary of Monroe Park, flanked by thick-trunked oak trees, all leafy branches that still showed no hints of autumn. A pair of robins chirped.

The café was as near as Dale had promised. It was a small corner spot with a crowd tumbling onto its sidewalk and a jumble of shops close by – lamp-makers and butchers and hardware stores – the kind of worn-in patch that had been there before any of them, and would linger long after they were gone. Even so, the march of the regime was too much even for these old arteries to neglect: every post draped in the Stars-and-Bars, curbs jammed with officers, Wanted-Posters for runaways crowding each other out beneath the streetlights.

Liza took a breath, as Dale used the privilege of his uniform to cut ahead. Inside, urgent-faced waiters were scurrying past cast-iron tables: there were women in pearls, men munching on chops and caviar, voices like snapping flames. "I don't know."

"What's the matter?"

She lowered her voice amid the commotion. "If people recognize me, they'll gossip."

"Nonsense."

"Not everything will bend to your charm, Dale."

"No?"

"I'm serious." Her voice was near a whisper. "My father will know I was out socializing, instead of heading straight home."

But he'd already spun forward: greeted by a maître-d groveling at his uniform indeed, ushering them in before Liza could stop it, towards a mahogany booth in the rear. She held herself stiffly as they moved through the starched air, ignoring the crowds as best she could.

They reached their seats, and Dale ordered teas and food for both of them. "Don't worry," he said, spinning back her way. "They're all caught up in their own nonsense! Not-a-one giving us a second thought."

The space grew louder. Crystal flutes were topped near to overflowing; the bow-tied waiters swung about like dancers; laughter boiled up and over. Soon the food was arriving in waves – sauces of every color, yellow hollandaise, green mint over spring lamb, black-soaked anchovies – and she tried to do as he'd asked, enjoying it, taking a re-fill of the tea, knowing all the while it would take only one wandering eye, one person to recognize her, to report back to her parents.

Dale grinned, watching her. "All this noise is good, you know. Makes it impossible for recording devices."

Liza nodded. How was it possible he talked about the government as though he weren't a part of it?

"You dab your lips between every sip, darlin'."

"If you don't have manners, mother always said, you don't have soul."

It made him guffaw, and she found she was glad.

When the meal was done, and they stood to go, again Liza registered the power of his uniform. People gave them clearance as they exited; one noblewoman in a violet hoop dress even spilled her drink curtseying too low.

"You want to know more about the Guard," Dale remarked matter-of-factly, as they returned to the streets outside.

"Not about the Guard exactly." They rounded another corner. Here were more roads lined with shops, and they strolled onto one of the new bridges over the James. The water looked rumpled, like sheets that had been slept in, and the whole city seemed to converge on its banks – voices loud yet distant, echoing off lampposts and narrow alleyways that spun in all directions.

"I do know what you mean," Dale said at last, leaning against the rail. "No one at the Guard has any idea about the meetings I attend. I work to keep it that way."

"How can you be sure?"

"I can't. But I'm careful: we rotate schedules, and I explain my time in the tavern by filing reports about it. The Village Field is a known hangout for agitators. So I took on the assignment of scouting the place out. I never report back real information, just the usual complaints – I tell them it's drunks whining over yeomen taxes, draft numbers, garbage pickup – nothing about proper Resisters inside."

"You're not terrified?"

"It's risky, yes." But his dark eyes were dancing as ever. "This week, we had to cancel a get-together because too many agents were on the next block over."

"What if you get spotted?"

"I can track them all on my phone easily enough. I make sure I'm free."

Liza had the thrill of feeling entrusted and wholly exposed. For years, she'd played perfectly the part of the southern belle. Now here she was, chatting openly about resistance, in a capital city doubling as the center of dissent. She'd long heard her father's talk of subversiveness. Apparently it was all true.

Dale resumed his walk. "You should come back to the tavern, Liza, make yourself visible next time. Tell folks of the latest slave rebellion firsthand."

"I wasn't even home!"

"Won't matter. You're from Rosewood Manor, you know the Planters' life. Just showing up would be enough. You wouldn't even need to talk about the indents – we have our yeomen to think about first anyway."

Liza pictured it.

"Why not?" Dale pressed. "It's past time for getting involved. The meetings are getting bigger, the government's anxious, the Guard's on alert. On top of it all, the slaves are acting up, and the U.S. is raiding the border. The cracks of aristocracy are showing. Nobles can't keep taking the pie and pretending no one else wants any."

She felt the urge to shush him, to be sure they were on their own. Yet wasn't he right? There were hints every day, making their way right through government filtering: in all the news stories about troop call-ups, slave-hunts, new Guard checkpoints.

Dale squinted into the sun. "Growing up, I was a proper Confederate, you know. I knew the words to every southern poem I came across. William Gilmore Simms, John Cooke, Timrod. I dressed up in soldiers' gray for each parade."

"Where?"

"Southwest corner of the commonwealth. Tiny town called Brownsville."

Liza couldn't recall the name. "Is it very nice?"

"It's beautiful. Thick forests, bottomless farmland." He exhaled. "But it's also poor."

"Oh," Liza said, not used to the word. "I'm sorry," she added.

"Don't be sorry, Liza. It was a nice place to grow up. But you see – and here's the thing – it wasn't just the town."

"I don't understand."

"It was also me. I grew up yeoman."

She swallowed. "Don't joke."

"I mean just what I say. In a yeoman family, with a yeoman pop who sold canned goods, and a yeoman mother who sorted mail at the post office." His gaze was intent. "Does it bother you?"

Now she was peering right back. "That you keep so many secrets?"

"That I'm not like you."

The breeze had picked up; the sun rose higher in the sky. Liza felt her heart racing, and all at once, she aimed to picture him as he might once have been, this man who carried himself with such swagger and ease, so clearly now accustomed to power. She wondered what Kevin would say. He was often reading about the yeomen, after all, always wanting to talk about the size of their cottages and their baggy modern clothes. In truth, he was the only person she knew who seemed to consider them at all. She herself had certainly never spoken to one. Not really. Not beyond asking after a price in a general store, or thanking one for filling her car. And taking in Dale's searching brown eyes, she began to see him anew, that rugged beard and those rapid intonations – hints at the dusty streets and cramped lawns that must've bred him. "No," she answered at last. "It doesn't bother me. I'm glad you've said something."

For a moment, he continued watching her; then his smile returned. "Well I suppose I'm just glad you didn't turn and walk the other direction."

"Did you really think I would? Is that how nobles are?"

"You tell me."

But Liza ignored that, absorbing the sun, breathing in the sausage and pretzels from the corner stands. "You didn't finish explaining, though. How'd a yeoman end up in the Guard?"

"I always longed for serving the nation as soon as I could. Everyone said yeomen couldn't end up at university, but I wanted to try. I shirked work at my pop's store so I could hit the books. Social studies came easy to me – I read that for fun. Science was harder, but I'd stay up late, and eventually that clicked too. In the end, they selected me for local scholarship."

Liza raised her eyebrows. Such scholarships were known as an exception to Confederate immobility. Back during the reforms, the New Confederates had introduced them; ever since, the resulting funding had sent a few yeomen each year to campuses normally reserved for aristocrats. Her father and his friends often grumbled about it. Only men were eligible, certainly, and the yeomen students had to perform superbly just to stay on, but it was a system that made the liberal wing in Congress feel better about itself than it should. "And the Guard?"

"I worked even harder in university than I had before. Hard enough that after military service, I could apply. It's what I'd dreamed of. I filled out the forms, collected all the recommendations from professors and commanding officers, was granted approval from local Council. The day I got my letter of admission, it came with a summons. They told me I wasn't to tell people about my roots: that was the deal, and it was more than fine by me. When they gave me the uniform, I couldn't believe it. I'd proven the Confederacy was what I'd always wanted it to be. A place where you can serve."

"What changed your mind?"

"I came to learn what the Guard really was. I grant you, I already knew nobles saw yeomen as servants, barely more than indents. But I'd told myself that was just habit, that it didn't run deeper. My fellow agents showed me I was wrong. We were no arbiter of justice. We worked only at snuffing out anyone who aimed to topple the order. If that meant screwing over yeomen, burying a legal case, so be it. In fact, all the better for it."

"Indents, too, I imagine."

"The Guard doesn't help a soul."

"You didn't already know that?"

"I'd glamorized them. Put agents on a pedestal."

Liza grasped he couldn't have been alone. For how else to explain their thousands of recruits, year in and year out, generation after generation? It just went to show the Guard was as nasty as she suspected, inviting an upstanding yeoman to enforce the very walls he'd been allowed to slip across – encouraging gratitude to shore up loyalty. "It's a shame," she said. "A shame they could inspire someone with so much faith, then give you no reason to believe."

"Except that's just it, Liza. They've given me what I need. It's not the kind of spirit they intended, but it's no less strong. Everything the Guard looks past – it's still worth fighting for. Stability's important. But it's nothing without justice."

"I think you must've recited that one before," and at that, he smirked. Still, it was easy to see how he got people to listen; he had a knack for finding a way to the unspoken. And without quite meaning to, Liza shifted closer, clasping his arm once more, as they made their way back toward the hotel.

"You better get goin'," Dale said when they reached the lobby's entrance. Though as he leaned in, and kissed her farewell on the cheek, she suddenly wished he would stay there. She could feel his warmth. She had half a mind to kiss him back.

Instead, she took a breath. "Thank you for everything," she whispered in his ear. "For speaking with me, and walking with me."

The grin returned. "The pleasure's all mine, darlin'."

Then he backed up and bowed, in the traditional Confederate manner, one arm behind his back, as Liza curtsied in return.

CHAPTER 20

Thanks to the lightness of Sunday traffic, the drive back was faster than expected. Most people were home after church, and with panic gripping the hinterland – the assault at Rosewood couldn't possibly be kept under wraps – Liza worried she'd be stopped by Confederate Guard simply for being out. Relieved when she wasn't, she gazed out the windshield, taking in old rubbed-bronze lamps by the roadside, winding dirt lanes spiraling outward, scattered steeples and weathered barns.

Thinking back on Dale, picturing that Richmond corner, she smiled at the way his long hair had brushed against her, and how his beard had felt surprisingly soft. But as she drove on, her thoughts also shifted to Kevin, and she fought off a rush of nerves in her stomach. He would never speak with Dale's naked conviction, nor strut with his bluster. Yet in his own way, wasn't Kevin also a radical? He considered life more intently than anyone Liza had ever known. He certainly thought about its inequities more extensively than any Confederate citizen was supposed to: seeking out where ideas came from, and how they affected people, rather than just granting they should be accepted.

What if Kevin's inaction had less to do with nerves than kindness? He'd always been governed by courtesy, never wanting to cause strife. She'd long found it frustrating, but on the occasions when she admitted it to herself, she also saw it was admirable. Kevin treated people well. Perhaps that was why it made her anxious to think of him. Obviously he'd be hurt by how much she was concealing.

It was almost suppertime when she turned into the long driveway at Rosewood, passing under the rigid rows of oak trees on either side. Antique hitching posts dotted the way; mulberries glinted like rubies in between. Stepping from the car, she saw the house's front door had swung open and her parents were rushing out to greet her, mother leading the way.

"Oh Liza!" Cathryn gave her a long hug. "Welcome back!"

"I'm coming too," Franklin added with a trademark chuckle, catching up.

She embraced them each in turn, feeling far more relaxed than she'd thought she'd be. In the wake of her defiance, being back here turned out to be soothing. And standing in the quiet dusk, with crickets all around and fine fluted columns ahead, it was hard to imagine it had all been a crime scene in her absence. "You're not angry I left?"

Her father pulled back. "We're just glad you're safe. We're glad everyone's safe. We have the Guard's protection now – they're stationing agents in town. The troublemakers are gone."

Cathryn was nodding. "You frightened us dear, leaving like that, but your father's right – we're relieved."

•   •   •

Later, after supper, a cozy affair after the extravaganza of the night before, Liza shuffled upstairs, and spotted bullet holes in the foyer ceiling, noticing how empty the landing felt without the fallen chandelier, carted off for repairs. Missing panes of glass had been replaced with ugly planks of plywood. Streaks of fresh paint butted up against the crown molding. And she shuddered. She knew what these parties were like: loud toasts and twirling dresses, the frequent "hurrahs" from old soldiers. To have it all torn apart by screams and guns and indents – it still seemed impossible. Bowing her head to the Lord for guidance, she asked forgiveness for her relief that she'd missed it – then too, feeling sheepish, for any part her country had played in necessitating such horror. Finally, she stepped to her room and closed the door.

As she did, Liza heard a crinkle in the hinge.

A small sheet had oddly been tucked inside, and reaching over, she yanked it down. The paper had no etched border, no engraved initials either. But when she flipped to its other side, she held her breath. *Dear Ms. Brooke* was scrawled across the top, in a crooked, hasty script. The lines were jagged, the curves uneven:

I have no reason to trust you, seeing as I've raided your family's home. But I've also witnessed your ways. You've brought lemonade and biscuits to our banquet hall. When we were both girls, you bandaged boys' knees in the fields. It's enough to think you might take notice of what's before you.

I fear this raid will fail. I gather in reading this, you know it already has. This means I am killed, or in prison, lined up to be killed soon. I write you anyways, with a hope you might look past our divisions.

I do not ask you to do anything hurtful to your own kind, but perhaps you can help in other ways. Perhaps in reading this, you'll at least reconsider what we did here. You'll understand why we fight, if you are anything like me.

Sincerely,

Clara "Brooke"

(I have no last name of my own – does this mean we are family?)

Liza read it again. Then, she crumpled the note back up and stuffed it in her pocket, considered burning it in the fireplace, decided that starting a fire would attract her parents' attention, and finally, sat down on the bed.

How could an indent possibly write? How could a person like that claim they were in the same family? This was a woman who'd fired those bullets out in that very hall, who'd terrorized Liza's parents, and all their friends. Amidst the terror, she'd found a moment to stuff this missive behind a door?

Liza took in several long breaths. Eventually, she showered, and brushed her teeth, and lay down beneath the covers.

Perhaps you can help.

She put the pillow over her face, hiding from her own thoughts.

It was obscene to get a note like that. Obviously she couldn't mention it to anyone. They'd wonder why she'd gotten it. Or why she'd even taken time to peruse it.

Yet why were her fists clenched? Why was her mind racing? Why couldn't she just drift off to sleep? And as she lay there, contemplating it still, trying to picture its author, Liza's indignation began slowly to soften.

She wondered where this woman was now – cooped up in prison indeed, according to the news reports. But what must they be doing to her?

She considered her own deeds in the meanwhile: meeting in that tavern, defying her parents, conversing with Dale that very morning. Already she'd crossed massive lines, it was true – betraying Confederate creed with every step she'd taken. Some might say she was even guilty of resisting herself. Was communicating with indents, then, just another form of the same? She bent back her head, facing the window, taking in the night stars framed like a picture on her wall. It was hours more before she could close her eyes.

Chapter 21

The van ride felt endless, and Clara's head throbbed the entire time. She hadn't slept long, she decided. At least she didn't think so. Whatever the agents had injected into her arm had worn off, and ever since, she'd been trying to figure out where she was being taken.

It was impossible to know. Nobody was speaking, and she couldn't see a thing through a new blindfold wrapped tightly around her face. Occasionally the van would slow, and she'd catch muffled voices from outside its walls. Other times, it felt like they were speeding, rocking across fields, with the crunch of grass and stones against the tires below. At last, the bumps and dips faded, and Clara could hear the sounds turn smooth, so that she wondered if they'd crossed onto roads smeared with black asphalt, the kind she'd seen at the Brooke plantation's loading stations, where trucks came to pick up the cotton bales.

Really, it didn't matter where she was going, for the fact was, it would end in jail. Richmond was said to have entire neighborhoods of prisons, and Clara leaned back tenderly, focused on alleviating the pain in her shoulders, finding a new position against the casing above the van's spare tire.

Her thoughts turned to the letter she'd written.

It had been unplanned, something she'd thought up only in the final instants before the attack, scratching it out just before she'd gone and met the others. There'd been nothing to lose. She'd noticed over the years how the Planter's daughter had carried herself, a friendly smile cloaking a nervous energy, a gaze that always seemed to linger an extra moment, as if she were actually taking in the world around her, rather than just taking it for granted. It was impossible that an aristocrat would ever consider a slave in full – but that's how it'd sometimes appeared. Even as a child, Ms. Brooke would come out to the fields, not to taunt the indents but to watch them. Clara had been a child then too, but she still remembered it: how every time, Elizabeth Brooke would check with the overseers to ensure they were providing the indents enough water.

She knew the very idea of stashing a letter was absurd, that the young noblewoman was all but certain to ignore it, that it would be the rarest of humans who would defy her own people to help another. But when she'd found herself in Elizabeth Brooke's room, about to be surrounded, Clara had snatched the note from her pocket anyway, stuffing it between the door and the wall, right as the Guard had come storming inside.

She shifted her body once more. Her stomach raged with hunger now; her wrists and ankles stung from being bound. Her eyes darted back and forth beneath the blindfold, her eyelids scratching its rough fabric, searching the blackness.

All the while, Atti never really left her mind. The thought of him fueled her conviction that the assault she'd helped plan – that had led to disaster – had still been the right thing to do. Any society that could sell a man was broken. It was deserving of whatever came to it. She prayed, anyway, that he was doing better than she was. She imagined him running through forest and fields, sleeping in caves or cutouts by canals, protected by God's grace. She shut her eyes to fight away new tears.

Finally, the van halted.

She stirred to the sound of boots.

Then the rear doors were banging open, so that she smelled fuel and hot pavement. Someone was reaching over, yanking her by the elbow, shoving the blindfold from her face. And all at once, the light was too much, blinding her as she blinked and tried to make sense of a set of figures before her.

There were four of them, all men, standing at the back of the van, staring in. Beyond them, she could make out the drab outer walls of a warehouse, a pale field beside it, cell towers scattered at its edge. Her gaze flitted back to the men. They had ruddy noses and rumbling baritones as they murmured under their breath, the one in the center clutching a pile of photographs, glancing between an image and her.

Clara caught sight now of the photo in their grip: her own face staring back in grayscale, she realized. It was her most recent plantation mug shot – taken annually, on the occasion of every indent's birthday – and she looked back up. But the men were stepping closer, and she saw the one in the front had another syringe ready – injecting her now with a sharp, speedy jab before she had time to protest. Once again, the world tilted. Once again, her sight went blurry. Once again, dreamless sleep was upon her.

•   •   •

When she woke next, the blindfold hadn't been returned, and she straightened, bleary-eyed, trying to lick her lips, which felt bone-dry. Quickly, Clara registered that she was being driven again, that the men she'd seen before were now inside the van with her, lined up on a bench opposite, sitting in silence, unblinking, as if she wasn't even there.

Growing more alert, she noticed that they'd changed their outfits. In place of the infamous uniforms of the Confederate Guard, these new ones were odd, and she wondered if they were some special division. The fabric was thicker, the color darker blue than normal. They had no matching slouch caps at all; their buttons were brass instead of silver.

Clara had never seen anything like them.

She tried to sit up further, but with her hands bound, she had trouble – until the agent who'd taken the blindfold surprised her, abruptly leaning forward and helping. She studied him in shock. His angled face was smooth; he had dusty brown hair that was a mix of curls and waves; his eyes were half-hidden behind tortoise-rim spectacles – unusual for a Guard member.

"Where are we going?" Clara asked him, keeping her voice steady.

For a moment, the man didn't respond. Then, he moved from the bench opposite, knelt before her, and retrieved a pocket knife from his jacket. When she recoiled, he simply shook his head, and started slicing the plastic binding from her wrists and legs. "Don't you worry," he said, his words split apart by hard *r*'s and too-flat vowels. "You're not in danger anymore. Everything will get explained shortly."

His words didn't register. Don't worry? She was under arrest, guilty of insurrection. "I don't understand."

But the man just smiled – smiled! – and shook his head. "Apologies, ma'am," he said. "I can't go into that for you – not my job. We're just here to bring you in. We'd have unbound you earlier, but needed to be sure you wouldn't fight. It won't be long now."

Clara rubbed her wrists with her palms. None of this clicked. It wasn't just what the man was saying, or the odd uniforms, or his clipped way of speaking, with sentences that came out too rapidly and instructions that made no sense. He just wasn't acting like Confederate Guard. He wasn't acting like any white person she'd ever met. He'd looked right at her when they'd spoken. He'd called her ma'am.

The van slowed to another stop. The agents stood up, and the one who'd spoken to Clara, apparently in charge, stepped to the door. He lifted a long metal handle, swinging the back wide open, and jumped outside.

The sky was dark. Clara realized that an entire day must have passed.

Behind the van, a whole line of official-looking men and women were waiting this time. All were white; all wore civilian suits. There were no hoop dresses. Instead, the ladies wore trousers, something Clara had never seen on a noblewoman before. The men's jackets were narrow and black, with no Confederate gray, no stripes, not even coattails on the backs.

In the middle of the group was a gray-haired fellow, with a cleft that made his chin look split in two and a long nose. He had a narrow neck and a wide tie, and he stepped to the van's edge and looked directly at Clara. His gaze was pointed; he was making more eye contact with her than any noble ever had.

"Hello Ms. Brooke," he suddenly said, in a voice that snapped like twine. "And welcome to the United States of America."

CHAPTER 22

Atticus had always heard the woods of northern Virginia were thick. Now he was seeing it for himself. A knotty root pressed against the back of his neck. The ground was littered with wet leaves, the branches above impossibly dense, like a netted web that had been cast across the whole sky.

Lifting himself from the earth, he rubbed his eyes, scanning every direction, feeling for his bag. The leaves slid beneath his boots, and his heart quickened against his ribs as he told himself to be calm, that he was still alone. Taking a breath, he listened. The forest's sounds were no longer strange: cracks of twigs, a white-tail deer startled and running off, the salvos of woodpeckers. All around, there were wide trunks that made it impossible to walk in a straight line. This was no accident: the land was all owned by the Confederate government, seized decades before through eminent domain and allowed to grow wild ever since, a buffer to block runaways like him, those who'd beaten the odds and managed to approach the enemy border.

He'd been moving steadily north, surviving on creek fish and berries, traveling mostly at night, but into daybreak and then at dusk as well, using the sun's location to keep oriented. He slept at midday, and woke by afternoons' close. The previous morning, he'd run out of water. He'd found no streams since.

He stood and pushed onward. His feet pounded the earth, as he batted brambles out of the way. His face was so scratched he couldn't tell when new wounds emerged; his ankles throbbed from his boots. It felt as though his muscles might give out any moment, but he wouldn't stop.

As he went, he wondered constantly where Clara was, terrified she was sitting against some awful, piss-stained wall in a Confederate prison. He prayed that somehow she'd gotten away, and resolved to devote his freedom to finding her and prying her loose if she hadn't. If only he'd gone back when he'd had the chance, perhaps she'd be with him now. The guilt that'd gnawed at him ever since dug in its claws further.

In truth, Atticus wished she hadn't revolted at all, waiting instead, that he might find money up north, purchase her labor, and get her out. He had no idea how he'd do that, of course; but it still seemed a more realistic option than rebelling outright against the power of Confederate civilization itself.

Sometimes, amid his hunger and exhaustion, Atti forced himself to imagine a new life for them together up north. He pictured them side by side, on a park bench, or at their own table at a pub, residents of a big U.S. city. He'd never seen a place like that, not even in a photo, but it had to be magic: where a man like him, with dark skin, could be paid for his labor, where he and Clara could share a meal or a stroll whenever they wished. He envisioned a mass of streets and fine buildings with front doors that he was supposed to use. Not for the first time during his flight, he dwelled on her smile. She'd always saved it; it was never a mere courtesy. That much was in her eyes – in their blaze, and their restraint. He bit his lip.

When all at once, he froze.

A clearing lay ahead, and an abandoned stone wall short of that – and there, on the far side of the clearing, out of nowhere, a building of some kind, the first he'd come across in ages. According to his map, there were still farming communities around. He'd heard about them before, centuries-old villages stubbornly avoiding government pressure to give up the land, surviving because public sympathy was on their side.

Atti slowed his pace and listened to his own breaths in the evening air. The benefit of finding food and water would outweigh the risk of getting closer, he decided. He'd just have to wait and approach under cover of night.

High-stepping through a briar patch, batting away stinging flies, he crouched silently beside the wall, studying the scene closely. Sure enough, the clearing marked the edge of a village abutting the forest. Some yards away, a farmhouse lay at the base of a narrow country road. Farther off, almost at the horizon, Atti could make out several other homes as well.

With nightfall, he'd scurry out to their trash bins and find some scraps. There were always leftovers in white people's garbage. These were yeomen homes, but that wouldn't change it: like nobles, even yeomen threw out decent food. As a boy, during trips to town, he used to smuggle corncobs and spareribs from yeomen dumpsters. And surely there'd be a hose for water.

His eyes settled back on the cottage that was nearest. Its shutters were freshly painted, the same soft jade as the grass, with gray stone walls and only a few windows. The roof was charcoal, the lawn tidy. In the background, a series of hills, unkempt but lush, rolled toward the sky.

But as he looked more closely, his vision caught on something unusual.

At first, he thought he was imagining it in the dim dusk light. Blinking, he looked harder, and shifted a half-foot closer, so that his head was just peeking out from the forest. He leaned forward, stretching his neck, trying to get as full a view as he could.

There, two-thirds of the way up the roof, amidst all the gray, a single, cloudy blue shingle sat on the near side.

Atticus rubbed his eyes.

Like every indent, he had heard of such blue shingles before. Clara had even mentioned them when she'd handed him the map. They were part of the stories of the Underground Railroad, offering a network of stops for runaways just like him, private houses furnishing rest and supplies during the dangerous journey north. Supposedly the U.R. was funded by northern abolitionists and sustained by Confederate yeomen, who sought, for some reason, to help their nation's indents. Blue shingles were said to mark every participating home.

But he'd never really believed it. It wasn't that it was hard to imagine indents keeping such a secret from nobles. But yeomen? Surely it would slip out.

Wouldn't it?

Atti stared ahead.

He could almost convince himself the shingle wasn't there, that the blue tint was just a different shade of gray. A fellow would have to really study the place to notice it. Maybe if he edged closer, he could be sure.

He hoisted himself up on his tired elbows, shimmying forward, trying to get a better look. His body was half out of the woods now, but he was so low to the ground, and it was getting so dark, that he'd be hard to spot. He imagined the feel of a cold canteen of water against his lips. He pictured warm bread too, filling his aching belly.

There was a shout from his left.

Atti leapt with fright. Someone was close – just yards away.

"Hey!" the voice was yelling, shrill and severe. "You there!"

It was a man's voice, a yeoman voice, tight and agitated.

Atti wanted to punch himself. How dumb could he have been? He tried to think fast, to slink back into the woods, to find a way out of being discovered.

Flipping to his side, he saw the man marching toward him. Here then was an old farmer, weary but strong, in denim overalls and hauling a shovel. The house's lawn sloped behind him. The farmer must have been down there, before striding back up.

Atticus racked his brain for ideas. Tall tales had gotten him out of pinches before, but how possibly could they work here? What could he say? That some Planter had ordered him to forage for mushrooms? No one would believe that. Besides, Atti's map made it clear no nobles lived in the area – he was too far north. Could he claim he was lost? Yet that wouldn't work either; the man would just call in help. What about asserting that he was a northerner, a spy of some sorts, and that arresting him would spark an international incident?

He was obviously a runaway. His heart urged him once more to flee.

Atticus wondered if he could put up a fight instead. He was weaponless, and as weak as he'd ever been, too hungry to put up any kind of proper struggle. Only what else was there? He swallowed back his fear, refusing the image of a jail cell, a long journey southward, some hot, stinking plantation in Mississippi.

The farmer had halted a yard or so away. He was over seventy, Atti guessed – thin hair, streaks of white – eyes of midnight blue. He had on a thick twill shirt, lined with loose buttons, sleeves rolled up, cotton apron folded over his belt.

"Well?" the man asked. "Name?"

"Me, sir?"

"Who else? Who are you?!"

Atticus had no idea what to say, so he simply answered the question. "I'm Atti," he replied from the ground. "I'm very sorry to be on your property like this, I – "

"Stop. I don't need your stories, and there's no one else nearby to hear them. Just follow. No tricks, or you'll be in a heap more trouble than you are now. Stand up."

Atti eyed the man carefully.

The best option, he decided, was to stall as long as he could, then somehow prevent contact with any authorities. He might have to knock the fellow unconscious, or tie him up even. In the meantime, he'd do as instructed, keeping the yeoman occupied.

Slowly, he stood.

"Good," the man muttered. "Now, walk beside me."

Atti blinked in surprise. He'd never walked beside a white man in his life. On the few occasions when he'd walked with a white person at all, aiding an overseer on an errand for fertilizer, or taking instructions from some visiting official, he'd always kept a good yard behind, as was Confederate custom. But there wasn't time to contemplate it. The farmer had already started toward the house, and Atti moved to keep up. His heart was pounding so hard he could feel his pulse in his palms, and though the evening had cooled, sweat poured down his neck.

The white man had perched his shovel over his shoulder, as if ready to strike. He walked with a stoop, and his knees bent dramatically as he cleared the top of the high grass, so that he looked like a bird when he stepped. Every so often, he glanced at Atti as if to say, "keep moving, and don't talk" – a look, Atticus thought, that white Confederates could have patented.

The trip took no more than a minute, as the man led them to a dark red door around the farmhouse's corner. He knocked, and to Atti's surprise – locks were supposed to be a rarity in the Confederacy, with criminals as terrified of the Guard as everyone else – the sound of a bolt scratched from inside, and the door squeaked open.

A thin woman with hazel eyes and long gray hair was standing just beyond its frame, wearing a shapeless purple dress. She held a large wooden bowl of water. And for the first time since hearing the farmer's voice, Atti recalled the sight of that blue shingle overhead. What if he'd been right in the first place?

The woman stepped forward. "Hello there," she said. "My name is Margaret Worthing – that's Maggie to you. Please come in, but watch the step down."

Atticus stared. The words came fired in staccato, crackling and untoward, a laborer's breed of talking. But there was a kindness underneath. No white person had ever addressed him with "please" before, and he wasn't sure how to respond. "Thank you," he managed. "They call me Atti."

·   ·   ·

Looking around the room, the first thing he noticed was that the windows were high, so that nobody from outside could see anyone within. It was the floor's sunken level that fully accomplished the effect, he realized, and he wondered if this was intentional.

The space ahead was small, with a worn wooden table at the center and matching benches on either side. An empty brick fireplace was in the corner, beside a cramped kitchen, and a hallway opposite. The walls were covered with framed pastels of Virginia countryside. "Come, come," Mr. Worthing offered now. "You were alone?"

"Yes sir," Atti replied, not sure whether this was some horrible, elaborate trick – or a glimpse at something else entirely: some broader network even, underneath all he'd ever known.

"We support whatever it is you're doing, son."

"Only what's that, sir?"

The fellow simply shared a sigh – a sag of his shoulders that seemed to say they were all now in the business of secrets – before continuing with the tour. The three next rooms were plain but sturdy – small bedrooms above, a crammed den below – then back to the kitchen. Oak beams lined the ceiling. On the window sills, nothing but pink blossoms spilling from small terracotta pots. The only hallway dead-ended with a parlor, a bookshelf climbing to its ceiling, a cloudy lamp, a wicker chair, several old boat oars resting in the corner.

It was a warm, tidy home, Atti thought, and when they'd returned to the main room in front, Worthing offered a water, and gestured toward another shelf of books, telling Atti it would be only a moment 'til supper, that he was free to read if he was literate, or simply rest while it was prepared. Mrs. Worthing was still smiling in the meanwhile, and Atti saw that her cheeks were splotched red, from sun and age. She handed him the bowl of water she'd been carrying. "Here, wash your face, and come have a seat. We'll go on and get you fed, then have a chat. I can only imagine the hell you've been through."

"Yes ma'am – "

"No, no – there'll be none of that here!" She was shaking her head. "I told you, I'm Maggie. And this scowling fellow is Lew Worthing, my husband. He's as much about helping you as I am" – the farmer grunted – "he just ain't able to shed his roughness they bred into him as a child."

Atticus took the bowl, dipping his face and letting the cool water soothe his skin. For a moment, the only sound was the splash. Then, unable to ignore his thirst, he put his lips to the edge and gulped.

"Oh, forgive me!" Maggie spun. "You're parched, of course. Let me get a cup." She returned with a plastic glass and handed it over.

After downing the whole thing, Atti regained some composure and whispered, "Thank you."

Then the farmer spoke from the counter, while he lifted a pot from the stove. His voice was softer than it had been before, gravelly, colored by years of tobacco. "Well, she's right, boy – " even here then, Atti thought – "I'm an old-fashioned Confederate, and I can be hard. But don't go and let it worry you. You ain't the first to pass through, and you won't be the last. We'll get you back on your way northward, better fed and better rested than when you arrived. No forest floors for you tonight. You'll have a bed."

Atti didn't move, the water dripping from his chin back to the bowl. He swallowed. "Is this the U.R., then, sir?"

And for the first time, Lew Worthing shared a smile, and showed his scattered yellow teeth. "That's what they call it. Though I've never understood why. There's no railroad – never has been."

Not long after, he waved for Atti to follow to the table, and his wife took the bowl back from Atti's hands. Out came a loaf of brown bread – thick and full of grain, just like in Atti's dreams – a plate of sliced ham, a whole platter of yellow corn with a pat of butter on top.

It was the finest meal he'd ever had.

He listened, then, as the farmer Worthing and his wife shared their story, acclimating to their sharp intonation and creative grammar. Times were changing, they said. Atticus was already the eleventh indent to pass through that year, and the Worthings agreed that the increase in numbers said something about the rumored cracks in Confederate stability.

Their commitment ran deep. Both believed the government had no business interfering in people's lives, that the Guard ought not exist, that this had been the original Confederate vision. They'd lived with yeomen restrictions all their lives – no real schooling, no say in policy, no chance at change – and they'd just never accepted it. Over time, though, both Lew and Margaret Worthing had come to believe that black Confederates also deserved rights. They told Atti this as though he ought to be grateful, but again he only nodded, glad enough for the food at least to keep listening. It was a radical view for yeomen, it was true, and they acknowledged it'd emerged only gradually during their first years of marriage. Together, they explained, they'd come to see that yeomen actually shared more with their nation's indents than with its aristocrats.

Eventually, they'd built up courage to ask after rumors of a Resistance leader living near the border, protected illegally by a contingent of northern veterans who'd come down in secret. In time, they'd discovered the rumors to be true, and in the years since, they'd never forgotten the man, though he'd long ago been seized by Confederate Guard. He'd been the one to introduce them to others, and it later became clear he hadn't betrayed one ounce of his knowledge to his captors. Now they toasted in his honor, and Atti raised his glass.

Then they went on, telling of how – in the words of Lew Worthing, switching from water to ale – they'd become conductors on the U.R. They'd found the first runaway in their backyard, shivering and scared, on a rainy December morning. It turned out he'd been there two days before Lew had spotted him from the window: an indent from Georgia, who could go no further, trying to catch the rainwater in his mouth, staring up at the blue shingle and unsure what to do about it.

Since then, the Worthings had kept an eye out every single day, hoping to spare future runaways the same paralysis. They'd taken in any who came, and though neither of them had ever been to the United States, every now and again they received anonymous cash in a package on the stoop. It gave comfort beyond the goods it provided, offering knowledge that there was someone up there who knew their runaways and that they'd made it across the border.

Atticus watched them the whole time they spoke, his gaze shifting back and forth, as though they were alien creatures – unlike any yeoman he'd ever encountered, part of a clan that in all his prior experience had only ever used indents as a stepping stone: overseers snarling in the fields, minions for the Planters. Yet here were these two, serving him a meal.

When the stories were done, and Lew stood to clear dishes, Atti sipped his water, and again peered back at his hosts. "Have you heard anything about a revolt over on the Brooke plantation?" he asked now. "Rosewood Manor? Down in the lower commonwealth, by the Blue Ridge?"

"'Course we have," Maggie answered. "It made the news. There was no escaping it at first: the TV spread fear as best it was able. It wasn't just the Brooke rebellion – there was a whole slew of others, all up and down the Confederacy. The Guard shut them down, but you couldn't help but feel it was part of something larger, some kind of tipping point, righteousness boiling up at last. There's never been anything like it."

Atti was nodding once more. "I know the Brooke place – "

But Lew stopped him, turning back from the counter. "No details, son." He lowered the dishes. "Alarms are up. Rebellions might still be spreading for all we can guess – the newsmen stopped covering 'em – that means the folks in charge are worried. The less we know about you, the better, in case we end up taken in, questioned."

Atticus hesitated. "Did the news say any more?" It sure sounded as though Clara's raid had made an impact, spreading trouble just the way she'd wished. He hoped that wherever she was, she got to hear that.

Lew lifted his glass and returned to the table. "Only that the indents tried to kill every white person there was, before they were stopped."

Atti was certain that hadn't been Clara's intent. "I don't think so," he said aloud.

Margaret eyed him, then reached out, surprising him yet again, patting his hand on the table.

They sat like that for some time before Lew pushed the bench back with his legs. "How 'bout some music before we slumber?"

Atti glanced up.

"Back in a moment," and with that, he was shuffling out toward the hallway.

When he returned, he was carrying not only a guitar, but an accordion and banjo as well. He handed the accordion to Margaret, the guitar to Atti. "You can manage?"

"A few chords maybe." Yeomen always presumed indents were musical – part of the Confederacy's endless, vicious cataloguing of stereotypes – but the truth was, in Atti's boyhood, there'd often been old instruments lying around the indent-quarters, and he'd learned a bit from the older men, eventually letting his fingers do his thinking.

Alas, when he'd been seventeen, regulations had been altered. The plantation had apparently gained a reputation for being too lenient, and General Brooke had changed the rules. Since then, Atti had played only a few times, and it stung his fingertips now simply to press the strings. Still, he found he didn't mind.

Margaret leaned over her banjo, tuning it. "'I'm on My Way to Canaan Land,'" she suggested with a wink.

Atticus wasn't aware white people knew that tune, and he couldn't help but grin back. It was one of the numbers he'd sung as a small boy – easy enough, since there were hardly any lyrics, aside from the title. And though he was still exhausted, anxious about the journey ahead and worried about Clara, some piece of his heart was lifted up, as the three of them started in.

CHAPTER 23

The next morning, Atticus awoke before sunrise to the sound of Lew Worthing's voice. He'd slept in a small extra room with a cot, just down from the kitchen, and already, he'd stirred more than once in the night, afraid he heard sounds – the squeak of a door, mutterings outside.

Now, though, Lew had pierced his sleep for certain, and Atti sat up. He'd planned on waking early anyway, and heading out, and pivoting to the cot's edge, he rubbed his eyes. Lew's words carried in from the kitchen, and Atti realized he was hearing one half of a conversation, and that the farmer was on the phone.

With growing horror, he listened more closely.

"We've got him here," Lew was saying. "Yes ma'am, that's right – he showed up yesterday evenin', and we provided a meal. He plans to keep on his way."

Atticus blinked in fear, as his mind funneled into clarity. Instantly, he stood – enraged at himself for trusting these folks as much as he had.

He stepped forward, fists clenched, unable to imagine anything but the worst. Lew must have dialed the Guard, and Atti couldn't wait another second. He swung open the door, charging straight to the kitchen, ripping the phone right from Lew's hands, hanging it up. Lew stared back with shock, and Atti saw he was trembling.

He was inches from Lew's face now, trying to see into those blue eyes, feeling the hate curdle in his own soul.

"Wait, son," the farmer whispered.

Atticus didn't budge.

"That was your owner – "

"How could you?"

"She's with us!" Lew continued.

Atti moved back just a touch. "She?" He wrinkled his brow. "My owner is Franklin Brooke. You know that."

"This is his daughter. I oughtta have said so." Lew pointed to the phone, where the name could still be seen on the screen. "Miss Elizabeth Brooke. She's a part of the U.R. network now. I'm telling the truth. Hell, I just found out myself!"

Atti was silent, staring.

"I was going to wake you before I called, but Maggie said you should sleep. We've got a contact here, a neighbor. Just two miles up the road. He's in touch with the U.S., and we keep him posted whenever we've got a runaway. He shares where the Guard is stationed, and what route might be safe. We all met a half-hour back."

Atti was chewing his lip. If Lew was telling the truth, that would explain the sounds he'd heard. If it was a lie, it was already too late. "Go on," he said quietly.

"When we mentioned you'd come from Rosewood Manor, our contact couldn't believe it. He said one of your owners just joined the network. Elizabeth Brooke, daughter of the general! It's true – she's on the U.R., I swear by God. I just spoke with her directly. Her phone line's protected because of who her father is. Word got passed, and she was ready for my call. Truth be told, Atti, she passed along her prayers to you. Said she'd never met you, but went on about how she wished she'd done something earlier, that she wished she could do something now, asked how to help us."

"What'd she sound like?"

"Talked faster than I expected."

Finally, Atti nodded. "That's her way." It was true, he thought. Elizabeth Brooke had always possessed an energy about her – whenever he'd spotted her, or overheard her giving instructions, she'd brought with her a kind of efficiency, a concentration, that wasn't normal among nobles, as though she were trying to get as much from every exchange she could. Still – could it be? General Brooke's daughter? He recalled occasions when she'd come out to visit the indents in the fields, wearing her hoop dresses in the mud, offering drinks on long days; but that was a long way from resistance itself. Having a mind of one's own wasn't the same as joining the U.R.

For a long moment, there was silence. Lew stayed against the wall, lips tight, eyes wide. At last, Atti passed back the phone.

Lew took a long sigh. "I'll tell you what, Brooke – things are changing even more than we thought." He paused. "But dammit son if you didn't scare me halfway to hell."

Atticus felt his own heart still pounding. "You did the same to me." He took a step back. "You think there are more like her?"

"Wouldn't have said yes before today."

"I hope so," and he turned to rest on the bench by the table.

At that, Margaret entered. "I was in the shower," she said, eyeing Lew still by the wall. "What in all the world did I miss?"

"Our friend here got a bit concerned is all. Not to worry."

She raised her eyebrows, but didn't respond.

It wasn't long until sunup now, and Atticus would need to get moving if he was to make any headway. Lew set about serving him a speedy breakfast: stewed oats with milk and a sliced banana – something he'd only tasted once before in his life, after General Brooke had canceled a brunch in the mansion and house-indents had smuggled out the unused food. He finished quickly, and when he was done, they gave him bread, apple, and water for the road. Then, he was standing at the door, with Lew climbing a stool and peering out the windows to make sure no one was there.

"You clear on where you're headed?" Margaret asked, with the tone of a worried mother.

"Straight north, along the forest, past town."

Lew stepped down and clasped him on the shoulder. "May the Good Lord guide you. One day, all this will change, and we'll get ourselves up there for a visit." It was obvious the old farmer was just putting on a show, reciting lines he'd no doubt delivered before: yeomen weren't allowed foreign passports. Even indents knew that. But Atti offered thanks nonetheless.

"I wish I had a way to repay you."

It was Margaret who shook her head. "No. You don't repay us, Atti. We repay you, for all you've suffered in our name."

Lew opened the door and stepped out first, to check once more it was safe. When he came back in, it was time.

CHAPTER 24

Kevin Donleau had been invited over to Rosewood Manor for supper, and the food, at least, had been delicious. There'd been spinach and strawberry salad, steamed yams, not to mention what seemed every part of every animal – patés and tartare, lobster and beef, deviled bones, grilled sardines, pig's feet, frog's legs, kidney of lamb – all of it shared among warm smiles, hearty drink, the eager clinking of glasses.

The conversation too had no doubt been stimulating. General Brooke had acknowledged that the recent revolt appeared to be part of a worrisome growing pattern. There'd been twenty-four attempted indent uprisings in the Confederacy in the last three weeks alone, six of them in Virginia – and that was a conservative count, marking only organized, armed rebellions. In dozens of other cases, indents had disobeyed orders, even assaulted overseers in the fields. No plantations had actually been overrun – the Guard still had plenty of agents, even with its resources shifted to the border – but the news was cause for concern at the least, amid the growing rumors of Resistance in the cities. "You must understand," the general had remarked. "I'm a realist. We've fretted over instability for a generation. Now it's here, and no one's quite sure what to do about it." It was then Mrs. Brooke had asked who'd be interested in pie.

Normally, Kevin would have been rapt. Yet tonight his focus was elsewhere. He looked across the table. Behind the candles' flicker, Liza's gaze was dark and radiant as she described wild blossoms by the roadside, and goofed her way through imitations of a cow in a nearby pasture – only wasn't it apparent something was also off? She wasn't verbally jousting with her father as she normally might. Her jokes felt rehearsed. What's more: she'd never once glanced Kevin's way.

Toward the end of dessert, stewing in his own impatience, spurred on by the Chilean merlot – sanctions on European wine remained intact, thanks to Brussels' incessant moralizing – he cleared his throat. "Perhaps an evening stroll before the light's completely gone?"

Liza's mother folded her napkin in her lap. "Oh I think it's a wonderful idea. We old folks ought stay back and digest. But you two make the most of it."

"What of the midges?" Liza asked.

"It's past their worst season."

So that after another moment, she stood, curtseying to her parents. "Sounds good then," she said. "Let's go."

•   •   •

It was still warm outside, a stubborn, late summer evening. The air was thick, the dimming fields draped in haze. But Kevin didn't mind. Liza led them along a path that ran beside the house, past a new botanical garden, beyond the tree nursery, toward a patch of periwinkle and a cluster of honeybee boxes. "So?" he began, as they looped behind the house, over to a hill at its rear. "How's August treating you?"

"How's it treating *you*?" she echoed back, a twinkle in her eye, marking the absurdity of small talk between them.

He grinned, an odd mix of relief and nerves. "Truth be told, I've missed you, Liza." The words hadn't been planned, but now he pursued them. "I've missed what we had at summer's start, I mean. Ever since you took off for Richmond."

She slowed. "Here," she said softly. "Let's sit." Together, they faced down toward the house, leaning their elbows against the hillside. Moonlight peeked over the ridge to the east, and she smoothed her hoop skirt. "The thing of it is, Kevin, I wasn't off to Richmond just to sightsee."

"I figured."

"I should have said so." She turned towards him. "I've something to share."

He waited.

"You can't tell anyone else. You understand?"

"Of course."

She hesitated. But he stayed patient in the meanwhile, admiring how her hair glistened black in the dusk. Somewhere, a barred owl started its call. Liza took in a heavy breath. "I visited a Resistance meeting."

He stared. The sentence seemed to stick to the air.

"I didn't intend to. It was on my first visit. I came upon it at a pub, and all at once, it was as if everything I'd ever wondered, deep down, was fair game – all the things you talk about, Kevin, yeomen voting, even indent rights – people serious about changing our country, about giving it back to the public."

"I don't follow. Who? How?" He rubbed his forehead. "When were you going to tell me?"

"I'm telling you now."

"You could've been hurt, Liza."

"It wasn't a call for violence. It was for justice. I haven't even told my parents."

"Certainly not."

"Only there's more. I didn't just witness the Resistance. I've done something else too. Something I still can't believe." She shook her head. "I helped it. I've joined it."

"Beg pardon?" His voice was too strident amid the quiet, and a rabbit went bounding into the brush nearby. All his life, he'd pushed Liza to be more engaged in the world, to ask the questions about their nation that kept him up at night. Now he felt like she'd done it without him.

"The Underground Railroad," she suddenly announced. Her dark eyes gleamed with a pride he didn't recognize; her voice shook with a restiveness that was more than her usual energy, a tightness of purpose that roiled his nerves. "I've been using my father's login on his computer, gaining his clearance, accessing uncensored sites. I worked up my resolve – eventually I called a number listed on a U.S. abolitionist page. I swear, Kevin, it still doesn't feel real. I left a message. I assumed I'd never hear back – worse, I worried it was a trap. But then a man phoned last week: a farmer, who knew about my family's runaway."

"You're kidding."

"He put me in touch with the couple providing a hideout. I offered money, but they said not to worry, just asked if I'd heard any tidbits about the slave-hunt. I told them my father doesn't share that kind of thing – that I'd call if that changed." She searched his gaze.

"My God, Liza."

"You still think it's too dangerous."

"I don't know." He realized that he meant it. While he'd been sitting still, studying the world around him, she'd gone out to change it. He marveled at the humility of her account, the courage she'd always had, finally boiling over the surface.

"I still haven't really done anything."

"That's not what I was thinking." Yet something was holding him back, it was true. It was in the fact that she'd waited, Kevin thought, in sharing all this – as if he didn't rise to its level somehow – and it made him wary, in a way he wished weren't so. It made him want to ask why.

Now, though, a new sound cut through the night.

Liza stood up quickly.

"Don't worry," he managed. Though he stiffened too. Vehicles, he thought. Loud ones. Everyone knew only the Guard was permitted to drive this late at night.

"Why would they be here?"

"Another check-in, probably. About the revolt."

"At this hour?"

"Let's go find out." Calmly then, they started down the hill.

· · ·

She knew Kevin well enough to see he was as uncertain as she was. She could tell from the way his blue eyes darted and the speed with which he'd moved. Still, she was grateful he was trying.

As they edged around the mansion's side, they bumped into her parents. "What's going on?!" Franklin boomed.

"I've no idea." Instantly, Liza was horrified at the notion of telling him the Guard was here for her.

They continued on together, until they were confronted indeed by a row of SUVs with flags on their sides, a familiar parade of jeeps and sedans idling farther back. All at once, the first dozen agents emerged in starched uniforms, marching briskly across the lawn. It was how they always traveled, she thought, so that there was never any knowing whether an actual emergency was occurring or not.

When in an instant, Liza froze.

There, at the front of the line, was Dale.

· · ·

Registering the three captain's stripes on his collar, and the robotically faced men shadowing him like disciples, she processed the extent of his power. She'd known he was Guard, of course. But this was something new. Stepping closer, she watched as he removed his cap, and the others followed suit. Then he began to speak.

"General Brooke," he trumpeted, and there was none of the joking flirtation Liza was used to. "Captain Dale Birch, Confederate Guard, at your service. It's an honor to meet you, sir."

"The honor's mine, Captain. Welcome to Rosewood Manor. May I present my family." Franklin gestured behind him. "My wife, Cathryn; my daughter Liza; that there's an old family friend, Kevin Donleau."

Dale nodded at each, showing no flash of recognition when he got to Liza. It was alarming how good an actor he was – even as she was doing her version of the same, formally curtseying in return.

Franklin clasped his hands. "How can we help?"

"We'd have called, sir, but for the possibility of providing warning to your indents."

"Any in particular?"

"The house-indents, General."

"You're serious?"

"We'd like to visit with them."

"They've served my home all their lives."

"No doubt you're right. But caution is the glue of our Confederacy."

Her father bowed curtly. Liza was so accustomed to seeing him issue the directives, it was bizarre watching it go the other way round. Yet the Guard was the Guard. Franklin Brooke clicked his heels and walked inside.

While he was gone, nobody said a thing. Dale turned toward his men, such that Liza could no longer see his face. She studied instead the rigidness of his shoulders, square and straight, and for a moment had trouble recalling his grin, or the way he'd strolled with such ease through the streets in Richmond. Then after a moment, she noticed Kevin watching her in turn, and she faced down.

It wasn't long before Franklin was back. Here alongside him were the chief butler, footmen, the upstairs maids, the kitchen staff still in their aprons. "As requested, Captain. The whole lot."

Dale shifted closer. Gravel crunched beneath his boots; the evening air shimmered purple. None of the indents looked up. Even at a distance, Liza could see them keeping their palms steady against their sides, and she wished she could tell them not to be nervous, that the captain before them was just putting on an act. "Boys and girls," he began. His voice shattered the quiet. "Raise your hand high if you were here the night of the revolt."

Every arm went up.

"Go ahead and keep 'em straight if you were surprised by it."

They all did.

"Well hell. Now I'm the one who's surprised. Hard to believe just a few indents could manage such a thing on their own, eh?" Dale's tone had gained a sting. "That's why we're stopping by, see. On account we're eager to learn more. To let it be known ya'all might teach us a thing or two – and that it'd be a hell of a display of loyalty if you did. Far more helpful than waitin' 'til later." Then, without warning, he moved toward the butler, a man in his seventies. "Well?"

But the old man just shook his head, eyes cloudy with age. "I only know what you're telling me, sir."

Dale snorted.

Liza felt her cheeks flush. How could this be the man she knew? Did the same capacity that let him corral free spirits also enable him to spew accusations with such venom?

Then – a flick of Dale's wrist, and the agents behind him were moving again. "The males with us," he commanded. "Females kept here." He faced Franklin as before. "Merely for questioning, General. You'll have them back by morning."

"Of course, Captain."

Liza was flabbergasted. It was dreadful – unnecessary! Why take in anyone at all? Just to frighten them, and remind them of the sweep of injustice? She clenched shut her eyes, ashamed at standing by, not sure what else there was, except to refuse to watch and pray for it to be over.

Not a moment passed, however, before she heard movement beside her, and opened her eyes to see. It was Kevin. He'd strode right past the rest of them, right up to Dale, who spun back. "There's no need," Kevin said quietly, coming face to face with this captain in the Guard. "This old man has already told you what he knows."

Dale squinted his way. "It's important he understand we don't believe him." His voice had turned tight as a whistle, his jaw so clamped it was almost hard to tell who was speaking.

"He got the message." Kevin straightened. "Now, if you'll excuse us, we should all think about retiring. It's getting quite late."

For a moment, Dale said nothing more. Liza could sense the other agents waiting to do as he instructed. Then at last, he broke into a something of a grin. It was nearly the same one she recognized from Richmond indeed – except this time his brown eyes were cold. "Mr. Donleau, is it?" He extended his hand. "It's good to know our nation's gentlemen still care for our nation's indents. It's that sort of sentiment that can keep our society bound together, and our country proud."

"Thank you, Captain."

"Certainly – and may you have a good night."

Kevin nodded, then angled back toward Liza and her parents, who were watching intently. "Heavens, Donleau," her father muttered now that the Guard were out of earshot. "I didn't know you had it in you."

"Neither did I, sir."

"I'll accompany you back to the road," Liza interjected, her voice louder than either of theirs – loud enough for Dale to hear. "That way we can finish our stroll."

. . .

Later, after the Guard vehicles sped away, Kevin and Liza chose to cut across the pastures that led to the Donleau Plantation. It would let them avoid the kicked-up dust from the SUVs. A breeze emerged along the way. The moonlight soaked through the whole sky. Liza studied Kevin's profile as they went – cheeks sharp and bright under the stars – the way he stood straight, yet unassuming. "That was impressive," she finally exhaled.

"If you say so." He paused. "After all, that was the reason I did it."

"Oh?"

"To show off for you, of course." He smiled gently, and now so did she. "I pray it doesn't lead to an arrest."

"Of that old indent?"

"Of any of us." He met her eye. "That man – that captain – he's the danger we were talking about, Liza. That's the type you're fighting."

She didn't respond straightaway. For he was right. Even then, she'd felt revulsion at how Dale had acted, and sadness at the idea he'd probably done it before. She felt it still.

"What is it, Liza?"

She looked at the overgrown grass beneath her hemline. Why, then, did she also feel more? Here she was, still thinking of Dale Birch, ignoring the honor and hope Kevin had just shared. What was wrong with her, concentrating instead on Dale's secret truth? – his unpredictability, the way he charged through life! – this time with her whole family watching and those poor indents terrified. And Liza scowled, annoyed at herself most of all, impatient with her own confusion. "I should've said something," she concluded. "I should've stepped forward too."

Kevin halted. He faced her in full. "May I kiss you, Liza?"

Again, she didn't answer.

"I've kissed you before."

She felt tears come to her eyes. "I've thought of it often."

"What's changed then?"

But she took a step back, regretting it even as she did, wishing she understood better herself, furious at her own lack of courage to explain. "I'm sorry, Kevin. If only I had it all sorted through. If I did, I could make sense of it for both of us." Why was she hiding from the one person she'd always gone to first? And yet – she also felt terribly certain that if she stayed and tried any harder, she'd only make things worse.

Kevin stayed put, watching as she began her retreat across the empty field. "Good night," he offered at last. "When you're ready, please tell me what's wrong. Or if I'm the one who's caused it."

"You didn't, Kevin. I swear you didn't." But at that, she was already gone.

CHAPTER 25

The crushed leaves were a giveaway.

No animal would sleep at the base of a big tree like that, making itself prey.

But it was the stench of dried human urine that confirmed it. Byron Sampson was sure now, and he walked around the trunk's perimeter, a sugar maple – furrowed bark, leaves not yet gone red – seeking covered tracks in the soil. He had enough experience to know when he'd found his man.

The runaway couldn't be far. This damned indent "Atti" had led Byron straight into the forest. But at last the slave-hunter was catching up. It gave him a thrill to know it. He'd spent a week on the fellow's tail, traipsing through the hellish backwoods of Virginia, scratching up his face, going without a proper drink, until he'd finally found a hint of success. It was still too bad the slave was sticking to the underbrush – it meant Byron had to stay on foot – but at least it wouldn't be much longer.

Triumph had come as it always did: from thinking like a damned indent – heading due north, staying with the trees and away from the Guard, looking for lush areas that might have a stream. Most whites never considered such a thing; it simply didn't occur to them. The other slave-hunters waxed poetic about all sorts of tracking techniques: salted sweat-stains on old leaves, broken anthills, impatient buzzards. But to Byron, it was all nonsense, no more than lore and tall tales. What was missing was *shamelessness*. That was his secret. A willingness to pretend to be one of them.

It was how he made his money. It was why General Franklin Brooke, High Command, was letting himself be fleeced. Damned fool. If he knew Byron's tactic, he could do it himself.

Instead, too many Confederates had talked themselves into the idea that black folks were different, that they didn't think the same, that nobody could understand another race no matter how hard they tried. Byron had never been so lucky. Desperation turned out to be a finely tuned meter for truth. He wouldn't let pride get in the way of cash.

Of course, that didn't make him fond of indents. They had their place, as did he. Like every other yeoman, Byron wished he were rich as a noble, sure, but did he want to be one of them? A pompous aristocrat in tight suits, forgetting his 'r's, mistaking manners for know-how? Please! He knew what he'd been born. So be it.

He decided he'd skip lunch. He knew too what mattered: catching this damned indent before the border. It was the only way to the rest of his payday. And he bent lower, striding into the next stretch of Virginia's north woods, right on the runaway's heels.

CHAPTER 26

To Clara, late summer in the United States of America barely warranted the name. The sun's direct heat felt downright muted. The nights could even turn crisp. It made her smirk whenever the soldiers nearby complained about the mugginess, or wiped their brows with their kerchiefs. More than that, it gave her relief from all the unknowing, the daily questions at the U.S. military camp where she'd been spending her time, located somewhere in the countryside, in a state called Pennsylvania.

Upon her arrival in the back of the van, she'd learned that the agents who'd apprehended her were not Confederate Guard at all, but U.S. military instead. They'd hauled her into a large compound and settled her into a moderately furnished room with small windows and the loud hum of air conditioning, where they'd begun the process of debriefing her and explaining where she was.

Clara was allowed out of the room whenever she wanted, so long as she wasn't scheduled for a meeting and so long as she didn't leave the grounds. There were eighty acres of open space out there, a set of gyms, even a sauna – whatever that was. The central building was a bastion of American bureaucratic rough-and-steady – men with loping strides, and women with loosely tied hair, all shades and colors. Star-spangled flags stood on brass stands in every corner; shining plaques graced every wall, tributes to liberty, always in stiff Yankee English.

In her first meeting, over coffee and circular bread loaves called bagels, Clara had been conscious of her new polyester slacks and button-down shirt, courtesy of the U.S. government, hoping she didn't look ridiculous, avoiding eye contact, taking in the endless officers barking orders. She'd learned that it was all part of a subdivision of their federal government called P.I. – the Primary Intelligence Office – that in fact, they'd been providing the weapons shipments all along. This was the office that'd made contact with the indents from the Brooke plantation, had monitored their planning through surveillance cameras planted on the main contact's clothes, had sparked their fight. But not just at Rosewood: as it turned out, the agents of Primary Intel had been aiding indent-revolts throughout the Confederacy.

They'd also made sure to stop them.

It was this last part that'd made Clara blanch. At first, she'd understood that the rebellion at Rosewood Manor must have come too close to failing, forcing U.S. officers to swoop in before the Confederate Guard could get there for real – donning disguises in order to apprehend the armed indents and keep them safe. But the men at the compound hadn't yet confirmed this, avoiding her questions instead, insisting there'd be plenty of time for filling her in.

The important thing, they'd repeated, was that she was in U.S. custody now, on U.S. land, and that together, they could work toward the goal of undoing Confederate society and its indent system all told. They'd assured her the other indents were safe as well, staying in compounds throughout the United States, being kept separate to maximize their time with northern agents. And despite her pleas to see them, the U.S. officers simply assured Clara that the future was more important than her bonds from the past, that everything was being done according to policy.

All the while, she couldn't escape her guilt – doubts, boiling within, that her need to take action had made her abandon the very people she'd believed she was helping. For what was it that'd led her to gamble the fates of her own partners, her own friends? What in her soul had made her believe she was the one, when others were not? She prayed on their behalf, and took on a new kind of sorrow, chastened by all that had occurred – humbled, she was certain – wiser, she hoped.

There'd been many additional meetings after that first one then, each more frustrating than the last. Every time, she'd ask if they'd heard anything of Atti, but the northern agents would only shrug apologetically and turn again to questions of their own, always laughably basic ones: how many hours a day had she labored – fourteen or more; how many calories a day had she received at the plantation – she didn't know; had she ever been beaten? – on occasion, but not for a while.

Already, a week had passed, and Clara had grown restless. It didn't help that she felt sick to her stomach. They'd been feeding her well – eggs and melon for breakfast, cold-cuts for lunch, steamed vegetables and poultry for supper. But she didn't react well to northern food; too much variety, more than her body had ever been trained to handle. More than that, she spent her days bored. Outside the meetings, she was on her own. Her room was spacious enough, with plenty of magazines and lots of screened-in windows, and the parkland outside was perfectly pleasant – playing-fields full of office picnickers, clusters of young bureaucrats and their flirts, soldiers playing softball – enough that if you twisted your head just right, you could almost believe it was some kind of resort. Still, the fencing at the perimeter was always visible, and she often found herself walking around the track on the compound's far side, picturing Atti and her fellow indents' faces if they could see her now, somehow trapped within this nation they'd all dreamed of as children.

Sometimes, she thought too of the Planter's daughter, Elizabeth Brooke. She guessed Ms. Brooke probably hadn't found her note, or had simply turned it in. Either way, why expect a thing? Why would a woman like that take a risk – let alone care? And Clara felt stupid for ever pretending in possibility.

Then, in her second week at the compound, a new guard arrived at her door. He was a fellow with slicked hair and a razor-thin part, and he smiled politely as he leaned in. "'Morning ma'am," – thirty years old, Clara guessed – loud-voiced, like all of them. "Won't you come with me?"

"Where to?"

The man looked back in surprise. "Just down the hall, ma'am," though his words were so fast she barely understood a thing. It was a recurring problem in Yankeedom, but catching enough of them, she followed beneath the fluorescent lighting, into a rectangular room ahead, walls painted off-white, a space she'd not yet seen.

It was there she was waiting now.

She'd been deposited at a narrow board table, staring at a painting on the opposite wall. It depicted several familiar well-heeled figures – George Washington, Abraham Lincoln, and a modern-looking man with a tiny chin, whom she guessed was the current U.S. president – all faces Clara recognized from propaganda back home: Washington always glorified there as a proto-Confederate, Lincoln vilified of course, the third man appearing frequently on the screens of overseers' phones in the fields. Here, the painter had used artists' prerogative to bring all three together into the same moment in time, standing before an ornate desk, above a caption that declared, "*U.S. Oval Office, New York, Their Spirits Preside as One.*"

She shifted her gaze to the furniture. It was nicer than any she'd ever been allowed to touch, let alone sit upon. The chairs had fine wooden armrests and plump red cushions. The table was gleaming, without a scratch to be seen. In the corner, a wide window looked onto one of the compound's lawns. Next to that, a plastic stand held pitchers of water and a bowl of walnuts, some of which she'd pocketed on the way in.

Only another minute passed, and a door at the room's far end slid open, as a man swiftly entered. He was the same who'd first greeted her when she'd arrived on Day 1, and had been present at every meeting since, often skimming through stacks of paper, like the one he was carrying now. He was near fifty, with short-cropped gray hair and lines in his forehead, but he looked fit, and wore a sleek blue suit with no tie.

He was on his own this time, and sat a few chairs down from Clara. She noticed a pair of reading glasses hanging from his chest pocket and smelled his cologne, and it almost made her smirk to think of the things that free people spent money on. For some time, the man just stayed there: hands folded, with a gaze so trained it didn't betray interest, disinterest, disbelief, a spark of anything. He just scratched his chin on occasion, and flipped through the papers before him. Finally, he squinted back Clara's way, as if a decision were winnowing into place, ready to be delivered with the same purr of action and snap of conviction as everything else around here. He smoothed the top of his trousers, then sat forward.

"'Morning," he offered with a nod. "I don't know that I ever introduced myself. My name is Sam Cooperman, and I'm the one in charge. I've been pursuing your case from the beginning, Ms. Brooke, and I must tell you, I've been looking forward to this. It's been hard waiting on all that information-gathering to be done. I'm sure you've anticipated its conclusion as well."

"Yes, sir. I have." Clara was surprised at how her voice echoed across the room.

"Is there anything new you'd like to go over?"

"I'd still like to know about the runaway I've mentioned."

"Is he your husband?"

"Like I've said – he's a friend. His name is Atti."

"Full name?"

"Atticus Brooke. But everybody knows him by 'Atti' – surname's the same as the Planter."

Cooperman pulled a tablet from his pocket and swiped the screen. He scanned it a moment, then clicked something, and scanned some more. "I'm sorry," he eventually sighed. "We haven't any indents by that name." He put the contraption away. "We'll let you know if we do."

Clara simply nodded.

"As you know, Ms. Brooke, they're getting nervous down in your country. Not just because of indents like you; a number of white citizens are starting to fight back as well. We've been receiving reports of Resistance, and we gather these folks are angry – some even lodging complaints in phone calls to their Congress. They're taking quite a risk, letting their views be formally known. But that's the thing – many Confederates just don't *believe* anymore. It's not just the old whining about taxes. They're questioning the restricted speech their government keeps drilling at them. They're finding ways onto social media. They're seeing images of life up here – life without curfews, without mass arrests, without enforced stratification – and they're asking why not for them?"

"I don't care about yeomen."

"Ah, but you should, Ms. Brooke. As we see it, the more instability in your Confederacy, the better. Which is why we've been helping it along. Along with supporting indents like yourself, we've been raiding the border to get more data. We just keep sticking our noses where the Rebs think we don't belong. And I don't mind telling you – we're making strides. We've intercepted government directives: we know they want the border stabilized, they've assigned the Confederate Guard to monitoring its nearest zones, they're mandating fuller indent surveillance too, they've begun a whole-hog hunt for white traitors in their midst. Every escalation is a sign of hope for us."

"Is it a sign of hope for me?"

Cooperman almost smiled – a simper that stretched his thin lips. "Ms. Brooke, that really depends on what we do next. We've fought for generations to topple the Confederacy, and unite our republic once again. But now we must acknowledge a new challenge: what if we actually succeed?"

She blinked. To contemplate the fall of the Confederacy was the stuff of dreams.

"Look out those windows, Clara. You see all those soldiers out there? Can you make out the ones your own color?"

"I've been thrilled about it, sir."

"Only there's the rub, Ms. Brooke. They make things look better than they actually are. Don't mistake me – we northerners have made progress. Our black citizens have homes and jobs. They can vote, they can walk and sit where they want – which wasn't always the case." He folded his arms. "Only, you see, that's just half the ballgame. The fact is, black folks still suffer. They still get stripped of justice, blocked from money and power, killed without consequence. The terrible truth is the North's adjustment from slavery to freedom hasn't been simple. And when the time comes, it won't be easy where you're from either."

Clara was growing unsettled.

"We want what you want, Ms. Brooke."

"And what's that?"

"Please." He lowered his arms, shuffling his papers, as if the answer were sitting right there. She waited. "The point, Ms. Brooke, is that remaking a whole society isn't quick. People need time to adapt. If we're actually to take in the Confederacy – with millions of former slaves living in peace – we'll need to put some care into it."

"Yes." She cleared her throat. "When the time comes. As you say."

He shook his head. "This isn't hypothetical, Clara. The shift from slavery is always thorny, not just here; if the Confederacy falls, then we're talking about far more souls than we ever dealt with on our part. Their freedom will shock your nation's way of life. We'll need everybody down there – Rebs, Resisters, Planters – to keep calm."

"Indents too, you mean."

"Everybody."

She was growing angry at herself for being surprised. "You're afraid. You're afraid the indents won't stay put. You're afraid if we get free, a whole bunch of us will try and move up here."

"Would I be wrong?"

She gazed right back.

"Alas, Ms. Brooke, if that were our only concern, perhaps we could manage our nerves." His hands were clasped on the table now. "What about your violence? What about the prospect of a new war, Ms. Brooke, at the conclusion of this one – a war of vengeance?"

"Spilling into the U.S., you mean?" She snorted. "That's why you're worried. You wouldn't care if it stayed tucked behind the border."

"We want to avoid jeopardizing our progress, if that's what you're after. We've papered over old cracks in our society we can't afford to re-fracture." Cooperman watched her, but she didn't budge. "I have to ask – why aren't you intimidated by me, Clara?"

"I was born a slave. What more is there to fear?"

"You've got me there." He squinted in thought. "Though perhaps it also explains so much you don't grasp." A shrug.

Another look out the window. "As I say, the more time you spend with us, the more you'll see – emancipation's a process, not a moment."

"Slaves are more than ready for freedom. They always have been."

"We've got to prepare everyone else, however. Before emancipation arrives, Ms. Brooke, we've got to convince them that freed slaves want to be part of their country – yours, as well as mine – not threaten it."

She jabbed her finger forward, and Cooperman flinched. "The slaves of the South are fighting right *now*."

"Yet if the rest of the Americas aren't ready in turn, a terrible backlash is what comes next. It's why we had to stop you, Ms. Brooke."

At that, she could only stare. So U.S. agents hadn't come to protect the indents at all. They'd come to ensure Confederate whites had time to process what was happening! Suddenly, she wanted to leap over the table and grab Cooperman by the throat.

He went on. "The Confederate Guard would've shown up anyway, Ms. Brooke. The revolt wouldn't have worked; you'd be tortured by now, even dead."

"We'd already taken over the house! The Planter was scared – he would have surrendered." Her eyes were smarting. "How could you?! You said yourself uprisings were happening all up and down the Confederacy – unless you went and stopped those too?"

"Not all. Some were simply defeated on their own."

She stood and slammed her fist against the table.

The door opened and an agent stepped in, but Cooperman brushed him away. "Please, Clara, have a seat." He waited. Eventually, she lowered back down; the agent exited. "We want these rebellions to work, I assure you. But it's a basic fact of our research that gradual change is the only form that's effective.

The first slave rebellions – yours included – went and failed. Now Confederates will have time to get used to the idea."

"And more bondage in the meantime."

"Success in the long run."

"You're exactly the same as the Rebs." Her breaths had gone short. "Just a different shade of blue."

"Nonsense. We merely want to be sensible – to ensure whites lead the new Confederate revolution, not blacks. It's the only way this works."

"You're a bigot."

"Not at all. Try and imagine a nation full of Confederates not just ready for change, but *pushing* it. It's how you'll benefit most. It's how we avoid unnecessary bloodshed." He neatened his papers. "That's why you're here, Clara. You're going to help us build this gradualist approach among your people."

"I'm not."

"You are." Cooperman's small eyes grew fixed. "You see, even by talking with you, we're breaking our armistice agreement with the Confederacy. The United States pledged a long time ago not to aid rebellious slaves in any way – not to arm them, not to harbor them, certainly not to discuss plans with them. In exchange, we live in the knowledge that the Confederacy won't launch an all-out attack at our border, no matter the skirmishing."

"The Rebs are dumb enough to believe your promises?"

"Under the agreement, we have every right to imprison you for life, Ms. Brooke. Alternatively, we could send you home, and your country could do with you as it pleases."

"Which one are you planning?"

"As I say, we need your help. We need you on the airwaves, sending our message. We feel confident you'll come to agree on our plan. First, yeomen will expand their rights; then slaves will gain their freedom. Phases, Ms. Brooke." Crisply, Cooperman stood back up. "Slaves, of course, will have to hear this from one of their own."

She opened her mouth to respond once more, but he was walking past her now, every movement planned. The door slid back open. He was gone.

She was alone as before.

Clara closed her eyes, leaning against the chair, and listened to the sound of the lights buzzing overhead. They were as loud as the locusts in the fields back home. She gripped the armrests at her side and held back a scream. She'd always assumed that with slavery gone, freedom would provide the answers. But here, slavery *was* gone. And freedom hadn't yet arrived.

CHAPTER 27

In the east, the border between the U.S. and C.S. shifted a few hundred feet every year. At the moment, it was situated precisely at the halfway point in Maryland. That was where the current trenches had been dug. It was where the artillery fire pierced the night. And it was where Ted Mercer and Raj Hayworth were now stationed.

There'd been times in earlier eras when the border had drifted farther south, closer to Virginia itself, and north as well, almost to Delaware. But for decades now, it had stagnated, even as the skirmishing had picked up. In recent years, nighttime raids into the Confederacy had increased, with attacks on armaments, rescue missions seeking runaways, and incursions – sometimes lethal – into border towns. These last were aimed at stubborn Confederate settlers, who stockpiled weapons and saw themselves as civilian defenders of their nation's sacred frontier, sometimes crossing into U.S. territory themselves. Still, through it all, the border endured, recognized by both sides of the conflict. Some pointed to conspiracy, arguing it was in the dueling governments' interests to avoid dramatic change for the sake of stability; others said it was proof the fanaticism of settlers was the answer and ought to be expanded; most simply saw it as the logical result of the new Cold War, two furious nations of equally matched strength and conviction.

Raj and Ted had been in place for three days now, after training camp in West Jersey. Time there had been brief – just a refresher week, since the draftees had already served their requisite stints after college – and it'd been hard getting to know the others. They'd come from all over, and had seemed friendly enough, but when it came time for border assignments, they'd been scattered to different sections of the line. Since then, there'd been a new routine of marching, weapons drills, and listening to lectures from commanding officers about staying alert. Raj still thought Ted overeager to join the fight, and Ted found Raj's continuing claims of apathy tiresome. But they'd both been leaning on their friendship in the face of military discipline. Neither could imagine stumbling through wake-up workouts or endless gunning practice without having the other for commiserating.

Just now, the two of them were sitting in one of the bunkers below ground – rooming together, thanks to the intervention of Ted's father – about a football field away from the official border line itself. This whole coastal region had become a stretch of pockmarked land, with buried bunkers on both sides, beyond the trenches. Ever since the armistice, each American nation had essentially agreed to use the space for sparring, perennially threatening to turn their Cold War hot. Even when the U.S. had developed nuclear weapons a generation before, things hadn't really changed. After all, there was no way for the army to use them – not without destroying itself, alongside the very place it hoped to reacquire. Instead, the soldiers just kept staring at each other, keeping the alleged peace.

So far, since Raj and Ted's arrival, it'd been more of the same. There were about two dozen men in their section, all still young, all plucked up in the same draft-call. The ceilings above where they stayed were barely seven feet high, the bunker walls hidden behind ammo crates and boxes of meal kits. Steel-backed chairs rested in the common areas, alongside video game consoles and chess boards. Lamps flickered; aging computer terminals sat unused. The previous afternoon, Raj and several others had spent hours playing the card game "War." The day before that, they'd gotten embroiled in a fierce discussion about whether baseball was still the national pastime, or whether football had taken over. Ted had suggested that football's popularity across the border even helped its case, making it a symbol of potential unity – though the others hadn't cared about that.

Today, as morning eventually became afternoon, Raj and Ted had been resting on their cots, eyeing apps on their phones that ostensibly kept track of Confederate formations on the border's other side. All they could really see, though, was a grainy feed of patchy grass, baking in the early autumn sun, and a few dead trees in the distance, destroyed by the sporadic shelling. It was like an empty stage set, a vague sense of anticipation up against the monotony of endless waiting. In a strange way, this wasn't so different from their old jobs back in the capital, when they'd sat monitoring chat rooms and social media feeds all day long for bits of intelligence about instability down south. Their first furlough wasn't for another two weeks, and in the meantime, they focused on getting through days like this one – often just a matter of exercising on treadmills, and texting with family back home, and once every twelve hours, getting sent above ground for thirty-minute shifts in the lingering heat.

On this particular rotation, their turn had come at three o'clock, as the sun was bearing down without mercy, cooking them in their heavy uniforms – inexplicably made of dark blue wool. Jagged honks rattled the air from jeeps on the bases behind them. Somewhere below, a radio blared. "Why in the hell doesn't the army just make summer fatigues?" Raj groaned, as they walked side-by-side, checking the missile silos for signs of rust, marking clipboards they'd been handed on the way up.

"Beats me."

"Well goddammit."

Ted laughed.

"What are we even doing here?"

"They say the government's trying to instigate more slave rebellions. It's pissing off the Rebs, so we've gotta be here in case they do something crazy."

"Great." Raj knelt down, testing a bolt, marking his form. "So you really still care?"

Ted looked over. "You know, I saw the Confederacy for myself once."

"You've been inside?" Raj lowered his pencil. "You never said."

"When I was little. A long time ago. My family drove down there. The skirmishing had calmed down, and my dad got us a special pass to take a trip – just to drive in and view the place – just through the car windows really. There was a government watcher assigned to us the whole time, to make sure of what we were doing. We took interstates all the way from New York down to Virginia. At the border, we drove right across the trenches – they'd put up some overpasses – then my dad flashed our pass at the border guards. He looked like a titan, doing that. We just drove right in. Like it was any other spot. Only it was different."

"He wanted to go because of your ancestors? To visit where they fought?"

"Who knows."

"So what happened?"

"We drove in, and then we just kept driving, for another hour maybe, straight into the center of Virginia. Pretty soon, the roads turned real crappy, all narrow and unpaved, and there were no signs, no modern buildings whatsoever. I mean truly, it felt like we'd driven back in time. It was actually kind of pretty." He stopped. "Only it wasn't."

"Why not?"

"The slaves, Raj. I saw them with my own eyes. We started spotting them at the sides of the road, working in the fields – tons of them. Just working away under this crazy hot sun – like today – torn shirts, soaked to the bone. Just bent over in the fields, working. And they looked *sick* – I mean, literally, physically ill. On their backs, through the rips, you could see they had scars everywhere. I still remember it. Some were kind of raised up, sticking out of their skin, a few were still wide open too – bloody, oozing, even as they worked."

"Jesus." Raj rubbed the back of his head. "Why'd you never say anything?"

"Just never seemed like something to chat about."

"I heard they've stopped whipping since we were kids."

"Supposedly."

Raj sighed. "What'd you end up doing next?"

"My dad had seen enough, plus my mom was mad he'd taken us at all. So he turned around, and we drove on out."

Raj could see intensity in his friend's gaze. "I'm sorry," he said, not sure what else he could offer.

"I'm not sure if I am. It helped me grasp things."

"Thing is, Ted – things aren't so great up here either."

"Well at least we've got hope."

Raj pondered that. It sounded right, and he glanced around. The torn-up landscape remained calm; there was a wind that smelled like chemicals and rot; scorched meadows sat nearer in.

"You've never thought about taking a trip down?"

He shook his head. "A friend's family tried once. I think his parents got a pass, same as yours. But while they were packing to go, there were news reports about artillery fire starting back up, so they never hit the road. He'd already gotten the currency exchanged in the mail; we used to make tiny airplanes out of the Rebs' eighty-dollar bills. That's the closest I ever came: touching their money." He paused.

"You alright?"

"Fine. Just hot." He rested a moment, leaning against one of the cement silos. "Imagine those slaves down there. How hot they must be every minute of every day."

"And you don't think killing is the way to help?"

Raj thought another moment. "No." He hesitated. "Hasn't helped so far. No reason it would start now."

CHAPTER 28

Liza felt panic rising in her throat.

"Confederate Guard agents came here?" she asked, telling herself it could be something minor, that there was still no reason to believe the Guard knew anything about what she'd done with the Resistance.

"This morning," Kevin answered. "Different men than last time. But they were asking about you." He'd greeted her on his front lawn with the news, as soon as she'd arrived to drop off a basket of her mother's vegetables.

"Why?" She worked to keep her voice from turning frantic. Suddenly the risks she'd been taking – until now making her feel brave and even a bit special – felt very real. "What'd they want to know?"

"I swear to you, Liza, it didn't seem serious. They were setting up checkpoints nearby, and were curious why your toll records showed trips to Richmond."

"They came to your house, not mine?"

He shrugged. "These guys were pretty low-ranking. I'd bet they didn't want to go to Rosewood for fear of provoking your father – their files labeled me a family friend, so they showed up. At first I thought it was going to be about that night I talked back to their captain. But they only stayed a few minutes. They told me your name came up on some computer back in Richmond, and the Guard was just covering its bases." He moved to the picnic table at their side. "I told them you've been sight-seeing. That you're interested in the city since your father talks about it all the time."

Liza nodded. That was a good answer.

"So what'd you bring anyway?"

"Your favorite." She placed the basket on the table. Amid the tomatoes and squash, there were hunks of mountaineer cheese and hickory ham, plus a slice of red velvet cake from Rosewood Manor's dessert the night before.

Immediately, Kevin grabbed it.

"Before sandwiches?"

"You bet," he managed, his mouth already full. "What can I say? Confederate efficiency."

They were lighthearted then as they ate, chatting about the cool relief autumn weather would soon bring, chuckling over a red squirrel wooing another that was gray. When they'd finished, Liza turned to him with an idea. "What if I went back to Richmond?" she suggested. "And you came with me this time?"

"When?"

"It's early yet. We could take one of my father's cars and still make it."

"Today you mean?"

"History's happening, Kevin. It's happening, and this is a chance to be part of it. I'll take you to a meeting. You'll see what I mean. You'll be fascinated."

He looked pensive. His eyes were the same color as the September sky.

"You're twisting your brain into knots, Kevin." She watched with frustration. This was the old version of him – more attached to Planter life here than he'd ever admit. "So then I should just go again without you?"

"You do what you think is best."

"Obviously you think I shouldn't."

"What I think isn't the point."

"You're the one who says so!"

"Well there you are."

Liza wasn't sure why she wanted his blessing so badly, but she did. And she couldn't help but feel a bit sad as she stood up. Still, she couldn't abandon another trip just because Kevin felt the need to be as cautious as ever.

"Good luck," he said quietly.

"Thanks," she answered, unsure how things could've turned so quickly, but unwilling to be the one held responsible for turning them back.

. . .

Richmond's skyline looked wonderful at sunset. It took on a rich brass color, with lights glinting from offices and apartment buildings, filling the horizon with their glow. To Liza, approaching in the car, it was gorgeous: magical and modern at once, making the most tradition-bound spot in the whole commonwealth also the most dazzling from the road. She smiled at the contradiction.

It really wasn't such a big place. Within a few minutes of reaching its outskirts, she was in the city's heart. It was just that everywhere else was so *small*. Here, there was a warehouse district – manufacturing Virginia's goods, everything from milk buckets to gun parts – the capital area, the residential and market streets, where she was headed now.

Nearing the Village Field Tavern, she parked and headed inside. Kevin was still on her mind, as he had been for most of the drive – she couldn't quite shake how his blue eyes had grown so anxious – but she was here now, and she strode to the bar. There was a large man serving drinks, wearing a black t-shirt and jeans, the clothes of a yeoman, with a round, shaved head.

He was tall – even taller than Kevin, she thought – and had shoulders like rocks. But every now and again, he broke into a loud guttural laugh, and when he did, everyone else laughed too.

Liza reached him. "I was wondering if you might let me through," she said in greeting, "over to storage in the back – I think I lost an earring there."

For a moment, the man peered back, and Liza could feel her heart beating in her chest. Then he shrugged. "Sure thing ma'am," and pushing himself from behind the counter, he told the other customers he'd be but a minute. Nobody seemed to think twice.

She followed him through the crowded room, toward the stairs and then the billiards table that she remembered from her last visit. The men playing there looked familiar, and when the bartender nodded to them, one reached down for the button by the electrical outlet. A second later, the hidden door in the rear wall opened, leading to the second bar beyond.

"Thanks," Liza offered – but the bartender was already returning to the front, and the door closed quickly between them. She saw a crowd gathered before her, applauding a speaker – and getting a better view, confirmed it was Dale. He'd told her he'd be scheduled today, and sure enough, he was standing on the bar in front of everyone, wearing a charcoal blazer instead of a Guard uniform, one arm up in the air, the other out to his side.

"Every nation must go through it," he was saying. "Outlive its Founding Fathers and survive to tell the tale. We never did! Incessantly honoring our past instead, never sorting out what we are in its wake. Lee and Jackson, Johnston and Stuart – clinging to their fumes, never a chance at igniting our own fire. Ours was a great democratic experiment. Then when the adventure was over, rights in Virginia began contracting! Gone was the vote. Gone was the belief that any yeoman-boy could one day become a full man!"

As he spoke, Liza leaned by the wall to watch. His hands were waving, voice bellowing, gorgeous dark hair flying.

"Friends, I shouldn't be the exception! I should be the *expectation*. When a fellow climbs up from yeomanry, it shouldn't be news. Wasn't that once the spirit of the South? Can it not be again? And if our northern brethren ask to be a part of it too, are we to go on alone, stubborn and stuck, or might we renew our grand experiment, recreate a world where a man is not what he was born to be, *but what he was born to become?*" With that, Dale descended into a theatrical bow, and jumped dramatically off the bar to cheers.

Liza realized she was holding her breath.

He'd just spoken treason, outright, undeniable: not merely endorsing democracy or rights this time, but proclaiming himself a Unionist, pledging support for a single merged nation of South and North. That was right up there with freeing an indent.

She stood to greet him, and he spotted her. "I'm glad you came!" he shouted over.

"Wow."

"Yeah?"

"Definitely – everyone was captivated." She studied him. "What about before I came in? Did you mention the slave uprisings?"

"Should I?"

"It'd fit with everything you said next."

"I suppose it would, Ms. Brooke." He smiled broadly.

"Does that mean you skipped it?"

"Liza – "

"The last time I saw you, you know, you were humiliating our family's indents."

"Come now, darlin'. You know that doesn't represent me. I had to. I didn't want to. I had orders."

"Still. Now I find you here, avoiding indents as part of the cause."

"Don't make connections that aren't there, Liza."

"No?"

"No. I'm a Captain in the Confederate Guard. I can't undo that now. If I don't do the job properly, I'll fall under investigation myself."

She considered that.

"You think it doesn't eat me up too?" he pressed. "The indents are the least of it."

"They shouldn't be. They ought to be at the center."

"I just mean they've always been part of our country, back to the beginning. With my job, I've got to uphold the whole damned hierarchy. I'm not just keeping indents in line, I'm ordering yeomen around too."

As she listened, Liza couldn't help but wonder how he'd react to her joining the Underground Railroad – if he'd be as understanding as Kevin had been.

"Listen to me go on, though!" He shrugged then, his brown eyes full of mischief. "Anyone's allowed to speak here, you know. Not just deceitful captains in the Guard."

"Don't be crazy."

"Come on, you'll be great!" He was turning now, facing the crowd.

"Dale, no – " Her throat caught.

But it was too late.

"Hey everybody!" He was back to full volume. "We've got one more before the night is through. This is Liza Brooke – " there were a few scattered gasps of recognition – "and she's got something to add." Dale spun back her way. "You're gonna be great."

Liza couldn't decide if she was furious or flattered – she knew only that she was mortified – but suddenly, she found her feet moving forward, aware of all the eyes upon her, unsure what else she could do. He'd used her real name, for heaven's sake! And lifting herself up, she slowly straightened, heart pounding, palms instantly wet. Afraid for a moment she was going to stumble, she glanced back toward the wall where Dale was now leaning against a banister, and saw him nod encouragingly.

Her face scanned the rest. There were dozens, many holding a beer in one hand, others draping an arm around the person next to them. Who were they all? What was she possibly doing in front of them? Then again, Dale had already put his whole life on the line with these people.

"Well," she began. "I didn't prepare anything. I have to say, I'm actually quite new to this…"

"That's alright!" a voice shouted from the crowd.

"We all are!" someone else called, as others clapped supportively.

"Why don't I tell you about an experience of mine?" There was more clapping at that. "You see, there's an indent whose labor belongs to my family back home: 'Atti' he's called, though I've never met him. And that's just the thing. We lived on the same land all our lives, yet I never met him. Not once. I don't even know which cabin he stayed in, or what he thinks about during his days, or even what he looks like." She took a steadying breath. "But I do know one thing about him. I know that he ran away. He just up and left, and he hasn't yet been caught. I've been thinking a lot about what he must be going through. About how tired he must be, and scared. It's made me think how badly he must want to be free – no different than any of us, really. I feel horrible that he had to leave for me to notice him. But at least by running, he's taught me that Dale Birch over there is right: that everyone has dreams, and that our country should make room for that. My family shouldn't have kept this man from what he wanted. That's the truth. Because no matter what our nation says, it can't be right that somebody who has dreams – even an indent – is too lowly to deserve them." She stopped. They were quiet. But they were listening. "That's really what I wanted to say."

Now she looked back to Dale. He was grinning wider than ever, eyes locked on hers – and then he began to clap as before, with others quickly joining in.

Liza felt herself laugh. "Thank you," she said, trying to make herself heard. "Thank you," she repeated, and crouching down, she climbed off the bar's ledge.

• • •

As soon as she'd returned his way, Liza confided to Dale she'd never had supper. He'd suggested they find a nice place, and soon, they were walking up the steps together, out into the main bar, toward the tavern's exit.

Only then did they realize something was wrong.

The block outside – crowded with passers-by when Liza had arrived – was empty.

She faced Dale. "What's going on?"

But a second later, a wave of sirens answered for him. They came crashing through the air, and suddenly two caravans of Guard SUVs and sedans were spilling into view, screeching closer from both directions. The first of them squealed to a halt, the others close behind. She could see the small flags on their doors.

Within seconds, agents were tumbling out, shouting toward the tavern, weapons drawn. "Stay inside – lie down!" they yelled from the street. "Nobody leave that bar! Stay inside!"

Liza had heard mention of such crackdowns: the Guard showing up unannounced, arresting everyone in the vicinity. It had allegedly happened in Atlanta a month before. Now it was happening here.

There'd be no denying she was involved. She'd just given a speech, for God's sake. It was hard to fathom how she'd gotten to this point, but it was certainly too late now. Each step of the way, she'd acted like she was simply learning a little more, trying to see a bit further. In the process, she'd become something more than herself.

Most people would say she'd become a traitor.

She blinked back tears. Kevin had been right, she thought. She was in danger.

At once, Dale's arm came around her, and he squeezed her shoulder. "Not to worry. Stick with me – don't drift away."

And then, just like that, he switched sides.

Though absent his uniform, he was suddenly striding forward as though he were in full ceremonial dress, making stiff his posture, his expression calm and unafraid. He even began blindly issuing orders, talking to no one in particular, as if he were the one leading the crackdown rather than serving as its target. Watching in amazement, Liza worked to stay close.

"Inside, men!" Dale had started shouting. "They're in the rear! Don't let them blend into the crowd! The Resisters are inside! Past the billiards table!"

As he shouted, leading Liza right onto the street, one of the younger agents scooted up close. The fellow was small, with anxious, darting eyes, and Liza thought she recognized him from the night the Guard had visited Rosewood Manor.

"Sir?" The young man saluted. "Captain Birch?"

"Yes, Private – do exactly as I say." Dale's voice stayed steady. "I've been scouting here undercover. You'll find Resisters in the back – there's a concealed basement – take the men; round up anyone you come upon. While you're at it, you might as well take in anyone from in front as well. We'll question them all."

The young agent nodded, then looked at Liza.

Dale shook his head. "Oh don't worry about her – she's just an old friend." And to Liza's horror, he gave a wink, so that the young man smirked in response, before saluting once more and sprinting onward as ordered.

Before she could say anything herself, however, Dale grabbed her by the hand and led her farther ahead, out of earshot. "Now listen." He spoke rapidly. "If anyone asks, you were simply visiting me for an evening get-together. It doesn't have to be scandalous. You can say we met in public precisely to keep it proper. Understood?"

She nodded, overwhelmed. Over Dale's shoulder, she could see Guard agents storming the bar, handcuffing the towering bartender.

He called her attention back. "Liza, listen – I wasn't careful tonight. I wasn't monitoring where the Guard was, and I'm sorry for that. But we have to think now. You're in a bad spot. Soon, they'll shut down all Richmond. This is too big of a bust – it'll be out of my hands. You need to head on back to Rosewood right now. You need to race. Do you hear me?"

"What about you?"

"I'll be fine. I'm on duty – I'll be fine. Now go!"

Once again, she had no chance to answer. He'd already spun back, his steps more purposeful, his voice ever more confident as he barked orders. He sounded just as passionate as he had down in the basement, such a short time ago.

• • •

It was past midnight when Liza pulled up her parents' driveway, on an almost empty tank of gas, hands sore from clutching the steering wheel the whole way back. To her relief, there'd been no checkpoints. She'd seen an array of additional Confederate Guard vehicles, but they'd all been going in the opposite direction, with no time to spare for a lone noble's car heading west.

Now, as she parked in front, Liza stepped out, exhausted. She was still trembling, gripped with a sorrowful mix of terror and pity, thinking of all those who'd been caught, wondering if they'd mention her name, pondering how possibly Dale could have messed up so badly. She felt as though she could barely stand, but she trudged up the porch steps, creaking open the door into the silent mansion, finding her way up to her bedroom, where she undressed and slipped under the covers.

In time, a fitful sleep descended.

·   ·   ·

There were only a few hours respite, however, before she was awoken by her mother. The door to her room had flung back open, and Liza could tell from the dim light pouring in from the windows that it was barely morning. Rubbing her eyes, she tried tugging herself from sleep. As she did, the night's events came flooding back, and for an instant, they seemed a horrible dream.

Cathryn Brooke shut the door hard, entering the room swiftly, sitting at the edge of her daughter's bed. "Good morning, dear," she said, and her clipped northern accent plucked the words like strings on a banjo.

"Good morning, mother." Liza sat up reluctantly, stuffing the pillows into a pile behind her.

"We saw you come in last night. Your father refused to sleep until the car showed up in the driveway."

Liza blinked. "I'm fine."

"Oh Liza." Cathryn's voice was suddenly shakier. "Tell me you weren't in Richmond. Is that where you were? On another of your visits to the capital?"

"I left before any of the trouble occurred. I heard about it on the radio."

"For goodness sake, dear. You worried us half to death, vanishing a whole night, in a city engulfed by revolution!"

"Don't exaggerate, mother – "

"What would you call it?"

"I heard they were just talking reform."

But Cathryn waved that aside. "Liza dear, tell me the truth."

She wasn't sure there was a way to answer. So instead she looked dully ahead, feeling like a child again, wishing for some escape.

"Answer me."

"Can't a girl just have a life of her own?"

"Excuse me?"

"Well can I?"

"Have you been seeing someone, dear?"

"Please."

But Cathryn Brooke raised her eyebrows. "Have you?" She paused. "You have! A mother always knows, darling. Now who is it?"

She sighed. "I'm not seeing him," she admitted. "We've just been meeting up. Nothing untoward."

"But who is he, dear?"

Liza took a breath, feeling her way through the conversation. She turned back. "Do you remember that Confederate Guard officer whom father spoke with? That night at our house?"

"That young Captain?"

"Captain Dale Birch, yes. I'm not *seeing* him mother, but we have been spending time together socially. He resides in Richmond, if you must know."

At that, she could see her mother's shoulders finally relax, a smile growing in place of her scowl, and despite herself, Liza felt some relief. She knew her mother: she'd be tickled at the idea of her daughter getting acquainted with a Guard officer. It would distract her. And Liza couldn't help but feel a twinge of satisfaction.

"What about Kevin, dear?"

"I'm not sure," she replied honestly.

A loud knock on the door interrupted. "Can't I come in?"

"Father, come in, yes!" Liza shouted back, almost too enthusiastically.

"Thank God you're safe and sound!" Franklin Brooke had twisted the knob and was looking upon them both. "I was telling your mother all night – I'm sure she's just on another one of her visits – that's what I said, didn't I, Cathryn? And here you are."

"Where else could I be?"

Franklin stood before the bed, hands clasped in front. "You're really alright?"

"Of course I am."

"And did your mother tell you the big news?"

"I was leaving that to you, Franklin."

"You'll hardly believe it!" he thundered. "I've been asked to head north."

Liza was confused.

"To the United States," Franklin explained after a theatrical pause, clearly more focused on this than dwelling on the unpleasantness of the night before. "I leave tomorrow morning, to negotiate for the Confederacy."

"They're allowing you in?"

"The border trouble's gotten far too delicate. The U.S. is afraid we'll retaliate. Our government's decided to seize the moment. We proposed a visit, and they've accepted."

"You're serious."

"Entirely. History seems truly to have arrived. I've been selected to go up for the preliminary meetings. If those go well, others will follow. It's not impossible we gain U.S. recognition, in exchange for nothing more than the stability we all desire. We obviously can't take their incursions much longer, let alone the incitement of our indents. But neither side is ready for all-out war. Everyone agrees it's a miracle that such a flimsy peace has lasted as long as it has – it's high time a proper treaty replaced the armistice."

"Naturally they selected your father," Cathryn added in now. "Congress knows northerners will be charmed by his good grace. I'm sure they were thinking about my own background too, though none would ever say so."

"The U.S. considers me a moderate." Franklin flashed a wide smile.

Liza gaped between the two of them. "Must you travel there alone?"

"It's the only way. If I come back with nothing, we can at least paint it as a minor summit over border concerns. If I succeed, then we'll set up a larger state visit."

"Bodyguards at least?"

"It wouldn't send the message we intend."

"Father!"

"I'll be fine, dearest."

She exhaled. Only what if people learned where she'd been in Richmond? Her father's career would be over.

"Now, now, Liza," he said, stepping forward. "I mean it. Why don't we have a celebratory supper tonight? I'll order up a feast. We can invite Kevin."

Liza felt her mother glance at her, but she didn't return the look. Could this really be happening? If the U.S. ended up easing its pressure, new resources would be opened up for the Guard. She had no doubt both yeomen and indents would suffer the consequences. Dale's optimism the previous evening seemed hollower than ever. "That sounds nice."

"Let's make it just the four of us," Cathryn cut in.

And Liza said no more.

CHAPTER 29

The next morning, General Franklin Brooke set out early. To reach the United States, he first had to get to Richmond. Tracks still ran between the Confederacy and the United States, reforged back in the 1940s for trade, amid the larger war with Europe and Asia. With Axis surrender, any softening between the two countries had vanished of course, and the tracks had become an anachronism. But they remained operational, if only for the rarest of missions like this one.

The clock hadn't yet struck nine when he spotted his government car waiting. By then he'd already enjoyed a big plate of eggs and toast, and with his wife and daughter at his side, Franklin retrieved his luggage, checked his phone, and made his way to the front hall.

In truth, Liza wasn't the only one worried by the trip. The weight of expectations was immense. The nation was weakened – some said at its weakest since the Revolution – with forces growing at the border, chaos rippling among the indents, the increasing Resistance roundups. And despite propaganda efforts to minimize talk of the trip, word had already spread among the aristocratic class. Hope was emerging that Franklin could find terms for an actual treaty. Barring that, the goal was an easing of rhetoric. At the very least, there was faith he'd return home with a promise of another meeting.

"Not to worry, my dears," he said, kissing them gently goodbye. Cathryn and Liza were standing beside him, as if in a royal receiving line, trying to look buoyant, though their nerves had already seeped through the house. "I love you both. And I'll see you in no time." Then, noting their tears, growing emotional himself, Franklin hugged them as one, cleared his throat, and turned to the door.

In a government vehicle with speeding privileges – and extra shocks for the dirt roads – the ride to Richmond promised to be quicker than usual; the views were soon a blur of finely lit hillcrests, curving stone walls, and ancient farmland. Still, Franklin couldn't stop fidgeting, tapping his thumbs, taking in deep, expectant breaths. By the time the car slowed, he realized he was sweating, and he stepped out with relief to board the single-car train, only a short distance away.

The station that greeted him was a domed behemoth, with a Confederate flag the size of a blimp planted on its main façade, and as Franklin glanced up, he saw the sky growing dark with thunderclouds. A crowd of sentinels escorted him forward, through the old red brick entrance in front, along cracked cement platforms beyond that. Several Congressmen were there to see him off, standing beneath a series of archways over the tracks – fine-crafted theatricalities, which architects had considered sleek eight decades before – slapping him on the shoulder now, delivering trite words of encouragement. Franklin suspected none of them wanted to be associated with the mission unless it succeeded – hence the lack of cameras. The only ones who'd shown up were on the Foreign Relations Committee. They'd probably drawn straws.

The train's operator was a yeoman who would exit when the train reached the border. There, a fence would slide open across the tracks, and the plan was for another engine car – this one with a U.S. driver – to link up with Franklin's and tug it into foreign territory, then all the way onward to New York. There'd be a severe lack of pomp, to be sure, but the trade-off was a lowering of stakes, not to mention the added security that came from staying free of the public eye. Arriving in the U.S. capital, Franklin was to be greeted equally quietly, and the diplomatic process would begin – probably over supper. He'd been wondering what sort of meals the Yankees would serve. Cathryn had long told him they ruined food up there, eating an anarchic mishmash of global cuisines.

Franklin hoisted himself up onto the train, saluting the young sentinels standing at attention in the door, stepping along the aisle and into a wood-framed seat by the window. As soon as he did, the train started creaking out of the station, its aged machinery grumbling with disuse. The clatter against the tracks was raucous, the wheels screeching terribly. In time, however, the engine accelerated, and he was swept into the countryside. He looked out the smudged windows toward gentle hills and rolling forests, and as the storm arrived in full, and raindrops hammered the car like broken little bullets, while thunder rattled the roof, he watched the glass panes fog up against the grace of fine pastures, grazing sheep, and brown-coated mares, reduced to blurred silhouettes against the green.

For two hours, the train passed through such scenes. Finally, when it reached the border area, Franklin straightened. The first Confederate trenches appeared outside, and he could see the men – his men – patrolling the dirt below. Some were checking weaponry, others monitoring screens, all glancing over in surprise at a train. A few saluted; most just stared.

Next, he entered the artillery zone. Here, the land was dented by craters, target practice for new-age weaponry from both sides, part of their massive game of chicken, the one he was going to try and end. He couldn't help but linger on the sight of fresh smoke rising from nearby holes.

Finally, the train slowed. It lurched the last few feet, then it stopped. Franklin couldn't see the fence directly ahead, dividing the track, but after a moment, he heard it sliding slowly open. He thought of the endless buildings and endless chaos that Cathryn had so often described of her home, all right there, all ready for him at last.

There was quiet then, until he heard a door creak in the front. From his angle, he could look down and see the yeoman driver hop onto the ground below. The man turned back and gave a salute like those of the soldiers; then a Confederate Guard jeep pulled up behind him, ready for the trip back to Richmond. Franklin saluted in return, faced front once more, and waited to be tugged ahead. Sure enough, the whole car knocked back a bit, and he guessed the U.S. engine had latched. The car rocked forward a moment later, and then moved once more, bumpy but sure, across the border itself.

He held his breath, watching the artillery zone again rolling by, until the fence that divided the rail line was directly at his side. It was a lone metal barricade, fifteen feet tall, crowned with barbed wire and laced with electric current, and it was hard not to frown that the two nations could agree to share such a nasty little door, but couldn't live in peace.

Then it passed, and Franklin was in the United States.

The dirt outside looked just the same, and he could again see craters from shells, now the handiwork of his own country's weaponry. In the distance, he spotted new trenches too, and as he listened to the fence groan closed, he waited for the speed to pick back up. Instead, the train trickled along for some time.

Until it stopped once more.

Through the window, Franklin saw a black jeep pull parallel, similar to the vehicles that the Confederate Guard used, though this one appeared to operate on gas. Another soon arrived behind it, and he peered out, watching. The passenger door of the first one opened swiftly, and a man stepped out in dark blue military garb. Double gold stripes ran down his sleeves, marking him a junior officer of some kind – a captain perhaps, though Franklin hadn't studied U.S. insignias since university.

The fellow stepped to the jeep's rear door, opening it up. And to Franklin's growing surprise, four young soldiers leapt out in rapid succession. They wore fatigues and carried M4 carbines, and as they appeared, the second vehicle inched closer – until it stopped too, and the same thing occurred: another officer exiting from the front, four other men streaming from the back.

They jogged from their vehicles then, out of view, too close to the train for Franklin to see. But an instant later, the door of his cabin slid open, and the soldiers were striding inside. The one in the lead guided the others; he had three stars on his shoulder confirming it. "General Franklin Brooke, CSA?" this young man demanded, his clipped accent a harsher version of the rhythms Franklin knew so well from his wife.

"Naturally, son." He stood stiffly. "No need for that tone."

"General sir," the soldier replied, more loudly than before. "You're hereby under arrest."

Franklin stared.

"U.S. Code 2381. Sir, you are charged with treason; you are to be taken in as prisoner of war."

"How can it be both?"

But the young man ignored that. "Any property on your being is now in custody of the United States government. All contact between you and any co-conspirators will be conducted with monitoring."

Franklin tried to remain steady. "Son, you're mistaken." But he could hear the tremble in his own words. "For God's sake, I'm here on a diplomatic mission."

The soldier, however, had yanked handcuffs from his pant pocket.

"Of all the ridiculous things. I'm a half-a-minute from my own country!"

But there was no arguing. The others were standing in formation, rifles gripped tight, faces steady as stone.

A new rage boiled within.

The sheer deception of it – the duplicity! It was everything he'd ever known about this country. Past contact had always been between government officers – politicians only. By sending a general this time, actually taking negotiations seriously, the Confederacy had opened itself up to something like this. How could they have been so dumb? Forsaking security as they had – mistaking correspondence for trust, that the Yanks would abide by the rules?

He wanted to roar. Technically, the U.S. was right it could arrest him: with no treaty, only an armistice, the countries were still legally at war, providing this young snot of a soldier his sanction, classifying Franklin as combatant instead of ambassador. He would be questioned, probably harshly. The U.S. would exploit this insidious legal maneuver to gain any intelligence it could.

He took a deep breath.

His own men would piece it together in no time. They'd hear nothing from him – first for a day, then another, and they'd know something had gone wrong. They'd enhance defenses, then threaten escalation. That should bring about his return in relative short order.

For now, though, Franklin looked ahead only in disgust, and gradually registered these men were actually going to take him in as a prisoner, for humiliation if nothing else. Turning his back, he folded his hands behind his waist, and felt the handcuffs clamp shut, tighter than was necessary.

CHAPTER 30

Ted was ecstatic. News of the arrest of General Franklin Brooke, by all accounts the most powerful man in the Confederacy, had hit the bored soldiers at the front like a rainstorm quenching a drought. Already, the story was becoming the stuff of legend. Apparently, it had all happened just a few miles from where they were stationed – according to reports, a brilliant ruse, executed flawlessly. Diplomats had persuaded the fool to come north for a summit, and he'd fallen for it. As soon as he'd crossed the border, he'd learned where he was actually headed: not to some bargaining table with a vase of flowers and a pitcher of water, but a stone-walled holding cell in an unnamed compound, exactly as he deserved. Ted would have loved to see the old traitor's face when he'd realized he'd been outmaneuvered.

"I don't know," Raj was saying, as he stretched his arms, and they made their way through the latest above-ground shift. "All that's happened is we tricked a has-been into jail."

"He's their top guy."

"We lied."

"We didn't lie. We said we'd accept a visit, and we did. They're the ones who sent over a general instead of a minister of state. We're at war, Raj."

"He was coming in good faith."

"Right. That's why they keep shelling us."

A sigh. "You're repeating what you're being told."

"By officers who know what they're talking about. Southern Resistance hasn't been able to reach out to us – it's too dangerous on their end. But we could reach *them* if we knew who they were. A guy like Brooke has that information – targets, people they're watching, suspected meeting places at least. We could find out what they need – money, weapons – send it over."

"Like Nicaragua all over again."

"Stop. The Rebs aren't foreign. We understand them. Remember that."

"You just said it yourself! We're at war. Always have been. They'll just end up attacking us outright." The midday sun was high above, and placing his hands on his hips, Raj leaned back his head, taking it in.

In the distance, the whistle of a new round of artillery shells had begun. They'd been sailing in more frequently the past few days, every hour even, no longer just a few times in the evenings. Of late, their own forces had responded in kind, so that both sides were re-obliterating the designated artillery zones, a contest in stubbornness as the standoff continued. Shifting to their side, the two friends noticed the whistling growing louder.

That's when the explosion happened.

It came like a clap of thunder directly overhead – and an instant later, chunks of earth were flying through the air, landing with a thud all around them.

The shell had landed too close.

As they stumbled, Raj turned, staring back at Ted, who returned his look with equally wide eyes – then dove to the ground, tackling his friend in the process, taking them both down for safety. In the distance, they heard a fresh pop – the sound of another shell launching. The whistling began anew.

Had the Confederates misfired? Was it a mistake?

"What the hell is going on?" Raj murmured, half to himself.

"I have no idea."

The whistling turned loud once again.

They both squeezed shut their eyes. It was too close.

The Rebs were no longer aiming for the artillery zone, Ted realized. Raj had been right. They were aiming for the trenches and bunkers instead.

Then – another explosion, even more powerful than the first, a crash that wouldn't stop echoing. The earth shook, and on instinct they started scrambling for the nearest trench they could find, even as the ground itself seemed to lose balance. Ted registered he couldn't hear anything. It was like his ears were clogged with water, and he shook his head.

Raj was grabbing him. "Ted!" he mouthed. "Ted!"

There was no sound. The explosion had been too much. It had done something to him.

Another moment came and went. Then an awful ringing started up – a steady scream that just wouldn't quit – and at last Raj's words started to make it through, faint but clear. "We've gotta keep getting back!" his friend was urging. "We've gotta get clear – they're firing right this way!"

Ted looked up, and noted he was on his back. The sky glowed an unnatural red: flames from things not meant to be burned, smoke billowing, as new bombs continued their reign, tearing apart a landscape already jagged and broken. He saw other men scrambling toward ladders on the back sides of trench walls, lifting themselves out, and he felt Raj take his hand and yank him forward.

Other shells were landing farther down the line. Over the ringing in his ears, Ted could hear more thuds knocking the trenches apart, even cracking the bunkers' roofs. Soldiers seemed to be shouting in every direction, telling each other to move; and gathering his wits, Ted went with the rest, back towards camp in the rear. He sprinted as hard as he could, still trying to shake the screeching in his brain, spotting a large section of the next trench collapsed in on itself, hoping no men had been inside.

"Come on!" Raj bellowed, and Ted caught up, pushing forward, legs burning. More men were beside them now, as every few seconds, there was another roar, a rush of dirt in the air, more shouts from the retreating soldiers.

Meanwhile, the U.S. had started its retaliation. Artillerymen in blue were sending their own shells now, with equal furor. Seeing them fly, Ted felt his heart pumping with charged-up vengeance, hearing his own side's shots sail overhead, landing back behind him, aiming to destroy the Confederate zones just as the enemy had destroyed his.

"Enjoy that," he heard himself say, his voice a growl, and he ran ever harder.

• • •

That night, the U.S. troops were briefed.

An hour after Ted and Raj had reached the camp, out of range of Confederate fire, the shelling had ceased on both sides. The border had taken on its old quiet – except the 'No Man's Land' had grown. The shelling hadn't been precise, and most of the above-ground men had been able to get out in time; meanwhile, the bunkers had held. Still, there'd been casualties. Counts would be released over the next few days.

Word from on high was that the Confederacy had been making a statement. The method was escalation. In keeping with history, the eastern sector was the target. Tensions always erupted there first – where the capitals resided, where the tradition of battle seemed to haunt the air.

The United States, of course, couldn't tolerate such an aggressive move. It would obviously keep pushing back, with further rounds of shelling, then a forward launch using air force and infantry. The goal wouldn't be conquest. Leaders had let go of that notion generations before. It would just be another salvo, a message in return, encouraging Confederate internal resistance, intended to add more pressure to the South, contributing to its turmoil and insecurity of its government. U.S. policy remained focused on bringing the Confederacy down from within. To Raj, that sounded an awful lot like conquest no matter what they said, and a hell of an excuse for more horror. But everyone else seemed on board.

After dismissal, he and Ted boarded a bus for their new lodging. They were being sent westward, to a border region seventy miles inland, which had escaped the day's trouble, but where more men were needed to firm up the line. The area would be more densely forested than what they were used to, apparently packed with wild growth that Rebel shells had never bothered blasting away. Old above-ground barracks, built several decades before, would be available, still intact because the trenches didn't extend that far. Rumor had it that the place might even be pleasant.

At ten o'clock, they boarded, scheduled to arrive by midnight. Nobody said much on the way; most dozed as best they could. At one point, Raj turned to Ted, half-asleep against the window. "Still don't think they'll attack?"

"Shut up."

"Just sayin'." But he kept his thoughts contained after that, listening to the bus rumble against the road, wondering when they'd see action again, hoping it would be never, knowing it would probably be soon.

Upon arriving, the men were assigned bunks. The barracks, it turned out, were small, musty cabins scattered among the woods; the beds were rickety and covered by flimsy mattresses. So much for rumors. But no one cared. As long as there were no explosions, everything else was easy by comparison, and Raj sat down amid the quiet, and removed his dusty boots.

CHAPTER 31

Byron Sampson was farther north than he'd ever been – and much closer to the Confederacy's limits than he liked. With border tension heating up, he'd grown fearful of nearby bombings. Worse, even if he skirted through, he was certain he'd soon have to report for duty. Another round of conscription, regardless of age, would be on its way. And yeomen always had to report first.

The last real flare-up had been a decade before, when a gaggle of fanatics had built a settlement on the wrong side of the border out in Missouri, and the U.S. had bombed it. Bryon had gotten his notice a few days later, ordering him to head down to the local draft outpost and sign up for active service. A month or two after that, to the relief of everyone, the dueling nations had agreed to scale back their posturing. Conscription had been rolled back.

He prayed that would happen again. But with neither side showing signs of backing down, he expected a call. He might be able to wiggle out of full duty, thanks to his age, not to mention growing demand for his profession, but he'd definitely have to report. He'd been receiving news alerts on his phone, and it was obvious the General's arrest was too much for the higher-ups to take. Every day the proclamations grew more pointed – pledges of vengeance, diatribes against northern imperialism and hypocrisy, hagiographies of Brooke and his long-lionized family.

That was reason enough to cancel this latest hunt. Forget the danger of traveling so close to U.S. shells; it would be foolhardy to antagonize a draft board by remaining in the woods like this, keeping its members waiting, unable to get back for an appointment in time. Besides, where was the guarantee he would now even be paid? It was Byron's current employer who'd been captured, after all – in the language of the official reports, "detained unexpectedly" – and as a noblewoman, Brooke's wife wouldn't have the authority to sign another paycheck while he was gone.

Nonetheless, he'd come this far. He might as well give it one last go. What's more, he didn't truly believe the general would stay behind bars for long. The man was simply too high-ranking, his imprisonment too provocative. It was worth betting he'd be released – and when he was, he'd no doubt be impressed with his man for sticking with the chase. There might even be more money in it.

Byron peered ahead. There was pine forest everywhere, but even that couldn't muffle the nearby shelling. In the last day, it had transformed from background noise – deep thuds echoing across the valleys – into sounds far sharper, slicing through the quiet, silencing the blackbirds, harder to ignore. His heart clanged against his chest. Not only might there be a wayward artillery shot, but U.S. raids would be more of a danger than ever. It was obvious Byron couldn't risk capture. If the bastards up there were willing to jail a general, they'd have no problem disappearing a fool like him.

Luckily, he suspected he'd finally found what he was looking for. He'd crested a ridge when he'd spotted the campsite. It wasn't much, but it was obvious. The slave had at last grown careless: tucked beneath a flat stone, a worn leather bag was peeking out, the kind Planters often gave their chattel for carrying supplies.

Byron quieted his heavy breathing, scanning the forest floor in front of him. Then he moved forward, keeping on the edges of his feet, stepping carefully across new piles of dead leaves. At last, reaching the bag, he lifted it up, finding nothing inside but an old paper bag, half-filled with peanuts.

A canteen was missing. He spun around, surmising his target must've gone to re-fill it. That would mean a stream bed nearby, or a valley where a puddle might have collected a little way's down. And just to his right, only about four yards off, Byron spotted a dip in the ground. He listened closely, becoming aware of water, the gentle flow of a creek. That was it then. The slave was a fool. This close to his destination, and he was risking it all by taking a rest.

•   •   •

The stream was narrow and rocky, but it looked clear enough, its current strong enough, that Atticus thought it safe to drink.

He was close to the border, he was sure. How else to explain the explosions? Folks always said there was warfare at the Confederacy's northern edge, and that it was noisy. Still, he'd had to pause. His throat was burning with thirst, and in the last hour, he'd grown fearful of fainting outright. The world had started spinning, so that on a few occasions he'd even slowed and leaned against the tree trunks in his path to steady himself.

When he'd heard the stream, he'd recognized salvation. Hastily, he'd dropped his bag, leaving it on the bluff so it wouldn't get wet and weigh him down. Taking the canteen, he'd slid down the hill toward a creek splitting two ridges – the one he'd just left, and another just opposite.

The water felt magical as he waded in. Frigid against his shins, its mist seemed to transfer him energy all at once.

Squatting low, he splashed his face and gulped it down, dumping more across his back.

At last, he was ready to go. With his canteen full, he turned, ready to scramble back up. Except that as he started to spin, something caught his eye downstream, over on the far hillside. He could swear he'd spotted a flash of navy-blue, amid the forest's brown and green, and he took a cautious step closer.

It looked to be a flag. He'd never seen one like it before – but he'd heard talk of them, he was certain. It boasted red and white stripes, and its corner square explained the blue. It was the U.S. banner, matching exactly what the indents had long described in old tales.

Atticus tilted his head for a better view, but it was hard to tell how the flag had been hitched. He started forward, moving there rapidly now, no longer taking much care. In a moment, he'd scaled the next ridge – steep but manageable – until he'd reached the top. He looked again.

Sure enough, about a half-mile off, he could spot an old cottage beneath the flag; he saw now it'd been hoisted to the roof. The place's walls were pale yellow; an aging brick chimney matched a slanted stoop in front. And it wasn't alone. There were more of them, nestled in a clearing – weathered walls, gray-shingled roofs, stacks of windows – each with its own flag up top.

All at once, Atti swallowed back tears.

It had to be the United States.

The autumn air among the trees was dry, and his mind wandered to this place's sights and sounds: pathways softened by fallen pine, the heavy flap of a turkey across the hillside, the whir of robins closer in. He was in the North, with home far behind him, and he shook his head, in wonder and triumph.

Glancing back, Atti thought of his bag. The only thing in it was a pile of stale peanuts. Were they really worth lingering in the Confederacy?

But at that, he halted.

There'd suddenly been a new set of sounds, though he couldn't place quite where: twigs cracked in a growing wind, old leaves rustling. Seeing nothing, Atticus twisted his head once more. Had the trees' shadows shifted? Somewhere, another branch snapped – from an animal, he told himself, maybe a deer or just a squirrel – and the sun snuck through the canopy. He heard a pebble bouncing down a hill somewhere close.

Was this just the clatter of a forest grove?

His eyes darted.

Then –

The burst of breaking branches was undeniable now. Jerking his head to the side, he scanned as far as he could. And his mouth went dry. There, scaling down the other ridge, was another figure, approaching fast. It was a man, covered in grime, with a gray shirt that might once have been white hanging loose from a skinny frame, and a warped straw hat nearly skidding down his greasy hair.

Could he be a Yankee? Is that what Yankees looked like?

But there was no time for debating. Perhaps the man hadn't seen him yet, and Atti figured his best option was to get toward those cottages. He shifted back in their direction. Until his right foot landed on an old sapling, and he broke it in two.

The crack seemed to split the air.

The man looked up instantly, his gray eyes fixed. Quickly then, he reached into his trouser pocket and pulled something out – a weapon of some kind. It looked to be a taser, the same type that overseers carried back on the plantation. One shot would put Atti on the ground.

Still, it wouldn't do to surrender. Abruptly, Atticus dropped his canteen, and started sprinting. Panic propelled him forward, as his legs took off, fast as they could go, bounding down from the crest of the ridge. He heard the weapon's crackle, and reflexively he ducked, knowing he couldn't afford to stay in range. His thighs stung; his ankles bent on jagged rocks, but it was no matter. He had to reach those cottages.

Only then – without warning –

He heard a new sound altogether, like the popping of a gas flame, and his feet skidded upon a collapsed pile of stones, disguised by moss, knocking off the uppermost rock. A stream of brown bugs squirreled from their home, as a second pop rang out. This time, he had no doubt what it was – the burning wind of a bullet, just inches from his shoulder – and he dove down, eyes frantic, head still pivoting.

It had to have been a rifle shot, unsettling the whole forest, echoing in every direction, nothing like the zap from the electric stunner a moment before. Had the man brought a second weapon? Was he firing it now?

From the ground, Atti twisted again to see.

But the slave-hunter had dropped to his knees, the taser slipping from his hand. There was blood now, lots of it, spilling down the man's shirt from his chest, and he'd started to tumble – rolling down the ridge as if he were a boy doing summersaults, except something was off – an angle in the way he was going, arms flopping out at his sides, head rocking up and down as though it were loose. Then, just like that, his body hit a small boulder and stopped – landing halfway down the slope, legs bent out like broken scissors. Atticus gaped. The man's face had come into full view: one whole side of his head turned to mush in an instant, his eyes – those eyes! – morphed to milky gray; lips gone slack forever.

Atti shivered to see it, scarcely able to breathe himself, to hear or think or understand, grasping only that those shots had come from somewhere below. Was there another slave-hunter nearby then, competing for the prize? He turned back around, frantic, panning the forest.

As he did, two new figures appeared from behind a cluster of trees. They were running right toward him, both of them tall, in dark blue uniforms he didn't recognize. The one in front had a square jaw and loose blonde hair and was holding out a long rifle of some kind. Behind him, the other soldier was sprinting as well. His hair was scruffier, darker – as dark as Atti's own – with skin that was darker as well. This second fellow looked neither white nor black, and Atti met his gaze, raising both hands high, in fear they'd shoot him too.

Other soldiers were emerging now as well – exiting from the cottages, Atti realized. He watched them warily. Had he come upon U.S. infantry? He wanted to be ecstatic, but he also felt the grip of uncertainty in his stomach – the danger of hope. What if such men didn't discern between intruders? And he clenched his hands behind his head, waiting, praying they wouldn't fire again.

The two soldiers in the lead were now just feet away. The blonde one in front lowered his gun. "Who are you?" he demanded, words tumbling forward like blades. "Who?! Are you with that man?" He was pointing to the slain slave-hunter. "Or was he chasing you?"

"I mean no harm," Atti managed.

"What's your business?"

"I'm an indent," he said, making his words distinct, trying to be calm. "I'm a slave. That man was chasing me, yes – as you say."

The blonde man blinked. He lowered his gun, studying Atti, his eyes moving across the runaway's face. Then he took another step forward. "Well you're not a slave anymore," he finally said. "Lower your hands, friend. You're not a slave anymore."

Atticus didn't move. He just watched the soldier, trying to take in the words.

The man looked at him intently. "I say you're not a slave anymore," he repeated once more.

Still, Atti couldn't react. He found he was unable to bring his arms down, or speak, or do anything at all. He simply ran the sentence again through his mind, as if it were another language, as if it required breaking down bit by bit.

"I'm Theodore Mercer, United States Army," the blonde soldier was saying now, straightening up. "You call me Ted – everyone does." The second soldier had arrived now too, panting, bent over, hands on his knees. "And this here behind me – this is Raj Hayworth, also U.S. Army, 15th Infantry Division."

The second soldier lifted his hands from his knees, extending one toward Atticus. "Raj works," he said, still breathing hard. "You call me Raj."

Atticus reached out his own hand in return. "It's an honor," he uttered, as they shook. "You both call me Atti."

CHAPTER 32

Atti's first meal as a free man was basic soldiers' fare, served at the barracks' mess hall near the forest's edge. It consisted of a packaged meal that didn't look like much, stored in vacuum-sealed packs amid thousands of others in one of the cottages nearby, but he appreciated it thoroughly, going through two beef stews and a whole pile of canned peas. The U.S. soldiers watched in awe, feeling guilty for complaining as often as they did.

Outside, in the darkness, the cabins were quiet. Nothing but wind, as if the world were still normal. Atticus, though, couldn't stop glancing out the windows, re-living the chase that had landed him here, still somehow unconvinced he'd made it. From habit, he studied his surroundings, timing the flash of floodlights now that the sun had set, measuring the barbed wire posts with his eyes.

This was an old camp, he'd learned, only recently re-purposed, where the latest recruits had been stationed in anticipation of more conflict to come. Nonetheless he shook his head at its scale – at the sudden, splintering possibility of having arrived – the boundaries pockmarked by guard towers, looming like spires out of joint over the cottages he'd first seen, narrow shadows at the tops of men and their guns, etched against the sky.

He turned back inside, scraping the soil from his nails, heart still pounding, and returned to his food. The hall they were in was one of two ugly buildings that sat parallel, the tiniest of alleys in between. After gaining permission from superior officers, the soldiers had taken him inside as dusk had settled, and he'd worked at ignoring the gawks from every direction, absorbing a pounding in his ears, walking along at their sides.

When they'd arrived within, the electric light had made him squint, and he'd noticed the smell straightaway: the stench of men, sweat mixed with wet soil from outside, startling after his days amid the woods – though nothing worse than what he'd known back home. He'd gotten used to it, and color had seemed to seep into view then – rich brown in the old wooden tables, faded brick at the sides, black streaks of dirt on the soldiers' boots.

After that, there'd been a screech of a whistle: too static for a train, blasting from loudspeakers instead. Movement had come an instant later, shuffling of feet, creaking of floorboards, and Atti had straightened, as a formation of guards had appeared from one of the larger structures across the way: a muffled barking of numbers to follow, with gaps between the voices, until the men had sat down to eat.

Hundreds of them.

No. Thousands.

Atti's eyes had darted fast, scanning every one, as he remained still, feeling a burn in his chest, thinking of where he'd been, how far he'd come, of Clara's warnings, and that slave-hunter firing on him. A lump had grown at the back of his throat – he'd squinted to be sure it all was real – wanting to shout with triumph and weep in despair, that he'd made it, but that he'd made it alone.

It was a sensation drowning out his breaths, and he'd shaken his head, letting the soldiers guide him further by the arm, showing him a seat in turn, until the minutes had piled up, one, then another, and another after that, and somehow he'd come to believe in his own prayers – still keeping tabs on the guards in the corners, minding the towers outside, avoiding the gaze of these strange curious Yanks, aware of every inch of space, every molecule of air, as he'd angled down toward a plate, and taken his first bite.

"You knew the way?"

Atti looked up and saw it was one of the soldiers talking directly to him.

"You got through your plantation's cameras?"

He nodded – then shifted again to his meal, his own gaze clouded, wet – blinking, until he'd simply nodded yet again.

"But how?" the soldier wanted to know. "How?"

"I'm not so sure," he whispered back. "Luck, I think. Luck."

And some of the men hooted, and clapped.

"I had help," he went on. "The U.R – friends on the way."

"Well we're glad," one of them said. "Welcome."

And this time when he looked up, he saw the soldier with the blonde hair – eyes bluer than the sky – peering back, and there was something in the transparency of his gaze, in the warmth that seemed to have found its way in, that made it so Atti had to stop himself from sharing more: of all the years behind him, how they'd beaten him, what they'd done – what they still could do – and he chewed his lip instead, not wanting them to see him sob.

In time, he learned that more questions were coming, and with the pain in his gaze hidden, his brow creased, his lips steadier than they'd been, and his hands held still, he found he was answering, no longer nodding, but speaking too, meeting more of their eyes, filling them in on what they wanted to know, what seemed every detail of his life – Rosewood Manor, field labor, the heat, overseers – not to mention his escape, and slave-hunting as well. For Atticus had never talked this way with non-indents before, and he was readier than he'd realized, starting out tight-lipped, steering clear of jokes or showing too much of himself, for fear that at any moment they'd change their minds, send him back across the border, scold him for saying something uncouth, but then, as the night wore on, he was even starting to relax. So that he found himself recounting not only the close call in the woods, but his time with the Worthing couple on the Underground Railroad – he kept their names to himself – and how it'd all begun when the Planter had moved to sell him.

The soldiers were shocked to learn the Planter had been Franklin Brooke himself. Atticus, in turn, could hardly comprehend it when they told him of Brooke's imprisonment, or the latest escalation it had sparked. That a noble could be an inmate! Though he also couldn't help but wonder: had he stayed, would his sale have been postponed?

He eventually asked if anyone had heard about the Rosewood rebellion; and though the soldiers didn't know of it, they assured him that slave revolts were sweeping the Confederacy. Atticus acknowledged what they described. But he had to accept that for now, Clara's whereabouts remained a mystery.

Finally, the evening slowed. The higher-rank officers had already told him he could spend the night, take an open bunk with the troops, before heading out come morning. They'd been apologetic about casting him off, but it was a war zone after all, and they couldn't just take him on without official approval. One sergeant, a heavyset man in his fifties, had mentioned that as a newly minted northerner, Atti would no doubt soon be joining up with the military himself – his best option for making a living, to boot. But for now it was agreed: he was untrained, unprepared, and undernourished from his escape. He could fetch a ride to a bus depot north of camp; they even gifted him an open-ended bus ticket, which would take him wherever he'd like to go.

It was here the conversation now turned.

Raj, sitting opposite, had spent much of the night in quiet, listening to the others' questions and the black southerner's responses. He leaned forward. "Where do you think you'll go?"

"Dunno," Atti answered. "I've never been anywhere before."

"You must have heard of places. There must be somewhere…"

Atti reached into the pocket of his new trousers. Before supper, he'd been shown a shower and given a fresh set of clothes, including a brand new pair of sneakers that felt like cushions on his heels. He retrieved the bus ticket. "They offered me this."

"They gave it free?!"

"I told 'em I'd pay with my savings." For a moment, the others just looked back. Then, sharing some true piece of himself at last, he winked. Gradually, they laughed. "People back home always talk of your cities. Are they far?"

"Never too far," came the reply. "That's where we're from. New York."

"Oh!" He was pleased to hear it. These two had saved his life. It was a fine thing to learn they were from just the sort of place he'd built up in his head.

"It's huge and intimidating and full of bastards," Raj went on. "But it's also the best spot in the world. Lots of people get started there. You wouldn't be alone."

Atticus nodded, and thought for a moment about asking their help, if they might know of a job somewhere. But he didn't see how two yeomen-types like this, stuck in the army as they were, would be able to offer aid. "How long since you've seen your city?" he wondered instead.

"Not long," Ted answered. "We were only drafted this summer. Still got a year to go."

"We're brand-new at it," Raj agreed.

"That slave-hunter – " Ted's voice had softened. "He was the first person I've ever shot."

Now Atti met his gaze in full. "He'd have sent me right back to Rosewood."

Ted nodded. "No regrets then," he answered. "No regrets."

But it was then the overhead lights flashed twice. And all at once, with barracks discipline, the soldiers were pushing themselves back from the table. "Just the call for bed," Raj explained.

"Your cottage is next door," Ted added in, pointing out the window. "Ours is farther off, down the other path." He paused. "Good luck, Atti."

"Yes good luck," echoed the others.

"Thank you," he replied, loud enough that they'd all hear. Then he got up too, and started off. He was glad for the company, he decided, but also exhausted. And reaching the door, he stepped out. The breeze had grown sharper, the stars making themselves known. He shuffled down a slight hill, as Ted had directed, and soon he was inside once more, nodding to a pair of guards at the cottage's door, smelling the evergreen nearby, hearing the same bubbling brook he'd found earlier that day. The crackle of possibility seemed again to blow past the branches, and as he slid into his assigned bunk, Atti exhaled. Gradually, his mind eased, his body too, thoughts of Rosewood ceding to dreams of something new: jumbled images, really, yanking him forward – of fast-paced shouts and busy corners, of breezes blanketed with whispers of war, an empire splintered, a new world too. Messages he couldn't yet decipher, he decided. Paths yet obscured. But all of it, somehow, a step towards home.

CHAPTER 33

The bus to New York contained the most remarkable chair Atti had ever encountered. Its back went higher than his head; its Union blue cushions conformed to his whole body. There were padded armrests on either side, and a lever at the bottom that allowed him to recline until he was nearly horizontal. It even included a belt for safety. It was as plush as any Planter's master-bedroom back home.

He breathed deep, and clutched the new card in his pocket. At the depot, they'd handed it over, explaining it was worth five thousand dollars. The officer had said it would be accepted at all stores, and Atti was so thrilled he'd almost wept. Apparently, the army had cash to spare for situations just such as this.

He'd waited anxiously for the bus to pull in, resting on a bench, only to stand back up a minute later as it'd arrived. Its silver side panels were gleaming, with fine tinted windows stretching from front to rear. What's more: the driver was black.

Atticus had stared, knowing that driving a bus wasn't an esteemed job, maybe not even a desirable one, but reeling nonetheless. He'd stared so long he'd gotten admonished. "Come on, man," the driver had said – though he'd done so with a grin. "What're you waiting on?"

Atti had handed over his ticket. "New York please."

"Take a seat where you want."

Atti had nabbed a spot by the window.

He was stunned at how fast they could go on these vast Yankee roads. It was enough to make him forget – or at least to ignore – the other passengers on the bus, white and black both, as they miraculously ignored him in turn: not only slipped from bondage, it suddenly seemed, but sitting in public without harassment. The world buzzed by, and if he looked too closely, it hurt his head, his eyes unable to catch up with the blur. Each minute, there were new sights – forested medians, countless buildings, some old brick or wooden houses like those in the Confederacy, but others mounted of fine gray steel, strong and rectangular, flanked by glowing signs; there were impossibly tall poles too, and thick wires at the roadside, and an incomprehensible number of cars. Only the sky seemed the same.

Eventually, there were smokestacks and tangled up metal structures as well, factories jammed thick with steam and haze; there were sharp bright colors on warehouse walls, and rows of crammed-together houses glinting in the lowering sun, narrow alleys among them, cramped corners overtaken by streetlamps and municipal storage vans parked all atop one another. There were also churches in between, Atti observed, steeples stretching high, alms-boxes languishing in front. The smell of petroleum was thick, seeping into the bus; the clatter of the other cars was constant.

Still, none of it was anything compared to what came last. There on the horizon, reaching out like an outstretched finger of God, the next sight seemed a painting at first, the imaginings of some crazed artist depicting another world entirely. Here were buildings twirling to the sky – pins made of stone and steel – lights like competitors to the sun. It was New York City itself, flanked by rivers like a sifting blanket holding it all in, and Atti found that his face was so close to the window that the glass grew fogged, and he had to wipe it clear with his sleeve.

To enter Manhattan, the bus sped through a dimly lit tunnel so fast and terrifying that Atticus couldn't help but laugh out loud. Some of the other passengers looked over, but he didn't mind. And when they finally re-emerged, he bent back his head as far as it would go, in order to see up in full. The buildings were so massive, he could no longer catch their tops. At street level, meantime, cars and crowds were everywhere, until as the bus finally parked, and he exited with the rest, Atti had to pause and gather himself.

The first thing he noticed was the air.

It was as if he'd stuck his face into the exhaust pipe of a cotton-picking module and couldn't get out. It made him gag, and cough, and eventually resign himself to the smells and smoke. He spun around then, making himself dizzy, figuring out where to go first, bumped and jostled by what seemed a million passersby.

First, he needed a meal. Then, a place to stay. From there, a pathway to work.

To think – just a day ago he'd been chased, nearly caught, by a slave-hunter in the woods of Virginia. Now that sham of a man was dead, and here was Atti standing firm, at the epicenter of the free world. The bus driver had pointed him toward a small door across the street, and he went there now, pushing through the throbbing streets. All around were faces as dark as his – not everyone, to be sure, yet not so few as to be dismissed – walking about unchecked, unstopped; and Atti blinked, disbelieving – still half-expecting them all to be halted, shouted down, told to show their papers, himself most of all – until he'd reached the building ahead.

Overtop, a small sign declared it a "Deli," alongside posters urging donations for the soldiers on the front, and rationing for the homeland. Tiny speakers rattled from window sills nearby, playing canned music Atticus didn't recognize. Blackout shades were rolled up and dusty – hints of fears that'd not yet been realized – the same types they had in tiny town squares back in Virginia; newsstands were crowded with endless periodicals, blaring eager headlines about the war – pride in what was, Atticus thought, rather than angst over what could be – the dignity of a people with a purpose. His eyes settled on the door front that awaited.

Its framework was a marvel of stone, glinting and gray, a tribute to U.S. modernity – focused not on frills or flourishes like buildings of old, but buoyed by the same purpose as the people. And skipping forward among the concrete and commotion, Atti entered through the heavy brass door, suppressing a rush that passed through him like a current, absorbing the echoes of hurried customers – some as black as he – on their way to meetings, to work, to making the world a purer place.

A whole counter of waiters looked ready for battle, standing beneath a glowing menu with a bottomless list of entries, and he followed the line to the register, shouting out when it was his time: a request for a ham sandwich, since the rest of the menu made no sense – *pastrami, Cajun turkey, veggie wrap* – cloaking his nerves as he handed over the card the army had provided. A fellow swiped it through a machine without a word, before passing it back. Apparently, the sandwich was now paid for.

Atticus stepped back out onto the sidewalk while he ate. As he went, he had to deliver apologies every few feet for bumping into someone – poised for the Confederate Guard to appear every time he did. It was a miracle he wasn't hit by one of the cars. Moving down darkening streets, he studied every nook he could find, every shadow, even gutters. Thirty blocks north, a few more east, he snaked past crooked awnings and cloudy lamps, moving fast and slow, peering every which way. The crackle of merchants greeted him; more overwrought buildings shone overhead; this strange northern world still glowed bright in the late sun. He spotted black laborers working on a new army office across the way, hoisting a beam, measuring granite blocks;

scattered beggars too, every color there was; handsome copper statues on nearly every corner, honoring U.S. leaders. Until at last it all was too much, and knowing he'd better lie down or he would collapse where he stood, Atticus spotted a hotel.

He noticed it wasn't daylight at all anymore. Dusk had arrived, and with it a realization: the city lights were so constant, they masked nighttime itself. It was as if the North had conquered God. Atticus decided a job-search could wait for morning; with the arrival of a new day, he'd purchase a newspaper. He'd heard of yeomen in the Confederacy seeking employment that way. Maybe that's how it worked here too.

The awning ahead declared, "The Lincoln Hotel." Probably named for Abraham, Atti thought, and accepting the good omen, he hurried right in. The lobby was grander even than the Planter's house at Rosewood. The ceiling was one huge dome; stone rosettes bordered massive arched windows; the air was scented with flowers in giant urns on pedestals. There were receptionists shuffling papers, and rich red carpets directed guests in all directions. At a counter at the room's edge, a young white man in a black civilian suit looked up.

"'Evenin'," Atti began, swallowing his angst, half-prepared to be tossed out just for making eye contact. "A room for the night, please. Or for the week I suppose."

The man looked casually down at a screen. "We have several still available. They've all got a king-sized bed. Will that do?"

Atti nodded. He had no idea what the fellow was talking about.

"And how will you be paying?"

He pulled the new card from his pocket.

"Excellent sir. And thank you for your service." And though Atti didn't really understand this either, the card was swiped through a machine, as it had been at the food shop, and handed right back, along with another the same size, a "key card," the man said, for accessing the room upstairs.

With directions in hand, Atticus moved toward a set of elevators and waited to follow a group inside, since he wasn't sure how to operate the thing himself. There were mirrors on all sides, and he lowered his head to avoid vertigo as the doors closed. A woman asked him "which button," and he said "twelve," pretending to be as unfazed as everyone else. Finally, a few seconds later, he was exiting, walking down a new carpeted hall and – after a series of failed attempts – entering his room.

• • •

Sun was barreling through the hotel window when he opened his eyes. His face was jammed on its side, and he could tell he'd barely moved, one arm pinned stiff beneath his belly, the other folded behind his back. He was lying atop a gargantuan bed, and his sneakers were still on. Blinking, he caught sight of the city outside, and as he slowly sat up, it made him feel as though he were slipping into a dream rather than leaving one.

In time, Atticus rubbed his face and shuffled from the bed to the bathroom, where he could hardly believe the enormity of the tub, or the way the white tiles shone as bright as precious gems. Back in the main room, he returned to the bed and sat on its edge, taking in a television screen on the far wall. He'd only watched TV once in his life. It'd been years before, when he'd accompanied an overseer into downtown Crotelle to pick up power tools for the plantation; at the general store, they'd learned of a delivery delay, and the overseer had left for the post office, telling Atti to stay put. Fiddling with his thumbs, he'd spotted a corner pub and a crowd watching a football contest, and shuffling over, had peered over their shoulders. Everyone had been so caught up in the game they hadn't bothered kicking him away, and for nearly an hour, he'd stood in place, sucked in by the colors and precision of images, and the way the screen appeared to capture entire men within its frame.

It had been a taste of freedom.

Now, Atti grabbed the black remote control from the nightstand. Finding the power-button, he squinted as the screen flashed on. A young white woman instantly appeared. She was speaking directly to the camera, with rigid yellow hair, and teeth so bright they seemed plastic. Quickly, however, he lost interest in what she looked like.

She was describing a hearing to take place that very day, and the cameras cut to a large, antique hall, filled with empty wooden pews and an ornate podium at the front. The news anchor said this was where the U.S. Congress would continue hearing testimony on the integration of freed slaves into society. She noted the proceedings had already captivated millions of viewers, boosted by the tale of a slave heroically rescued from the Confederacy by skilled northern agents – during that summer's raid at the Brooke plantation, Rosewood Manor.

Then the photograph appeared.

Atti blinked, and stood from the bed. His brain felt slower than usual. His thoughts were underwater.

For that was a photo of Clara.

She was wearing a civilian suit like those of the women on the streets outside, sleek and gray, with a man's jacket on top. She had a hard gaze, and her hair was done in a new style. But it was her. The photo dissolved, and she was being shown now in a film clip walking down the center of the large hall – only this time the pews were jammed with spectators. Her stride was strong.

His heart beat nearly through his chest. By God, she appeared just inches away on the screen, but how in hell had it happened? Had she escaped the Confederate Guard and dodged arrest? The television had said she'd been rescued by U.S. agents – perhaps they'd raided a prison?

Atticus studied the footage. She looked well-fed, her shoulders pulled back, her skin clear. She was alive. Not just alive, but secure – thriving – clearly prominent. Like him, she was somehow in the North. She was testifying for the U.S. government. But there was something else too.

Her stomach.

She had a small bump.

His pulse quickened even more, and he tried to collect his thoughts, to understand what he was seeing. The voice on the screen was saying now that Clara Brooke had argued eloquently in her testimony the day prior for "gradualism" – step-by-step progress for former slaves, in place of full citizenship rights all at once.

Perhaps he'd misheard. Clara would never argue for gradual emancipation. Obviously some piece of this was getting lost in translation, a cultural clash between him and the United States that he didn't yet grasp. It wasn't worth dwelling on, anyway. The main point was if he could locate that Congressional Hall, he'd find her.

He was jarred from his reverie by a banging on the door.

Atticus glanced over, shutting off the TV. Whoever was out there knocked again, and this time didn't stop. Cautiously, he placed down the remote, and walked over.

As he opened the door, he was confronted by three U.S. soldiers in the hall.

They were standing in loose formation: one in front, the other two making a triangle. All three were white men, and all were wearing the dark blue uniforms that Atti now recognized. Each boasted a holstered handgun at his side. Their expressions were serious.

The one in the middle looked right at him. "Mr. Brooke?" His voice was calm.

Atticus nodded.

"You were brought by military transport to New York yesterday afternoon?"

"I took a bus," he answered. "Your men gave me a ticket, though."

The young soldier's brown eyes were stern. "You didn't report to Enlistment Services when you arrived."

"No one told me I was supposed to." Atti thought back to the military camp. "I really don't think I heard that from anyone," he repeated, though it was true some of the soldiers had referred to his enlisting.

"It was assumed you understood. Your information was communicated to our offices in New York. Your arrival was confirmed by your debit card."

Atticus tried to process it all.

"Mr. Brooke, as a registered unemployed resident of the United States, you've been selected for full service. This is your notice of conscription. Effective today."

One of the other two soldiers shifted in back. "Would've been yesterday," he muttered, "if you'd signed up like you were supposed to."

Atticus rubbed his eyes. How would he find Clara if he went with these men? "How long will I be gone?" he asked.

"Your enlistment will be five years."

He took a step backwards.

"Standard for African heritage. That's the law." A shrug. "After all, Mr. Brooke, it's more your cause than anyone else's."

Atticus recalled the soldiers he'd met a day before. They'd been drafted for only a year's time. Then again, none of them had been black. "Why didn't they just keep me down at the border camp if I was to be drafted?"

"They've got enough going on, Mr. Brooke. Bureaucracy's beneath them." The soldier checked his watch. "You got luggage or no?"

He shook his head. This city, this dream, was about to vanish, he realized. The injustice he'd borne all his life was intact. Some voice within him told him what he'd already suspected – that it knew no border, only color – that it'd followed him straight up from Virginia. That none of this had been his to begin with.

He wondered if there was some way out. He'd escaped the plantation. Couldn't he slip past three soldiers in a hotel?

But the lead one read his mind. "Don't think about running, Mr. Brooke. It's not jail – it's the military. Everyone's serving these days. You included."

• • •

The bus waiting outside was the exact same model as the one Atti had ridden the day before. But as he stepped on, he saw that the passengers inside were all like him: young, black, and male. Some glanced up as he boarded; most kept staring out the window. A few were asleep. Several were wearing handcuffs.

Was this the United States? Had he come all that way for this?

Bitterness swelled. Running from one *master* only to serve another! The kindness he'd received the previous day seemed suddenly empty.

He felt a shove. "Find a seat!" a soldier ordered.

Atti took a short step forward. He thought back to the snippets he'd heard on the television. Had Clara been pressured by the same hypocrisy he saw here? By the same types elbowing him onto this bus, forcing what they wanted, exchanging emancipation for exploitation? Was that what was behind her alleged advocacy for gradualism?

"Sit down, Brooke!" the soldier shouted now. "No one wants to wait for your tired southern ass!"

Atti looked over his shoulder, examining this young white private doing all the yelling. He was a kid, with mousy hair and big ears. The shoulder pads in his jacket looked oversized on his narrow frame, and Atticus was certain he'd never make it as an overseer back at Rosewood: his frenzied eyes betrayed his fear, seeking respect he didn't even grant himself. He looked afraid to use his own gun. Not that it mattered. This nasty little northerner was more than himself. Atti grasped that, even if the kid didn't.

Slowly now, he made his way down the aisle until he found an open seat, next to a burly man about forty. "This one free?"

"More than you or I," he said with a sad chuckle, and Atticus sat down. "Get comfortable. Picking up draft-dodgers like you all over the city."

Atti offered thanks. "I just got here last evening. From Virginia."

The man turned.

"Name's Atti Brooke."

"I'm Bill Rollins – friends just say Rollins. You say you were just down there?"

"Sure did. Ran from the Confederacy. Got here, now I'm drafted."

Rollins was still taking him in. "I'm sorry for it. Used to be a runaway could get some peace without enlisting, at least for a little while. Now, these goons are nabbing everyone they can. Folks seem to think we might even beat those Rebs, so the draft-board's been cracking down. I figured they'd let me out since I served twice already. I figured wrong. Only a year since my last stint."

"And your first go-round was five years?"

"I'm black, aren't I?" He gave a grunt, and closed his eyes. "Don't fret, son. We'll work at our own rights once our southern brothers are free. You know it better than me."

"You're a born northerner?"

"As much as anyone. My mother, God rest her, was a runaway. Made it all the way from Alabama. I grew up on stories of the South." He paused. "It's true we got nothing – but you got less."

Atti faced frontward.

"Get some rest, friend." Rollins leaned against the window and folded his arms. "We've got a long ride. Use it."

Atti nodded, but he wasn't tired.

CHAPTER 34

The walls of the prison cell – for that's what it was, she'd decided – were as unforgiving as ever. Clara squinted straight ahead. From outside, the last of the day's sun reflected back in her eyes, making them sting. She sat on a stiff aluminum chair, at the edge of a narrow table, tapping her fingers, steadying her gaze, unable to find solace in the emptiness before her, or relief from the guilt at all she'd uttered for the cameras – bowing down as she had, surrendering to her captors just the way they'd asked.

During the van ride to Congressional Hall, she'd grown ever more nauseous, nerves jostling, palms as wet as rotted cotton, cooped up at least two hours, maybe three, watching bland, flat countryside whir relentlessly past: yellowing fields, stubborn and sterile; hints of frost; narrow swaths of maples beneath the tight northern sky. She'd been told they were headed east, toward Manhattan, its southernmost tip. No radio. No conversation. Only silence on the way.

At last they'd arrived. There'd been shops and cafés, boulevards wide and gleaming; men in Union-blue, women laughing on the corners – enough at least that Clara had been distracted – untold throngs, and towering shadows overhead, pointed clocktowers cutting against the sun, soaring arcades, walls smooth as glass. The Hall that awaited had been the grandest of all.

Inside, it was more palazzo than exhibit of Yankee restraint: endless cornices and panels of marble, windows as tall as trees, unending paintings and busts of Yankee governors. They'd given her a change of clothes, and a woman did her hair and put makeup on her face, and then they'd led her up the stairs while the cameras had watched. She'd stood straighter as she went, eventually moving down the aisle, as the whole place murmured, then onto the dais, telling herself that the clothes were the same dress uniform as all the rest had on, the same brass cuff links, gleaming shoes, kerchief stuffed in her pocket. She'd found her chair, folded her hands, taking in that inner sanctum, government types and journalists only, all of them white, same as in the Southland, their awful chattering in its very own staccato, the entire Union nation accelerating along beneath them.

A pudgy fellow had moved to the podium then, a comb-over hairdo dyed black, standing beneath a row of bright flags, lifting his arms as he began the session in full. *"Fellow patriots! Leaders of the United States!"* His tinny voice had ricocheted off the back wall, while the clocktower bells clanged outside, and every conversation had funneled into one: gaggles of Union bigwigs applauding, as he'd bowed and grinned ear-to-ear. *"Governor Kennedy IV presiding! Let's welcome our guest, straight from the belly of the beast, a model for us all. Grit, defiance, patience personified! Ms. Clara Brooke of Rosewood Manor, Virginia, CSA!"*

Her pulse had quickened as she'd stood, and the cheering that'd been raucous went hushed. She'd raised her head, rigid as a rifle at present-arms. She'd thanked them for having her, and the microphone had crackled as she'd exhaled. If silence could somehow grow quieter, she was sure that it had.

If only she'd done something with it.

"War is hell." That was how she'd started. "One of your generals once said so." Those were the words she'd been given, the ones they'd written on her behalf – in exchange for pledges

of liberty at last. "It was true then, and it's true today. It's why we must work so hard, you and me! For what's freedom without peace? That's why we must seek a new balance, away from all the blood." The politicians had pounded their fists, nodding earnestly, and she'd known in that moment, from their postures and their stares, that they were desperate.

It was the desperation that had her doing their bidding – that made her believe them – fearing their punishment, that they meant what they said: no different from her masters of old, promising prison, dangling promise, forcing her with no more than their cowardly gazes. So that she'd re-doubled her focus, undoing her pride, ducking her memories: fighting off a flash of the uprising – of Atticus, she realized – telling them what they wanted to hear, when she could have said anything at all.

"*My fellow Americans* – " and with that they'd roared with swift, sudden, hysterical approval, enough that she'd had to wait – "*We indents require only freedom, nothing more. We know stability is at stake; that citizenship is a privilege to be gradually bestowed.*" Never a mention of schools or voting booths; no call to action; not even a word for the soldiers who'd lain down their lives in anguish and pride and regret. "*We ask only this,*" and they'd nodded with vigor, as she'd spewed their nonsense back at them. "*Only the same birthright as you – God-given air to breathe, that's all!*" Some of the men had stood then, even stamping their feet, and she'd wanted to spit. "*We know what's reasonable. Gradual rights when their time has come!*" From there, the cheers had grown, hurrahs and huzzahs, the thrill of those who told themselves their puppet was their hero; that such gratitude was their due; that their future would be as fine a plaything as their present.

Now, as she recalled it, Clara felt a lurch in his stomach, and a tightening in her throat. Her fingers trembled, and she flattened them against her thighs, stretching, finding a speck on the floor to stare at. She was going to be sick, it was only a question of when – and as it came upon her, she hurried to the silver basin in the corner and let herself be.

It wasn't just the speech that'd done it of course. It wasn't even the expectation that she somehow would have to repeat all of it again, in the days and weeks and committee hearings to come. It was a greater truth still.

She was carrying Atti's child.

Now, she was sure of it. Her new belly was still barely noticeable, but there was no denying the truth. She wiped her lips with the back of her wrist. She let loose a wobbly breath. Finally, she exhaled.

She'd been cocky indeed – quick in taking command, bragging of her abilities, insisting a new world would follow. If she'd known then, back at Rosewood, that she was with child, would she have acted? Would caution have taken the place of fury? Yet the answer was there in her deeds – in a deeper charge, a deeper demand – one that'd been with her then, that was here with her now, that would remain even when the baby arrived.

And finally, she was letting herself imagine it anew – the world she still sought – the one she still had to believe was there. She pictured a caress on a baby's warm skin, a kiss atop its brow. She could envision Atti's broad smile too, the tiny infant in his fine arms, and the life they might forge together, garden vegetables bright and crowded in summer, and trees turned rusty in fall; errands in town, and laughter at supper; his wide, free gaze every time he suggested an evening stroll. The three of them as one, alive and intact, building a home in crisp free air.

Would Atticus reclaim his old spirit then, in this country he'd longed for? Refusing to be flattened as she had been, by the knowledge that a land of promise and freedom still lacked both? Had he been flattened already?

What if he'd never even made it at all?

CHAPTER 35

On a dreary Wednesday afternoon, the winter's first foray below freezing, Kevin Donleau was ambling about his ancestral mansion, looking for tasks that could prove diverting. Already, he'd mended some loose shelves in the second story library, mopped the century-old blue tiles of the kitchen floor, dusted antique tin soldiers he didn't have the heart to throw away.

It was still only two o'clock.

In the weeks since the government's crackdown in Richmond, he'd been worrying incessantly – about Liza and her involvement in the Resistance, about Liza and himself. Still, he'd kept quiet. After all, his earlier objections had only driven her away. It hadn't kept her from risk. And these days, she had not only the Guard to worry about – there was also the problem of her missing father.

They hadn't yet heard from General Brooke, and rumors swirled he'd been taken prisoner by the U.S. Normally, Kevin would have discounted these as gossip, but even Liza seemed uninformed. The television insisted he was taking part in intense negotiations.

Pacing the old living room, brushing clean the marble mantle, he shifted his view to the windows behind him, a smeared vista of sleet and rain. In truth, uncertainty gripped the whole country, and General Brooke's absence had only made it worse, spurred on by U.S. mischief at the border – more shelling, people said, talk of raids and harassment – and the constant stories of indent unrest. The Confederacy's contradictions were becoming harder to ignore.

He plopped down in an armchair, and took in the drenched eastern fields, when the doorbell chimed. There'd been increased reports of conscription, but Kevin had assumed his noble status would protect him. Now he wondered if he'd been wrong, and he pictured a posse of Confederate Guard agents outside, armed with military orders, ready to take his information with relish. Letting his imagination run wild, he hurried to the door. He'd hated army service after university, filled with drills, marked by empty nights on the base without enough books.

He unlocked the bolt – installed after the Rosewood Uprising – and opened up. But rather than Confederate Guard, he saw Liza instead, her dark hair sopping from the rain. Her eyes were wet too – from the storm, or had she been crying? She was out of breath. "Can I come in?" Yet already she was through the doorframe, without awaiting a response. "Can I trust you?"

"What sort of question is that?"

"I'm sorry." She shook her head. "Of course I know that I can." Her gaze was wild, desperate, and Kevin reached out, gripping her shoulders, hoping to calm her.

"What are you talking about, Liza? What's happened?"

For a moment, she let herself be embraced; then quickly, she took a step back. "There's someone I've just met." Her words came out rapid, sliced together. "Only I'm terrified. The Guard is everywhere. She has to go someplace. She can't stay."

"Who?"

"It's why I haven't been around so much. After I joined the U.R., I was using our house line, talking with contacts to the north. I had to stop. They worried it would get tapped by the Guard – with my father gone, we've lost privilege and protection. After that, I didn't hear anything more – not 'til today. I was upstairs when I saw her – she was suddenly running up from the culvert at the roadside. She's so frail. Her eyes were swollen from not sleeping – she'd been hiding there waiting for me, spotting me through the window. She's made it all the way from the Carolina border. Contacts near Danville told her I was in the network." Liza caught her breath. "Her name is Rebecca."

"By God." Kevin's heart raced with new fear. He couldn't process the immensity of what he was hearing.

"I had no choice." Her gaze locked on his. "You said I can trust you, Kevin." And with that, without another word, Liza turned back, beckoning out to the rain. A thin black girl, no more than twelve, wearing a drenched yellow dress that Kevin recognized from Liza's own wardrobe, darted out from beside the porch stairs. She hurried to the top, sheltering from the chill of the storm. There she stood, trembling with terror and cold. Like a ghost, he suddenly thought. Skinnier than seemed possible, dark eyes gone dull, posture stooped.

What sort of a place could do such a thing?

What sort of a land? What people?

Except even as such notions rushed upon him, Kevin stopped them where they landed – for there could be none of that, he told himself. Not right now. Not when there was work to be done. He extended his hand. "Kevin Donleau," he said, quite formally, not knowing what else to do.

"Rebecca."

"You were unseen?"

She nodded. Her hollowed-out eyes traced his face.

"Then come inside," and it was as if he was hearing his own words before he'd even forged them, unsure if he was doing this for Liza, or for this girl, or for himself. "I'll get you a towel. We can find some new clothes too."

The enslaved girl took a tentative step forward.

"Come in, come in."

He backed inside then, hurrying around the corner while they waited, fetching a towel from the linen closet, beginning the hunt for something his mother might've left behind - flinging aside shirts in the closets, racing through the dresser, finally coming upon an old drawer of sweaters that looked small enough.

Until suddenly, Liza was beside him, and he turned. She was very close.

For a moment, Kevin forgot everything, seeing only her, filled with a warmth he hadn't been expecting. In silence, she leaned up, kissing him softly, all too briefly, on the lips. He closed his eyes, keeping them shut an extra moment as she pulled away.

"I'm glad you care as I do," she said quietly, her face still nearly touching his.

"I can't say that for sure."

"You're helping." Already, she was stepping back. "That's what matters."

"You won't stay?"

"They'll notice," and she was moving back down the hall. "Our family's being watched. They say it's for protection - in case the Yanks reach out for a deal with my father gone. But I think they suspect something - about my trips to Richmond - about my phone calls."

Blinking, trying to slow down time, Kevin reached out his hand, but she was off. He heard her say goodbye to Rebecca; then he heard the front door closing once more. What had he done, agreeing to this? But he found himself turning back to the closet, aware of the indent shivering out in the hall, uncovering a pair of faded pants from his old school uniform, folding them alongside the sweater. They'd look ridiculous, but they just might fit; if nothing else, they'd be dry.

• • •

By the time Liza returned from the Donleau Plantation, the sleet had colonized the meadows with ice, and was hammering Rosewood so loudly the whole manor sounded like a stream of static. Reaching the porch, she brushed the wet from her face, noting the edges of her skirt had frozen in place, as brittle as shards of glass – when a familiar voice reached her from the door's other side.

Her throat tightened. She hadn't seen Dale since he'd sent her fleeing in Richmond, and she looked up, surprised by a flush of guilt over where she'd just been – whether because of the runaway, or that briefest of kisses, she wasn't wholly sure. The door swung open.

Out he came, in full Confederate regalia, with golden tassels atop his shoulders and a powder blue jacket underneath. His cap was under his arm, just the way he liked; his thick hair was down past his ears. He looked dashing as always, though after seeing him switch sides so effortlessly the last time they'd been together, she found it harder than ever to get past the uniform. "Well hi there, darlin'," and he knelt over and kissed her frigid hand.

"Sorry I'm such a fright – this weather!" She was trying to sound normal; the result was as if she were performing lines.

"Well, I'm sorry too." He stood back up straight. "Sorry to surprise you like this. Your poor mother didn't know where you'd gone."

"I was on a walk."

He raised his eyebrows. "In the sleet?"

"I just – " Feeling ridiculous, she pushed her lie. "I wanted some space, and I hoped the ice would feel good after all those months of heat. Come in. I'll order us tea." How absurd, she suddenly thought, to be served by one slave even as she worked to save another.

But Dale blocked her. "Liza, I can't protect you much longer." His voice was quieter than before. "Don't make it harder by keeping everything to yourself."

"I'm not."

"What were you really doing out there?"

She stared back. She knew she should trust him – of course she should! – but he was always so convincing, whichever side he was playing, and it made her feel increasingly out of sorts.

"Whatever it is, you're putting yourself at risk. You must realize your name was mentioned – as was mine, darlin' – by the Resisters we arrested in Richmond. We're lucky my cover worked; their testimony was thrown out as an attempt at distraction. But now you've come up again. The Guard's captured some runaways. Under questioning, they've said you're part of the U.R."

"That's absurd."

"You don't have to lie to me, darling." He'd winced when she'd said so. "Just listen: my commanders don't believe them. They think the indents made it up, trying to throw them off the real scent. It's impossible for anyone to grasp the Brooke family could ever be involved in proper insurgency. Only I'm worried. What if I wasn't around to help? What if someone else had come by today?"

Wordlessly, she made her way forward, finding her way to a window seat by the door, not minding that when she sat, the cushion seeped wet.

He followed, standing over her. "I care about you, Liza. I could protect you better if you were with me, you know. If we were together."

She tried to make sense of the words. It was impossible that Dale could mean what it sounded like. In the Confederacy, a nobleman and lady could never simply "be together." Short of marriage, there was no such thing as a public relationship.

"You know it's the only way for someone of my rank, and a blue blood like you, to be proper." He took a deep breath.

"Say it aloud," she demanded. "Say what you mean."

"I'm talking about getting engaged. That's what I mean. A wedding."

"You want to be married so you can protect me?" Liza's eyes flitted across his. She cared for Dale. She admired his poise, and adored his charm, and she couldn't help but be impressed by the way he grabbed ahold of life. But even with all that, why did he always surprise her? It was that which made him magnetic, but also meant she never truly relaxed when he was near.

Looking at the uniform yet again, it was obvious how comfortable he seemed in it. And it occurred to her now, as it should've long ago, it was as though he enjoyed both sides – the power of each – the way people listened to him, extolling him wherever he was. It was the adventure of it all that swept him up, so that she wondered now if he even knew what he wanted most.

"It's not just to protect you, my darling." He was taking her hand. "Liza, I swear, I love you. I'm certain I have for some time."

She looked away, and bit her lip. "I don't know."

"What don't you know?"

She watched the water tumbling from the gutters outside, and suddenly she could see Kevin's face in her mind, his blue eyes and warm smile, his words so cautious, his expression honest and true. She turned back. "I don't know if I can live with the deception."

"This?" He glanced at the uniform. "Come now. You do just the same. I've told you."

"But it's not the same."

"No? The perfect southern belle?"

"I just need time, Dale. Please."

He seemed ready to say more, but the door opened.

It was her mother. "Hello dear." She faced Dale. "I saw you two talking, and I hate to interrupt – but I wanted to let you know, Captain Birch: it looks as though some of your men have come up the drive. They're milling about, looking rather aimless I must say."

"Mrs. Brooke, I'm so sorry they've turned you into a messenger."

"Not at all. It's my pleasure to help the Guard."

"And ours to serve. Naturally, our alert's been up ever since the uprising. We're in the area – we've some new folks to question – reports of runaways about. I've told them to meet me here."

Cathryn was nodding. "Of course. Anything we can do?"

"I don't believe so – the men would have mentioned it." Dale bowed to them both, before turning back to Liza. "I'll check in soon, Miss Brooke. 'Til then," and he stepped back into the storm.

CHAPTER 36

General Franklin Brooke had never been so hungry in his life.

His captors fed him twice a day – and only ever Spam. All that time proclaiming their own virtue, and no attention to the virtues of life itself. Staring now at his plate, he pictured buttered sausage in its stead; closing his eyes, he lifted a forkful, leaning against the cinderblock behind him, chewing determinedly. He was on a stone floor – his right hip stinging, both legs asleep. But his only other option was the bed, and he'd spent too many hours in that already.

The room was dismal. During the day, it boiled from the blasting radiators. At night, it got drafty and buzzed with incessant fluorescent light. The walls were gray. The cot had neither pillow nor blanket. It was enough that the questioning had even come to be a spate of relief: about transport schedules, indent classifications, Confederate Guard, Resistance.

He'd have to retire upon his return home. He knew that. He'd already answered too much, melting under their mix of serums, pain, and threats to his family. No doubt his fellow Confederates would pretend to honor his service – all the while hating him for his failure. Let the next generation try again, then. In the meanwhile it would be enough to simply get back to views from the Rosewood porticoes. Back to the taste of ham and grits, the crackle from the fire, the feel of Cathryn's caress in his hair, and the sound of Liza's laugh at supper.

Franklin let loose a lengthy sigh, praying God would keep his family safe in the meantime, and he looked out the tiny window above the bed. He was somewhere in Pennsylvania, one of the guards had slipped, but all he could see were fallow winter fields, stretching to the horizon. Confederates would have turned them green, he thought, never allowing land like this to go to waste, never ignoring the offerings of God. But the North was a land of industry, where fields were disregarded. Here, the grass turned brown.

Franklin paused in his chewing.

There was a new set of footsteps now. Heavy, and unfamiliar – and he made himself stand, as the door was unlatched. A brawny man in dark blue military dress stood in the hall: thick hair and a fine jaw. Stronger than most Yanks, Franklin decided.

"Brooke," the fellow said, ruining the vowels, hands clasped round a manila folder. "Follow."

He did as he was told, flanked now by a pair of helmeted lugs with rifles – into an empty room with a black lacquer table and a hard metal chair. So it was to be physical pain then. On any given morning, he never knew which medieval tactic they'd choose. The chair had an electric current running through its frame. It was attached to a lie detector, and it gave Franklin a terrible shock whenever he strayed from the truth, shattering any semblance of honor, attaching humiliation to falsehood.

A moment later, after they'd strapped him in, the major appeared, the one who seemed to run this whole place, retrieving a pair of reading glasses, scratching the back of his hair, while the guards waited unnecessarily at the door. He took the folder – the younger man clicked his heels on the way out – and started perusing the papers as if he hadn't seen them before. "Good morning, General," he said calmly.

Franklin didn't respond.

"Let's get to it then." The Yank sat down in a chair opposite. "Just to put it in the record" – it was clear they were being recorded – "this is Major Sam Cooperman speaking, Primary Intelligence, here with Confederate General Franklin Brooke."

Franklin braced himself. He despised such men, building their lives around deceit. At least back home, the Guard's Intel unit existed not for conquest, for the sake of a nation's defense.

"Listen, Franklin." Cooperman's voice was ice. "You've said you made this trip to pursue peace negotiations. Are we really to believe that?"

"Why else would I come?" The machine didn't zap him, and Franklin exhaled. It was getting to the point where he couldn't even be secure in his own honesty, until after he'd gained the contraption's approval.

"Under such a settlement, what plans would be pursued regarding the slaves?"

"Indents."

"Let's call them what they are, General."

Franklin shrugged. Shifting in the chair, he worked to make sure he got this one right. "You're referring to my indents personally, or those of the nation as a whole?"

"Both."

"We no longer own their bodies, as you know, only their labor. In theory, over time, they'll pay off their debt to the owners."

"How?"

"Through their production efforts."

"And how long will that take?"

"It could be some time."

"But you believe it'll happen?"

Franklin paused. He didn't want to feel the charge. Still – it was better than the serums, he told himself. At least with the chair, he had some agency. "I do."

The electricity reacted instantly. He felt as though his skin was on fire – every muscle pulsating against his will. He sputtered and squeaked and felt the sweat pooling in every crevice he had. Then, quick as it'd come, the current subsided. Franklin grew still.

"You've lied," Cooperman sighed. "Why?"

"I was sharing my official position, not my personal belief." He readied himself for another current, but none came.

"Did your government ever consider true emancipation?"

Franklin shook his head. "The indents have greater numbers than they know."

"And why would that be a problem?"

"You know the answer to that."

"Tell me anyway."

"If the slaves are given rights, they'll use them for revenge."

"So you delay their freedom."

"Naturally."

"And it's safe to say you'll continue delaying it? If the indents were ever let off the plantations, they wouldn't just gain full citizenship, would they? Voting for example?"

"Our yeomen don't even have those rights." Franklin raised his head. "You could learn from us, you know. The way your soldiers talk to their superiors – I hear them in the hall – there's a lack of respect."

"Answer my question: if the indents left the plantations, would your government ensure their progress was gradual?"

"I just told you that."

Cooperman reached to a shelf beside the table for a water bottle. He didn't offer one to Franklin. "Would the Confederacy ever agree to restoration of Union?"

Franklin snorted.

"That's a no?"

"There'd have to be total conquest, and then there'd be total revolt."

"You'd stand by your government in such a scenario?"

"Certainly."

"Yet you acknowledge the hollowness of Confederate claims. You say you fight a defensive war, yet you employ troops from one ocean to the other. You have 'indents,' but you know they're slaves. You call yourselves a democracy, while only nobles vote."

"Not a democracy. A constitutional aristocracy."

"Now you're spinning things."

Franklin gave another shrug. "When was the last time a black citizen became an officer in your Primary Intel?"

"Don't turn this around."

"Seems like I've touched a nerve."

"You can go ahead and pretend our flaws match up against yours. Yet you ignore what we know, General. That your fellow Planters murder their slaves, and that your government covers it up. That every spring, you celebrate the traitors who destroyed our country, whilst imprisoning your own people for questioning yours. We know you don't pay taxes, that you've got ancestral trusts, all while you live off the toil of others. We know you have no immigrants, because they'd never want to come." Cooperman's eyes turned to fire. "General, talk big all you want. Tell me how you grow your own food, and care for the land, and live with order. But the fact is, if you had a real country, a real life, you'd also talk about what's wrong. You'd talk about how the extremists have you trapped, and you're embarrassed by your antique feudalism. How you've earned rogue status among the nations of the world." He leaned forward. "That's the difference, Brooke. I live in a place that admits it's not perfect; yours is so sick it can't even look in the mirror. We brought you in so we could learn more. But there's nothing there. Turns out you're every bit as sorry as we thought."

CHAPTER 37

Something was wrong. Kevin knew it the instant he opened his eyes.

It was early – barely light – and he sat up, trying to think through the grogginess. Listening hard, peeling back the house's quiet, he heard voices outside.

Male ones.

He couldn't make out the words, but he was sure of their rhythm: choppy and brusque, piercing the air. His stomach churned. There shouldn't be anyone on his property – not at this hour. Not ever. He swung from the bed and threw on a pair of pants draped over a chair, jogging across the room to see. The wooden floor creaked, frigid against his feet, as he stepped forward, already out of breath. Bending down, he peered through the sliver of space between the frame and the shade.

He stopped short. Directly below, jumbled just outside the front door, a crowd of Guard agents had arrived – every one of them in crisp tunics and fine slouch caps. In the thin dawn light, Kevin could see a row of black SUVs and sedans behind them, more arriving every second. One of the men was barking orders, gesturing around the mansion, directing the others to form a circle around the main lawn's perimeter.

Kevin retreated from the window.

The whole world seemed to shift on its axis, the color drained straight from the morning air. And all at once, he saw his situation with sudden, terrible crispness – how they all now must view him: a known consorter with an indent, tolerating resistance – even tarred as a Resister himself.

He thought of the poor slave girl Rebecca, down the hall. Had they spotted her muddy tracks on the steps? Had someone seen her arrive? He prayed they hadn't already arrested Liza.

He did his best to shake such thoughts aside. There wasn't time. Turning toward the hall, he tried to figure a way to help, to warn her, to usher her to the attic for escape, possibly to the roof – even tell her to slip out the back and hide in the higher grass beyond, while he distracted the agents.

In the days since they'd met, he realized, they hadn't really spoken. Not in any way that meant something. He'd never hosted an indent before – who had? – and he hadn't been sure what to say. His brain had urged him to speak as he would with any other child. But he'd felt instead only a growing shame, like an anchor around his neck, a sense that this girl Rebecca must be judging him, that he'd only make it worse by uttering something inane. They'd ended up eating suppers in silence.

Now it was too late to do any different.

There was a terrible thud from downstairs.

"Donleau! Let us in!" The voice was coated in a false friendliness, like a glaze of spoilt cider. "We mean you no harm!" But already, the men were prying open the entrance.

Kevin struggled frantically for a response, but none came. He could only stare down the hall, wondering if Rebecca remained mercifully asleep, as yet unaware that her prayers were at an end.

Then – the door below came crashing open, and he looked down from the hall, leaning over the railing. An agent looked right back, a fellow cut from steel, his pale chin sharp as a blade. The rest of them angled in as well, and Kevin held up his hands.

"Good morning," he said stupidly. "I just awoke – my apologies – I was on my way – "

"Where is she?" the one in front yelled, already skipping up the stairs.

"Who?" He thought his heart would shatter right through his ribcage.

But then he heard the door behind him squeak open.

"Still don't know who?" the agent muttered, reaching the second story, close enough that Kevin could see the sunburn on his nose.

Kevin spun back. Rebecca was standing alone there, draped in the striped cotton clothes she'd borrowed. Her thin lips shook, her dark skin went gray.

"I'm so terribly sorry," he managed.

She shook her head – reached out her hand – but before she could answer, he was being dragged away. The agents had him by the elbows, and were shoving him down the stairs. "You're being charged with concealment, deceiving the Guard, treason."

He was trying not to trip. The events seemed to be happening to someone else. He'd never run afoul of authority before, not even as a boy in school. Hauled outside, through the icy morning wind and into the rear of one of the SUVs on the grass, Kevin tried to recall a single instance of such uncertainty. He couldn't. Somehow, a lifetime of caution had led to this moment. The vehicle door banged shut, and the agents piled in from the other side and in front.

"What'll you do to Rebecca?" Kevin suddenly shouted, swinging back his head, trying to get a glimpse of the mansion through the rear windshield. "What'll happen to her?"

One of the men snorted. "Missing your harlot already, Donleau?"

The others simply laughed.

·   ·   ·

Liza was already awake when she heard the sirens.

She'd been up all night, on and off, retiring early after a supper of guinea fowl and frozen garden peas. Under her mother's watchful gaze, she'd pretended her mind was empty. Now, ten hours later, she was propped up in bed, listening.

It had to be the Guard. Only they owned sirens like that, blaring against the Virginia quiet; only they would be audacious enough to use them.

The noise was growing louder, from the west – from the direction of Kevin's house. She sat up stiffer. She'd hoped Rebecca could stay with him until they figured out a path for her escape. In the meantime, the Donleau Plantation had seemed the likeliest harbor. Liza had planned a visit for later that very day.

Shooting out of bed, she quickly changed and went to the stairs in the hall. She reached the ground floor in seconds, and worked at keeping calm, her suspicion under control. But dark ideas were already brewing. As her panic built, she grabbed a coat from the hall tree, hurrying straight outside, ignoring the indents sweeping the floor to start the morning. The sky was still gray, the air chillier than she expected, and Liza shivered, slicing across the front porch, peering out at the front pastures, not sure how she could possibly help.

If only her father were here to intervene.

She paused then – pulling out her cell – texting the only person who might be able to help.

Please come, she typed. *Now.*

Then she paced, wondering what more she could do, counting the seconds, praying for a reply. Until to her surprise, scarcely a few minutes later, a large vehicle spun into the driveway from the road up ahead, clouded by morning mist. Liza froze, waiting for a clearer view – when sure enough, she could make out that it was one of the Guard's SUVs, its telltale black doors bedecked with Confederate banners, rumbling towards her, across the icy patches in the driveway.

Behind the steering wheel, she saw Dale.

Liza leapt down from the porch as he pulled in, heart pounding, baffled as to how he'd been so quick. He was opening the car door now, stepping out, and she saw that he was again in full uniform – front jacket fully buttoned, white shirt crisply ironed – as if he'd been on duty already, not just stirring in some nearby barracks, to be awakened by the buzz from her text.

And all at once, like a terrible swift strike from above, it hit her.

"How could you, Dale?!" she cried, her voice cracking with emotion.

He looked at her blankly.

She pointed out toward the road. "Kevin Donleau! " She was frantic. "The indent!"

"You heard the sirens?"

"Of course I heard them! Did you know about this?!"

"I only heard a few minutes ago – I'm so sorry, Liza. It sounds like Donleau's under arrest." He looked full of pity, but she knew he was a fine actor. He'd never much cared for the Underground Railroad, or the plight of the indents; that piece of the Resistance had never appealed to him – whether or not the rest of it ever truly had.

"Don't you try and fool me," she said, closing in on him. "How can you be so cold? How can you pretend to care?"

"What are you saying?"

"You're dressed for service, Dale. You're on duty. You knew what I was talking about before I said a word!"

He opened his mouth as if in surprise. "You think I turned them in?"

"I do." Liza was gathering herself now, her voice growing steady. "No one else could have known."

"But darlin', believe me – "

"Stop. Just tell me where they've taken them."

He looked stricken. "They're at the nearest holding cell, I'm sure – but let me come with you." His voice sounded suddenly scratched; a blue vein tensed in his brow.

She was already turning back toward the house. "Crotelle Jail?"

"Yes. They'll keep them there for transfer, while they figure out what to do with them. But – "

"No more!" Liza shouted over her shoulder, searching for the keys she'd used for her car trips to Richmond. "Don't be here when I get back. Don't try to contact me anymore."

"Let me help you, Liza, really – I'm sure there's something I can do."

But swallowing back the lump in her throat, she wished he wasn't so convincing. "You've done plenty already, Captain Birch. Just leave me be."

•   •   •

The holding cell at Crotelle County Jail had an old stone floor and a water-stained plaster ceiling. In front, a set of rusted bars was flaked and brown; the rear was the same stone as the floor. Through the bars, Kevin could see a dilapidated hallway running to a door. Beyond that, he could hear the Guard agents gathered, awaiting orders from superiors about where to take him next. Out the window behind him, he could glimpse the rest of the prison complex. Watchtowers stood like chessmen on some bleak, giant board; farther out, the Blue Ridge foothills peeked from behind barbed wire fences.

Suspecting he was being filmed, Kevin worked not to frown. He angled back around towards the cell door, hiding the shake in his knees, no matter how it begged to be let out, asking only for the Lord instead.

Poor young Rebecca wasn't even here any longer. One of the Guard had mentioned she was being sent directly back to her owner in Carolina. And Kevin resolved to ask after her whenever he was assigned an attorney, no matter how hollow his own trial, to task his parents with tracking her down, purchasing her labor themselves if need be, providing her a life. He was certain he'd failed her somehow, by not thinking of a better hiding place – certain he'd failed some larger cause in the process.

He heard heavy strides down the hall. One of the agents appeared on the other side of the bars, a fleshy fellow, with a lieutenant's insignia on his collar. "New visitor, Donleau. You've got five minutes," he said, before ducking back out.

Who could already know he was here?

Then a new shadow appeared – and a second later, it was Liza who walked in. Her hair was untidy; she wore a wrinkled hoop dress without the hoop. Kevin swept right up to the bars, clutching them with both hands. He saw that her cheeks were flushed, the lines around her eyes gone red.

He shook his head, willing her not to say anything. It was bad enough they had him – it was far too dangerous that she was visiting as well.

"Let me take the blame, Kevin."

"Don't be absurd." He knew whatever the two of them uttered could be recorded and used in court. "I made my own choices."

"You shouldn't be here."

"I don't know, Liza – I've been waiting all my life to find a spot that suits me." He tried to grin. But in truth, he also meant it. He'd finally done something that felt right. His blue eyes shone with conviction. "I owe you for that, at least, for helping me see what I believe."

She wiped a tear, then stepped forward, so that her lips met his through the bars, kissing him for all that he'd said, and all that he was.

The guard interrupted. "You'll have to leave, Miss Brooke."

"I'll see you soon," she mouthed.

"But how did you find me?"

She hesitated.

"How did you get here?"

"There's a captain I know in the Guard," she finally whispered.

That made sense. Liza knew the whole of the commonwealth through her father; she was bound to know someone in the Guard. Not that it mattered. "I'm glad."

"You think I'd let my own neighbor sit alone in jail?" And despite everything, she smiled.

The lieutenant stepped in from the door. "Enough, you two – Miss Brooke, it's time to go."

CHAPTER 38

The ceilings of Congressional Hall in New York City were so high, and the walls so widely spaced, that echoes were inevitable. The result was that whenever anyone spoke, it sounded authoritative. Sam Cooperman was pleased. He'd been at the podium nearly twenty minutes, and now he was wrapping up, confident the drooping eyelids of Senators and Representatives in the audience meant nothing. All that mattered were their votes.

Frankly, Cooperman enjoyed the capital. Its ivory buildings and grand mahogany interiors reflected the might of the place. Being invited here meant access. It meant victory. Three times this year alone, he'd made a visit asking for funding. At the first, he'd sought construction of bases near the border; approval had swiftly been granted. Next, he'd pushed for drones that could destroy Confederate crops without collateral damage – the media had grown hysterical, but eventually consensus had been reached. Finally, he'd requested sanction for another year of going in and apprehending indents, a hearing that'd been camera-free. Both parties had righteously agreed.

Compared to all that, this was a breeze. Today he was merely padding the nation's sense of virtue, making this whole lot feel better about dipping into their pocketbooks. Looking to the rear, he could see anchors from all the networks, transcribing the sanctimony, blanketing the back wall with cameras. That was good. The more attention the better.

Some out there were growing antsy, it was true. It didn't help that U.S. allies wouldn't offer any more aid to the cause; everyone knew western Europe didn't want a unified American power; even friends like Japan and Canada remained coy. Meanwhile, the hawks in Congress were furious over the paltry progress on the border, and the doves – well, they were the doves.

Today was a chance to buoy them all. And the life jacket he'd be tossing their way came in the form of their favorite new darling, Clara Brooke. Over the course of the fall, she'd already told them that the indents would accept gradual emancipation, that no slave would ever seek vengeance, or demand full citizenship, let alone come north to disrupt society here. Now, she'd be appealing to Congress's heroic sense of self. She'd quote Lincoln, summoning their better angels; she'd remind them resistance was already well underway. Cooperman was sure it would work. No one could be as persuasive as an actual slave. Besides, he'd written every line. By day's end, the cash would be flowing.

"Ladies and gentlemen," he declared now. "It falls to one who's suffered more for the cause than any of us. Allow me to reintroduce, from the fallen commonwealth of Virginia, the so-called 'property' of that infamous general whom we now have in our custody" – there were jeers and hoots and general glee – "please welcome Ms. Brooke."

· · ·

She took her place, feeling as though the microphone would pick up every thump of her heartbeat. The nerves got worse each time, and she gripped the podium as she leaned forward. The Yanks were shifting in their pews waiting, this remarkable tableau of white power, ready to hear from a black slave. "Good afternoon." Her voice echoed from the speakers. There was a siren outside, louder, then fading; aside from that, nothing. Just the stillness of a crowded room. She knew what Cooperman wanted. She knew what they all wanted. The same as always. The words they'd written. The words she despised.

She'd made her decision.

She wouldn't stomach the lies any longer. It was the knowledge of the baby that had done it. On some future day, either in heaven or before, she wanted to tell Atti she'd raised their child in truth and pride from the beginning. She pictured his charged, curious eyes, and she knew in her soul he'd approve.

Anyone with half a brain would already have seen the truth, anyway. The slaves wanted property, and schools, and the vote of course. So why not say it? She looked out at these men with their expensive suits and their thoughtful, practiced expressions. If they were going to shirk their moral duty, why must she? What good would her release do, if it came at the expense of dignity and fact, if it meant being ostracized by her own?

Their rot could no longer be permitted to make her forget who she was.

"Folks, it's time you know something real about my people." The words were crisp, clean, undaunted; she'd practiced them in her room. "*We won't be satisfied.*" She let the phrase sink in. "We won't be satisfied leaving our cabins. Would you? We won't be satisfied just calling ourselves 'free'! We won't be satisfied simply bidding our Planters farewell. We'll fight for *full* freedom, as long as it takes." The politicians out there looked frozen now, lips drawn tight, hands clasped in their laps. "That means rights! It means citizenship. It means freedom to live in your nation, and make it *ours.*"

Sure enough, Cooperman was back at her side now, already yanking her from the stage, so that she had to shout her last few words. "It's our war, folks!" She was being lifted by a guard. "Ours! Not just yours! Remember – we won't just be satisfied!"

They were carrying her out, her face angled up to the ceiling, and she heard the crowd rumbling. She was tugged through a door, then down a hall – until she could smell the outside city air, smoke and fumes and asphalt and rubber, and glimpse a winter blue sky. She was shoved into a rear seat in the van. Someone strapped her in. Somebody else started the engine up front.

Clara simply smiled. The van was moving then, ready for the ride back to the compound, and she thought again of Atti. She prayed he could one day be free, as free as she'd just been, up at that podium. She prayed for their child too, and she rested her hand on her belly, leaning back in the seat, knowing, at last, she'd done right, remembering that freedom had never been theirs to give, but hers to take. And so she had.

CHAPTER 39

Dale Birch wasn't used to this feeling. All his life, he'd been good at getting what he wanted, persuading people. Now, the person he'd come to care for most – the one he needed to listen to him – had walked away.

He wished desperately that he'd explained why he'd been nearby, clarifying he was always close whenever there was an operation, that he'd been summoned to overnight-duty all week, and so of course he'd been awake when Liza had texted. If he'd just gotten the words out quicker, maybe she'd have listened. He'd never seen her so determined, so fierce as that; it hadn't given him time to collect his sentences the way he usually did.

An hour had passed since she'd stormed off, and he found himself sitting on a stone in a pasture, between the mansion and the woods. The Brooke family had allowed the patch to grow wild, a touch of untamed nature for admiring from the house. Winter berries gleamed, an echo of the red brick chimneys crowned by frost.

Dale sighed, picked up a twig, and scratched at the hardened dirt in front of him.

Liza was right, of course. The Guard hurt people. His time in the Resistance didn't undo that. He just hadn't ever done the math – hadn't ever been forced to hold himself to account – always assuming it wasn't enough to derail him, that the only thing that mattered was his talent for spreading the gospel of change.

Shutting his eyes, Dale let the sun warm his face. All his life, he'd separated himself from the indents, naturally. Yet what of Liza's insistence that yeomen and indents shared a certain angle in life? – each of them trampled by the aristocratic class, both sustaining the nation, threatened by the Guard. Why had he brushed her aside? Self-interest? Arrogance? Rank prejudice, probably.

It could've been either indent or yeoman who'd discovered Kevin Donleau. So why had he instantly suspected the former – keen to be closer to family, or simply scheming for an escape, passing along information in order to curry favor? Weren't there just as many yeoman informants? Equally eager to butter up the powers that kept them in place? Either way, it certainly hadn't been him.

God he wished Liza had believed that.

Dale stood.

.   .   .

By the time he was nearing Crotelle County Jail, he had a plan.

He couldn't simply make up a transfer-order and take Donleau with him. Word would travel too quickly, and they'd both be tracked down and arrested. Instead, a half-mile out, Dale slowed down his SUV. The ride had stayed quiet; there were no checkpoints to be seen – with the runaway captured, there appeared to be no panic. Still, he steered onto the grass and parked out of view, finding a dip in the fields just to be sure.

Jumping out, he moved quickly, stepping through overgrown reeds, until he'd spotted the jail's antique holding cell, a brick building a few rooms at most. It was separate from the modern main prison complex – a mile farther back, thank God. Here, only two Guard vehicles sat out front, and staying low, he scurried close. He counted five men. That would mean one more in the building, with agents always traveling three per jeep. They looked bored, their breath misting, rubbing their hands together for warmth. Four were against one of the SUVs, chatting. The straggler was under a tree, a few yards from the jail's entrance.

Dale stayed patient. From the look of things, Donleau hadn't even been processed yet. The agents were probably waiting on instructions, no doubt for transfer to a higher-security facility. He inched forward, his own fingers growing numb from the cold. Ten minutes passed, then twenty. Finally, the man under the tree made a move. He ambled toward the others, forging a semicircle for conversation. The result was a briefly unguarded opening.

Dale stepped faster now, aiming for the rearmost jeep. He'd have to dart the last short distance through open air – and taking a breath, he leapt forward. As he slung himself to its back corner, he could hear the men chatting about football, and he slipped out of view. He allowed himself a rush of relief.

Creeping silently alongside the SUV's doors, peeking under its base to confirm the agents' feet hadn't moved, he slid to the next vehicle. Reaching its front bumper, just feet from the jail entrance, he glanced inside, down the hall.

Kevin Donleau was right there, sitting on a warped bench in his cell, eyes fixed right back on Dale. Apparently he'd been watching the whole time. Now he shifted his gaze ever so slightly to his left.

Dale nodded.

He sprang inside the building, lowering his head to hide from the cameras, and immediately stepped to the side. A lone agent sat in a stainless steel chair, facing Donleau, scrolling through his phone in his lap. Dale moved directly behind him, latched his forearm around the man's throat, and squeezed. Gasping, the young agent tried to yank himself free; the phone fell to the floor. He kicked at the ground, and the chair squeaked nastily. Dale was sure someone outside would grow suspicious, but no one came. Finally, the young man went limp.

Dale let go. Killing the kid would only make more trouble. Leaving him unconscious was all they needed, and he looked toward the cell.

Donleau had tiptoed forward. When he spoke, it was in the tightest of whispers. "The card's on the desk. Swipe the keypad next to the bars."

Dale spotted a white badge, a metallic strip along its back. Staying hunched, he found the machine on the wall and did as directed; the cell's two middle bars detached. Swiftly, delicately, Kevin swung them open.

"Follow," Dale mouthed, sticking the card in his pocket to avoid leaving fingerprints. He paused by the door. The agents were still gathered beyond the SUVs, and he pointed to the fields.

. . .

Kevin was untrained and had trouble keeping light of foot, but he managed it. All the while, he kept his eyes fixed on the boots in front of him, puzzling over this agent's help, and why he'd risk everything.

He'd noticed right away that they'd met before. This was the pompous captain from that night at Rosewood Manor – the nasty one, who'd taunted the indents. For how many long-haired Guard agents could there be?

Together, they were jogging now, through bare, rolling farmland, cautiously picking up their pace, toward the road beyond. These fields near the prison were deserted, casualties of the winter months, as well as of the advancing paranoia of the age, a buffer around the jail complex – a few depressed paths where cattle might once have trampled, a rotting timber fence to the side – overgrown enough to allow for staying low and blending in. In time, Kevin pulled closer to Dale, looking over at this savior silent at his side, hands still clenched tightly to keep away the cold.

"You must know Elizabeth Brooke," he murmured at last, once they'd made some distance. "That's why you're helping me. She asked you to."

"We have to be quiet," the agent answered. "We can talk later."

"Come on Captain, they can't hear us now. Tell me I'm right."

· · ·

Dale looked at the man beside him in turn. His words were careful, his voice earnest; he had a sincere face, and probing blue eyes. So this was Liza's oldest friend – and the man who had her heart, he suspected. He was also the fellow who'd once embarrassed Dale at her house, talking back instead of doing as he was told. He had more spine than he let on.

"Well?" Kevin pressed. "Did she ask your help?"

They were nearly at the road, and Donleau was right they'd gotten out of earshot. What's more, the agents almost certainly wouldn't notice a thing until their unconscious friend woke up. By then, Dale could have Donleau back to Liza, and they'd figure out next steps. "She thinks I turned you in," he finally acknowledged. "Please make sure she knows I didn't."

Kevin studied him.

Dale let out a sigh. "It's you, Donleau, if that's what you're wondering. You're the one – not me. You should've seen her face when she realized you'd been taken. And like a damn fool, here I am, going and fetching you for her, throwing you two right back together."

CHAPTER 40

Despite rumors that funding might cease, U.S. forces continued their advance into northern Virginia, marching ahead as ordered, unsure if they'd be called back. The troops were exhausted, Raj Hayworth among them. Their battalion had been moving through frigid woodland since dawn. The swift progress aimed to allow commanders a claim of control over as many new districts as possible, before a halt was announced. In the wake of the artillery attacks at the border, the U.S. offensive had truly arrived.

Farther south, reports were coming in that Resistance fighters, standing tall against their own Confederate government, were now actually organizing and taking abandoned rural territory themselves. The dream was that the two forces would eventually converge, squeezing the Confederate troops between them. In the meantime, the diversion southward was allowing the invasion to march right in.

Raj's legs felt like mush, and he was sure he'd lost weight. Day after day of army food didn't help. Neither did this latest cold snap. He paused among the others, leaning against a white birch, for a sip from his canteen.

As he did, something crinkled against his back, and he turned.

It was another Confederate broadside, posted by enemy forces as they'd fled, intended for discovery by the oncoming northerners. Raj had read a million of them before, but Ted was striding over, stepping over branches.

"What's it say?"

Raj shrugged. "Same crap as always."

"Come on."

He lowered the canteen from his lips. "Fine," and he reached over his shoulder for the posted sheet, straightening it out in his hands. "*Soldiers of the enemy –* "

"Nice touch."

"*Welcome to the Confederacy –* " they both snorted – "*and the War that Never Ends. Ask your commanders what you fight for! A distraction from your own sins! Following in the treacherous steps of your ancestors!*"

Raj stopped reading.

"Is that all?"

"It goes on like that."

"Keep going then."

But they were cut off by a roar from the sky.

They looked up. F-16s. U.S. flags on the wings, thank God.

This was rare. For the most part, the two nations had neutralized each other's air power; but every now and again, one side or the other was able to sneak by the aging anti-aircraft terminals at the border for a bombing. They'd been doing it for generations, though in recent decades, it'd grown controversial. It wasn't just liberals anymore who saw the strikes as savage relics of a less progressive time. Northern media had grown universally critical of it; no one would endorse it in polite conversation. Still, the military readily insisted the targets were weapons caches or new army bases – it was probably even true – no matter that the real goal was to terrorize the other side.

Over beers in pubs, lounging at home with a joint, Raj had often argued against such efforts – *brutal*, he used to proclaim, *unnecessary!* – yet now, watching the squadrons screaming by, he also felt a stirring inside. Their authority was hard to ignore. He glanced back down and realized Ted was shouting.

"Get flat! The jets are low – it'll be close!"

They dove to the ground then, just as the explosion struck, shaking the earth and rattling the trees. Branches dropped down, a few old bird nests too, and Raj felt his own bones vibrating within. The planes were targeting something nearby.

But the attack was also short-lived. After only a few terrific bangs, an uneasy quiet returned to the woods, and a sergeant came running from behind. "Radio report says they hit a slave-hunting headquarters. Undercover center of some kind – using residential areas as a screen."

"There's a town?"

"We'll head there now." The sergeant was catching his breath. "Seek out wounded civilians, offer first aid." He kept running, beckoning the troops to lift themselves from the forest floor and follow. Ted and Raj jogged along with the others.

When they arrived, only a minute or two later, they found a ruined collection of farmhouses. A few soldiers were already in place, putting out scattered flames, stepping through smoke tumbling from the charred grass. Some stray chickens had survived. There were scattered stones from flattened buildings, a splintered fence. At first, the people were few, stumbling alone, crying quietly; but there were also hidden screams of the suffering, tucked behind rubble, puddles of blood. And soon the soldiers saw more of them: men in overalls leaning against burn-stained cornerstones, laborers in notch-collar vests blinking at barn walls that might yet come tumbling. A few women hugged their children tight, moving in silence; others hardly had strength at all, lying still in the meadows. The cratered road glistened; shards of glass from shattered windows lay like knives. Pockets of ash drifted like summer haze; fires still crackled on the lots where hoses hadn't yet arrived.

"Primary Intel says not to be fooled," another officer was saying, pointing ahead, focusing the men on the lot in question. "Sketchy details, but apparently we had cameras in these woods. They caught an operation here – tracing runaway routes, looking for slaves – didn't even own any themselves. Just hunted 'em down for others."

Another soldier lowered a fire extinguisher as he came upon the broken top of the place's mailbox. *Lew and Margaret Worthing*, read the name-plate above it, and the man spat in disgust, placing a new sign above it. *Evidence of Confederate Crimes – Do Not Disturb.*

"Come on, let's go," Raj murmured, turning to make sure the civilians nearby were alright, ready to collect information for reparations to be applied to their destroyed property.

Ted was slow to follow. "Slime." He shook his head. "Profiting from slave-hunting."

"Enough of that now."

"Too bad we can't tell Atti about this."

But in time they made their way. As they moved down the main road, they spotted a small boy staring out from a window, barely as tall as the sill. He wore a miniature Confederate coat, and a slouch cap too big for his head. Raj waved, but the boy just looked back, before his mother whisked him away. "They're terrified of us," Raj said to no one in particular.

CHAPTER 41

Kevin waited in Liza's room on the mattress edge, thinking not of what he'd done, but of all that he hadn't – a whole life spent simply minding his own, never worrying a moment about so many others. Somehow, all of that was now altered. Here he was, a fugitive, afraid to trust anyone but Liza, or step outside without a plan, and he wondered if the indent Rebecca must have felt this same way during all her days in hiding – afraid to show her face, afraid even to make a sound.

Around midday, Dale had dropped him off at the plantation, before speeding off to join his unit. He'd told Kevin that the agents at the jail would suspect Resistance fighters had broken him free. Rumors abounded about their growing strength, and rosy, government-funded news reports had done nothing to stamp such tales out. Word from the Guard was that farther inland, activities were no longer confined to tavern meetings. Stories flowed of angry crowds and forces assembling.

Kevin had walked up the main porch at Rosewood Manor, and Liza had greeted him with joyous tears, quickly hustling him up to her room without a word. She hadn't needed to ask how he'd gotten there. She'd seen Dale driving away.

Upstairs, he'd filled her in on the details, until she'd insisted they wait until evening to talk more. Her mother's nerves were on edge with her father still gone, and she needed to help with the accounting books. So it was that he was still waiting, hours later, for her return. He hoped she'd come up from supper soon, perhaps with some leftover food. In the meantime, his mind drifted to easier days, admiring the countryside together, enjoying lazy afternoon picnics. That hadn't been so long ago, he thought.

Yet now even the plantation itself seemed to have shifted. Perhaps it was just because the general was gone, taking his parties along with him. Or maybe it was the worry Liza wore on her face, brown eyes gone distant, lips etched in a frown. Perhaps, it wasn't really the place at all, but in how Kevin saw it – all that had always been present, right there in front of him, if only he'd looked – the echoes of happier times, muted by the knowledge that an uprising had boiled in their midst, the bullet holes still visible in the walls, visits of Confederate Guard seared into the mansion's memory.

More than that, though: a bitterness from indents he'd never paused to examine, embedded in every piece of life within these halls, infused into the lifestyle they made possible – the radishes and cream sauce passed about at cocktails, prepared by their tired hands; the lush peacock-colored carpets on the floorboards below, an affront to the warped and dangerous planks in their cabins just down the hill – and the runaways they prayed for and remembered, millions just like Rebecca, standing alone on his own landing that very morning, a woman he'd abandoned and failed, without even letting himself know her in the first place.

Kevin turned toward the window. Chestnuts lay scattered on the lawn, glinting in the twilight; wooded hills sat peaceful at the horizon, some climbing high, others cresting without warning. It all would have been beautiful, were it not suddenly so terribly ugly.

· · ·

At last, Liza entered the room. She was wearing a green dress; her hair fell loosely over her face. "Hi," she said quietly, placing a paper bag on the nightstand. "I snagged you chicken and apples."

"I knew you would." Kevin stood, and offered a bow. She was exquisite.

"I hurried as best I could."

For a long moment after that, neither one of them said anything. They simply stood, only inches apart. Until the kiss that came next, tender and gentle, extended much longer than ever before. Kevin closed his eyes, holding her close, knowing what was to follow without another word – and together they lowered to the bed, trying to be quiet, suddenly finding it impossible they'd waited quite this long. Feeling her smile against him, he moved them to the quilt. Carefully, he undid the bows that kept her dress together, and when his fingers fumbled, she slid it away herself, as his eyes trailed down – taking his jacket in turn, unclasping his belt – and they lost all notion of being careful after that, laughing when his boots toppled to the floor, focusing only on the here, the immediate – thinking no longer of the Guard, nor of the world outside – not of how any of this would end, but only that it was theirs right now.

·　·　·

It wasn't long after sunrise when Liza opened her eyes, and saw Kevin getting dressed beside the bed.

He smiled, and leaned over to kiss her good morning. "I know it's early."

She nodded groggily. Still, her mother would be awake soon, wanting company for breakfast, and so Liza stood too and shuffled to the dresser. The house was chilly, and she quickly pulled on a dress.

"I'm off," Kevin said from behind her. "I'm headed to the Resistance."

She spun back around. "The only thing now is finding where you can be safe."

"This is the best answer." He'd considered it overnight. "Better with them than in hiding."

"How?"

"Dale told me there are fighters gathering to the west. I'll leave through the fields."

"The government's cracking down."

"They already know I'm involved." He stepped forward. "Besides, I can't just stay here."

There was a sound in the hallway. A floorboard's creak. Subtle, sharp – and both of them froze. Their conversation was halted, as Liza met his eye, raising a finger to her lips. She stepped towards the door, then paused at the handle. Finally, opening it just an inch, she gasped.

It was her mother. Holding a phone.

"No!"

"Don't you use that tone, Liza dear."

"Tell me why." There was new panic in her voice. "What did you do?"

Cathryn took a breath. "I've dialed the Guard, if you must know."

"Tell me that's not true."

"It was necessary." This time, Cathryn's voice was cracking too, even as her eyes were steady. She pressed open the door and faced Kevin in full. "I still can't fathom it."

"Mrs. Brooke – you've known me all my life."

"Apparently not very well. The Guard's put out alerts."

Liza was frantic. "I'm the one who brought him into this. I'm the one who's been in the Resistance."

"Stop it, Elizabeth." Cathryn's voice wobbled now near to breaking. "You're a part of this family."

"Mother!"

"You don't understand: disregard for the law – it's what I grew up with. It leads only to horror – never more freedom. You couldn't bear such a life, in chaos, everyone fighting over their beliefs." The phone was still in Cathryn's hand. "You don't know what it is to live like this. My father – your grandfather – always running off to border skirmishes, building trenches, hunting enemies. He was a zealot, Liza. And God rest his soul, he was killed. It's because of people like him that this war doesn't stop. The stubbornness of it, Liza – the fanaticism! People refusing to live their lives – craving fighting, rejecting how things are, delivering anguish to everyone else for so-called ideals. They bring terror and call it liberty." She was shaking her head, tears streaming at last. "Don't you become your grandfather, Liza. Don't let this young man drag you in."

But Liza was retreating. "Turning him in is the same as if it were me."

"Don't be absurd."

At that, the sound of vehicles shattered the room. They were already close, Liza realized. They were in the driveway. And she spun round to see Kevin peering out the window. "We can't just wait here," she urged, joining his side. "We need to at least try. We need to go!"

"Where? They're surrounding the house."

Her mother interrupted. "It's better if you just surrender." She stepped up from behind. "They won't hurt you, Kevin – you're a noble. They'll sentence you to military service, then you'll be out. You can still make a proper Confederate life."

But neither he nor Liza were listening any longer.

They rushed past Cathryn Brooke in a flash, into the hall, toward the stairwell as fast as they could manage. Liza led the way, leaping down the steps with Kevin on her heels, until they spun toward the kitchen, where a second set of stairs led to the basement. Liza had hardly ever used it – the indents stored supplies down there – but she knew it housed a small exit at the house's rear, one the Guard might miss.

Together, they pushed through, past the cooks preparing breakfast. Liza yanked open the door, and chilly air tumbled up.

The stairs were no more than loose planks, wobbly and lacking a banister, but there was light enough from behind them. They moved quickly.

"The door leads to the rear pasture," Liza yelled over her shoulder. "Not far from the eastern woods!"

They cut across the room diagonally, dodging shelves covered with spare flowerpots and tools. The stone floor had divots and holes; there was dirt as old as the house piled at the corners. Liza reached the next door, and in an instant, morning light was streaming in; she jumped to the grassy hill against the house, with Kevin still just behind. The Guard hadn't yet circled around, and without a word, Liza sprinted ahead. "Close it behind you," she directed. "They won't know which way we went."

"Your mother will tell them – "

"Close it anyway!"

From there, they galloped upwards, straight towards the woods. At least there they'd have cover. In the meantime, the Guard would waste its time in the mansion. Alas, they were leaving tracks in the frost, but there was nothing for it. Liza looked at Kevin as they came upon the first trees, twigs splintering in their path, winter sparrows rushing off. "We just have to keep at it," she panted, lifting her legs to scale a rotten log, irritated more than ever by her dress.

She glanced back and gulped.

There was the Guard. Six of them.

"Damn," Kevin said from her side. The agents must have moved to the hill just as he and Liza had left the house. He squinted. "Wait."

"What?"

"It's Dale!"

"You're sure?"

But he was right. That beard was unmistakable – that long stride, cutting a tall figure against the muted brown surrounding them. Liza held Kevin's arm.

"Stay in place!" Dale suddenly shouted their way. "Donleau – you're in the clear!"

Kevin stared back.

But Dale had turned to the other agents, saying something out of earshot, before resuming the pursuit alone. His strides were quick; in a moment, he was near, meeting them with the smallest of grins. "Well I doubt I can fool 'em in Richmond much longer. But for now I had Mrs. Brooke's call patched through to me – I listed it as a local dispute – stress from the General's absence." He even shared a wink, as if it were all still a game. "Then I worked some real magic." He caught his breath, wiping his brow with his glove. "Convinced the bosses the indent was only in your house, Donleau, because you'd caught her yourself and were planning her return. If I'd known they'd buy that, I'd never have snuck you from jail."

Kevin stared. "You're serious."

"Honest to God."

"What'd Rebecca say?"

"Who?"

"That's the indent. Her name's Rebecca."

"Ah."

"What'd she say, Dale?"

"Apparently she corroborated it." He paused. "She'd already told them you hadn't aided her at all."

Kevin took a step backwards. "By God." He shook his head. "I didn't even know her last name."

"Donleau. Relax."

"It's just – she's helped me far more than I ever helped her."

But Liza was eyeing the men milling at woods' edge.

Dale met her gaze. "Not to worry. They're not here for you. There's talk of skirmishes in the vicinity." He lowered his voice.

"You'll be livin' under house arrest for the time being. You don't want to push it with the Guard – not after the prison break today. But it shouldn't be long. Richmond will forget. The Resistance requires too much of their attention these days. Besides, your father will be back soon, and they won't want to upset him."

She shifted back her focus. "I'm sorry I blamed you, Dale."

His brown eyes were steady. He offered a nod, and extended a hand. "Good luck from here."

"To you too."

Then, brushing his hair from his face, leaving them stunned, Dale sauntered back to the other agents, saluting them briskly as he got close.

CHAPTER 42

Atti's regiment entered the Confederacy along with the rest of the invasion forces. For while the military was still segregated, its battle plans were not. The unit had crossed the border a few days before, in Virginia's northwest corner. With spring's first buds sprouting, he was back in his own country.

After marching east then south, the men had reached a remote stretch of the commonwealth, not far from the old abandoned U.S. capital in Washington, a city still in northern territory – barely – but known for its deserted corridors and flourishing black market with the Confederacy, an arrangement that had long protected it from full-on Rebel occupation. The old government buildings were now mostly public housing projects, with jarringly ornate exteriors, an unacknowledged model for re-occupation, and even reconciliation. Indeed, the city's open flouting of cross-border commerce regulations demonstrated some level of cooperation between the two sides. The underclass suffered, but that was nothing new for either.

So far, the regiment's march had involved only limited action. On the advance's second day, the soldiers had encountered a group of cut-off troops and exchanged brief fire. A few men had been injured, but none had been lost. Prisoners had been rounded up; reports filed. Forward movement had resumed after that.

Most of the journey had come through forest and empty pasture, land historically too near the border and its threats to entice farmers. Nearing the coast, the troops had reached more settled regions; just a day ago, they'd passed through their first yeomen village. The civilians there had taken the sight of black soldiers remarkably in stride. Atti had expected their faces to register horror; instead, the town's residents had mostly ignored them, too afraid to provoke conflict, too occupied with their own daily concerns, apparently too cynical and fed up with nobles to care.

Or maybe the Resistance really was growing. Maybe it was taking hold in people's minds. He'd even nodded to an old white man sitting on a stoop a few days ago, a fellow long enough in years that his great-grandfather might have fought in the Confederate Revolution itself, and the man had nodded back; no smile or tip of the cap, certainly, but nor had he spat his chewing tobacco out either. If that wasn't progress, then what was? Racial doctrine, after all, was the only thing keeping yeomanry in line.

Now, resting by a dying campfire under a darkening sky, his stomach filled with crackers and cured meat, Atticus grew drowsy. He was sitting beside Bill Rollins. They'd stuck together after meeting on the bus to camp – first training, then marching – and Atti had concluded Rollins always had something useful to say. Listening to the flames pop and the coals hiss, admiring the distorted images of trees through the rising smoke, he leaned back on his elbows, staining his blue sleeves in the mud. "Those white folks we saw yesterday in town..."

Rollins grunted.

"They didn't seem near so mad as I thought they would."

At that, Rollins poked the last few coals with a twig, his knapsack serving as his pillow, not much better than a stone. "To what end, Atti? That salvation has come?"

"Who knows?"

"Never stop fighting, right? Isn't that what your girl said on TV?"

Atti nodded. It sure was. Clara's speech had made the rounds at training camp, everyone trading the clip on their phones, watching it on a loop, cheering at all the best lines. "*We Won't be Satisfied*" had even become a kind of mantra, with men shouting it whenever they broke for a training session or started a march.

It gave him pride. It also made him sick; for it was hard to imagine the U.S. government would ever let her free, now that she'd so obviously carved her own path apart from theirs. She was as full of fight as ever, and when word had gotten round that Atti knew her – that they were to have a child together – some of the men hadn't even believed it. Others had patted him on the back, telling him his girl had spoken words they'd long held inside. Still, all he really cared about was the chance to see her again.

Rollins was watching him. "You've been doing better, Atti. Not thinking on her all the time."

In fact, Atticus had been thinking about her every minute, but he didn't say so. He just looked back at the popping fire, picked up a pebble, and tossed it in.

CHAPTER 43

The footsteps were Major Cooperman's.

Franklin Brooke had become expert at recognizing U.S. agents out in the hall. He could detect immediately if it was someone he'd never met, if it was the youthful guard who delivered food, the one who took him for strolls in the courtyard, or the one who brought him to the interrogation room. And he knew when it was Cooperman.

For the latter walked with special urgency, a quick stride driven by some unquenchable urge to make up time whenever possible. It was a profoundly northern trait, Franklin had concluded – as if before bed each night, a fellow could count up all the minutes saved and store them in a savings box for morning.

He would always be a foreigner here. A Virginian, and a Confederate. His life had taught him when to pause, and when to breathe, when to lean back and accept God's plan. It meant that he didn't rush reflexively, didn't require every conversation to end in victory or defeat, and certainly didn't need to parade around the way the major did, making sure everyone knew he was there, one foot clicking in front of the other.

The door opened, and Cooperman appeared, wearing a silver suit to match his silver hair, holding one of his manila folders, nodding curtly. "General," he said stiffly, stepping into the room. "Have a seat."

Franklin was already seated on the floor, but now a junior agent entered with two plastic chairs and placed one in front of Franklin and the other across the room. As the young man left, Cooperman let the door shut, then opened the folder in his lap, sighing demonstrably.

Franklin watched and waited. He wasn't going to placate his prison-keeper by growing curious. Instead he lifted himself onto the chair and placed his hands on his knees. He could easily act as silent and stubborn as Cooperman, and for a long moment, the only sound in the room was that of the papers in the folder, one against the other – until at last the northerner looked up, peered over his reading glasses, and cleared his throat. "Do you want to know what I'm reading about, General Brooke?"

Franklin shrugged. Of course he wanted to know. "I imagine you want to tell me."

"These are the latest press updates about the war. They say the United States is winning."

"Of course they do. They're propaganda."

Cooperman shook his head. "No, General. We don't do propaganda like you " – Franklin wasn't at all convinced that was true – "our journalists are permitted to report whatever they see fit. It just so happens that in this case, they all agree with our assessment. And how could they not? Our forces have penetrated your border all across Virginia. Our special-ops are freeing slaves from your plantations without opposition. In the meantime, we're getting more reports of runaways each week; and now we're in communication with your country's own Resistance, not just in its Virginia hotbed – in Tennessee, Carolina, even Oklahoma. See for yourself."

Cooperman handed the folder to Franklin. Back home, the Confederate government dreamed of getting its hands on northern summations like this one – intelligence agents pored through old hard copies, and strove constantly to pierce on-line security walls – and gazing down, unable quite to contain himself, Franklin at once took in the lists of cities and headlines, celebrating U.S. pressure, successful campaigns, territorial gains. Alas, there was no real intelligence here, just morale-building, and he handed the folder right back.

"I can assure you, General Brooke, you'd find our direct government reports even more disheartening. We've got firsthand accounts of Confederate forces retreating against orders, leaving entire districts for the taking. We've got maps showing U.S. troops farther south than they've been in years, ready to meet up with your domestic Resistance." Cooperman smiled coldly. "And of course we have in custody the Confederacy's most venerated military official, whom I'm sure must be missed."

"Well so what?" For the fact was, Franklin was unfazed. Even if the border was shifting the way Cooperman claimed, that wouldn't be apocalyptic. The Confederacy had faced invasion before, and despite U.S. numbers, it had always pushed back, its spirit carrying it through. That was something northern men like Cooperman had never understood.

The real problem, admittedly, was the news of the Resistance, but how much of that was to be believed? To be sure, if this part were real – and Franklin had heard enough reports before his arrest to account for at least some of it – then his nation really would be in danger. Yet never once had yeomen and indents actually tied themselves together. It was true they would vastly outnumber nobles if they did – organized indent uprisings, coupled with yeoman sympathy, would be the one thing to sap the spirit of aristocrats and force them to compromise; with enough instability, sentiment for democracy could even return to the Confederacy – but where was evidence that class would ever trump color? That yeomen would ever delude themselves into thinking the slaves were some of their own?

"If you're winning the war so completely," Franklin pressed, "why talk to me? Just go ahead and topple my country then."

Cooperman folded the papers back together. "General. Even if our progress in Virginia spreads west across the continent – as we expect that it will – we'd require more conscription. In order to take your Mississippi bases, let alone those in the Plains, we'd have to increase pressure in the east far more than we already have. You know that as well as I. Even then, there's no guarantee you wouldn't revert to your guerrilla strategies. It would be a slog."

Franklin nodded. Finally, some truth. He knew what Cooperman was really saying: it would be a challenge to keep his own people on board. That had always been the problem for the United States. Its people were weak – incessantly told that each of their voices mattered, no matter that their rulers didn't believe it themselves – enough that all Yankees felt entitled to a say. It destroyed their sense of community, and undermined their nation's goals. Their constant mantra of individual rights meant they couldn't stick together for long.

Over the years, of course, the prime beneficiary had been the Confederacy. Every time the U.S. started to make advances in the war, its people tired of the bloodshed, or wearied of taxes, or decided to tend to their own economy. Whatever the excuse, they always turned back.

And from what Cooperman was implying, it sounded like the Confederacy could rely on it again. Even now, amid its triumphs, the U.S. didn't have the heart to expand its assault. No matter the U.S. papers trumpeting victories, the U.S. government was still concerned. Its people's infirmity was on display.

Franklin studied Cooperman more fully. Lines of concern creased the northerner's brow; he was fidgeting, crossing and re-crossing his legs. "Am I correct in thinking the jailer has come to negotiate with his prisoner?"

"We're ready to end the armistice."

"Come again?"

"You heard me."

"Why?"

"Because we seek some reward for our success."

Franklin was searching for the trick. "A permanent treaty is what we've always wanted. You know that. We'd welcome it."

"You say so, General, but it's clear this war serves you. It provides your people a common enemy amid your divisions. A treaty would take all that away." Cooperman shrugged. "I don't mind sharing that with you, General. You won't change your mind anyway."

Franklin drew in a deep breath, ignoring that, trying to hide his eagerness. No matter how Cooperman wanted to spin this, it would mean Confederate victory, exactly as his country had long sought: recognition from the United States, peace along the border. It was clear indeed: for all Cooperman's bluster, the people of the United States weren't behind him. The Confederate Dream was within reach. The founders must be laughing in heaven. "You have specifics in mind?"

"Both nations would pledge no more war. We'd give up claims of reunion, and in return, your government stops stoking your people's anger by calling for conflict. That will be hard for you – harder than you admit – for it will mean finding new ways to build a national Confederate spirit." Cooperman removed his glasses, folding them, placing them in his shirt pocket.

"Spare me your patronizing."

"We'll announce terms upon your release. At that time, we'll deny you were ever imprisoned, as will you, claiming instead we've been involved in intense top-level negotiations. Coming from you, this will be easy for the Confederate people to accept. Same with the leadership. You'll chalk up your silence to communication challenges. They'll be too blinded by their excitement to care. It'll all be seen as a feat of brilliant diplomatic maneuvering, amid a war that's been going against them. You'll be a hero as before, General. That's our offer. Peace, recognition, details to be worked out within the border zone."

Franklin gaped. Cooperman was right that Congress would celebrate. The state presidents would sign eagerly. It would enable their economy to be unleashed, bringing time to mend lives and relationships, forging community, not destroying it. He straightened in his seat. "On behalf of a noble people, I accept your offer, major."

· · ·

Cooperman stood. It was a sour pill, but he and the rest of Primary Intel were convinced such a treaty would not only force the Confederacy to face its own fault lines, skillfully letting it crumble, but would outpace the U.S. Congress amid its endless torpor and timidity, at last overcoming the paralysis of partisanship. The top Senators had already agreed, of course, their enthusiasm betraying their cowardice – salivating over the notion of an end to votes for or against the war's funding, embracing instead just endless blather about principles and pride. Meantime, this would allow his agents to focus on espionage rather than raids. And it would certainly free up the military; the army men would be delighted to turn to the globe's other hotspots, ending the border's stranglehold on their attention.

He looked at the ridiculous, antiquated man in front of him. Perhaps Brooke would appear less absurd if he were still in his Confederate uniform and not the prison's regulation white shirt and slacks. Perhaps not. This fellow embodied everything that was wrong with the soon-to-be country to the South. Self-regard without merit. A warped sense of dignity over any real curiosity.

Aristocracy above everything else. Cooperman was convinced Brooke was signing the Confederacy up for its own doom. To be sure, it would arrive in murkier form than a surrender in war, more like poison in the blood than a single blow to the head. But arrive it would: without a common cause, the Confederacy was nothing but noble bastards stepping on everyone else. It couldn't last.

He clicked his heels. "My people here will draw up the paperwork," he announced. Then he saluted.

CHAPTER 44

As the Americas' fortunes shifted, and General Brooke was flown from an airfield in Pennsylvania back to Richmond, Clara Brooke remained in her room at the very same compound. She'd heard the helicopter humming outside, and she'd had no idea why.

Cooperman had never mentioned to his Virginian visitors from Rosewood Manor they'd been staying so close, answering questions in near-identical rooms, existing within yards of one another. There'd never been any reason. Still, he'd taken some private satisfaction in knowing that the Planter and the indent – owner and slave – had been sleeping under the same roof, eating the same food all this time.

Now, finished with lunch, he headed to Clara's room. Word had arrived that General Brooke had landed and the treaty was announced – the cable news shows were in hysterics – so there was no reason to delay. The Confederate Congress was in emergency session, on the verge of voting unanimously – as its members always did, following clearance from the generals – ready for thunderous ovations in the Confederate capitol dome. The war would be over, Franklin Brooke's whole life removed of its purpose. He'd be a peacetime officer, heading toward retirement. The world would have a noxious new nation. America would have its latest new border.

This was how history happened, after all. People waited entire lifetimes, then zero-hours arrived in a blink. Later on, there'd be time for commemoration; in the meanwhile, history-making days were easy to miss as they occurred. The sunlight lasted no longer than usual, the sky grew no brighter, the sounds and sights no sharper than before. Minutes ticked by at their regular pace; a fellow still had to eat and drink, shower and shave and use the toilet.

Cooperman found Clara resting in bed. She'd gained a new room; with her pregnancy advancing, they'd moved her to a larger space. The bed was wide, the windows tall, a blue carpet hid the ugly gray concrete of the floor. The bathroom was enclosed, and there was a small laminate table for meals. A few weeks before, she'd even relented and started reading the books on her shelves.

•   •   •

As Cooperman unlocked the door from the outside, Clara looked up. Ever since her impromptu speech to the U.S. Congress, he'd barely spoken with her, sending in assistants to check how she was feeling, assigning her a doctor, providing her boilerplate updates on the war's progress. As he entered the room now, he looked tired. Behind the rims of his glasses, Clara could see dark circles.

"'Afternoon," he said quietly.

She said nothing. She'd stopped being civil some time before.

"Good news. You're being released."

Now Clara's hands slid from her pregnant belly. "What about holding me for more information? Or punishing me? Or however you all say it?"

"Not anymore." Cooperman leaned against the doorframe. "The war's over."

"Speak truth now."

"But I am." He seemed almost to smile. "You see, Ms. Brooke, you scared the hell out of those representatives back at Congressional Hall."

"I just told them what's true."

"I believe you did. They're convinced your people would keep fighting, even after we set you free."

"So you'll abandon us instead?"

"We'd have abandoned you eventually anyway. You just helped accelerate it. You know what half of them were thinking? 'God help us if we turn this into a black republic.'"

Clara cocked her head. She appreciated his honesty at least. "When do I go?"

"I think the bigger question is where."

But that she already knew. She thought of asking Cooperman if he'd heard anything about Atticus Brooke. Only she was sure of the answer. Escape was too hard. It was all too easy to imagine Atti still toiling down there now, plotting his next attempt at freedom. She couldn't just stay here and pretend the struggle was over. "I'm headed back."

"To slavery?"

"You just said it yourself: beating the Confederacy depends on us indents, no one else."

"I didn't mean you personally."

"That's what I heard."

"Well." He shook his head. "I wish our Congress had your spine."

"So do I."

He hesitated. "If you're sure, we can get you on a train south. It'll take a spell – there's still only the one track, and no doubt demand will spike with the treaty, but we'll get you there. We can forge a Southern pass back to the plantation so you won't be harassed by Confederate Guard. Then you can go undercover. Build operations. We'll stay in touch, of course."

Slowly, Clara stood. She wondered if this was what the major had been planning all along. But the truth was she didn't care. The offer was what she wanted, and she already knew she'd accept.

Chapter 45

Cathryn Brooke rested her head on Franklin's shoulder, and together, from a wicker seat on the house's eastern portico, they watched the Virginia sunset over blooming fields. The indents – those who remained anyway – were mostly in their quarters, tallying crops or keeping still, now that warmer nights had arrived. The evening was mild enough for sitting outside, under the fans anyway, and they took in the view from their second story. "There, there," Franklin murmured, as he often did now. "I'm here. I'm not leaving again."

Almost nobody believed the story that he'd been negotiating without ever contacting his own government, and most officials correctly suspected he'd spent his time away in a U.S. prison. As a result, despite his hero's status, he'd lost access in elite circles. The result was that these days, he learned about the progress of the Resistance the same way everyone else did: through the rumor mill, and reading between the lines of government-issued statements. He'd miss his reputation, to be sure: it was nice to be listened to, to be able to avoid the Confederate Guard, to squelch questions about his daughter's trips to Richmond, to know that Tax Services never paid close attention to his finances. But it also meant he had more time for moments like this one.

As it stood now, the Resistance apparently had forces in every district, with reports of sightings even in Crotelle itself.

Some Guard agents had stopped by to tell him as much, and there was nothing he could do about it. The indents, meanwhile, were abandoning their posts every day, and without overseers to stop them – yeomen were all off fighting now, on one side of Resistance or the other, drafted, or picking up their guns in defiance – and with the Guard focused on the fast-encroaching frontier, there was nowhere to turn.

Franklin exhaled. As it turned out, that Yank Cooperman had been more right than he cared to admit. Despite the treaty, there was no denying the nation was in trouble. That it was happening at what should have been this moment of historical triumph only added to the despair. He kept his thoughts within, though. He didn't want to alarm Cathryn. Besides, after being cast aside, a new phase really was upon them: one in which the world puts on a show, and you become the audience. The young take over, and you realize you're not one of them anymore.

"What is it, dear?" Cathryn asked, glancing up from his chest. "Is it Liza?" At first, she'd tried keeping the truth from him, but that had been silly. He'd heard the rumors already.

He didn't look back. He just shook his head.

• • •

Early the next morning, with the sun barely back up in the sky, Franklin stirred. At some point in the night, after dozing together on the portico seat, he and Cathryn had moved into the bedroom for a proper rest. Now he opened his eyes to the sound of a door squeaking down the hall. Sitting upright, he listened, gazing through the room's dim light. After a second, he could hear footsteps, and the door squeaked again, swinging back shut.

Silently, Franklin swung his legs from the bed and put on a robe, working not to disturb his wife. He walked quietly from the bedroom, wondering if it was an indent, readying to prepare breakfast, or possibly even to thieve. Either way, it was worth a check, and arriving at the main stairwell, he started down – only to stop halfway.

There, at the base, was Liza, facing back. The cheeks he used to pat were flushed; her fine hair had been left to roam; her gaze was burning. "Father."

He didn't respond.

"I gather you've heard the truth about what I've done."

"They didn't want to embarrass me before my departure," he replied. "They told me some."

"I'm sorry."

Nodding slowly, he hunched, and lowered himself to the step behind him. The chatter was real. She'd allegedly helped the U.R.; she might even be in contact with yeomen. Some captain in the Guard – apparently one he'd met – had gotten Liza protection; that plus her surname would keep her secure for now. But she was obviously well on her way to getting involved. "Going against your own nation?" he asked faintly. "Against your family too, Liza?"

She watched him, this man who'd held power for so long, now slumped against the carpet on the stairs. He looked suddenly old and worn out, his gray hair flopping down over his ears, lifting a tired hand to block the first rays of sun leaking through the windows high in the hall.

"I've made my decision, father."

His own daughter. Alive with confidence. She'd inherited his pride, and he took solace in that at least; in a nation that denied women the right to make their own choices, he had a daughter unable to do anything but. Alas, why must it be for the Resistance, the one cause he couldn't abide? In fighting for her country as she understood it, she'd be standing against everything she'd been taught, pursuing her urges instead of her duty, seizing on cracks instead of working to reinforce a foundation. She'd be standing against his whole life. "Liza," he tried now. "You must think you know what you're doing. But the danger…" His eyes were pleading. "There are ways to change things without mutiny. There must be ways to serve your people without frightening them."

"We don't have time for this, father. I have to go. But please know – when this is all over, there won't be retribution. There will simply be a new order to things. There will be real rights, for everyone in the Confederacy, as God intends. That's our aim. You won't be punished."

Franklin stood. For a very long time, he stayed on the steps, looking down at her, meeting her eye. "I love you, Liza dearest," was all he said.

"I love you too, father," she answered. Tears came to her eyes, and she moved forward. She stepped up the stairs and into his arms, as she'd done as a little girl. "Tell mother I forgive her," she said into his chest. "And that I love her too."

He nodded, and kissed her atop the head.

CHAPTER 46

Atti had decided to ignore the caution coming from Bill Rollins. He knew his friend was right, that he should be careful and think his plan through. But the news reports had said the U.S. government had released prisoners with the treaty, and word was Clara Brooke was among them – the famous slave-turned-congressional-speaker, who'd inspired civil rights activists across the land. Ever since, Atticus had been wondering how to find her.

He wanted to believe she'd have faith in his escape, but told himself to be reasonable, to think as she would, and follow the odds. He looked down the line. His regiment was among the last U.S. forces still in the Confederacy. Along with every other unit, they were being deployed back north in the treaty's wake, though with the lone rail line out of Virginia clogged with troop transports, they were still waiting at the main depot just north of Richmond, a collection of brick buildings half a century old, covered in red ivy begging to be trimmed. It'd been a wait full of long mornings and longer afternoons, as the men played cards, dozed on their bags, and hoped for information. The white units had been shipped back first; Atti and his fellow soldiers were all that was left.

Rollins was shaking his head. He couldn't fathom the desire to turn around; he'd spent weeks pleading with his friend to get to the U.S., use resources there to track Clara down. "You're nuts, Brooke. She won't go back. Last she heard, you were running or sold."

"She'll assume I got caught. She'll think General Brooke's capture voided my sale." He stood. "Things are changing: you've heard the reports. The Resistance is real. She'll aim to raise that child in a better age. She'll be part of that fight. She'll aim to change our country."

"It's not your country."

"Not yet."

Rollins sighed. He heaved himself up. "Come here then, you damned fool," and he reached out, and hugged Atti tight. "God bless you, son."

Atti hugged him back, then whisked around and walked toward a sheltered passageway that cut to the other tracks. A southbound train was arriving – they'd heard it whistling – the first one in all the days since they'd been stuck here. Picking up his pace, he sidled up to its side, shedding his uniform, switching to civilian clothes from his bag, seeking a car that looked empty as it slowed. If he was right, and Clara was heading south, this is how they would've sent her.

If he was stopped by Guard agents, he was ready with his story. He'd tell them he'd been sent to Richmond to serve his owner, General Franklin Brooke, upon the famous man's return to the Confederacy. He'd mention he'd lost his transport papers and ticket. It was believable enough; he'd be using his real name and could show his old identification card.

Ascending the steep train steps, he turned right.

Alas – there was a whole throng of them. They were standing in a circle just beyond the door, and hadn't been visible from the platform: six in total, gathered in their crisp uniforms, rigid and perfectly coiffed. His heart beat in his throat. All the old feelings of slavery came flooding back at once. He cursed his own recklessness.

Picturing Rollins, Atti wondered if he should leap from the train, sprint to the northbound track, re-join the other soldiers. But the Guard agents were too close. If he ran, they'd just grab him. His mind raced.

Then one of them pointed at his shoulder. "Make sure you stow that bag properly."

Atticus nodded. "Yes sir, of course – " Only before he did, the agents had miraculously already turned back, speaking in hushed tones among themselves. Atti eyed them another instant, registering they had no interest in him at all.

It seemed impossible. Confederate Guard agents always had interest in slaves. They had interest in everyone but their own kind. That's all they were known for. In the old days, they'd have wanted to know exactly who he was. They might even have sent an escort to ensure he went straight home.

He bit his lip. It must be the Resistance, he thought. It had them distracted.

He walked on.

•   •   •

It was then, halfway down the next indents' car, that he saw her.

She was sitting by the window as the train pulled away, staring out at the depot, a mesh cap pulled tightly down on her head. Her old cotton clothes had been replaced by one of the North's tightly sown frocks. Her hair was flattened back to her shoulders, hands resting, fingers interlocked atop her stomach – much larger now than it had been in the television images.

Atti halted in place. All this time, all the interference of governments and history, and God had put them back in the same spot. His lip quivered, and he took in a breath. For a long moment, he could scarcely do anything but gape. He'd wanted this moment more than anything, more than freedom itself, he realized – yet now he could hardly move, as if his soul was insisting on savoring it instead, ensuring it was real. His own hands clenched at his sides; his breaths turned shallow.

She shifted in her seat, and for a moment he wondered if she'd spotted him too. Atti blinked. But she only leaned back instead, getting lost in the ceiling tiles. The tilt of her neck, just so, brought with it the rush of the familiar. The sun from outside seemed to shine only for her.

Beyond the windows, the hills rose higher; the clouds drifted in the sky. On one side, a new pasture floated to the horizon, treeless but overgrown. On the other, the maple and birch grew dense. The tracks clattered. The seconds vanished. Until at last he took the next step down the aisle.

Still wary of drawing attention, he kept his gaze fixed. It was just another twenty feet – ten now – past rows of drab leather seats, flickering bulbs, smudged windows lining the way. Was it a trick somehow? Some insidious plot, arranged by those Guard agents behind him? But no – he stayed steady.

When he reached her seat, Clara's lips were taut, her shoulders and face leaner than he remembered. And suddenly Atti wanted to yelp, to lift her straight up and twirl her round, so that her cap flew back as they laughed, so that the world was theirs and theirs alone. "Clara."

She peered upwards, lifting her hands as if shielding herself from the sun, pushing back the cap. She gasped. "How?" was all she said at first. "How possibly?"

His cheeks flushed. It was as if her voice had become the only sound in the world – like the rush of an entire river, he thought – triumphing over his every sense, erasing his caution, his plans, his awareness of the Guards or stray passengers or anyone else, all while he just kept staring – at her clothes, at her very being – so that he swallowed, and tried to nod. At once his memories were spiraling, recalling all their time apart, and how it'd all begun, the way he'd sprinted from Rosewood, into that woodland and those hillsides and the North beyond.

The train rattled ever louder, but so what? – the distance between them narrowed, and now she was up too, standing the same as he was, wrapping his body in her arms. Again, he struggled to believe it. Again, he nearly failed. His forehead scrunched; his lips pursed. "Clara," he uttered again.

Tears came to her eyes. And reaching up, she brought him in close. "Atti!" she replied into his ear, trying to remain quiet in turn. "They were after you, weren't they? How'd you make it out then? How'd you get by?"

He was kissing her cheeks, feeling her grip around him, conscious of her stomach, her breath upon his face. "Clara, I'm sorry."

"There's no reason – "

"I should've come back that very first night. I should've helped. I heard the sirens."

"Atti, no – " She pulled back, held her finger to his lips. "We're here now. We're here." Their eyes locked. "I was on my way south to find you, Atti. How'd you reach Richmond? How'd you find *me*?"

"I only just got out of the army."

"The Resistance?"

"The United States," he answered, staying hushed. She listened rapt then, as they sat down and he told her his tale, breaths still thin, eyes still watering, drying their cheeks with the backs of their hands, confirming the car had stayed empty. "I saw you speak to their Congress, you know. The whole regiment was riveted. You were a power, Clara."

"I made a scene."

He offered a smile, in place of a sob. "It's why folks follow you – why they always have. It's just this time you reached so much farther." He eased closer, placing his hand gently alongside hers, atop her belly. His throat caught.

She glanced back. "It's ours, Atti."

"How much longer?"

"Weeks now."

The idea to hop from the train came roaring back. "What if we get off? Duck away, catch up with the Yanks, go north with them."

But finally, Clara shook her head.

"What then?"

"I've heard the Resistance is taking slaves into its forces."

"I heard the same."

Her voice was filled with purpose. "We'd be risking it all."

"Not for the first time." He was considering it, picturing their next steps. His words came stumbling out. "Brooke has other concerns – he won't be looking for us. He's retired; rumors say his own daughter has up and joined our side, though there's no telling what's real."

Clara blinked. A tear sprung loose, and this time she let it. "How'd you hear that?"

"Soldiers get to talking. They say the Guard almost arrested her a while back."

"I wrote her a letter," she murmured now.

"Come again?"

But at that, she merely gave another shake of her head. The moment passed. "Maybe we really can win," was all she said next.

"I think so." And he squeezed her hand in return.

THE END

ACKNOWLEDGEMENTS

I would like to thank those who read and commented on the manuscript and helped make this novel possible: my wife, Phoebe Geer; my dear friends and colleagues, including John Valliere, David Gelber, Mario Dell'olio, Dexter Davenport, Kate Carcaterra, and Melissa Blair, and my mentor and former doctoral advisor, Gary W. Gallagher. I am profoundly indebted to each for their support. I am equally profoundly indebted to Black Rose Writing and everyone there for their belief in me, their editing, effort, and their guidance through this adventure.

ABOUT THE AUTHOR

Matthew Speiser is author of the novel *Sons of Liberty*, in addition to numerous pieces grappling with American history, in publications ranging from the Tennessee Historical Quarterly to McSweeney's. His doctoral dissertation examined battles over our national memory of the Civil War, which were waged long after the actual battlefields had quieted. As Chair of the History department at the Marymount School in Manhattan, Dr. Speiser engages with the legacy of America's past every day. He holds a PhD in U.S. History from the University of Virginia.

Other Titles by Matthew Speiser

"Speiser makes his command of history and love of storytelling evident on every page."
—Allison Pataki, *New York Times* bestselling author of
The Magnificent Lives of Marjorie Post

SONS
OF
LIBERTY

MATTHEW SPEISER

Note from Matthew Speiser

Word-of-mouth is crucial for any author to succeed. If you enjoyed *To the Manor Born*, please leave a review online— anywhere you are able. Even if it's just a sentence or two. It would make all the difference and would be very much appreciated.

Thanks!
Matthew Speiser

We hope you enjoyed reading this title from:

www.blackrosewriting.com

Subscribe to our mailing list – *The Rosevine* – and receive **FREE** books, daily deals, and stay current with news about upcoming releases and our hottest authors.
Scan the QR code below to sign up.

Already a subscriber? Please accept a sincere thank you for being a fan of Black Rose Writing authors.

View other Black Rose Writing titles at www.blackrosewriting.com/books and use promo code **PRINT** to receive a **20% discount** when purchasing.

www.ingramcontent.com/pod-product-compliance
Lightning Source LLC
Chambersburg PA
CBHW020556120726
47903CB00001B/281